THE LOST GIRLS

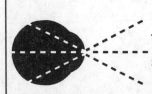

THE LOST GIRLS

HEATHER YOUNG

THORNDIKE PRESS

A part of Gale, a Cengage Company

Farmington Hills, Mich • San Francisco • New York • Waterville, Maine
Meriden, Conn • Mason, Ohio • Chicago

LIBRARY OF CONGRESS CATALOGING-IN-PUBLICATION DATA

Names: Young, Heather, MFA, author.
Title: The lost girls / Heather Young.
Description: Waterville, Maine : Thorndike Press, a part of Gale, a Cengage Company, 2017. | Series: Thorndike Press large print peer picks
Identifiers: LCCN 2017027750| ISBN 9781432843304 (hardback) | ISBN 1432843303 (hardcover)
Subjects: LCSH: Family secrets—Fiction. | Missing persons—Fiction. | Large type books. | BISAC: FICTION / Family Life. | GSAFD: Psychological fiction | Mystery fiction
Classification: LCC PS3625.O96433 L68 2017 | DDC 813/.6—dc23
LC record available at https://lccn.loc.gov/2017027750

Published in 2017 by arrangement with William Morrow, an imprint of HarperCollins Publishers

For my father — my inspiration
and my mother — my hero

Sister — if all this is true,
what could I do, or undo?

— Sophocles,
Antigone

LUCY

I found this notebook in the desk yesterday. I didn't know I had any of them left, those books I bought at Framer's with their black-and-white marbled covers and their empty, lined pages waiting to be filled. When I opened it, the binding crackled in my hands and I had to sit down.

The edges of the book's pages were yellow and curled, but their centers were white, and they shouted in the quiet of the parlor. Long ago, I filled these books with stories, simple things the children enjoyed, but this one demanded something else. It was as though it had lain in wait beneath stacks of old Christmas cards and faded stationery until now, when my life has begun to wane with the millennium and my thoughts have turned more and more to the past.

It's been sixty-four years. That doesn't feel so long, strange though it may seem to you, but Mother is dead, and Father, and Lilith;

I am the last. When I am gone, it will be as though that summer never happened. I've thought about this as I sit in my chair on the porch, as I take my evening walk up to the bridge, and as I lie awake listening to the water shifting in the dark. I've even taken to sleeping in Lilith's and my old room, in the small bed that used to be mine. Last night I watched the moonlight on the ceiling and thought of the many nights I have lain there: as a child, as a young girl, and now as an old woman. I thought about how easy it would be to let all of it pass from the earth.

When morning came, I made my buttered toast and set it on its flowered plate, but I didn't eat it. Instead I sat at the kitchen table with this book open before me, listening to the wind in the trees and feeling the house breathe. I traced my finger along the scratches and gouges in the elm table my great-grandfather made for his new wife in the century before I was born. It was the heart of the cabin he built on their homestead, and of the home their son built in the town that came after, but their grandson thought it crude, fit only for this, his summer house. Its scars are worn now; the years have smoothed them to dark ripples in the golden wood.

As I said, I am the last. Since Lilith's passing three years ago, the story of that summer has been mine alone, to keep or to share. It's a power I've had just once before, and I find I am far less certain what to do with it now than I was then. I hold secrets that don't belong to me; secrets that would blacken the names of the defenseless dead. People I once loved. Better to let it be, I tell myself.

But this notebook reminds me it's not so simple as that. I owe other debts. I made other promises. And not all the defenseless dead, loved or not, are virtuous. Still, I have no doubt that I would have remained silent, waiting for my own death to decide the matter, had I not found it. Its empty pages offer me a compromise, one that I, who have rarely had the fortitude to make irrevocable choices, have decided to accept.

So I will write my family's story, here in this book that bided its time so well. I will tell it as fully as I can, even the parts that grieve me. When I am done I will leave it to you, Justine, along with everything else. You will wonder why I've chosen you and not your mother, and to that I say that you are the only one to whom the past might matter. If it does, you will come here when I am gone, and Arthur will give this to you,

11

and I will trust you to do with it as you see fit. If it does not — which may well be, for I knew you so briefly, and you were just a child — then you won't come. You'll be content to let the lawyers and the realtors do their work, to continue your life without seeing this house or the lake again. If that is the way of it, I will instruct Arthur to burn this book unread. For I believe it will then be all right to let that summer slip away, and Emily with it. Like all the other ghosts of forgotten things.

It was 1935. I was eleven, Lilith thirteen, and Emily six. Our family lived in town then, in the brown house my grandfather built, but we spent our summers here, in our yellow house on the lake. The day after school ended, Mother packed our trunks with our sundresses, swimming suits, and hats, and Father drove us the twenty miles that spanned our known world. Lilith, Emily, and I sat in the back of the Plymouth, I in the middle as usual. When I pressed my foot against Lilith's, she pressed back.

You knew Lilith for such a short time, that one summer twenty years ago when you and your mother came, and I imagine to you we were just two old women living out their days on a screened-in porch. I wish you

12

could have known her — really known her — because any story of which Lilith was a part became her story, and my story is no different. My earliest memory is of her directing me to place my feet in the footprints she made in the sand, leading me in twirls and spins until I lost my balance and fell. It was only a game, but it was also how we spent our childhood years: I followed her everywhere and did everything she did, though never as quickly or as well.

Then, in the spring of 1935, something changed. We still went everywhere together, but she no longer wanted to go to Seward's Pond or into the tree house Father built in our backyard, and she wouldn't play hopscotch or swing on the swing. Instead she spent a great deal of time looking in her mirror, brushing the dark curls that fell to her waist. She had an odd sort of face, with a too-long nose and a too-wide mouth that conspired with her delicate cheekbones to make something improbable and arresting. Now she studied it as if it were a machine she was trying to figure out.

She was taller, too, and though she still wore last year's dresses with the hems let down, her body was changing. In April she pulled me into the bathroom we shared to show me the small buds on her chest. In

May, Mother bought her a brassiere. At first she needed my help to hook it in back, its tiny claws slipping into fragile eyes. Afterward, wearing it with her shoulders squared and her chin high like the girls in the Sears & Roebuck catalog, she looked like someone very different from who she'd been.

Of course, there's a big difference between eleven and thirteen. I know that now. But then, I saw only that I was being left behind on a journey I didn't understand and didn't want to make, and as spring deepened toward summer I decided the three months our family would spend at the lake offered my best chance to pull Lilith back to me. Surely, as we played our games in the woods, sat on the bridge over the creek, and lay in our twin beds whispering in the night, she'd shed this odd veneer of adulthood she'd been trying on. When her foot pressed mine in the car, that hope expanded even as the road narrowed around us.

We arrived in that afternoon hour when the sunlight turns from white to gold and the water is its deepest blue. The house, shut up for winter, was chilly and dark, but as we opened the curtains and raised the window sashes, it breathed in the warm breeze and shook off the gloom of the long cold season. It has always seemed a living thing to me, this house, and I felt its spirits lift as it filled with our voices and the clattering of our shoes across its pine floorboards.

Lilith and I carried our trunk to our airy green bedroom. We loved the annual ritual of hanging our summer dresses in the closet, lining our shoes on the shelves, arranging our hats on the hooks over the dresser. In town we slept in separate rooms, so our unpacking here was more than a simple filling of drawers and closets; it was a ceremonial reclaiming of a shared territory. As we unpacked that day, Lilith was very like her old self, making plans for us to visit the Hundred Tree as we laid sheets on our beds and shook out the quilts that had spent the winter sealed in the hallway linen press. Meanwhile, Mother settled Emily in her small bedroom across the landing, and Father unloaded the rest of the suitcases and trunks, which seemed to get more numerous every year. Outside, up and down the dirt road that fronted the lake, our summer neighbors greeted one another as they, too, opened their houses to the sun.

There are seven houses here, all built between 1905 and 1910. That was when our self-styled Minnesota aristocrats, emulating New York's Vanderbilts and Rockefellers,

15

built summer homes to which they escaped while the lesser citizens sweltered in town. The Joneses, who owned the general store, were the first. Then came the Pughs, two generations of whom were the town's doctors; the Davieses, whose grandfather was the circuit judge; the Lewises, whose father was our dentist; and the Williamses, who wrote our wills and gave the town its name. My own father ran Evans Drugs, which his grandfather had founded. The biggest house belonged to Robert Lloyd, who owned almost everything else and who, like his father and grandfather before him, was the town's mayor. All of us were descended from the small group of men who fled the coal mines of Wales to found Williamsburg some eighty years before, and we considered our prosperity and social prominence to be our birthright.

Today these houses are in disrepair, but surely you can see how lovely they once were. In the summer of 1935 they were just beginning their decline: paint was fading and would not be freshened; a broken screen here and there would not be replaced. As a child I didn't know the extent of the hard times, although I saw Mother's little economies — the let-down hems, the resoled shoes — and resented them. The very next year, the Joneses and the Davieses would not come to the lake at all. Their houses would sit closed until they were sold to families from Minneapolis who came up for a week and rented them out for the rest of the season. Within a few years the other lake families would do the same, until Lilith, Mother, and I were the only ones left.

As I look back, knowing everything that was to come, the first day of my family's last summer together takes on a melancholy it did not have then. To the contrary, I loved that day as I had loved all the first summer days that came before. It was one of the few times when I felt our family was like all the others, not just in appearance, but in truth. Father's stern manner softened as he deferred to Mother in the domestic matters of unpacking and moving in, and Mother's voice had a lilt that I never heard elsewhere. Emily, normally so somber, skipped around like the six-year-old girl I often forgot she was. Best of all, Lilith chattered and laughed as if she were twelve again. I watched all this, the normal happiness of a family on holiday, and I smiled until my cheeks ached.

For supper that first night, as we did every year, the lake families prevailed upon the Millers, the half-Chippewa family who owned the fishing lodge, to cook for us. The hours we spent laying out our bed linens and placing our clothes in freshly papered drawers the Millers spent roasting chickens, boiling corn, and baking bread. No doubt they worked for days to feed all of us, more than sixty people, but times were hard for them, too; I imagine they were glad to have the money we paid.

Abe and Matthew, the Miller sons, brought tables and chairs to where three picnic benches sat on the sandy grass between the road and the narrow beach. There the women, cheeks rosy from the exertion of moving in, clustered in knots and patted wisps of hair into place while the men rattled the ice in their cocktails and speculated on the season's walleye catch. They wore cardigans and light coats; in June the evenings were cool, though the sun hung high above the hills that crowded the lake's western shore. When it was time to eat, everyone bowed their heads as Father, the closest thing among us to a minister, said grace in a quiet that was as profound as it was temporary. Then the feast began, the children eating as quickly as their mothers would allow so they could resume running up and down the dock and around the trees. Even Lilith and I, who otherwise kept to ourselves, always joined the games of tag and kick-the-can that heralded the start of summer.

But this year, Lilith sat on a picnic bench with her hands folded in her lap while the other children chose up teams. I sat beside her, digging my toe into the grass, unease shifting the creamed corn and chicken in my belly. I couldn't bring myself to join the game without her — she was my conduit to the others, her imperious confidence paving a way for me and my small awkwardnesses.

"Don't you want to play?" I asked.

"We're not children, Lucy," Lilith said.

I wanted to say that all the teenaged boys were playing, even Stuart Davies, who'd just graduated from high school, but I knew she was talking about the teenaged girls, who sat nearby, whispering as they watched the boys run about on the sandy road. So I said nothing and tried to remind myself that tomorrow we were going to the Hundred Tree. She'd promised.

I heard Mayor Lloyd's voice booming from a picnic table behind us. "If you keep giving everything away, Hugh, it'll be my name over your door before long." I glanced over my shoulder. He was smiling at Mr. Jones, but Mr. Jones's timid features were flushed. Father had told us the grocer wasn't collecting on the accounts of families that were struggling to put food on their tables. He was a true Christian, Father said. Mayor Lloyd reached for another roll from the bread basket.

Mother and Father sat at a separate table with the Williamses and the Lewises. Father and Mr. Williams had grown up together, the sons of best friends, and Mrs. Williams and Mother had become close over the years of their marriages. As usual, Mrs. Williams was doing most of the talking in her quick, laughing voice while Mother nodded and Father rested his elbows on the table, his dark eyes quiet. Like us, he'd spent his childhood summers at this lake, and the tension that always simmered in him seemed to ease when he was here.

Emily sat between Mother and Father, her feet dangling almost but not quite to the grass. She rarely played with the other children, either. She was a serious child, not inclined to play the kinds of games children that age play, and even had she been, she was Mother's pet, so Mother kept her close. In fact, in her six years I don't believe she'd made a single friend. I suppose that's why, before long, Mother, Lilith, and I were the only ones who remembered her as anything other than a local mystery. Aside from Abe Miller, of course. Though he would never speak of her to us.

As the kick-the-can game got under way, Emily left Mother and Father and slipped onto the bench beside Lilith. She adored Lilith, although Lilith paid her almost no attention and the little she did pay was invariably unkind. Now Emily sat, hoping to catch Lilith's eye. Lilith and I refused to give her a single glance.

In the course of the game the can rolled close to us, and big-faced Charlie Lloyd chased it down. He was fifteen, with his father's heavy good looks but none of the politician's easy manner. The summer before, he'd sent Lilith a love note that we burned in the kitchen sink, watching with satisfaction as the plaintive phrases turned to ash. Now he gave Lilith a shy glance over his shoulder as he ran back to the game. I expected to see disdain on her face, but to my surprise she smiled at him, a close-lipped smile that tilted higher on one side. Charlie's face blazed red and he tripped over his feet.

Jeannette Lewis, one of the nearby girls, saw this, and said something to Charlie's twin sister, Betty. Betty's rosy apple face dimpled at Lilith with a new, calculating regard that I didn't like. Lilith looked straight ahead, that smile lingering, her long, silky curls gleaming. All the teenaged girls wore their hair in bobs that curved around their ears to the collars of their dresses. I knew Lilith was desperate to cut hers, too, and that Father would never let her, but I thought her long hair was much prettier than their blunted locks and that she looked, with her odd smile and strong features, older than any of them at that moment. With my unruly, sand-colored hair and my dirty feet, I felt like Emily: an unwanted, tagalong little sister.

I leaned around Lilith to where Emily sat. She straightened, her eyes hopeful. "Go away," I told her, my voice as vicious as I could make it. She blanched, then slid off the bench and ran back to Mother and Father. I felt the slippery, cold satisfaction I always felt when I hurt her. I glanced at Lilith, hoping for an approving smile, but she was still looking at Charlie. Behind us, Father lifted Emily onto his lap. Over her dark ringlets he watched Charlie, too.

I imagine we don't seem unusual to you as I've described us on that first summer day. We were an oldest sister growing up, and a middle sister being left behind. A youngest sister wanting to belong. A father watching a boy who flirted with his daughter. Nothing you wouldn't see in countless other families. But if I am to tell you the story of what happened to us, I must start at the beginning. And in these few things, ordinary as they may seem, lay the beginnings of everything that came after.

JUSTINE

She wasn't thinking of leaving him. Why would she? He was everything she wanted; everything Francis, her daughters' father, had never been. He was faithful. Reliable. Home every night at five thirty. And he made her feel safe. Especially after the burglary. She was lucky to have a man like him when there were people out there with lock picks and violence on their minds. At least, that's what she told herself as she lay awake beside him the night after it happened.

The police said the burglars must have been watching the apartment building, because their timing was perfect. Justine had picked up Melanie and Angela from the elementary school aftercare on her way home from work as usual. Then, five minutes after they walked in the apartment, Angela said she needed supplies for a school project — poster board and colored pipe cleaners. Patrick wasn't home yet, so Justine left a note saying she'd be back at six and would bring takeout. They went to the Walgreens and the In-N-Out and got back at six exactly.

As soon as they walked in the door Justine stopped, instinctively pressing the girls backward. The apartment was completely trashed. The sofa was on its back, its cushions off. Both lamps were on the floor. The coffee table was tipped over, and magazines were everywhere. In the kitchen the cupboards stood open, their contents emptied on the counters, and pots and pans covered the linoleum.

Patrick's black messenger bag sat in the hallway at Justine's feet, but he wasn't in the kitchen or the living room. "Patrick?" She called, in a half-whisper. There was no answer. The air went thin around her. "Run!" she hissed to the girls. "Go to Mrs. Mendenhall's! Tell her to call the police."

Melanie and Angela fled back to the landing and down the stairs. Carefully, Justine lowered the shopping bags to the carpet. She stepped into the living room, every muscle tensed. She called Patrick again. Again there was no answer. She crept down the hall to their bedroom, her back pressed against the wall. She held her breath and peeked inside. The covers were off the bed and clothes spilled out of the drawers, but no one was there. Across the hall, the girls' room was the same. No one was in the apartment.

Justine ran back to the living room, panicking now. Where was he? Had he been here when the burglars came? He must have; otherwise he'd be here now. She pressed her hands against her head. They'd done something to him. They'd taken him. Or he'd chased them and they'd hurt him. She heard the distant whine of a police siren. The police would find him. She would meet them in the parking lot.

She turned toward the door and jumped, a scream in her throat. Patrick was standing in the doorway, watching her.

"Patrick! Oh, my God!" She staggered with relief — he wasn't hurt; he didn't have a mark on him; he was safe. She ran to him, tripping over the sofa pillows, kicking one of the lamps, falling against his chest. His arms swallowed her as she inhaled the tang of his sweat and the acrid scents of ink and toner, sobbing into his white Office Pro shirt. His fingers dug into her ribs as though trying to unlock them.

"It's okay," he murmured into her hair.

"I was so scared."

"Me, too." His voice was tight. "I came home, and you were gone."

She raised her head and saw in his taut, pale face what he'd been through. He'd come home at five thirty, as he always did, and found the apartment wrecked, and her gone. With her note buried in the mess, he hadn't known she and the girls were safe, buying pipe cleaners at the Walgreens. The errand might have saved their lives, but she knew what it had done to him to walk into the ruined, empty apartment. He'd thought his worst nightmare had come true.

"Patrick, I'm so sorry." She embraced him again, tenderly this time. He sagged against her. They stood for a long time like that, his weight heavy on her. When her back began to ache, she eased him away, kissing him in solace. His cheeks were soft, like a baby's.

After the police had come and made their notes and dusted for fingerprints, Justine and Patrick cleaned up the mess and made a list of what was missing: the television, the VHS player, Justine's few earrings and necklaces. Then, while Justine retrieved the girls from Mrs. Mendenhall and fed them their cold In-N-Out burgers, Patrick drove to the twenty-four-hour CVS and bought a new lock that he installed himself. It took the girls a long time to settle into sleep, but once they did, Justine and Patrick made love like survivors in the tangled sheets of their bed.

Afterward, Justine lay with Patrick's arm heavy across her waist and watched the digital clock measure out the minutes in silent red lines. He made her feel safe. He did. But something about the burglary niggled at her. Part of it was the enormity of the mess — why would a burglar flip over the sofa and strip the beds? — but it wasn't just that. Finally, as the sky lightened toward dawn, she put her finger on it: it wasn't how excessive the violence had been, but how orderly. The lamp shades had still been on the lamps, even though the lamps lay sideways on the floor. The pots and pans were stacked on the linoleum as if set there rather than tossed. Things were missing, but nothing had been broken.

She thought, too, about how she hadn't left her note on the counter but on the kitchen table, which wasn't really in the small kitchen but practically in the living room, where Patrick might not have found it right away. For a few minutes, when she'd been at the Walgreens and her note wasn't in plain sight, he might not have known where she was.

She drew her legs to her chest. Patrick

28

always wanted to know where she was, insisted upon it, even. It was one of the things she found most endearing about him, after Francis's painful disinterest those last years. She stared at the gray light that seeped through the gaps in the oatmeal curtains that had come with the apartment. Where had Patrick been when she got home? When she called his name, fear making her voice tremble and crack? How long had he been standing in the doorway, watching her?

Outside, birds began to chirp and chatter. Patrick's body, curled around hers, was warm and solid and reliable as always. What was she thinking? That he'd staged an elaborate burglary just to make her feel what he'd felt when he came home and she wasn't there? To see if she would feel it? Because that would be crazy. This was Patrick. Dependable, meticulous Patrick, who couldn't abide any sort of mess and never raised his voice to her, much less a hand. She was thinking like her mother. Her mother, to whom every man was a prince — until he was a liar, or a pervert, or a nutcase, and she had to leave town. She wasn't her mother. She'd found a good man. She felt his breath on her shoulder and forced her suspicion to hold its tongue.

But the next day, she left him.

That day started like every other day since he'd moved in ten months before. Justine got up first, even though she'd barely slept, and spent half an hour sitting in one of the Windsor chairs at the kitchen table with her knees pulled up under her chin and her eyes closed. She'd done this every morning since she was a girl, sitting alone while her mother slept, storing up silence against the noise each day would bring. If she listened, she could hear the low voices of the couple next door, but she didn't. She listened only to the quiet of her own apartment in the pale light.

When Patrick's alarm went off, she woke her daughters for school and made breakfast. At precisely eight Patrick appeared, ruffled Angela's hair, and said good morning to Melanie. Justine stood on her tiptoes to kiss him, and he didn't smell like sweat and toner; he smelled of Irish Spring and Walmart laundry detergent, the fresh-bitter scent she associated with him. By the light of day, in the tidy kitchen that bore no traces of the burglary, her nighttime suspicions seemed even more preposterous.

He had his eggs over easy, as always, and as always he told her they were great. She'd learned to make them exactly the way he liked. He needed his eggs done exactly right because he sold office equipment at the Office Pro, mostly desktop printers and other small machines. When he proved himself, he could sell the copiers, which was where the big money was, because once you sold one you got to sell the paper and toner and ink that went with it, forever, but his boss wouldn't let him do that until he got his quarterly numbers up, and to do that he needed eggs that were not too hard and not too soft. After he ate he wrapped her in a hug and tossed his keys in the air as he walked out. Just like any other day.

On her way to work, she dropped her daughters at the elementary school. She watched Melanie trudge to the blue doors and wondered if she was going to get another call from the assistant principal that afternoon. Her eldest had been surlier than usual, even disobedient, and last week there'd been shoving on the playground during which another fifth grader's backpack had landed in the mud. The assistant principal said if it didn't stop there'd be counseling, maybe special classes. Justine watched with a frown as Melanie climbed the steps with her shoulders hunched like a tiny boxer. Then she drove to Dr. Fish-

baum's office, where she was the receptionist, and she didn't think about anything but
work until lunchtime, when her cell phone
rang and everything changed.

She answered, assuming it was one of
Patrick's check-ins — it was why he'd given
her the phone, an expensive luxury in 1999
— but instead her mother's voice breezed
in from Arizona or New Mexico or wherever
she was now, cruising the warm lands with
her latest boyfriend. Justine hadn't seen her
in three years, but Maurie called every
couple of months and, of course, she sent
all those postcards — pictures of beach
towns and mountain towns and desert
towns with a scrawl on the back: "Mesa is
wonderful!" "Gotta love Austin!" Justine
threw them away immediately. Now she
rubbed her left eyebrow, where the headache
a call from her mother always awoke opened
its tiny eyes.

At first Maurie chatted on in her usual
way about Phil-the-boyfriend, the RV park,
and how she was learning to play golf, and
Justine's attention wandered to the stack of
patient files on her desk. She wasn't supposed to read them, but she liked the small,
ordinary stories they told, so she opened
the top one. Edna Burbank, 84. Arthritis,
bursitis, a prescription for Xanax.

Then Maurie said, "Do you remember my aunt Lucy? Up at the lake?"

Justine closed Edna's file and sat forward in her chair. She hadn't thought about Lucy for years, but at the mention of her name a riot of memories broke out in the front of her brain. When she was nine, Maurie had driven them to a lake in northern Minnesota where there were green trees, clear water, and blue nights filled with the sound of crickets. They'd lived in a yellow house with a screened-in porch with three women: Aunt Lucy, Grandma Lilith, and their mother, Justine's own great-grandmother. "Yes. Yes, I remember her."

"Well, she died. I just got the notice. Thank God I set up the forwarding this time." Ice clinked in Maurie's glass. "She never should have stayed in that house by herself. After Mother died I told her she should move to the retirement home over in Bemidji, but she wouldn't. God knows how she made it through those winters."

Justine had loved that lake. Not only because it was beautiful, but also because Maurie laughed differently there. Instead of the brittle laughs Justine had heard in the diners and cheap cafés that crowded her memory, Maurie's lake laugh let you see all the way to the back of her mouth. She'd seemed different in other ways, too. Relaxed. Not looking ahead to the next big adventure. For a while Justine even thought they might stay, that they might live there longer than the few months they spent in most places. But in September they piled their things in the rusty Fairmont and drove away. Off to Iowa City, or maybe Omaha. She couldn't remember. Another apartment, another job, another boyfriend, another school.

Still, all that next year, Justine hoped they'd go back. Maybe it would become a tradition that they went to the lake every summer. Other people had traditions like that, she knew. But she never brought it up, and when summer came and went with no mention of the lake she wasn't surprised. After all, Maurie never went back anywhere. When they left a town she wouldn't even let Justine look back at it. "Shake the dust off," she'd say. "Shake the dust of that town off your feet." She'd take her foot off the gas and shake both feet and Justine would, too, even though she never wanted to leave, no matter where they were.

She wondered what Maurie had done when her mother died. Had she gone back then? Would she have broken her rule to see her mother buried? "When did Grandma

Lilith die? You never told me."

Maurie ignored her. "The letter was from some lawyer. Turns out Lucy had some jewelry of Mother's she wanted me to have. And he wanted your number."

"Why?"

"Well. Apparently she left you that house."

"She *what*?" Justine had to tighten her fingers to keep from dropping the phone.

"Not that it's worth much, stuck up there in the middle of nowhere." The ice clinked again. "She always wanted me to come back. Your mother misses you, she'd say. But my God, it was awful growing up in that place. Nobody lived there, just the summer people who didn't give a crap about some local girl. I got out as soon as I got my driver's license."

It had never occurred to Justine that the lake house was where her mother grew up. Maurie rarely talked about her childhood, and as an adult she was such a creature of the road that Justine had always pictured her screaming her way into the world in a caravan somewhere, a modern-day gypsy. "Minnesota," was all she'd say when anyone asked where she was from, somehow making an entire state sound like a bus stop. Now Justine remembered her lying on the porch swing at the lake house as the sun,

35

silty with motes, spilled through the front windows onto golden pine floorboards. Her hair was in a loose ponytail, her face was young, and she laughed with her mouth wide open.

But Lucy had left the house to Justine.

The elevator chimed. Phoebe, the office manager, was back from lunch.

"Mom, I have to go," Justine said. "Do you have the lawyer's number?" She wrote it down and slid the phone back into her purse just as Phoebe opened the office door. "Angela's sick," she said to her, without meeting her eyes. She'd never asked to leave early before.

Phoebe sighed. She didn't much care for Justine, but she had a fatherless child of her own, so she said she'd cover the desk. Justine walked out without looking back.

In the apartment she paced, holding the phone in one hand and the lawyer's number in the other. Finally she sat at the kitchen table, pulled up her knees, and closed her eyes, as she did during her morning minutes. Only this time she couldn't hear the silence. Instead she heard the low hum that came from the refrigerator, the fluorescent lights, the clock on the wall.

The apartment was crappy. The walls were scuffed, the carpet was matted, and the sliding door was held shut with duct tape. Still, it was the only place she'd lived since she stood with one hand in Francis's and the other on her belly, where the secret clot of cells divided and grew, and told her mother, who'd decided to give Portland a try, that she was staying in San Diego. She was eighteen, Francis nineteen. They'd picked it because it was the closest place to the ocean they could afford. Eight blocks, so not that close, but when she stood on the balcony at night with Melanie in her arms Justine could hear it whispering beyond the low-slung buildings that made up their neighborhood. The night they moved in they drank champagne out of paper cups in the empty living room. The worn nap of the carpet was soft on Justine's shoulders as they made love, and she'd sworn she'd never leave. That her child would grow up in one place, whole.

She opened her eyes. Patrick's coffee cup, half empty, sat on the table.

She dialed the lawyer's number. Just to find out what was going on. To see if her mother had her facts straight, which wasn't a certainty by any means.

The lawyer's name was Arthur Williams. He and his uncle before him had handled the Evans sisters' affairs for decades, he said. Lucy had died three weeks before, in her sleep. It had been sudden but peaceful, and her neighbor had found her the next day. His voice was soft, the consonants that bracketed the broad vowels crisp.

Justine pressed the handset against her ear. "My mother said you wanted to talk about Lucy's will?"

"Yes. You're her sole beneficiary." This meant, he explained, that Lucy had left Justine everything she owned, except the jewelry she'd left for Maurie. The house was old and in need of updating, but it was unencumbered by any liens. Lucy had a checking account and an investment portfolio, too; he would fax her the details.

"How much is in the accounts?" Justine asked, then wished she could take the question back. It sounded like something her mother would ask.

The lawyer answered as though it were a perfectly acceptable question. The checking account had about $2,000, and the investments were mostly stock and worth about $150,000. "You might want to come and settle things in person," he said, "if there are things in the house you want to keep. Or you can contact a lawyer where you are, and we'll handle the probate by fax. Then I can recommend a realtor to sell the house for you."

He paused. Justine knew she was supposed to say something, but her head felt as if it would float straight up and away if she didn't hold on to it. There was $150,000 in an investment portfolio somewhere in Minnesota. She and Patrick had $1,328 in their account at the Wells Fargo. The lake house had been the color of butter in the sun.

"Can I call you back?" she asked. Of course, he said.

When she hung up she took Patrick's coffee cup to the sink. She washed it and dried it and put it in the cupboard. Then, from the storage unit in the basement, she pulled the faded blue duffel she'd kept from when she was her mother's daughter. In it she put her jeans and the three sweatshirts she owned. Two pairs of shoes that weren't sandals. Bras, underwear, socks, pajamas. Toothbrush, shampoo, hairbrush. She zipped up the bag and put it by the front door.

From beneath the sink she took a stack of brown grocery bags. In them she put the photo albums she'd made when the girls were babies and the more recent snapshots magneted to the refrigerator. From inside the refrigerator she took bread, peanut butter, and jelly. From the pantry, crackers, chips, and cereal. At two thirty Patrick called on her cell. She stood motionless in the apartment as he crowed about his day: two fax machines and a printer sold before his lunch break. When he asked what was for dinner, she told him they had leftover spaghetti. He asked her to pick up that garlic bread he liked on her way home. She said she would.

After they hung up she called the lawyer. "We're coming," she said. He sounded pleased. He gave her directions and told her Lucy's neighbor, Matthew Miller, would have a key to the house.

Her daughters didn't have suitcases, so Justine took the pillowcases from their beds and filled them with their warmest clothes and shoes. Then she used more brown bags to hold their jewelry boxes with tiny ballerinas inside, stuffed animals, plastic horses, dolls with tangles in their hair. Barrettes and scrunchies, drawing paper and markers. She put the bags by the front door with the rest. It didn't look like much, but it filled the back of the Tercel.

When she finished loading the car it was four thirty. She was supposed to pick up her daughters at the aftercare at five. At five thirty, Patrick would be home.

She put her apartment key on the kitchen

counter and her cell phone beside it. She pulled a Post-it off the stack. The clock inched forward another minute while she debated what to write. Francis's note had said he was sorry. She didn't know if she was sorry. She didn't know what she felt, other than a buzzing anxiety pegged to the sweep of the second hand around the clock face. In the waning November afternoon the living room furniture she and Francis had bought on layaway looked dark and strange, as though it had never belonged to her at all. A shiver ran across her shoulder blades. She'd forgotten how easy it was, to slip out of a life.

Dear Patrick, she wrote, *the spaghetti is thawing in the refrigerator.* She laid the note on the counter, smoothed it once, and walked out. Her feet on the steps were light. When she reached the bottom she heard her cell phone ring, faintly.

Later she wouldn't remember driving to the school. But she would remember that her face felt like dried icing as she walked her daughters to a picnic table on the playground and told them they'd inherited a house on a lake that had a porch and a swing, and that it was in Minnesota, but that was okay, because they'd get to see

41

things along the way, like the Rocky Mountains and Las Vegas, and it would be an adventure.

The girls stayed quiet until she was done talking. Then Melanie's eyes narrowed. "Wait. Are we moving there?"

Melanie was not an attractive child. At eleven she'd long since lost her baby fat, revealing severe features and a too-long nose that rode high into her wide brow and gave her a haughty air. Now her suspicious frown made her look small and cunning, like a fox.

Justine forced her voice to remain even. "It's a house, sweetie. We'll have a great big house just for the three of us, with a lake right out front. For free."

"The three of us? What about Patrick?"

"I thought it might be good to be on our own for a while, just us girls."

Melanie's frown deepened. Angela looked stunned. Both girls' arms in their short-sleeved shirts were thin and straight and brown from the San Diego sun. Behind them Justine could see other parents picking up their children. Taking them home for dinner, then homework at the kitchen table, maybe some television before bed. "I've got all your stuff in the car."

"We're leaving now?" Melanie's voice slid up half an octave.

"I know it's sudden. But it's better this way. A clean break."

"What about Daddy?" Angela said.

Justine opened her mouth and shut it again. Francis had been gone a year, and they hadn't heard a word from him in all that time. Neither girl had asked about him in months. After Patrick moved in, the picture of Francis and the girls at Coronado Beach had disappeared from the girls' room. Justine had thought this meant they were shaking him off their feet like dust, the way Maurie always told her to, the way she was trying to, but the hitch in Angela's voice told a different story.

Melanie said, "Daddy's not coming back, you idiot." She looked at Justine, her eyes flat. Justine muffled a flare of anger. Her eldest daughter's sullen temperament and brusque manner often made Justine dislike her, something she felt ashamed of and guilty about. Besides, she knew it wasn't Melanie she should be mad at this time. Toward the end Francis had hardly come home at all, but that hadn't diminished his daughters' love for him. The opposite, in fact.

Justine put her hand on Angela's arm. "I'll tell Mrs. Mendenhall where we're going, and if Daddy comes looking for us, she can tell him." This was a lie. She wasn't going to tell Mrs. Mendenhall anything. Mrs. Mendenhall liked Patrick.

Angela's eyes filled with tears. "What about Lizzie and Emma?" These were her best friends, the three of them the most popular girls in the second grade.

Justine's tongue tasted like metal. She remembered how she would come home from school to find her mother sitting at the kitchen table with her cigarette and her can of Tab. "Sit down," Maurie would say, and Justine would know they were leaving.

"We can send them postcards when we get there, sweetie," she said, just as her mother had.

Angela looked back at the school. Through the open door of the aftercare center Justine could see children coloring and playing with LEGOs. Angela's face puckered, and Justine's simmering anxiety bubbled into panic. It was five thirty. Patrick was walking into the empty apartment right now. Would he come to the school? He probably would. A familiar, claustrophobic sense of failure mixed with her panic, making the world feel small and tight. What was she thinking, doing it like this? She should have waited until tomorrow. Kept the girls home from school, had them help her pack. It would have been easier on them. And easier for her to get them in the car.

Then Melanie stood up. "Angie, you know what? It sounds like fun to live on a lake. And Lizzie and Emma can come visit." Justine watched in mute astonishment as she continued, "Plus you'll go to a new school and you'll make all new friends. You'll be the most popular girl in class because you're so pretty. And maybe" — she shot a dark-eyed glance at Justine — "you can get a kitten."

Justine leaned forward. "Of course! We can have cats, dogs, whatever we want."

Angela's face was a study in misery. She'd wanted a cat ever since she was small, but Francis had been allergic, and Patrick, the farmer's son, thought cats belonged outside.

"Come on, Angie." Melanie reached out her hand. After a precarious moment Angela swallowed a throatful of snot and tears and took it. Justine tried not to show her limb-loosening relief as she rose to follow them.

An hour later they were on Highway 15. None of them said a word as they drove through the California dusk into the Nevada night. Justine could hear her mother's voice, braying over the wind that whistled through the open windows of the Fairmont: "See any place that looks good, honey?" In the rearview mirror the salvage from their apartment crowded the Tercel's back bay, looming like a slag heap over the small forms of her daughters. She forced her eyes forward, to the yellow ribbon that un-spooled before them.

LUCY

It's hard for me to remember what Mother looked like then. She was slender, I do remember that, with blue eyes and curly light-brown hair she wore in a snood. Sometimes I heard people say I looked like her, and sometimes I heard them say she could be pretty if she tried, but I didn't want to look like her and I didn't think she could ever be pretty. Although I will grant that she had fine bones — years later, her cheekbones and jaw made delicate craters into which the flesh of her face sank. What I remember most are her hands: chopping, kneading, washing, mending, combing. How the tendons worked as she made her samplers, or picked at the quilt that covered her when she was dying.

In the kitchen the morning after we arrived, her hands were wet with soap as she scrubbed the pot she'd used to make our oatmeal. Father was fishing, so it was just us girls for breakfast. Lilith and I filled our bowls and sat at the table, Lilith's face a portrait of martyrdom, and mine, I'm sure, its studied mirror. We knew what awaited us: every year we had to spend the first full day of summer cleaning the house. But this year I felt a relieved pleasure beneath our shared misery, because it tasted the same as always, and as always it belonged only to us. Emily never had to help with the cleaning. She never had to do any chores at all, an inequity that had rankled us for years. Just looking at her that morning, immaculate in her pink flowered dress and matching hair ribbons, was enough to raise a righteous bile into our throats.

Lilith spooned up a large bite of Emily's oatmeal and ate it. Emily looked at Mother, whose back was to us, but didn't say anything. Lilith laughed, and so did I.

After breakfast, we worked. We washed the curtains, beat the rugs, and wiped the cupboards clean of the curled-up insects that had died there during the winter. We scrubbed with Borax, swept under bureaus and beds and parlor furniture, and dusted the tops of the picture frames. Father was fastidious, so Mother kept a nice house in those days. She checked our work, found dust we missed, and told us to do it over.

She said it kindly, though, and promised us ice creams at the end.

At first Emily crept along behind us, her eyes always on Lilith, but when we got to the upstairs bathroom, Lilith pushed her backward hard enough that she nearly fell. "Stop following us," she said, and shut the bathroom door in her face. After that, Emily gave up and went back to Mother. Then Lilith's mood lightened, and she started to do one of the things I loved most about her: she made things fun. She staged contests to see who could clean the bedroom windows faster (she won), and who could hit the Lewises' house with the dirty water we threw out the window from our buckets. We pretended we were Cinderellas, slaving away in anticipation of our princes, and Lilith used a funny British accent as the voice of the evil stepmother, and I could barely breathe for laughing. We hadn't played like this in a while, and as we scrubbed I shared in the pleasure the house seemed to feel in shedding the dirt of winter. Once our cleaning was done, we would go to the Hundred Tree, and summer would begin in earnest.

We were mopping our bedroom floor when we heard Father return. At the sound of his voice we both stopped, listening as his feet came light upon the stairs in that quiet way he had. When he reached the landing, he paused in our doorway.

Mother's long-ago appearance may be hard for me to recall, but I remember Father's as though I saw him yesterday. This is partly because, unlike with Mother, my memory of Father in his youth wasn't displaced by the image of him in his old age, but it's also because no one who met Father forgot him. It wasn't that he was handsome. His face was narrow, and he was shorter than most men, with spare bones. It was his eyes, which were deep-set, with bottomless dark irises that seemed unusually large, like those of babies. Like a child's, too, they looked at you for longer than was comfortable and seemed to see things that others did not. I used to love it when he looked at me.

That morning, though, he looked only at Lilith, and he frowned. She'd fastened a skirt to her head so it hung down her back — it was part of her Cinderella costume — and the makeshift wimple gave her fine cheekbones and arched brows a proud austerity that made her look, to me, every bit the beautiful servant girl destined to be a queen.

"Take that off," he said.

Lilith's shoulders twitched in the smallest

of flinches. I didn't know why Father was upset with her; we were just playing, and our game was the innocent sort of play he'd always told us God loved to see. Lilith dropped her eyes, pulled the skirt from her head, and went back to mopping. Her long hair fell forward, hiding her face.

I expected Father to leave then, but instead his eyes slid to me. He didn't look at me often, and the unaccustomed weight of his attention slackened my fingers so that my mop clattered to the floor. My face burned as I bent to pick it up. When I stood, he was gone, into his bedroom to change. Lilith and I went back to our cleaning, but we didn't play anymore.

After we finished, I wanted to go straight to the lodge for our ice creams, but Lilith made me wait while she changed into a blue plaid dress and brushed her hair. Only when she'd checked herself in the mirror for the fourth time did we go to the kitchen, where Mother was cleaning the walleyes Father had caught. Her bloody fingers were quick with the knife, and a pile of severed heads stared dully from the counter. Emily stood on a chair, watching.

Mother brushed her forehead with the back of one hand and gave us a tired smile. "Go get your ice creams, and get those

51

things for me. Take Emily with you." She motioned to the table, where a five-dollar bill sat next to a grocery list. Lilith put it in the small blue purse she'd selected to match her dress, and we went out the back door.

We didn't want to take Emily, of course, and we didn't think she deserved an ice cream, so we walked faster than her legs could go. Lilith glanced at our neighbors' houses as we passed, and I was peevishly glad no one was out to see her parading in her summer glory. The happiness I'd felt during our cleaning, which even Father's disapproval of Lilith's costume hadn't erased, dissipated into the dust that clouded our feet, hers in trim white sandals and mine in dirty Keds. The moment she'd changed her clothes I'd known we weren't going to the Hundred Tree.

The lodge was the only commercial structure on the lake, so it served many purposes. On the second floor were rooms for the fishermen who drove up from the lakeless counties downstate. Downstairs, a screened-in porch ran across the front, with couches and chairs and two pinball machines. Behind that was a big, high-ceilinged room with a bar, a pool table, an old upright piano, a half dozen tables, and, in the far corner, shelves that held a dusty collection of souvenirs and the most basic of groceries.

It was empty when we arrived, but as we gathered our groceries Abe Miller pushed open the kitchen door. The night before, when the Millers served our supper by the lake, I hadn't paid him any attention, but now I saw how much he'd changed since the previous summer. He must have been fifteen then, and he'd gotten his growth; he was taller than Father now, with large hands dangling several inches below his sleeves. His black hair was cut short, and his face had lost its childish softness, revealing strong features with a straight nose and full lips. To my horror, Lilith smiled at him — a close-mouthed smile that canted up on one side, like the one she'd given Charlie Lloyd.

Abe's swarthy skin reddened. "Can I help you?" His voice was slow, the consonants labored, the way it had always been, but now it was the deep voice of a man.

The kitchen door opened again, hitting his shoulder. Matthew, the younger brother, nearly dropped a heavy tray stacked with coffee cups, and blurted out a word I'd only heard grown men use when they thought children couldn't hear them. Abe took the tray and carried it easily to the bar, his shoulder muscles knotting beneath his white shirt.

Matthew saw us, and wiped his hands on his apron. "Do you need anything?" He stammered a little, no doubt remembering his curse word of a moment before. His head was lowered, and he looked at us through straight black bangs.

Lilith and I hadn't had much to do with the Miller brothers before that summer. The little I did know about them came from overheard talk among the grown-ups: their father was a white man from Williamsburg who'd married a woman from the local Chippewas, and after they'd both been cast out by their tribes they managed to get property along the lake and build this lodge. The lake families disapproved of them, of course, but they liked the lodge's amenities, so the women smiled at Mrs. Miller when they bought their groceries, and the men shook Mr. Miller's hand when they rented their fishing boats.

But as we stood there that day, it struck me for possibly the first time that the Miller boys were almost the same age as we. We'd lived our childhood summers not one hundred yards from one another. Lilith and I had spent those summers exploring the woods and swimming in the lake. What had the Miller boys been doing? I couldn't remember seeing them in the water, or even fishing off the dock. Had they, too, explored the woods? With a start I realized the woods might even belong to them.

Abe was standing by the bar. He'd gone back to staring at Lilith, his mouth hanging slightly open. Matthew moved in front of him, as though shielding him.

"We'll want ice creams," I told him, then gathered the rest of our groceries as fast as I could. Lilith went to the bar and leaned there, still giving Abe that off-kilter smile.

Matthew went to the freezer box. "What flavor do you want?" He was talking to me but his eyes cut between Abe and Lilith.

"Strawberry," Lilith said.

"Me, too," I said, even though chocolate was my favorite. I wanted the transaction over quickly.

"What about you?" Matthew said. I'd forgotten about Emily, who stood a few feet behind us.

"Butter brickle," she said, in her high, little-girl voice. I looked at her — I'd never even tried the butter brickle. She smiled, and I turned away.

Matthew scooped out our cones and began to make the tally. Lilith handed me her cone and rooted in her bag for the money Mother had given us. She smiled again, this time showing Matthew her white, even teeth, and Matthew fumbled with the change. She thanked him sweetly, took her ice cream from me with graceful fingers, and walked to the door, leaving me to carry the groceries. Her hips swung in her blue dress as she brushed past Emily. Abe stood like an oak tree, his liquid gaze following her. As I picked up the groceries I glanced at Matthew, expecting to see him similarly transfixed. But he was looking at Abe.

JUSTINE

The drive took four days and $493.

They drove nine hours a day, stopping only for gas and food. They had the $26 Justine had left from the allowance Patrick had given her on Monday and $600 she took from their joint account on the way out of town. She didn't want to pay with the credit cards or the checks because Patrick would know where they'd been used, so they bought lunches at gas station convenience stores and dinners at fast-food restaurants to make the cash last. At night they stayed in Motel 6s and Travelodges, paying $19.99 for a single and sleeping sideways on the bed. Every day the weather grew colder and the trees fewer and more barren. In Salt Lake City they found a Salvation Army store and spent $67.50 on down coats and wool gloves. In Idaho Falls, the girls walked in snow for the first time, twisting to see the treads their sneakers left in the thin dusting that covered the motel parking lot.

Sometimes Angela asked what was happening in school. Was it recess? Was it math time? Instead of answering, Justine talked about the lake, surprising herself with the details she dredged up: the feral cats who lived under the lodge, the white butterflies in the grass at the edge of the woods, the green smell of fresh water. Angela listened with a worried crease between her brows, but Justine thought she looked intrigued despite herself.

Melanie didn't ask about school or the lake or anything else. She just drew in her sketchbook or looked at the landscape with the intensity with which she looked at everything, as though it were hiding something on purpose. Still, she seemed thoughtful rather than sullen, and this made Justine feel hopeful, speeding like an arrow across the high desert. On Highway 90, between Bozeman and Billings, she lifted her feet and shook them, just a little.

But when her daughters slept, their heads lolling against the shoulder belts, Justine watched the snow-frosted brown land roll past and thought about Patrick. His absence was so present it was like a living thing sitting in the car with her. It accused her from the passenger seat, its silence a shout in her head, the air ringing with its charges of abandonment and betrayal. I loved you, it said. And you left me, just like Francis left you. Like your mother leaves everyone — without even bothering to say good-bye.

"I wasn't planning to leave you," she told it. It was true, but it sounded more like an excuse than an apology.

She'd met Patrick six weeks after she came home to find Francis's two-word note next to an empty can of Coors. Those six weeks had been the worst of her adult life. She'd staggered from one day to the next with two little girls asking where their daddy was and none of his so-called friends answering her calls until reality hit in the form of the rent payment, which she couldn't make on her own. They needed to move, but she couldn't do it; couldn't send her daughters to another school in another part of town — it would be like moving to a new town altogether, a trial she'd sworn she'd never put them through. So she begged her old manager at the Sunny Kitchen for dinner shifts and went straight there from Dr. Fishbaum's, waiting tables until midnight while her daughters fell asleep without her and Mrs. Mendenhall watched her television and knitted.

It was probably the exhaustion that made her careless. She remembered a shout, the squeal of air brakes, and then someone tackled her like a linebacker and landed heavily on top of her. When her rescuer pushed himself up on his hands she saw blue eyes and square, even features etched with concern. She recognized him: he was a salesman from one of the medical supply companies. He'd been in the office the day before, pushing his syringes and gauzes. Over his shoulder a San Diego transit bus was stopped in the road. Its door swung open, and the driver yelled, "Watch where you're going!"

The man helped her to her feet and promptly asked for a date. "I saved your life. The least you can do is let me buy you dinner." She felt herself blush. No one had asked her out since Francis offered to drive her home from the Sunny Kitchen twelve years before, and that hadn't been a proper date. Not dinner, she said; she needed the money from the evening shifts too desperately. So she met him for lunch at a diner down the street.

She'd liked him from the start. He was handsome in a mid-western way, with reddish hair and white teeth that filled his wide smile. He ate his sandwich neatly, his fingernails clean and square, brushing the occasional crumb off the table as soon as it fell. And he talked — how he talked! There were none of the awkward pauses that marked so many of her conversations with other people as he told her about his job, his life growing up on a dairy farm in Indiana, the 1969 Mustang he'd rebuilt. She returned to work exhausted and exhilarated.

After that, he wound himself into their lives quickly. On weekends he took them to the pier in Santa Monica or fishing near Mammoth Lake, and after her night shifts he waited in the parking lot with beer and doughnuts that they ate before making love in the cramped backseat of his truck. He called her beautiful, sexy, irresistible — words Francis had never used — and made her feel she might be those things, at least some of the time. He won Angela over with presents and magic tricks, and though Melanie wasn't so easily bought, Justine didn't let that bother her. Melanie wasn't going to like any man who tried to replace her father, even a man like Patrick, who was better than Francis in every way that mattered. So when, after a month, he told her his landlady was a nightmare, she didn't need convincing. He was a miracle, she thought as she gave up the night shift.

Once he moved in, he obliterated the faint footprints Francis had left. While Francis almost never touched her, Patrick always had his hand on her hip, his arm around her on the sofa, his body pressed against hers in bed. Francis's lovemaking had been gentle and rare, even nonexistent the last few years, but Patrick's was exuberant and frequent. Francis had disappeared when he worked his bar shifts, but Patrick e-mailed from work a dozen times a day. His name on her screen was like a finger reaching from the supply company or, after the layoff, the Office Pro, to touch her on the shoulder.

And she'd loved it all. No one had ever needed her the way Patrick needed her. Not because of biology, as her children needed her; or as an audience, as her mother needed her; or intermittently, as Francis had needed her; but fully and constantly. His every mood depended on how she touched him, the words she said, the way she made his breakfast, the way she folded his shirts. It was hard work, managing him like that, and when she didn't do it right it could take days of soothing and capitulation before he recovered his equilibrium, but it made her feel like she mattered to someone for the first time in a very long time. And she needed him, too. He took care of everything, from fixing the leaky faucet to managing their money to making their weekend plans. She could depend on him, and she loved that, just as she loved his smile, his easy way of talking, the mimic's way he had of bringing people to life in his stories. When he talked about how they met he'd say "I swept you off your feet," and it was true. He swept her up inside his world, and she loved him for that most of all.

But now, when she pictured him finding the apartment empty and reading her note on the counter; when she looked out at the brown grass and the small white houses alone in the vast land and thought about calling him — she didn't. She drove, and felt the distance between them open like a sail, pushing her forward.

In the late afternoon of the sixth day she turned the Tercel from a rural Minnesota blacktop onto a nameless, snow-covered dirt road where a wooden sign said MILLERS LODGE — FISHING above an Indian-style arrow pointing into the woods. The letters were a dirty white, the background once red but faded to brown. The sign itself stood in waist-high weeds. They'd seen no one for miles, and the sky threatened more snow, its chill ceramic pallor pressing against the black-fingered trees.

The road was just wide enough for the Tercel. It was so pitted and ridged that Justine steered carefully along at ten miles an hour until, after a mile and a half, they drove over a small bridge with low stone walls and down a long hill to the lake. Justine stopped the car in front of a square, log-bound structure that looked as if it had been hewn from the forest itself — the fishing lodge, where Arthur Williams had told her she'd find Matthew Miller.

The three of them sat unmoving on the vinyl seats. The lodge brooded over them, its massive porch jutting like a mouth. A smattering of cabins receded into the woods behind it. Farther along, a row of seven weathered houses dating to the early days of the century huddled together like dowager sisters, looking across the dirt road to where the lake lay embalmed in gray ice. The lake was bigger than Justine remembered, its frozen surface running between two narrow points of land half a mile away and into the distance beyond. No other structure interrupted its watchful black borders. Not a soul could be seen.

Melanie said, "I thought you said it was pretty."

"You said there would be butterflies." Angela's voice was small.

"That's in the summer," Justine said. "This is winter. Remember, I told you it would be cold at first. Soon it'll get warm and sunny, and it'll be pretty then. In fact, I think it's kind of pretty now, don't you?"

Both girls looked dubiously at the austere landscape.

A hand rapped on Justine's window, startling her. An old man stood there. He wore a stained brown coat and a wool hat with heavy earflaps, and his black eyes were sunk deep in the webbing of his skin. Justine had no idea where he'd come from. She rolled the window down two inches, her eyes watering in the icy air.

"Justine Evans?" His voice was low, roughened by cigarettes.

"Yes. Are you Matthew Miller? Arthur Williams said you'd have a key to Lucy's house."

The man's eyes slid to her daughters. They paused, then came back to her. He reached a slow hand into his pocket and withdrew a set of keys on a silver ring. He jerked his head toward the decrepit row of houses. "It's the yellow one. Third one up. You can park in the back." Without another word, he walked around the front of the car and up the steps to the lodge. Despite his age he held his shoulders erect, and he walked quickly.

"Who was that?" Melanie asked.

"That's Aunt Lucy's neighbor. He had the key for us. Wasn't that nice?"

"He's creepy."

For once Justine agreed with her. Matthew Miller was decidedly creepy. She kept her voice light as she said, "I'm sure he's perfectly nice. He wouldn't have been Aunt Lucy's friend otherwise." Neither girl said anything, but she could feel them looking at her as she coaxed the car along the road to a clapboard house whose color did seem, on closer inspection, to be yellow. It was narrow and plain, with two windows in peeling frames above a battered screened-in porch, and it seemed to lean toward them, as though the effort of holding itself up had made it weary.

"Is that it?" Melanie asked.

"It's big, isn't it? Think how much bigger it is than our apartment." Justine turned the car into a lane between the house and its equally dilapidated neighbor, finding a covered parking area in the rear where she wedged the Tercel beside a green Subaru. Her mouth was dry. In her memory the house had seemed to glow, its yellow paint fresh in the sun.

Snowflakes began to fall bleak and fine as they walked to the front of the house. Justine was cold even in her coat. It was just four thirty, but the sun had already set and the temperature dropped by the second.

When she unlocked the door, they stepped into a gloomy entryway lit only by the pale light that filtered through heavy draperies in a living room to the left. Dark wainscot pressed close, and shadowy portraits watched from the walls. To the right a staircase vanished into a deeper darkness upstairs. Though it was warmer than outside, it was still very cold.

"Mommy, it's awful," Angela whispered.

Justine didn't answer as she led them down a short hallway to the kitchen, where she found a push-button switch that lit a fluorescent ceiling light. This room, at least, held an echo of what she remembered, but the years had been as unkind to it as they'd been to the outside of the house. The white cupboard doors were scratched, and several hung askew on their hinges. The linoleum floor needed patching and sloped toward the back wall, and the ceiling had an ominous brown stain that probably meant something in a bathroom above was leaking. She clutched the bag of groceries she'd bought in Fargo close to her chest. Arthur Williams had said the place needed updating, but either he'd understated things or he hadn't been here in a while.

Yet — here was the old wooden table where she'd had breakfasts of cinnamon rolls and dinners of roast chicken. The flowered plates she'd loved still sat on the shelves, and the teacup collection hung in its wooden rack. Justine felt her shoulders unwind a little, and she set down the groceries. In the corner next to an antique white stove stood a radiator. She turned the knob and heard the clank of hidden pipes.

"Why is it so cold?" Melanie asked, her jaw tight.

"I don't think they knew we were coming today." It hadn't occurred to Justine to call Arthur Williams as they got closer. She'd assumed the house would be warm and waiting, as though Lucy had lived here until yesterday morning. In reality she guessed the heat had been left on just enough to keep the pipes from freezing.

The radiator soon warmed the small room, though, and when they could take off their coats Justine made peanut butter and jelly sandwiches for dinner. Afterward she washed the flowered plates, looking out the window over the sink to the blue-dark night.

The forest was a curtain of black velvet a hundred feet away. The ground in front of it was luminous with new snow, tracked here and there by the hopping prints of something small, and the light from the kitchen fell upon it in a golden square. The journey's end settled over her, weighing on her eyelids.

Angela's head rested on her arms. Melanie's face was drawn with exhaustion. "I think we should find your bedroom," Justine said.

The rest of the house was still bone-chillingly cold. They would need to turn on the radiators in the bedrooms or they'd freeze even beneath the covers. Justine led them upstairs to a square, pine-floored landing with four white paneled doors. She groped at a flitting memory, then opened the one to the left and pushed the light switch inside.

"Oh, look!" she said, relief and delight mingling in her voice.

It was a girls' room, without question. The walls were a delicate green, the baseboards eggshell white. Twin beds with matching wrought iron headboards and faded star quilts bracketed a tall window that faced the lake. An oak dresser stood on the opposite wall, with brass hooks above. The furniture was worn, but the air smelled like pine soap, and everything was as neat as a room in an inn awaiting its guests.

Justine found the radiator and turned it on. She sat on one of the beds, and after a moment's hesitation, Melanie and Angela sat beside her. The mattress sagged under their weight. Melanie looked around, picking at her nails, something she did when she was thinking things through. Angela leaned in, and Justine put her arm around her, feeling her shoulder blades flared like wings beneath her sweatshirt. The room was so cold she could see her breath.

"It'll be fine once it warms up," she said. "The walls are such a pretty color, like spring. And look at these quilts. I wonder if Aunt Lucy made them."

"I want to go home," Angela said.

Melanie's fingers stilled their restless motion. Her eyes glittered as she looked at her mother. Behind her, through the darkness outside the window, snow fell like ash.

Justine took a slow breath. Beneath the pine soap other odors lurked. Mildew, maybe. Old age, definitely. She bent her head to the penumbra of Angela's wheat-colored curls and inhaled their apricot scent that bore the memory of sunshine, hot pavement, and close-cropped grass. She tried to find the lightness she'd felt when she'd left the apartment key on the counter, but she couldn't. Instead she felt her inner compass teeter and spin. What was she doing? Her daughters had never lived anywhere but in that San Diego apartment. Yes, it was worn and poor and stank of striving and failing and overcooked brussels sprouts. Yes, their father had left it, and Patrick had moved into it. But in its constancy she'd given Melanie and Angela what she'd promised them that first night with Francis in the living room, something far more important than the poverty of circumstances and the comings and goings of men. They would have friends they'd someday say they'd known since grade school. They would have a mother who came home at night, who was there in the morning when they woke up. They wouldn't eat dinners of stale crackers and warm soda. They wouldn't tell the landlord to come back later because their mother was sleeping. And they would never, ever disappear overnight in an overstuffed car, unable to say good-bye to the friend they'd just made, at the whim of a woman consumed by the promise of the next good thing.

Yet here they were, sitting on a faded quilt in a dead cold house by a frozen lake that was practically in Canada. She'd pulled them from the life of certainty she'd promised them after a conversation with a man she didn't know about a house she barely remembered. Why? What was it about this place that had unmoored her in a way she'd sworn she never would be? Yes, Patrick was needy and manipulative. Yes, Melanie was struggling at school. Still, these were problems other people faced every day, weren't they? Problems other people faced without ripping up the footings of their lives and disappearing without a good-bye.

Her eyes skittered around the room until they landed on a small framed picture on the bedside table, a black-and-white shot of two girls, maybe ten and twelve years old. Their arms were around each other, their dresses tugged by a long-ago breeze. The younger one, her blond hair a frenzy of curls, looked up at the older one, whose light eyes smiled into the camera. The photograph was faded, but behind them Justine could see the lake, and could tell from their dresses and sandals that it was summer.

She herself had rarely worn shoes here. Not even sandals. She, who'd never had even the rudest patch of yard to play in, had roamed the forest barefoot for hours that summer. She found old structures made of branches and twine — remnants of forts built by long-ago children — that were the first places she claimed for her own. The lake was busy with fishermen and water-skiers, and the lodge that now seemed so grim was filled with children playing pinball, fathers and sons playing pool, teenagers flirting over malts, and mothers buying ice cream for their toddlers. She and Maurie and Aunt Lucy and Grandma Lilith ate dinners at that table in the kitchen, and she could see the happiness that suffused the older women's faces as they reached across to pat Maurie's arm or smooth Justine's disheveled hair.

She hadn't slept in this room, she remembered now. She'd slept in a smaller bedroom across the landing with a single twin bed and lavender walls. This mint-green room was where Aunt Lucy and Grandma Lilith had slept. Two old women sleeping still in the room they must have shared as children, beneath the quilts that sheltered them from the nighttime breezes of their youth. She looked at the lace curtains, frayed but freshly laundered. She saw for the first time that the beds had sheets on them. Someone had made them up. For her girls.

She ran her hand down Angela's back.

Felt the fragile bones beneath.

The doorbell rang. Justine froze, listening to the crashing silence that followed the jangle of the bell.

"Wait here," she told the girls. She went downstairs. Through the door she said, "Who is it?"

"Matthew Miller."

She opened the door halfway, bracing it against her hip. The old man stood there, snowflakes dusting the shoulders of his coat. He held a grocery bag and a flashlight. His eyes lifted, and she turned to see her daughters at the top of the stairs. He looked at them for a beat more, then he held out the bag.

"I thought you might need some things to tide you over until you can get to the store."

Justine took the bag and looked inside: a pint of milk, four eggs lodged in a broken half-carton, a stick of butter, and most of a loaf of sliced bread. "Thank you," she said, surprised.

"You're welcome." He stepped back so his face, just outside the reach of the light, was shadowed. Then he went down the steps and back to the lodge, stepping almost delicately in the snow.

LUCY

Nowadays, twenty miles is not that far. When I worked at the library, I drove it twice a day, and I still go on Saturdays to read to the children and do my shopping. But when I was young we took car travel less lightly, and the men had businesses to run, so they came to the lake only on the weekends, leaving the weekdays to the women and children. Because of this, our lake retreat was really two places: one when the men were there, and another when they were not.

On the weekdays, the strings of our mothers' aprons hung loose. They drank iced tea on one another's porches in the late afternoon, reveling in the fact that supper need only be cold sandwiches and that no one with any authority would ask when it would be served. During the heat of the day they played bridge at the picnic table underneath the elm tree or walked along the lane, car-

75

rying umbrellas against the sun. We children ran about unheeded, and no one told us to be quiet because Father needed to think.

On the weekends, when the men were there, our mothers fixed their hair and wore their better housedresses. They did laundry and cleaned house while the men fished in the mornings and napped or read in the afternoons until cocktail hour. On most Saturday evenings, the Joneses or the Lloyds hosted a grown-up party. Our parents hardly ever went, but Lilith and I watched the other couples walk past, the women in pearls and starched dresses and the men in light summer suits, and later we heard their laughter through our window.

Suppers were a more formal affair, too, when the men were there, or at least they were in our house. Mother made roasts or fried the fish Father caught instead of serving the leftovers and cold plates she gave us during the week. Lilith, Emily, and I had to come to the table in dresses, not our play-suits or, God forbid, our swimming suits. Father wore a tie and sat at the head, where he helped himself first, then passed the dishes around and said grace. Only when he lifted his fork could we lift ours, and we couldn't be excused until he finished. He and Mother talked, sharing news from their separate lives, but we girls were not to speak. Lilith and I endured these suppertime vigils by carrying on conversations below the table, pressing our feet on one another's in a rudimentary Morse code while keeping our faces frozen in perfect decorum. How Emily managed I have no idea.

After weekday suppers, Lilith and I were free to go back outside, but on weekends we had family time, just as we did in town. We went to the parlor, where the curtains were still drawn against the afternoon heat, so the room was dim and cool. Lilith and I sat on the davenport, Mother and Father in the chairs, and Father held Emily on his lap. From outside came the hoots and cries of the other children playing, but I never wanted to be out with them. I loved family time. I loved that none of the other families had it. It was a secret of the best sort, the kind others would envy if they knew.

It began with Father reading aloud. He'd gone to the Methodist seminary outside Chicago for a while, and he still had much of the preacher about him, so he'd read from one of his books of philosophy or the big leather Bible his father gave him, then speak for a time on what it said about how we should conduct our lives. I liked the philosophy books quite a bit — Kant was my favorite — but I loved it best when Father read from the Bible. He had a voice like a cello, deep and melodious, and it made of the language of God's chosen people a wrathful and mesmerizing poetry, as I imagined it sounded when first spoken by the mad prophets of long ago. We weren't churchgoers; Father left the seminary over an ideological dispute, something about how the church defined sin "in the hand rather than the heart," as I once heard him tell Mr. Williams. But it didn't matter. From his lips the Word of God rang more awfully in our parlor than I ever heard it from the pulpits of the churches I visited later in life.

That first night, as he did every summer, he read to us one of his favorite passages from the Gospel of Matthew:

And Jesus called a little child unto him, and set him in the midst of them, and said, Verily I say unto you, Except ye be converted, and become as little children, ye shall not enter into the kingdom of heaven. Whosoever therefore shall humble himself as this little child, the same is the greatest in the kingdom of heaven. And whoso shall receive one such little child in my name receiveth me. But whoso shall offend one of these little ones which believe in me, it were better for him that a millstone were hanged about his neck, and that he were drowned in the depth of the sea.

The words, spoken in his beautiful voice, colored the air with tones of darkest purple. When he was done, he placed his hand on Emily's knee, tracing gentle circles on her skin with his fingertips. The slow gathering of his thoughts ripened my breath, even though I knew what he would say.

"There is no such thing as original sin," he began. "The ministers who say so are cowards, excusing the transgressions of those they depend upon for their livelihoods. The truth is here, in this passage. We're all born pure, and while we remain that way, we are children. As soon as we take our first step into corruption, we are no longer children in the eyes of God. We must then strive to return to that state of grace as best we can, trusting that if we get close enough, and try hard enough to wash away our sin, Jesus's forgiveness will open the gates of heaven for us."

I nodded. The purity of my childhood self was one of the few things I took pride in. I wasn't compelling to look at, like Lilith, nor was I funny or charming or brilliantly imaginative, as she also was. I didn't have Emily's more conventional beauty, either, with her long-lashed eyes and heart-shaped face. But I saw the reverence with which Father touched Emily's hair as he spoke of Jesus's godly child, and I thought I, more than she, might be one of the "least of these" whom Jesus loved most especially, and whom Father, too, might learn to love, if he ever noticed.

"Your mother and I," Father went on, "bring you here every summer, even though it means we must live apart, because it is a refuge for innocence in the corrupt world. We want you to be children here. Swim in the water, play in the forest, look at the stars. Enjoy the simple pleasures of nature and family, and keep your innocence as long as you can."

This, too, was something I loved hearing every year, a blessing that bestowed upon all of our summer games and adventures something of the character of religious observances. But Father's words had an unusual intensity tonight, and he looked at Lilith as he spoke. For a shivery moment I thought he'd seen her flirting with the Miller boys in the lodge, but he hadn't been there. Then I remembered the way she'd smiled at Charlie the night before, and the expression on Father's face as he watched, and I knew he was warning her.

"When did you stop being a child, Father?" Lilith asked.

I stiffened. No one ever interrupted Father's sermons, and questions most definitely were not allowed. That Lilith would ask this, especially in the face of his clear warning, shocked me. Mother's hands stopped their needlework, and Emily watched Lilith with a worried crease between her dark brows. Even the children playing outside fell quiet. Lilith sat with her eyes wide and blue in her pale, strange face, waiting.

Father regarded her. I felt in his gaze the power of his will bearing down upon her, and for once I was glad he wasn't looking at me. Then we heard a shout from the shore — a little boy's crow of triumph, followed by a chorus of youthful outrage like geese squabbling over bread — and the lines of Father's face eased. He gave an indulgent laugh and patted Emily's thigh. "That's not for you to know. All you need to know is that I'm trying to become like a child again, through the example of my own children."

He closed the book and, to my relief, the odd moment passed. It was time for our nightly prayer: Psalm 51, which we knew by heart, even Emily. *Have mercy upon me, O God, according to thy lovingkindness: according unto the multitude of thy tender mercies, blot out my transgressions.* As I recited it I closed my eyes, searching for recent transgressions for which I might beg forgiveness. I didn't find very many. As I said, I was quite certain of my goodness, then.

When we were done, Father kissed Emily's head. Then Mother lifted her from his lap and settled her on her own, smoothing the hair that Father had mussed. The rest of the evening passed in quiet pursuits. Lilith and I played cards on the coffee table, Father read one of his philosophy books, and Mother continued her stitching while Emily pillowed her head on her breast, her eyes sleepy. When the light that came through the curtains turned from gold to navy, and the voices of mothers calling children home sang in the air, Mother carried Emily upstairs. Then she changed into her nightgown and slipped into Emily's bed with her, where, as always, she would sleep all night long.

Lilith and I took their departure as our cue. We kissed Father good night, brushing our lips on the rough skin of his cheek. He smelled of cinnamon and Arabic spices, the subtly wild smell of his aftershave lotion that, as a child, I thought belonged to him alone.

Soon after, settled between our sheets, we heard the crunch of his feet on the lane. I raised my head and looked out the window. It was almost full night by then, but the gibbous moon was up, so I could see him walking up the road toward the bridge, black against the silvery water. He went for a walk every night he was at the lake, after everyone had gone to bed. Once, years ago, I heard Mother ask him why. He told her he loved to count the stars as they came out, one by one, until they filled up the sky. I still remember the hush I felt when he said this. The way he spoke made it sound like church, or how I imagined church to be. Worshipful, and quiet.

JUSTINE

When she woke up, Justine checked her watch to see how many minutes she had before the alarm. Then she remembered: she was in Minnesota, in a double bed in the room next to her daughters'.

She ran her hand across the cool, empty space beside her. She'd slept in her sweatshirt and jeans, missing, against her will, the warmth of Patrick's body pressing against hers. She wondered how Lucy had stood it, sleeping alone in this room where the radiator fought a loud but losing battle against the cold.

The night before, she'd been so tired she hadn't cared that this was probably the bed Lucy had slept — and died — in. She'd only cared that, like the girls' beds, it had fresh sheets. Now she slid from beneath the covers and stood on the small rag rug, rubbing her arms in her sweatshirt. This was definitely Lucy's room. Though it was as immaculate as the girls', it bore the unmistakable tracings of a life. Cotton balls and hairpins filled porcelain pots painted with yellow daisies on the dresser. On the bedside table sat a pair of reading glasses, a small photograph in a gilt frame, and a library copy of *The God of Small Things.*

Justine picked up the novel and fingered the leather bookmark lodged two-thirds of the way through. How terrible to die without finishing a book, she thought. Never to know the end of the story. She read the inside flap. The story sounded exotic and sad. She wouldn't have chosen it. She loved to read, but she liked cozy mysteries, romance novels, the occasional thriller. Trashy stuff, Lucy probably would have thought. But it was distraction she was after, not intellectual stimulation or emotional engagement.

As she set down the book the photograph caught her eye. She picked it up with astonishment. It was a snapshot, the square sort taken by cameras in the late 1970s, and it was of a dark-haired woman and a blond girl. Maurie never kept photographs, claiming she didn't want to look over her shoulder at anything, or at any time, but Justine recognized the woman as a younger version of her mother, and the girl as herself. They were sitting side by side on the porch steps of this very house. The summer sun was bright on their faces, and Maurie looked so young they could have been sisters. Her arm was around Justine, her hand hanging loosely over her shoulder, and they were both laughing at the person taking the picture. Justine looked closer at the image of her younger self. Unkempt hair, bare feet. Too thin. But happy, in that moment, with her mother's arm around her.

It was so quiet here. A thick quiet that pressed on her eardrums. She looked out the tall window that was the twin of the one in the girls' room. The bare branches of the trees were bowed with snow, and the lake looked as if it was covered with white felt. It wasn't snowing now, but the sky was a pearlescent white, and for a moment the monochrome of the world made her dizzy. She set the photograph down.

Her daughters were still asleep, so she went downstairs. The entryway was only slightly less gloomy by the light of day, but at least she could see the pictures that had been shadowy, watchful squares in the dark the evening before. They were black-and-white photographs, the black faded to gray by years behind glass. Two were portraits of a man and a woman in Victorian clothes, the woman's face severe, the man's angular behind a wiry black beard. The third was of a couple posed stiffly in a photographer's studio. The man had striking dark eyes below wavy dark hair. The woman was small and fair, her hair in a chignon that couldn't quite tame her curls. She looked bewildered, as though she couldn't think how she'd come to be there.

The photographs must have been here twenty years before, but Justine didn't remember noticing them then. Now she studied them. These people had to be her ancestors — her great-grandparents and her great-great-grandparents, judging from the clothes. The blond, bewildered woman might even be her great-grandmother, the woman who, the summer Justine had come, lay wasted and dying in the bed she'd just woken up in. Justine had been afraid of her then, but in the photograph she was younger than Justine was now, and in the wan vulnerability of her face Justine saw something she recognized. They were the first pictures she'd seen of anyone in her family besides her mother, and she looked at them for a long time, her fingers working at the collar of her sweatshirt.

Then she went to the living room. It had the pine floors she remembered, but they were the color of dust in the thin light. Maroon velvet curtains framed the wide front window. A sofa and two armchairs upholstered in faded rose-colored fabric faced an ancient television on a metal stand, and on the far wall were a curio cabinet filled with figurines and an oak rolltop desk. Through a set of pocket doors was a small dining room with a table and six chairs. Both rooms swam with silent, chilly eddies of air.

Justine wrapped her arms around her chest and eyed the old metal radiator under the window. It must cost a fortune to heat this place. She should probably close both of these rooms off until spring. Except the living room had the only television in the house. She chewed her lip. They would just have to be careful. She shut the pocket doors to the dining room and made a mental note to turn off the radiators in the bedrooms once the girls were awake.

As she started back to the entryway, she saw an oil painting to the left of the door. It was of a little girl in a blue dress, her dark hair coiled in gleaming ringlets, a calico kitten in her arms. It wasn't very good; even Justine, who knew nothing about art, could see that; but the painter had captured a watchfulness in the child's eyes and a somberness in the turn of her mouth that made Justine feel almost as if she knew her. Below the painting, two candles sat on a walnut stand with an old Bible between them. Twin smoke stains darkened the gilt frame.

Unlike the photos in the hallway, Justine remembered this painting. One day, as she and Lucy sat on the porch, Justine had asked Lucy who the girl was, and Lucy said she was her little sister, who had disappeared in the woods on the last day of summer a long time ago. Her voice was light, as though it were nothing, just an old story, but her eyes went far away, beyond the lake, and Justine felt uneasy. Later, when she played in the forest, she imagined she was the lost girl living there in secret. She imagined she could go home if she wanted to. But she didn't want to.

Then, not long before she and her mother left, the older women held an observance of sorts. Lucy turned to Lilith and said, she's been asking all day, and Lilith said, we might as well get it done. Together they carried their mother down the stairs and sat her in one of the armchairs, which they'd turned to face the painting. Lucy drew the curtains and lit the candles in the day-dark, and she and Lilith stood on either side of their mother, their hands on the back of her chair. Justine and Maurie stood behind them, Maurie's arms crossed in silent, long-suffering irritation. The scene felt heavy with remembrance and mourning, and Justine waited for something else to happen, for Lilith or Lucy to say something, or to read from the big Bible, but other than lighting the candles, they did nothing. The old woman's dry, fluttering sobs were the only sound, and they were so quiet they sounded like mice chirruping under the floorboards. When she was done, her daughters carried her upstairs again, their hands dutiful.

Now Justine walked over to the Bible and opened it. It was a beautiful book, with gilt-edged pages and an embossed leather cover that was cracked with disuse. On the title page was written "To Thomas — An Enquiring Mind," signed "Father," with the date August 12, 1915. Gently, she turned the pages, which were riddled with underlinings and margin notes in a neat but crabbed hand. A red satin bookmark marked a page with a rectangle drawn around Psalm 51. *Have mercy upon me, O God, according to thy lovingkindness,* it began.

Who was Thomas? Was he Maurie's grandfather, the father of the three Evans sisters? Perhaps the severe, dark-haired man in the photograph in the hallway? Justine thought he must be. She looked up at the painting. The girl's black, pupilless eyes looked back at her as though they were actually seeing her. Unnerved, Justine took a step back.

She heard footsteps on the stairs: Melanie. Justine closed the Bible and went out to the entryway. Even as a baby Melanie hadn't been a morning person, so from long habit Justine didn't try to talk to her; she just led her to the kitchen and made them both toast. As they ate in their usual silence, Justine gave the room a closer look. It wasn't any less shabby in the light of day, but now she noticed more of its homey touches: a set of rooster canisters on the counter, a clock made from a barn door on the wall, and on the table a set of salt and pepper shakers shaped like fat bakers. With the radiator on, it was practically cozy.

One day that summer, she'd come inside, sand on her bare feet, and heard her mother, Lucy, and Lilith talking in here. Her mother's voice was higher than usual. "No," she said. "Absolutely not." And, "You have no idea what you're asking." A softer voice in reply: Lucy. "Think of her, Maurie. Think how it is for her." Justine must have made a noise, for they called out — "Justine, is that you?" — so she had to come in. Her mother, leaning against the counter, caught her as she passed and pulled her close. "We Evans girls stick together, don't we?" she asked, her voice too bright. Justine nodded because her mother wanted her to nod, and the old women looked back at her with something sad in their faces.

Now Justine turned to Melanie, whose hair hung in limp black curtains above her plate. She found herself smiling. Lucy had found a way to ask again, hadn't she? A way to ask Justine directly, without Maurie's interference. Now they were here, Justine and her own daughter, in that very same kitchen. "I think this house could be nice if we fixed it up a bit," she said.

Melanie raised her head. The colorless light of morning fell on the sharp angles of her face. For a moment she looked like someone different, someone older. "I hate it," she said. "It's freezing, and nobody lives here."

Stung, Justine looked away, at the teacups in their rack. When Melanie bent over her toast again she went to the sink and washed her plate.

After breakfast they went to see Arthur Williams. The dirt road was even more treacherous with four inches of fresh snow — the low stone walls of the bridge they'd crossed the day before were nearly covered — and Justine wondered uneasily who would plow it. Fortunately, the county road was clear. They followed it through winter forests and small hamlets barely large enough to justify signage: Kishawnee, population 120; West Liberty, population 179; Six Arrows, population 86. Each one a scattering of dirty white houses and a small, understocked-looking general store. Justine turned on the radio. The rock station from Fargo was fuzzy, but she didn't care.

After twenty miles they passed a sign that said WELCOME TO WILLIAMSBURG, POPULATION 2,425, and the small houses gave way to larger ones, some sturdy and plain, others with wraparound porches and fussy Victorian woodwork. Large oaks lined the street, their roots rippling the shoveled sidewalks. After a few blocks, the street ran into a small central square framed by quaint nineteenth-century storefronts. The Jones General Store anchored one corner. On the opposite corner sat Lloyd's Pharmacy, twin wrought iron benches framing its door, and there was a gazebo in the center of the square. The little town looked like a Rockwell painting, even with the dirtying snow and the metal-gray sky.

"It's cute, don't you think?" Justine asked the backseat as she slid the Tercel into an angled parking space. Neither girl answered, and as they picked their way down the sidewalk, cold air biting their faces, Justine saw that up close the stores' signs were worn and paint was peeling on many buildings. Several shops were closed, with faded FOR LEASE signs in the windows. She walked quickly, hoping the girls wouldn't notice, but a glance at Melanie told her that she, with those sharp eyes that found fault in everything, had.

The law office was on the first floor of a plain two-story building facing the square. On its plate glass window the firm's name was stenciled in chipped gold and black: WILLIAMS & WILLIAMS, ATTORNEYS-AT-LAW, EST. 1885. Its waiting area was furnished with four straight-backed chairs and a coffee table on well-worn parquet floors. At a small desk a woman with neat gray hair looked up when they came in.

"I'm Justine Evans. I'm here to see Mr. Williams." Justine glanced at the lettering on the window. "Arthur Williams."

"There's just the one. Mr. Williams's uncle passed ten years ago." The secretary picked up her phone and motioned them to the chairs. "I'll let him know you're here."

Justine and her daughters sat. Angela swung her feet until Justine stopped her with a hand on her knee. Melanie picked at her fingers. It was quiet except for the clacking of the receptionist's fingernails on her keyboard until the door beside her desk opened on a slight man of about sixty, stooped in tweed pants and a light blue dress shirt. His gray eyes behind wire-framed glasses followed Justine with keen but friendly interest as she and the girls entered his office, which was surprisingly opulent after the austerity of the waiting room. Its shelves were heavy with law books, an Oriental rug lay on the floor, and the mahogany desk was the size of a small boat. Justine took one of the two leather chairs and lifted Angela onto her lap while Melanie took the other. Arthur sat in the enormous desk chair. It made him look even smaller.

"This office was my great-uncle's," he said with a smile, as though he'd read her thoughts. "Apparently it was important to him to have the biggest desk in town. How are you faring at Lucy's?"

Justine smiled back, liking him. "It's cold." She cleared her throat. "But the house is clean. The beds were made up for us."

"I told Matthew you would be coming. I trust he's been helpful."

"He brought us some groceries."

"Well, don't hesitate to ask him or Abe if you need anything."

"Abe?"

"Matthew's brother. They keep to themselves, those two, but there's nothing they wouldn't do for Lucy's family."

Justine tightened her arms around Angela. During the drive from San Diego she'd tried to remember what Lucy looked like. All she could remember was the reading glasses she wore on a chain around her neck and that she smelled of talcum powder. Now, as she thought of the unfinished book on the bedside table, the porcelain bowls with their unused cotton balls and hairpins, and the photograph of herself and Maurie, her chest felt hollow.

"I don't want you to think I'm being ungrateful. But I'm not Lucy's family. Not like family is supposed to be. I only met her once, when I was a little girl. I hardly remember her." Surely, she wanted to say, there must be someone else — if not Maurie, then some cousin, or even a friend — who was closer to Lucy than she. More deserving.

Arthur templed his fingers and looked at her over the tops of his glasses. "There were just the three sisters. Lucy never married. Lilith had the one child, your mother. And Emily died young."

Justine nodded but didn't trust herself to say anything more. Arthur reached for an accordion folder and walked her through the paperwork, instructing her where to sign and giving her copies of everything. When he said the probate would take four months he was quick to reassure her that, as Lucy's trustee, he'd requested an early disbursement of the two thousand dollars in Lucy's bank account. "To tide you over," he said delicately. When he was done he handed her a small jewelry box. "Lucy gave this to me a few weeks ago. She said Lilith would want Maurie to have them."

Justine took the box with numb fingers. As she'd signed the papers and listened to him talk about transfers and court orders, the reality of her changed circumstances had struck her with full force. Two thousand dollars was more money than she'd ever had at one time. The investment portfolio could send her daughters to college, which was something she'd hardly dared hope for them. She felt a manic elation, yet at the same time she felt chagrined, even guilty.

She could not remember Lucy's face.

"There's one more thing," Arthur said. "Lucy asked that her body be cremated and the ashes deposited in the lake. I arranged her cremation before you arrived, and will keep custody of her remains until the lake thaws. But I wanted you to know, in case you were wondering about funeral arrangements, or burial."

Justine hadn't wondered about any of that. She swallowed, her throat thick. "Thank you."

Arthur took off his glasses, relaxing now that their business was done. "How long will you be staying?"

It took a moment for Justine to realize what he meant. "We're going to live in the house permanently. If that's all right."

Arthur looked at Melanie, then back to her. "It's awfully isolated out there."

"I know. But the girls will be at school during the day." She didn't know where the school was, but surely it was here in town.

"What about you? I imagine you'll need a job."

Justine hadn't given this much thought, either. She'd never had trouble finding the sort of work she and her mother had always done — waiting tables, tending bars, working in stores. Now she thought of the empty shops on the square. "I was a receptionist in San Diego, but I can do most anything, if anyone's hiring."

"People are losing jobs rather than finding them around here. You might try over in Bemidji. There's a Walmart there, and a Home Depot. If you're willing to work a cash register, there might be a place for you."

"Thank you." Justine had seen Bemidji on her map. It seemed far to the southeast, but maybe it wasn't as far as all that. Besides, she reminded herself, her situation was different now. She had two thousand dollars and no rent to pay. She could take her time.

LUCY

I've moved the parlor table to the porch so I can feel the breeze as I write. It's a lovely day, cool and almost cloudless, and the lake is that midnight blue it takes on in the late afternoon this time of year. Most of Matthew's summer guests have gone, all but the young family. The mother is in her chair by the water, stretched out in her pink bikini to catch the last of the sun. Her children are playing with their sand toys next to her. Her son, the elder, is quite gentle with his sister. He touches her on the shoulder as they walk and fishes her toys out of the water when they drift too far for her to reach. Watching him, I wonder what our lives would have been like if we'd had a brother. Or if Lilith had been a boy.

Matthew stopped by earlier. He's curious about what I'm doing, I can tell. I haven't been so clearly pursuing a project in a long time, not since the days when I wrote my stories, one after the other, in notebooks like this one. He didn't ask, though; he wouldn't. As usual, he offered to do some shopping for me in town, as he was going. I asked him for coffee and some of Millie Conroy's jam that I love. I find I haven't been hungry lately.

I realize I'm writing to a nine-year-old girl who lives only in my memory. I have no idea who you've grown up to be, Justine, and sometimes, I confess, I hope you won't read this. Lilith would say that an old woman's secrets should be allowed to sink beyond the reach of recollection, and maybe she's right. Still, I will keep writing. There is no harm in the writing. It is only in the reading that the damage would be done. Even then, what will it matter? I will be dead, along with anyone else the truth would hurt.

It was late spring when your mother called. When Lilith hung up, the look on her face astonished me. That was Maurie, she said. She'll be here in a week. Her voice was even, as though her daughter's coming to visit wasn't at all remarkable. As though it wouldn't be the first time she'd see you, her granddaughter. I said only that we should get Emily's room ready. We always called that room Emily's, even though it had been Maurie's for nearly eighteen years.

I still don't know why she came. I do know she hadn't a penny when she arrived and she left with several hundred dollars, but that was between her and Lilith. I think there'd been a man in St. Louis, which is where you came from, though she didn't say much about it. She seemed to want to pretend this was just a visit to her mother's house for a summer vacation, but it was the first time she'd been back since she left twenty years before, and that phone call was just the second one we'd gotten in all that time. Those postcards were the only contact we had. She did send a lot of them, though. Letting us know, I suppose, that she was seeing the world we'd kept her shut away from.

She arrived three weeks after she called. We were beginning to think she'd changed her mind. Of course, we'd been telling ourselves that all along: she won't come. We didn't even mention it to Mother; we didn't want to get her hopes up. But we cleaned the house, bit by bit, without seeming to. One day I cleaned out the pantry, throwing away past-dated jars of spaghetti sauce and boxes of stale crackers. When I did our shopping I bought a few treats I thought a nine-year-old girl might like — Fig Newtons and apple juice, things like that. Lilith put away her creams that cluttered the bathroom and moved her magazines to the basement, all those celebrity and travel magazines that had collected in foot-tall piles on the coffee table. I put sheets on Emily's bed, just in case.

We were sitting on the porch, as we often did in the afternoons while Mother slept. When we heard the car we didn't mention it — it was the time when the first summer guests arrived to stay in Matthew's cabins, so it could have been anyone — but when your station wagon pulled up, full of suitcases and boxes, I didn't dare look at Lilith. I went to the screen door, to be sure.

Maurie got out of the car. She was wearing tight, high-waisted jeans and those high-heeled plastic sandals the young girls wore in those days. A yellow halter hugged her small bosom, and her midriff was flat below it. Her hair, as dark as Lilith's, was parted in the middle and flipped out in feathery wings. She was almost forty, but in that light, in that outfit, she looked just like the girl who had stormed out our door twenty years before. She smiled the crooked smile I remembered, and there were tears in my eyes that I couldn't help.

She climbed the steps, looking me up and down. I felt frumpy and soft in my polyester

pants with their waistband sinking into my
stomach and my short-sleeved blouse from
Milligan's in town, cheap and practical. I
wished I'd thought to wear something less
old-ladyish. I wished I'd known for certain
she would come that day.

Lilith came up behind me. Maurie said,
"Hello, Mother," and her smile didn't falter
for an instant. Her eyes were that intense
black, shining with points of light like stars.

Lilith said, "Pull your car around back,
then we'll get supper on." Her voice was
casual, as though Maurie lived in town and
we saw her three times a week. Maurie
didn't like it; she wanted the Prodigal
Daughter welcome. She tossed her head,
that old gesture.

"I need to get our suitcases first." She
turned to the car, and for the first time I
noticed you standing there. Your arms were
folded, your fingers picking at your elbows.
All of us looked at you, and you looked
back, your gaze shifting from your mother
to me to Lilith.

The picture of you that I carry in my mind
is the image I saw that day. A small child,
too thin, in a dirty pink tee shirt with flowers on it. Your legs below your denim shorts
were beginning to lengthen as girls' legs do
at that age, your knees bony and scabbed

with patches of eczema. You wore navy Keds with frayed laces and no socks. Blond curls that needed cutting straggled unkempt to your waist. Your eyes were pale and wary, and you worked your lips between your teeth in a way that must have been habitual, for they were chapped. I felt a small, sharp pain in my chest. It seemed to me that by looking at you I could see everywhere Maurie had ever been.

The moment stretched longer than was comfortable, until you dropped your eyes and shifted your feet. Then Maurie called you over. I opened the screen door, and the four of us gathered in a circle on the porch. Lilith stood next to Maurie, and I thought how similar they looked, still.

"Justine, this is your grandmother," Maurie said, "and Aunt Lucy."

You watched us with those careful eyes and didn't say anything. I started to say hello, but Maurie laughed a brittle laugh. She wore dangling earrings with turquoise stones that looked like something the Millers might have sold in the lodge, years ago. "God, Mother, this place looks exactly the same."

Instead of answering, Lilith bent down to you and took your hand. Sometime in the last week she'd colored the roots of her hair so no gray showed in the flat L'Oréal black. "You can call me Grandma Lilith," she said, and you smiled just a bit. Until then I'd seen little of Maurie in your face. But as you smiled, one corner of your mouth tugged higher than the other, and I could see her there.

I never knew who your father was, but it's no mystery who you were named for: that boy Justin Yeats, the doctor's son from Minneapolis whose family used to rent the Lloyds' house every August when Maurie was little. Of course, by then it wasn't the Lloyds' house anymore — they had sold it to a family from Duluth after Charlie died in the war, and its new owners rented it out by the week to people like the Yeatses.

Justin and Maurie were four when he started coming, and they were inseparable from the beginning. They ran around building forts, pretending to be Indians and cowboys and whatnot. Maurie always decided the game, ordering Justin about in her high, bossy voice. His parents thought it was sweet; Justin wasn't the sort for rough play, and I think they were happy to see him having some adventures. But I never liked it.

One day I walked past the fish cleaning

shed to our kitchen garden and surprised them there. They were seven, eight at the most. As I came around the corner Maurie jumped backward, away from him. Justin was standing against the wall of the shed, his hands behind his back. His cheeks were red and his lips were shiny and wet. Maurie wiped her hands on her shorts and looked at me with those glittery eyes, and as I said, I didn't like it. They weren't doing anything wrong that I could see, but the air was charged with something, and it made me uneasy. I shooed them back to the beach.

Later I told Lilith about it. We were making dinner while Mother watched one of her programs, the muffled voices coming through the door. They were probably playing doctor, Lilith said; it was nothing to worry about. She knifed through a peeled potato with brutal dexterity.

I told her it hadn't seemed like they were playing doctor.

Lilith laughed a singing little laugh, the knife flashing up and down through the white meat of the potato. "How would you know? Is that something you did with Matthew?"

I had been draining the lettuce but I stopped, putting my hand on the counter. I was twenty-seven years old that summer.

No one had ever kissed me, and Lilith knew that. In fact, no one ever was going to kiss me, and I was beginning to realize this, and she knew that, too. Here I was trying to be helpful, pointing out that her daughter might be a bit wayward, and perhaps this tendency ought to be nipped in the bud, but instead of thanking me Lilith couldn't miss the chance to cut me, the virginal, unclaimed sister. I hated her a little bit in that moment. But all I did was turn back to the lettuce.

She knew she'd hurt me, though, and she continued in a milder tone. It was normal, she said, and she wanted Maurie to be normal in that way.

I'm sure she did, but I was right. The Yeatses eventually saw it, too, because after the summer Maurie turned fifteen, when it was obvious to everyone where things were heading — indeed, probably had already gone — they never came back. For a while, the two of them wrote to each other, but then Sylvie Yeats called and asked me to intercept Justin's letters, as she was doing with Maurie's, and I did. I know it was hard on Maurie. Still, I was surprised to see the name on the birth announcement, ten years after she'd gone.

Justine, indeed.

JUSTINE

After they left the lawyer Justine found the elementary school, a squat, brick cube with 1924 stamped in its cement cornerstone. Inside, it stank of sweaty sneakers and microwaved noodles. Melanie made an explosive noise with her lips. "Gross, Mom." Justine ignored her and led them to the office, where the secretary gave her the enrollment forms and said the girls could start on Monday. She offered a tour, but Justine thought of the airy San Diego school and declined.

Then they went home and unpacked. As the girls bickered over the drawers in the green bedroom, Justine replaced the photo of Lucy and Lilith on their dresser with one of Melanie and Angela at the Padres game Patrick had taken them to that summer. Her own room was less easily claimed. Its closet and drawers were bursting with Lucy's elastic-banded pants, polyester blouses, broad-bottomed underwear, and nylon stockings. The thought of clearing it all out was too much, so she left her clothes in her duffel bag.

The next day they drove forty-five miles to the Bemidji Walmart, which sprawled like a cow patty across from a snow-covered field and a Burger King, and Justine bought each girl two pairs of jeans, three sweaters, and a pair of rubber snow boots. As they headed for the cash registers they passed an aisle stocked with backpacks and lunch boxes. Angela stopped in front of a pink backpack with zebra trim. She fingered the strap and looked hopefully at Justine.

"The one you have is fine," Justine told her.

"It has a tear in it."

Her backpack did have a tear in the front pocket; she'd had it for two years, and Melanie had carried it before that. It wasn't a big tear. Not so big that it needed to be replaced. But Angela stood on the scuffed linoleum beneath those horrible Walmart lights that made every color too bright, and in two days she'd go to a new school where a rip in your backpack could tell everyone exactly who you were and who you were not, and she was so small, and so worried, and so perfectly made that Justine said, "Do you like that one?" Then she let both girls choose new backpacks and new lunch boxes. It was a spree compared to the stinginess of their San Diego lives, but she would have liked the same, once or twice, when she was their age. On the way out she picked up an employment application.

Back at Lucy's, she pulled out the chocolate chips she'd smuggled into the Walmart shopping cart and announced they were going to bake cookies. Melanie's eyebrows shot up so fast that Justine laughed. "It's a starting-over time," she told her, "and that requires cookies." The girls sat at the table, Angela bouncing in delight. Justine was a little giddy herself. New clothes and homemade cookies surely would make them forget the cold, shabby house and the grim school.

She'd never made cookies from scratch. When she was young, Maurie would buy a refrigerated roll of cookie dough and they'd slice it into hockey pucks they ate right out of the oven. It was a real treat, Maurie said, but Justine was secretly disappointed in the cookies' perfect roundness and the overblended texture that tasted of cut corners. She'd sworn she would bake from scratch when she was a mother, but she'd never found the time. She had a moment of panic in the pantry, but the dry ingredients were there, and they had the eggs and butter from Matthew Miller. As she lined up the ingredients, she felt she was keeping a promise.

She turned the oven to 375 degrees and read from the recipe on the back of the bag of chips. "Start with the flour. Two and one quarter cups."

They needed a separate bowl for the butter, eggs, and sugar, so Justine pulled one out and got the butter from the refrigerator. She dumped two sticks in the bowl, then Melanie and Angela cracked the eggs and the yellow hearts slid around the butter. The girls watched them silently. Justine made a mental note to get a radio. She could put it on the counter, next to the microwave.

She couldn't find a mixer, but she did find a sturdy, wooden-handled whisk. "This is what people used before they had electricity," she said. She expected an eye roll from Melanie, but Melanie just took the whisk and began to stir. The butter was hard, so she pulled the bowl into her lap and pounded it until it was the texture of tapioca, her face determined. When she was done she set the bowl back on the table, and she and Angela added the dry ingredients. Finally Justine opened the chocolate chips with a flourish and poured them on top. She was proud of herself, not just for the cookies, but also for how well she was managing things. She'd driven them halfway across the country, met with the lawyer, enrolled the girls in school, found the Walmart, and baked cookies from scratch, all on her own. Neither Francis nor Patrick would have thought she could do any of it, except for the cookies.

"Have some chocolate chips," she invited. Melanie and Angela each collected a small handful, then Justine set a cookie sheet on the table and they placed dollops of dough in four neat rows. When they were done Justine held the tray up as though it were a crown. "Now we cook them for eight to ten minutes, and then we eat them!"

But when she opened the oven it was cold. She jiggled the knob. The stovetop was working, a quick turn of a burner knob confirmed, but the oven definitely was not. Behind her the girls ate their chocolate chips. Justine looked under the stove for a pilot light. She didn't see one, but she wasn't sure there should be one, or where to find it. How old was this oven, anyway? She played with the knob again. Nothing happened. Her hands on her hips, she looked at the microwave. It was fairly new. And there were a dozen microwave dinners in the freezer. "Damn," she said, quietly.

"What's the matter?" Melanie said.

Justine kept her back to her daughters. The cookies lay in their raw balls on the silver sheet. "The oven isn't working."

"So we can't cook them?"

She forced herself to turn around. Angela's pewter eyes were wide with dismay. "No, I'm afraid we can't."

Melanie flicked a chocolate chip across the table with one finger. Disappointment mixed with scorn on her narrow face.

Then Justine remembered something. Sometimes Maurie didn't want to wait until the cookies were baked, and they ate the store-bought dough right from the plastic wrap. Maurie said it tasted even better that way. Justine pinched a fingerful of dough. It was delicious, buttery and grainy with sugar. "We can still eat the batter. It's almost as good."

Angela shook her head. "Mrs. Fitz says you can't do that. There's something bad in the eggs that you have to cook them to kill."

Justine wiped her finger on her jeans. Mrs. Fitz was Angela's teacher in San Diego. Was she right? Justine had never gotten sick from eating uncooked dough, but maybe the store-bought kind was different. Pasteurized, or something. She looked at the raw cookies. The sweet sugary taste was gone, replaced by a bitter one she knew well. "Okay. I'll have somebody out to fix the oven. And then we'll make them again. This was just practice."

Melanie gave a harsh laugh. "Sure, Mom." She walked into the living room. When Angela heard the television snap on she followed. Justine leaned over the sink. Through the window the forest looked like a tangle of barbed wire.

Patrick, who'd rebuilt a 1969 Mustang, could fix the oven. He'd get out his toolbox and sit on the floor with the contented look of a man doing something he knows he can do well. "We'll have cookies tonight," he'd say with his wide grin, and they would.

Damn it, Lucy, she thought. Why couldn't you have gotten your oven fixed? And Matthew Miller, creeping around, washing the curtains and changing the sheets. Why hadn't he noticed the oven wasn't working?

The dough made a sodden thud when she scraped it into the wastebasket.

She was washing the bowls when the phone rang, a harsh, old-fashioned jangle. On the third ring the ancient answering machine kicked in, and a thin voice spoke into the room. The house seemed to catch its breath

115

at the sound of it, and Justine froze. "You've reached the home of Lilith and Lucy Evans. Please leave a message."

After the beep came Maurie's much louder voice: "Justine, I know you're there. Call me."

Justine hesitated, then lifted the receiver. "Mom. How did you know we were here?"

"I called your cell phone. Peter, or whatever his name is, said you'd gone. He didn't know where, but I figured you'd head up there once you found out you got that house."

Justine should have expected that — both that Maurie would call her cell and that Patrick would answer it. Carefully, she sat down at the table. "Did you tell Patrick where we were?"

"Of course not. Believe me, sweetie, if there's one thing I know, it's when a girl leaves town without telling her boyfriend, she's got her reasons."

For once Justine was grateful for her mother's horrific track record with men. "Thank you."

"Artie Williams told me he gave you Mother's jewelry," Maurie said.

"He did. I'll send it right away."

"Never mind that. Just tell me what's there."

Justine got the box from Lucy's room and described its contents: a strand of pearls, a half dozen necklaces studded with semiprecious stones, a few rings, a gold locket, and several pairs of clip-on earrings. Justine didn't wear much jewelry, but she was pleased for Maurie. The pieces seemed like things she would wear, and it was nice she could have some jewelry of her mother's.

"Isn't there a diamond ring?" Maurie asked. Justine looked again; there was not. "Damn it, where did she put it?"

"What diamond ring?"

"She had a huge diamond engagement ring from my father. He was killed in World War Two before they could get married, but she kept it. It's got to be in that house somewhere. You need to find it for me."

Justine ran a hand through her hair. She knew what this was about. Whatever Maurie had going on, with Phil-the-boyfriend or without him, she needed money. Again. "I'll try." She dreaded going through the house, sorting through a dead woman's stuff from the bedrooms to the dank, mildewy basement, but she knew Maurie wouldn't leave her alone until she did. Besides, she told herself, she needed to do it anyway, if the house were ever to feel like theirs.

After she hung up she reached for the

answering machine, intending to replace Lucy's message with her own. But as she placed her finger on the "record" button, she hesitated. Erasing that whispery voice, the last echo of her great-aunt, felt like a desecration, somehow. The air stirred around her face in a cold caress, and she gave a quick shudder. There must be a draft somewhere. In fact, she could hear it: a whispering all through the house, as if the house were breathing. She shook it off, and went back to washing the bowls.

LUCY

At the lake, some children were younger than I, and others were older than Lilith, but none were our age. We didn't mind this, because we took little interest in other children anyway. On weekday evenings we'd join their game if we liked the game and were feeling sociable, but usually we walked up the hill to the bridge by ourselves. The bridge had low stone walls that Father, along with the other lake fathers and sons, built one summer when he was a boy. They were only a foot or so high, so they made a perfect bench for us. There we'd sit as the night fell around us, our feet dangling over the water, and talk about our future selves: rich, beautiful, and far away.

Lilith had it all planned. We'd go to Hollywood, where she would be discovered and become a movie star. I would be her assistant, the one person she could trust. We'd marry handsome men who adored us, and live next door to each other in houses that overlooked the Pacific Ocean and were linked with a covered walkway. Back in Williamsburg, people would read about us in magazines and marvel at how the Evans girls had made such sparkling lives for themselves. Night after night Lilith spun this tale to the sound of the creek that ran below the bridge, a shallow trickle of water over rocks. As she talked, I closed my eyes and let her voice replace my blood with air until it seemed all I had to do was take her hand and we would float away, as light as the fireflies that blinked all around.

When the stars were all out, we walked down the hill and home. The other mothers would have called their children inside by then, but not ours. Emily's door would be open, and Mother would raise her head from Emily's pillow when she heard us on the landing, but that was all. Lilith and I would close our bedroom door, change into our nightgowns, slide between our sheets, and keep talking, in whispers now, until we fell asleep.

At first, to my relief, our nights that last summer were like this. During the day, Lilith had no interest in roaming the forest or playing the games we'd always played; she wanted to sit on the beach near Jeannette and Betty and the other teenaged girls. But she was the Lilith of old in the dark, where it was hard to see the shapes of her breasts and her dreams were the same as they'd always been.

Then one night she stopped in front of the lodge on our way to the bridge. The sun had just dipped behind the hills, casting the lake into copper shadow, and the lodge's lights glowed like embers. The air was warm; it was late June and summer had overtaken the cool spring evenings of three weeks before. Laughter, high pitched and young, floated through the screened windows of the big porch.

"Let's have a Coke," Lilith said. I followed her, my steps heavy with misgiving. The lodge was the evening hangout of the teenaged crowd, who played cards and drank pop on the porch until ten o'clock, when the Millers closed up. That night Jeannette and Betty, Charlie Lloyd, Ben Davies, Harry and Mickey Jones, and Felicity and Sincerity Pugh sat on the porch in a circle they'd made of couches and chairs. I'd known them all since before I could walk, but it still startled me to see what they'd become overnight: bosomy girls with rouge on their cheeks and pimply boys who seemed made of elbows, the cheekbones of men pushing

121

up beneath the soft skin of their faces. I kept my eyes down and followed Lilith to the main room.

Mr. Miller was at the bar. I was a bit frightened of him — he rarely spoke, and his face sagged in heavy lines around his mouth, so he looked like he was angry all the time. Lilith ordered our Cokes in a light voice and he poured them from the fountain. I headed for a table in the corner, away from the group of lodgers playing pool, but Lilith walked to the porch. She sat on a couch near the teenagers and motioned for me to sit beside her. The teenagers didn't pay us any mind, but Lilith watched them with sideways glances as she sipped her Coke. She crossed her legs at the ankles like Jeannette and tucked her hair behind her ears like Betty.

I asked her if she wanted to play the pinball. "No, you go ahead," she said, but I didn't.

After a few minutes Charlie rose to go to the bar, and as he passed he gave Lilith a blushing smile. Lilith shifted her foot just enough that he kicked it as he went by. His apology was so awkward I almost felt sorry for him. Lilith rotated her delicate foot in its sandal. "I'll forgive you if you buy me a Coke," she said, waving her nearly empty glass. He ran a hand through his short brown hair and said sure he would.

"Why are you getting another Coke?" I asked her once he'd gone.

She winked at me. "I'm thirsty."

When Charlie came back he sat on the couch opposite us. Lilith thanked him for the pop, and soon they were in a conversation — halting on his side, astonishingly cool and flirty on hers — about how dull it was to be stuck at the lake all summer. This was the first time I'd heard her say our summers were boring, and I took it painfully to heart. I was the only one she spent her time with, after all. I finished my Coke, draining the dregs in a noisy gurgle. They ignored me.

Before long Harry and Ben came over, and then the entire gang. They pulled in more chairs and resumed their party, but now with Lilith and me at the center of their crowd. Or, rather, Lilith. I sat with my arms folded over my flat chest, my little-girl legs skinny below my skirt. But Lilith talked as though she were one of them. She, who normally ignored everyone but me, talked about the movies they'd seen as though Father had let her see them and the music they liked as though Father let her listen to the radio. Her hands gestured and her wide smile beckoned. Through the open button of her gingham blouse the tops of her new breasts glowed with an early summer sunburn. The boys darted looks at them when no one but me was watching.

When the last of the supper crowd was gone, Abe came out to wait on them, and they kept him busy wiping up their spills, bringing them French fries, and refilling their pops. He moved among them with barely a word. Though he was the same age as the other boys, he was bigger in every dimension: taller, his arms more muscular, his shoulders broader. Lilith smiled at him when he took her order, and I noticed he served her first when he brought the trays of pops and fries. I thought about Father, and what he would say about this whole business, and my stomach clenched. I wanted to leave, but I was stuck between Lilith and Ben, and of course I wouldn't have gone without her anyway. So I stayed, listening to their silly talk about the dance hall that had opened in Lexington — everyone seemed to know someone who'd gone, but none of them had ever been — until Mr. Miller told them it was closing time.

The boys shoved one another as they walked up the path. Jeannette linked her arm through Lilith's, and Betty walked on

Lilith's other side. I trailed behind, watching their heads bend close together as they talked. When we got to our house they called after her: "Good night! See you tomorrow!"

In our bedroom, Lilith was giddy almost to the point of mania, twirling about the room so her nightgown wound around her thighs. "Did you see Charlie bought me two Cokes? And Ben couldn't stop looking at me. I would love to go to that dance hall. Can you imagine?" She didn't notice I said almost nothing in return.

After that, she went to the lodge every night Father wasn't there. When supper was over, she went upstairs and primped, leafing through the *Vogue* and *Harper's Bazaar* magazines Jeannette and Betty loaned her, studying the models while I sat on my bed in silent misery. She'd never look like them, of course; not with her hair that Father wouldn't let her cut and the babyish dresses Mother bought for her. This gave me some comfort, though secretly I wished she'd offer to do my hair in the new style she devised: swept back and pinned in a glorious mass that gave the illusion, at least, of short hair. I knew I'd never be pretty no matter what anyone did. But I would have liked to feel her fingers in my tangled curls and have her eyes meet mine in the mirror.

"Why do you want to go?" I asked her one night.

"It's fun," she said. I told her I didn't see what was so fun about playing cards and drinking Cokes for hours on end. She stopped in the middle of pinning her hair and turned to face me. Pressed against the dresser, with her hands gripping its edge and her face set in tense lines, she didn't seem like someone who was about to go have fun. "I'm practicing."

"Practicing for what?"

Her pupils were large in the blue fields of her irises. "I'm getting out of here, Lucy. I'm going to go far away, and live a fabulous life. To do that, I need to make people notice me. So I'm practicing."

I looked at her raven hair, her bold face, the graceful young curves of her body. We had talked about leaving for as long as I could remember, but in that moment I knew it had been just a game to me. I couldn't really imagine myself anywhere but here.

"You should come to the lodge, too," she said, and I knew she did want me to come, but I couldn't go to the lodge and watch, ignored, while she sat among her new admirers, practicing, so I shook my head.

126

Not going, though, was almost as bad. Without Lilith I had no idea what to do with myself. I tried to join the evening games, but as the older children had become the teenaged crowd, only the youngest ones remained to play, and among them I felt out of place. One night I walked up to the bridge by myself, but this was an exercise in self-pity that even I, feeling hard-done-by though I was, could not abide. In the house my moping distracted Mother and Emily, whom Mother was teaching to stitch.

"Where's Lilith?" Mother asked one evening as I leaned against the doorway.

"At the lodge," I said, "with Jeannette and Betty and them." I watched her. She pursed her lips, and I could tell she didn't know what to make of this. Lilith and I had never separated before, and although Jeannette and Betty were nice girls from good families, they were older, and she had to know what that meant. I think I was hoping she'd intervene, perhaps forbid Lilith from going, but I shouldn't have hoped that. Even then I knew she'd relinquished any power she might have had over Lilith and me long ago.

Emily was watching me from Mother's lap. I frowned at her, indulging a small flare of resentment. Once it had been my hands Mother guided in embroidery, and my bed she shared at night. My bed, where I'd pull Mother's arm over my head so its soft weight closed my ear to everything but her heartbeat and mine, a thrum-thrum that sent me safely into sleep. Until the night, soon after Emily outgrew her crib, when Mother sat beside me in her white cotton nightdress, her long hair in its plait, and looked at me with a sorrowful apology in her face that in those days I thought was sweet and plain, a perfect mother's face. "Good night, baby," she said. Then she laid her hand on my forehead, smoothed back the curls, and kissed me, her lips light and dry, before slipping away to Emily's room. Ever since, I'd fallen asleep alone, except in summer, when Lilith and I shared our bedroom at the lake.

What saved me in the end was books. Lilith and I had never read much; quiet, internal pursuits like that didn't suit her. Now, with these long evenings to fill, I began to investigate the lodge's makeshift lending library, two shelves of castoff books left by earlier guests. All the children's books were for boys, but I was so desperate that I picked up Tom Swift, the Hardy Boys, *Huckleberry Finn,* and *Treasure Island,* and soon I was immersed in the worlds of these messy, swaggering adventurers. Each night after Lilith left me I lay in my bed and read about rocket ships and pirates and orphaned pickpockets until she came home. Years later, when I got around to reading the books girls my age were supposed to read — *Little Women, The Secret Garden, The Little Princess* — I found their staid rhythms difficult and the melancholy that seeped from their pages distaff and secondhand when measured against the loneliness of my eleven-year-old self reading *Tom Sawyer* in that empty bedroom.

When at last Lilith opened our door, I'd slide the book under my pillow, because I knew she'd want to talk then. I tried not to mind that the topics of our conversation had changed; that instead of talking about Hollywood and the glamorous lives we'd live there, she talked about how Charlie adored her, how desperate Ben was to catch her eye, and how, through clever gesture and insinuation, she flattered first one, then the other, with her attention. Practicing. I listened and made the assenting noises she wanted. I was just glad to have her there, alone with me, who knew her best, after all.

JUSTINE

On Monday the girls went to school. Justine drove them to the end of the dirt road, and they waited in the car for the bus to rumble over the hill and collect them on its way to Kishawnee and West Liberty and Red Arrow before getting to the school an hour later. It was still dark at seven thirty, and bitter cold. Justine watched Angela's shoulders sag as she climbed onto the bus, and tried not to think about the sunny six-minute drive to the San Diego elementary school.

The night before, she'd scrabbled through the coupons, paper clips, and buttons in Lucy's junk drawer to find a piece of paper and pen. Then she made a list of the things she needed to do. She needed to find out where Lucy got her mail. She needed to send her mother the jewelry and find that diamond ring. She needed to get the oven fixed, and she needed to find a job. Now the list lay on the counter next to the blank Walmart job application while she sat at the old elm table, still in her coat. The draft had kicked in again, and it fingered the nape of her neck. In the empty room it felt as if the house itself were watching her.

Over the weekend she'd confirmed what she suspected: nobody lived in any of the other houses. They were probably summer homes, so she supposed she and the girls would have neighbors come June, but right now there was only the vastness of the woods and the silent, frozen lake, and creepy Matthew Miller and his unseen brother in the lodge. She couldn't stop thinking about the San Diego apartment. It was five thirty in the morning in California. Patrick would still be sleeping, and if she were there she'd be tucked against him, feeling anything but alone.

The doorbell rang. It startled her — she'd just been thinking about how isolated this place was, and now somebody was here. She answered the door to find Matthew Miller standing with his neck thrust forward like a buzzard in his dirty coat. She stifled a sigh. Of course it was him. Who else could it be? She hoped he wasn't going to keep dropping by like this.

He made a wet, gurgling noise in his

throat. "I'm heading to town. If you need anything, I could pick it up for you."

"No, that's all right. I'm going myself, in a little while."

He nodded and left. Ten minutes later, a heavy motor turned over, and Justine watched through the living room window as he drove his black pickup onto the ice, heading to where the frozen lake collided with the hills in a colorless line. There was no way she was trying that in the Tercel. But as she watched, she decided she really would go into town. The thought of spending the day in this cold house filled with a dead woman's clothes and unused coupons was unbearable. In Williamsburg she could get some coffee, maybe find a library, and pick the girls up after school so they wouldn't have to take the bus back.

She found the coffee in Ray's Diner, a café down the street from the Williams law firm. It was a small place built in the 1950s and unimproved since then, but it was warm inside, and humid with melted snow. Two older men sat at the blue Formica counter, remnants of egg and toast on their plates, and three middle-aged women were talking in a booth. Justine stood at the door for a beat too long, and the women looked up, curious, and scanned her secondhand coat:

the new girl in school. Justine grabbed a newspaper from the stack on the counter and slipped into the nearest booth.

She'd just finished reading about the local movie theater's impending closure when a voice said, "Hon, we don't have table service until lunch. You want something, you gotta order at the counter." The woman who spoke was about sixty, with dyed black hair in a misshapen bouffant, heavy brows, and thick lips painted a red that disagreed with her sallow skin. When she caught Justine's eye she smiled, and the smile made her oddly appealing, like a friendly goblin.

Justine obeyed, ordering coffee and a cinnamon roll. As she walked away with her cup and plate one of the men at the counter said, "Ray, fill me up, why don't you," and the woman answered, her voice low and musical, saying something that made both men laugh.

Next Justine found the library, a new-looking building with its own parking lot two blocks off the square. Inside, she breathed deeply and happily, inhaling the familiar library smell of wood and paper and dust. All around were the sibilant sounds that libraries make: the turning of pages, the shelving of books, and the whispering of librarians colluding to make a

133

shush like the ocean on a still day. Sometimes Justine imagined this was how the world sounded to babies listening from the womb.

She had spent many hours in libraries. By the time she was ten she'd stopped trying to make friends at every new school and instead spent her time at the closest library. She'd been in all sorts, from small town libraries no bigger than a double-wide to the city libraries of Kansas City and St. Louis. She went after school, on weekends, and in the evenings if they were open. She walked to them, took buses to them, begged her mother for rides to them. To be fair, she hadn't had to beg very hard — dropping her daughter at the library was easier for Maurie than convincing a neighbor to watch her.

She went to the counter and put *The God of Small Things* in the returns box. When the librarian greeted her, Justine told her she'd like a library card. "Where are you from?" the woman asked as she gave her the form. She was in her mid-fifties, with dyed blond hair, and though her smile was warm, she had gossipy eyes.

"California." Justine filled out the form and slid it across the desk.

The librarian gasped when she saw her

name. "Are you related to Lucy Evans?" When Justine gave a reluctant yes, the librarian looked as if she wanted to jump over the counter. "That's wonderful! We heard she had a relative somewhere! I'm Dinah, so happy to meet you. Oh, but I'm so sorry for your loss. So sudden. But such a blessing, to go in her sleep like that." She leaned closer. "Did you know she worked here, at the library?"

Justine took a step back. "No."

"Well she did, for decades. We even had a party for her fiftieth anniversary. She retired about three years ago, but she still did her weekly story hour for the kiddies. Although I think the driving was getting to be too much. I told her she should sell that place, move into town, but she wouldn't hear of it. She loved it out there, she said. But with her sister gone, she was all by herself. Except for the Miller brothers, of course." She gave Justine a significant nod, and when Justine didn't say anything, went on, "She was supposed to come in for her reading that Saturday, but she didn't. That's how we found out she'd passed."

Justine had taken her girls to a story hour at their neighborhood library in San Diego when they were younger. The reader was a rangy woman with a severe face, but when she opened the book, her body curved toward the children.

Dinah was watching her expectantly. Justine said, "How long until the card is ready?"

The librarian squared her shoulders. Justine had offended her. To mend the breach she asked where the fiction stacks were. Dinah pointed to the back of the library. "We don't have a big selection. Not like what you're used to in California."

"That's okay." This, too, felt like the wrong thing to say, so Justine hurried off, anxious to put several bookshelves between herself and the front desk.

The stacks were indeed small, but the mystery collection was impressive for a library this size. Justine picked out an Elizabeth George — she loved the character Barbara Havers, the awkward and homely deputy to the handsome, highborn detective. She sat in a chair, and before she knew it, it was past noon and the library was busy. Half a dozen people were browsing or sitting at the computers by the wall.

Dinah was still at the desk. Justine debated coming back later, but she took herself in hand and put the book on the counter.

"I've got your card right here," Dinah said, all-business as she swiped the barcode.

"You have a beautiful library," Justine said, tentatively.

This was the right thing to say. Dinah puffed up like a rooster and stroked the wooden counter as though she'd built it herself. "We're the only town in the county that has a new library. All the others are falling apart." Williamsburg, she explained, had received a large gift from a local patron, Agnes Lloyd. "If you like to read, you've come to the right place." She paused. "You know, I have something you may want. Wait just a minute." She disappeared through a door and returned with a large cardboard box. "Lucy read the children all the usual things. Dr. Seuss, Winnie-the-Pooh, and all that. But she also read them stories she wrote, and those were the children's favorites." She slid the box toward Justine. "Now that she's gone, we don't know what to do with them. She read them in such a particular way. Maybe you'd like to have them?"

Justine lifted the flaps. Inside were two dozen notebooks with black-and-white marbled covers and black spines. She pulled one out and opened it. On the first page was written, "Emily Catches a Star," in the neat, careful cursive of a young girl. The rest of the pages were filled with the same handwriting, story flowing into story, all with titles beginning with the name Emily.

"They're set at the lake," Dinah said. "Of course, the children didn't know the history. They thought Lucy made Emily up."

Justine ran her hand over the spines of the little books. "Are all the stories about her?"

"Yes, isn't that sad? She must never have gotten over it, poor dear. They searched for weeks — they dragged the lake and everything — but they never found the slightest sign of that child." Dinah shook her head, her enjoyment of the tragedy palpable. Justine felt a twinge of affront on Lucy's behalf. To cover it she reached for the box and thanked the librarian. She made sure to smile at her before leaving.

At three o'clock she was in front of the school, the box of Emily books on the seat beside her. She called to her daughters as they shuffled toward their bus and saw relief burst upon their faces. Her heart felt spongy in her chest: she hadn't been so long without them since leaving San Diego. When they climbed in she asked how they'd liked the school.

"It's awful," Angela said. "My teacher made me stand up and tell everybody where I was from. When I said San Diego somebody said that must be why I wore such stupid boots." She kicked the back of Jus-

138

tine's seat. "Everybody else has big fuzzy boots, not these dumb ones."

Justine looked at the clots of children passing by. Several girls wore thick suede boots with fluffy lining. They looked expensive. "Sweetie, the first day is always hard. I've been the new kid lots of times. After a while they'll forget you're new, or another, newer kid will come along." She didn't add that she'd made few friends at any of her new schools; that wouldn't be Angela's fate, she knew. "How about you, Melanie?"

Melanie's eyes met hers in the mirror, then looked away. "It's just a school, Mom."

Justine turned on the radio for the drive home.

That night, when the girls were in bed, Justine carried the Elizabeth George mystery and the box of books the librarian had given her up to Lucy's room. She changed into her pajamas, intending to get into bed and read the mystery. But instead she opened the box.

The bindings of the notebooks were creased from many openings and closings, and she pictured an old woman in a chair, reading them to a circle of children. She lifted out the one that started with "Emily Catches a Star."

Emily had always wanted a star, it began. They were so bright, and she thought if she had one, she could use it as a night-light. She was a little bit afraid of the dark, even with Mimsy to keep her company. The story went on to tell of a night filled with shooting stars, and how one of them landed in the lake. With the help of her friend Mimsy, who was a talking mouse, and the night nymphs, a shy form of fairy, Emily persuaded the water sprites to give her the star, which she hung on a silver chain by her bed, and she was never afraid of the dark again.

It was a simple story, but sweet, like the children's books of an earlier day. Justine lifted the box to the bed, and over the next two hours she read through the rest of the notebooks. Lucy had written more than a hundred stories in all, and in each one Emily and Mimsy had an adventure in a benign world populated by fairies, fauns, and other forest creatures. They lived in a tree house in a massive oak, with pulleys for raising treasures, buckets for catching rainwater, and bedding made of dandelions and cattails. They ate honey, berries, and the edible gifts of the forest denizens. There were no adults or humans of any kind, and it was always summer.

When Justine was done she wrapped her

arms around her knees. The librarian was right. When you knew the history, the stories were incredibly sad. Lucy must have missed her little sister terribly. In her schoolgirl notebooks, in handwriting that evolved from the looping cursive of a girl to the spiky hand of an adult, she'd invented a benevolent world for the lost child in the forest into which she'd disappeared. She'd continued to invent it for what must have been decades.

It was past midnight. The house was quiet except for the low hiss of the radiator in the corner. But Justine felt the forest pressing against the house from behind, and it did not feel quiet. It felt stealthy. Somewhere in its black tangles, under dead leaves and fresh snow, lay the bones of a child. A little girl who died alone and scared, without a night-light. Once Justine conjured that image — the small white bones, curled among shreds of rotting fabric in the hollow of a tree or the heart of a thicket — she knew she'd never stop seeing it. How long had it taken Emily to die, as summer chilled into fall? How many days had she wandered, trying to find her way home, before lying down in that last, desperate shelter? A six-year-old girl. One year younger than Angela.

Stop it. She shook her head. It was a long

time ago. Three generations. This was a starting-over place for her and her daughters. The past didn't matter — not their own, not Lucy's, and certainly not the house's. All of it was nothing but dust. Emily most of all.

She put the box back on the floor. Then she lay down, pulled Lucy's quilt to her chin, and closed her eyes. She left the light on.

LUCY

There is nothing so quiet as this place after the summer guests have gone. It's my favorite time of year. The leaves are beginning to turn, and the air is crisp, but it's not cold yet. The geese fly south in great dark vees that span the sky, and the lake is calm.

Matthew's teenaged summer hires are working their last days, cleaning the cabins and closing down the kitchen. Right now he's pulling the boats out so he can tow them to Olema for the winter. He'll leave one for himself until the lake freezes. It's the only season he has time to fish, and he'll go out every morning. If he catches more than he needs, he'll bring a couple of small ones by for me, cleaned and ready to fry.

Yesterday he brought in the old pontoon. A wooden platform mounted on oil drums, it's been a summer fixture since 1935. The children love to jump off it, though when they swim out there, their dark heads bob-bing, I want their mothers to call them back. I mind my own business, of course. Besides, it's not anchored as far from shore as it was that summer, when Lilith and I swam to it.

It was shortly before Independence Day, and summer had arrived in earnest. It was hot by midmorning, with a haze that leached the color from the water and the sky. Lilith and I were sweaty, bored, and trying to think of something to do as we wandered down to the dock. Most people were inside their houses, trying to stay cool, but the two littlest Jones brothers were building a sand fort on the beach, and Abe and Matthew were working in the boat shed. As we passed, Abe raised his hand to wave, but at a glance from Matthew he put it down again. Lilith didn't look at him, but she ran her hand through her hair in a way that told me she'd noticed.

We tucked our skirts underneath us and sat on the end of the metal dock, wincing a little at the filtered heat on the backs of our thighs. Lilith took off her sandals and dipped her toes in the water. I wished the dock were lower, so my feet could touch it, too. It didn't occur to me that my legs would grow.

Lilith looked back at Abe, and I said, irritated, "Why are you looking at him?"

"He's handsome, don't you think?"

"He's a retard." I tossed the word off as if I said it as often as I'd heard it on the schoolyard. I knew it wasn't fair, though. Abe wasn't retarded. He was just a little simple, and he had a childlike way about him that his body had outstripped years before. He has it even now.

Lilith shrugged. "I think he's sweet."

We sat without speaking for a while. Then I said, "Maybe we could go to the Hundred Tree." We still hadn't been there, and this had been troubling me.

We'd found the Hundred Tree four years before. The forest around the lake is dense, and most of the lake children never went farther into it than their mother's voices could reach. But our mother's voice never called, so Lilith and I went wherever we wanted, which meant we went wherever Lilith led us. One day we came upon a clearing deep in the woods that was dominated by a magnificent oak, its trunk ten feet across at the bottom. Its base was split and it was hollow inside, but despite this it was strong and alive.

"This will be our secret place," Lilith said. Light filtered through the tree's branches in a patchwork on the mulchy earth, and on

Lilith, making her elfin and strange, her dark hair struck with silver and her pale eyes flat like new nickels. "No one can find us here."

We called it the Hundred Tree because we thought it must be the unimaginable age of one hundred years old. We cleared the inside and smuggled pillows from the house and set them in a circle around a large flat rock we dragged and pushed through fifty yards of forest. We brought egg cartons to hold the beads, marbles, and Cracker Jack trinkets we hoarded like magpies. We sat for hours in the cool dark, feeling the living tree around us as an embrace. We talked. We were silent. We escaped there as often as we needed to during that summer and the summers that came after.

But now, when I brought it up, Lilith smoothed her skirt as if brushing away dust. I tried to stifle my fear that the Hundred Tree had gone the way of the tree house and the playground in town. Then her eyes lit upon the pontoon. "I know what we should do. We should swim out there."

I peered at it. As I said, it was new that year, and it wasn't for children then. It was for people who didn't like to fish from a boat or who wanted to picnic while they fished, so it was half a mile into the lake, almost to the westernmost of the two points. Through the wavy summer air it looked even farther away than that.

We weren't allowed to go there, of course. The lake bottom dropped off past the dock and we weren't permitted to swim beyond it. But Lilith's eyes snatched at mine, sparking with that devilish light I could never resist. I thought about the Hundred Tree, and how she'd led me there. I thought about the Miller boys, too, and how far away from them the pontoon was. I said, "Okay."

She clapped her hands and ran for the house, and in her excitement she looked like the young girl she still was. We changed into our swimming suits and grabbed towels from the linen press. When we came back out, Abe was standing at the edge of our front yard, talking to Emily. When Emily saw us she ran over, her feet skip-skipping in the dirt. "Can I come swimming with you? Please? I'll ask Mother."

Although Mother didn't keep as close an eye on Emily during the week as she did on the more straitlaced weekends, she never let her leave our yard without permission. She would probably say no, but we couldn't risk it. If she did let Emily come, she'd come out to the beach herself to watch over her, and we would be stuck dog-paddling in the shallows. I started to run past without answering her, but Lilith stopped, standing over her with her hands on her hips. "We aren't going swimming. We're going to do something secret, and you're not invited." She put her hands on Emily's shoulders. Emily was so small that Lilith's thumbs met in the hollow of her neck. "If you tell Mother, I will pull out all of your eyelashes."

Emily's hands flew to her eyes. Of course she believed her. Lilith had carried out many a threat and perpetrated many a small meanness on our little sister; even I believed she would do it. I stood beside Lilith, relishing, as always, my exclusive position as her chosen comrade. To Emily I said, "You couldn't do it anyway. You're a baby."

Lilith laughed and grabbed my arm. We ran to the beach, our bare feet still soft enough that the pebbles on the road pricked at the soles. The Jones brothers were deep into their sand excavations and didn't notice us, but Lilith veered aside anyway, to the far edge of the beach. I stole a glance back at Emily. She was sitting on the porch steps, her hands still pressed to her eyes. Her shoulders were hunched close to her bent knees, and she looked so miserable that for a moment I felt a little bit sorry for her. Abe walked over in his slow way and sat beside her, putting an arm around her. Maybe, I thought, he wouldn't be so impressed with Lilith if he knew what she'd said to Emily.

I forgot about Emily, though, as Lilith wrapped our towels around our heads so we looked like Arabs, and posed and walked about as she imagined an Arab might, making me laugh. Then we were paddling through the water, our towels dry in their makeshift turbans. Within fifty feet the bottom disappeared, and we turned toward the pontoon.

Oh, it was exhilarating! The water splashed around my face, smelling musky and fecund in a way it didn't in the tamer places close to shore. My arms were brindled with sunlight as they carved neat arcs just beneath the surface. I felt like a water sprite, graceful in my natural element, and as I swam I thanked the sister whose adventurous spirit led me to do things I would never otherwise dare.

But Lilith was a stronger swimmer than I, and although I strained to keep up, she left me behind. Soon I tired, and as my legs grew heavy beneath me I craned my neck and was shocked to see how far away she'd gotten, and how much farther still was the pontoon. I looked back: the shore was a thin brown line, the Jones brothers like ants scurrying among their tiny battlements. A finger of fear tickled the edge of my mind, and just like that I was no longer a water sprite; I was an eleven-year-old girl in the middle of a lake, a towel on her head, treading green water that had no bottom. My heartbeat slammed in my ears. The water, so buoyant when I'd set out, clutched at me with fingers stronger than gravity. I called Lilith, but my voice was high and weak, and she didn't hear. She was too far away to save me anyway.

I forced my lungs to slow down, to draw great, shuddering breaths. All I had to do was keep swimming. I fixed my eyes on the pontoon in the distance, and ordered my limbs to propel me toward it. For an unmeasurable time I concentrated on moving forward, trying not to think about how deep the water was or how far I had to go. I swam until my legs felt like they were made of concrete, my arms felt filled with lead, my side burned with a cramping stitch, and my neck ached from holding my head with its towel-turban above the water. Finally, nearing the end of my strength, I looked up — and there! The pontoon was a mere hundred feet away, and Lilith sat on it, relaxed and mocking in the sunshine. She waved, telling me to hurry up, lazy-bones.

One hundred feet. I could do it. Water ran into my eyes and I blinked it away. My mouth was barely above the surface now. Then the towel, already half undone, fell in soggy clumps around my shoulders, and its sodden weight dragged me under. I fought my way up to take a breath, but I sank again, and this time I couldn't get back — the surface was a bright, shimmering veil that floated away from my reaching hands. I held my breath for as long as I could, but at last it burst from my lips in loud, glossy bubbles. My empty lungs burned, then they spasmed open and the lake flooded in, thick and cool and sweet, and filled me all the way up.

A deep, soft silence fell. Without the thrashing of my limbs or the frothing of air from my lungs, my ears filled with the quiet pulse of the water. The water was golden, stabbed by the sun, and tiny motes of algae floated in the slanting rays of light. Below me the gold filtered into green, the green dimmed to black, and the black dropped away to the deep, cold heart of the lake. The towel slipped from my shoulders, and I watched its sinuous descent, a pale thing spiraling into the darkness. My fear was gone. In its place a great calm descended, languid and cool, whispering of homecoming and safety and infinite secrecy. My arms drifted, dappled still by surface light as I sank through the deepening water.

Then something grabbed my hand and yanked me upward, and my head burst back into the bright, screaming world. The screaming came from Lilith, who was shouting at me to swim as she dragged me toward the pontoon by the strap of my bathing suit. I couldn't swim, so I lay on my back, coughing up water and gulping air that tore my lungs like shards of glass while she pulled me along beneath the violently blue sky.

After I hauled myself onto the pontoon she shrieked at me: What was I doing? I knelt on my hands and knees, retching up the last of the lake water. When I was done I fell forward onto my face, feeling the warmth of the wooden planks on my cheek. I looked up at Lilith with one eye. Her shoulders were heaving and her hair was matted to her head. Her hands were shaking by her sides.

"The towel got wet and dragged me under," I said, my voice hoarse.

"Why didn't you just drop it?"

I had no answer. She had tied it on my head. It hadn't occurred to me to let it go.

She combed her fingers through her hair,

calming herself. Then she wrung it out, twisting it into a knot. "Well. If I'd known you were such a lousy swimmer, I never would've brought you out here."

I felt the sudden prick of tears. Lilith flopped onto her back on her towel and closed her eyes. Her face was still flushed and her breathing was still fast. The sun glittered in the water droplets that lay upon her cheeks and brow like diamonds.

We stayed like that for a long time. My heartbeat slowed and the sun dried my skin and the cotton of my swimming suit. Eventually I could tell that Lilith had fallen asleep. I lay still, feeling the pontoon sway gently beneath me. The oil barrels pinged in the heat. My arms and legs felt like they were filled with sand.

The sun was high overhead when Lilith stirred, then sat up. "It's almost time for lunch. Let's go." She wrapped her towel around her head and sat on the edge of the pontoon, ready to jump in. I dug my fingers into the wood as the platform rocked with her movements. "What's wrong?" she asked.

I tucked my knees under my chin. I couldn't get back in the water.

She made an exasperated sound. "How do you think you're going to get back, then? Is someone going to have to bring a boat for you?"

I studied my knees some more. Yes.

"Mother will be furious if she finds out we were here."

I couldn't imagine Mother feeling anything as strong as fury about anything we might do. It didn't matter; I still couldn't do it. I was paralyzed with fear.

Lilith stood up. She was quite capable of fury, and hers was an electric thing, charging the very air about her. I could feel the hair on my arms stand on end as she glared at me. Then I felt her soften. She sat down and put her arm around me. With her other hand she tucked a stray curl behind my ear. "Don't be afraid, Lulu." Her old nickname for me, unused for too long. Her eyes were as clear as the sky. "I'll swim beside you the whole way. I promise." She touched her index finger to her lips, then to her heart, then held her hand up, waiting.

Shakily, my hand repeated her movements, my palm pressing hers in the private seal that had marked our allegiance for as long as I could remember. Her hand was warm and firm. My lungs expanded and filled with the soft summer air, and together we slipped into the lake.

That night I lay in bed and watched the lace

curtain float in a breeze that smelled wet and green. My breath moved in and out of my body with easy sweetness. My limbs felt as heavy on the sheets as they'd felt when I'd drifted down through the water.

"What was it like?" Lilith's whisper pulled me from the edge of sleep. It held an urgency that raised bumps on my skin. Although the moonlight shone on her face, her eyes were shadowed, unreadable. Still, I knew what she was asking.

I could have told her, then, how the lake had fallen away below my feet, and about the silence, serene and watchful, that waited there. But I didn't. I said, "It was cold. That's all I remember."

It was the first lie I ever told her.

JUSTINE

Two weeks went by. Justine still couldn't bear to spend the day alone in the house, so she drove her daughters to school, ate breakfast at Ray's, ran a few errands, and read in the library until it was time to pick them up. When they got home Melanie and Angela watched the fuzzy picture on the television while Justine made dinner in the microwave or on the stove top: spaghetti, hamburgers, sloppy joes, Lucy's frozen dinners. She'd figured out the house was heated with propane, and that the tank was only one-third full, so she turned the radiators down when they left for the day. With no wind the kitchen heated up quickly, but the living room stayed cold for hours. The girls watched TV with their coats on.

Though she saw Matthew Miller from a distance a few times, Justine still hadn't seen his brother. Nor did Matthew stop by again, which brought her a mixture of relief and regret. Now that she'd been here for a while she realized she took comfort in the glow the lodge lights cast upon the snow. Once night fell, they were the only lights she could see besides the stars.

Her list of things to do still sat on the counter, with a pen beside it. She'd figured out Lucy got her mail at a post office box in town — check — and dropped off the job application at the Walmart — check. But the oven stymied her. O'Keefe & Merritt, it said in chrome letters on its white porcelain finish, but neither of the appliance repair shops in the Yellow Pages serviced that brand, or any oven as old as this one, which apparently dated to the 1920s. She also hadn't looked for Maurie's ring, or sorted through any of Lucy's belongings. All she'd done was clean out the bathroom to make room for her own things, and throwing out the prescription bottles and half-empty jars of face cream made her feel horrible, like a janitor sweeping up after a life.

The worst thing, though, was the cold. She'd lived in cold places before; she and Maurie had spent winters in Iowa City, Omaha, and a few other midwestern towns, but the cold here was unlike anything she'd ever experienced. It was a raw, windy, toothsome thing that whipped through your coat when you were outside and forced its way through windows and floorboards to trace its icy fingers against your cheek when you were inside. And it was just November. In San Diego it was still warm enough to barbecue. Every Sunday, Patrick had barbecued for them on his meticulously maintained Weber grill. He wore an apron that said KISS THE COOK, and he'd hold Justine's plate above her head until he collected his kiss.

His absence still felt like a phantom limb. She missed him; missed his laugh, missed his broad shoulders. And he was so capable. If he were here, he would take charge of fixing the oven, filling the propane tank, even going through the house. Often she turned around to say something to him as she washed the dishes, expecting him to be sitting at the table, or reached for her cell phone to see if he'd left a message, only to remember she'd left the phone in San Diego. At the same time, she reveled in the silence and the additional space she felt around her body without him. At night she read in Lucy's bed for an hour or more before turning out the light, something she'd never been able to do when Patrick lay beside her. He hated when she read — he wanted all her attention for himself — so she'd only been able to read during her lunch breaks.

She was watchful the way the unnoticed often are, the way she'd learned to be when Maurie brought her to whatever restaurant she was working in, put her at a table with a coloring book, and told her to make herself invisible. Every morning she sat in her booth at Ray's and watched the other customers from behind her newspaper. Of all the places she and her mother had lived, she'd liked the small towns best, because the people there made for better watching. Unlike city people, who moved quickly and cultivated a lot of artifice, small town people were slow and transparent, even when they thought they were being secretive. So Justine could tell that Maisy the shoe store owner irritated everyone with her constant chatter, and that Mike the barber was desperate for a friend but made everything worse by standing too close to people. And when Quentin, one of the two brothers who ate breakfast at the counter, talked about his soldier-son she could tell from the way the other man, Nate, hunched his shoulders that his own son wasn't worth bragging about.

As for Ray herself, she was something of a town oracle. The neighboring business owners stopped in every morning to get their coffee and ask what she thought about everything from the high school football team's chances to the drifter panhandling outside the general store. Her opinions were succinct, often funny, and no one ever disputed them. T.J., the Chippewa cook, loved her with a forlorn fervor, and Justine liked her for the way she spoke to him, as if he were fragile.

She also liked Ray because Ray left her alone. Everyone seemed to know Justine was Lucy's great-niece, but whenever anyone asked Ray anything else about her, like where she'd come from, whether she was planning to stay, or whether she was married, Ray just shrugged. Eventually, just as they had in all the new schools, people stopped asking, and Justine felt herself slide into the background where she belonged.

She watched her daughters, too. Angela in particular worried her. Her normally cheerful child cried on the way home from school, saying she didn't fit in. Despite the new backpack she didn't dress right, in her Argyle sweaters from the Walmart. No one sat with her at lunch or wanted to partner with her for projects. They were studying Minnesota history and all she knew were the missions and gold strikes of California.

She missed Mrs. Fitz and Lizzie and Emma. Justine tried to placate her by letting her write postcards that she secretly didn't mail, but it didn't help.

Melanie was a worry of a more familiar sort. Justine had allowed herself to hope her oldest daughter's grim nature might be lightened by the chance to start over in a new town, but the child who lived in Lucy's house was the same sullen girl who'd lived in the San Diego apartment. She gave monosyllabic answers to Justine's questions and barely spoke to Angela. She shoved her homework in her backpack without showing it to Justine, her eyes defiant, just as she'd done back home. Justine hadn't known what to do about it then, and now she let it go without a word.

Thanksgiving came. When Justine was young, Thanksgiving was haphazard, celebrated or not depending on whether her mother had a boyfriend she wanted to cook for. So Justine had always tried to create for her family the kind of Thanksgivings she imagined other families had as a matter of course. She made centerpieces out of corn husks, used recipes from *Better Homes and Gardens,* and lit candles. This year, with the oven still broken, she bought a roast chicken at the Safeway and served it at room temperature with microwaved mashed potatoes and canned peas she heated on the stove. The girls ate without comment, as if it were any other day. Justine looked at the empty fourth chair and wondered with a pang of guilt what Patrick was doing. He was probably eating takeout in front of the television. This would have been their first Thanksgiving together, and if she'd stayed, she would have cooked all day for him.

She got up, found two candle stubs in the bottom of a drawer, and set them on tea plates. Angela smiled, but Melanie didn't seem to notice.

On Friday the girls had no school, so they went to the Paul Bunyan Mall in Bemidji, a modest indoor mall with a JCPenney and a Kmart at either end. The mall was gaudy with red and green bunting and packed with people shopping the Black Friday sales. In the central plaza children lined up to whisper their hearts' desires to Santa while a middle-aged lady dressed as an elf took their picture. Justine thought of the many disappointments of her own childhood Christmases: the roller skates she'd wanted so she could skate with the other girls; the Barbie Dreamhouse everyone else got that one year. She thought about her daughters opening their Walmart presents on the brown carpet of the San Diego apartment year after year and wondered what secret, futile wishes they had made. She pulled them away from the North Pole and into the JCPenney.

Ten feet inside they ran into the makeup counter girl. "Care for a makeover?" she chirped. "It's free with any ten-dollar purchase!"

"Mommy, do it!" Angela's face was bright, her silver eyes reflecting the Christmas lights like twin mirrors. The makeup girl nodded at Justine in vigorous encouragement. She looked about nineteen. Her nametag said CARRIE in swirly handwritten letters. Hired for the season, Justine thought, trying to make it permanent. It was only ten dollars.

Carrie beamed as Justine sat on the metal stool. "You have a fabulous complexion. We'll just even it out with some foundation." She pawed through a drawer, her inexperience with the product line obvious, before seizing a bottle of foundation and a sponge. As she bent close Justine smelled jasmine perfume, chamomile shampoo, and cigarettes. Angela sat on the stool beside her. Melanie stood behind Carrie, her fingers picking at her cuticles.

"You don't wear much makeup, do you?"

Carrie said. "Are you married?" Justine shook her head. "Then you need come-hither eyes. We'll use Sapphire Jewel on the creases and blend it with Smokey Mist."

Carrie's hands were surprisingly gentle with the eye shadow wand. With her eyes closed Justine couldn't see her daughters, but she could feel their attention. She found herself enjoying this, sitting on a stool while another woman made her beautiful.

"What do you think?" Carrie asked the girls when she was done with Justine's eyes. Angela's face wore an expression of fascinated surprise. Melanie was frowning, but Carrie moved in with a lipstick and blocked her from Justine's view. "Honey Blossom will make all the men want to kiss you," Carrie said as she painted it on. Her own lips were plump and red, traced with liner and parting to reveal crooked teeth and the tip of her pink tongue.

Two women had stopped to watch. Justine looked away, but now she saw that all the shoppers that passed glanced at her, and all of a sudden she felt ridiculous. She thought about what she'd gotten for those childhood Christmases instead of the toys she wanted: brushes, bows, lip gloss, perfume, makeup. Maurie wanted someone to play dress-up with; she'd thought that was what daughters were for. But Justine never liked the way men looked at her mother when she had her "face" on, so she'd been a disappointment that way.

At last Carrie turned her to the mirror. Justine didn't recognize herself. Her narrow lips were full and pink and shiny. Her eyes were enormous, with thick, curly lashes. Her skin looked waxen, the pores and her light spray of freckles invisible, and pools of rose bloomed on her cheekbones. She looked unreal, like a mannequin.

"Mommy, you're beautiful!" Angela said.

"Do you like it?" Carrie asked, proud. Behind her Melanie scowled, her eyes hard.

"It's great, thank you." Justine slid off the stool and began to walk away.

"Hey, wait a minute!" Carrie put her hands on her hips. "You gotta buy something. Ten dollars, remember?"

"Oh, yes, sorry." Justine grappled with her bag. "What do you have that costs ten dollars?"

"Well, the cheapest thing we got is fourteen." Carrie's face was crafty and embarrassed at the same time. Justine handed her a twenty and left with a tube of mascara. Her face felt brittle. She kept her eyes on the scuffed floor tiles, but she was sure everyone they passed looked at her longer than they looked at anyone else.

Melanie was glaring at her with such disdain that finally Justine stopped. "What's the matter with you?"

"You look like a clown."

Justine pulled her purse tight against her stomach. A woman in a pink velour sweat suit navigated a stroller around them.

"No, she doesn't! She looks beautiful!" Angela patted Justine's arm. "You look beautiful, Mommy."

"Why do you want to look like that?" Melanie hissed. "So you can get another boyfriend? Another great guy to be our daddy?" Her eyes were slitted with fury.

Justine's face flamed beneath the creamy foundation. The woman with the stroller stopped, her features avid with piggish curiosity. Justine grabbed Angela's hand and walked away. She didn't look back to see if Melanie was following. When they reached the car she helped Angela inside, then got behind the wheel and waited until she heard Melanie shut the rear door before slamming the car into gear and driving away. It took an hour to get back to the lake. No one talked the entire way, and Justine didn't turn on the radio.

At home, Melanie walked straight to the living room, and Angela, after a quick look at her mother, followed her. Justine went upstairs to the bathroom, where she picked up the hand towel and wet it with soap and water.

Above the green porcelain sink her reflection stared back at her. The bulb buzzed in the metal ceiling fixture, and Justine rested her hands on the sink. In the muted light the makeup looked less garish than it had in the store. She turned her face from side to side. Melanie was wrong. She didn't look like a clown. She didn't look beautiful, either. But she did look like someone you might notice.

She considered her reflection for a while longer, then scrubbed everything off.

When she got back to the kitchen the girls were watching television, some Disney thing, by the shrill voices. Justine's skin felt prickly-clean from the rough nap of the hand towel. It was five, and already it was night. They'd have sloppy joes and Tater Tots for dinner, with frozen corn on the side, and an early bedtime. Tomorrow they'd go back to the mall. What else was there to do? What had they done on Saturdays in San Diego? She couldn't remember. Patrick had planned it, whatever it was.

The phone rang, and she picked it up,

bracing herself to tell the caller — last time it had been a dentist's office — Lucy was dead. Instead it was her mother.

Maurie got right to the point. "Did you find the ring?"

"Not yet, but I'm looking," Justine lied. At least she could cross calling her mother off her list. "There's a lot of stuff here."

"Believe me, sweetie, I know. Those two never threw anything away." Maurie paused. Then, as though the notion had just occurred to her, she said, "I'll tell you what. I'm kind of at loose ends right now. How about I come up there and help you look?"

Justine sank into a chair and closed her eyes. She should have seen this coming. Of course her mother would come up here. The diamond ring was one thing, but the house was quite another, and then there was Lucy's investment portfolio. Justine wondered if Maurie knew about that. She'd been thinking about giving her some of it — it felt wrong that Lucy had cut her out — but the transparency of her mother's plotting made her think again. When she opened her eyes the red and white saltshaker on the lazy Susan looked back at her, its rosy baker's smile cheerful and dead. She wished she were brave enough to tell her mother not to come. She wondered if the woman in the bathroom mirror would have been.

"You don't have to do that," she said, though she knew it was hopeless.

"Don't be silly. We can have Christmas together. It'll be like old times."

The last time Justine had seen Maurie, her mother had called from a gas station outside Roseville and showed up in San Diego eight hours later. For six months she slept on the couch, scattered her stuff all over, flirted with Francis, and followed Justine around, offering unwanted advice on everything from her clothes to her parenting. When she left she took $1,200 with her, almost all the money Justine had managed to save since she'd started working at Dr. Fishbaum's. A loan, supposedly.

But it was also true that Melanie and Angela had adored her. To them, their grandmother was a beautiful gypsy in glamorous clothes and Navajo jewelry who painted their nails, did their hair, and gave them necklaces she picked up from sidewalk vendors. Justine would come home to find all three of them on the couch, her mother's legs crossed like a child's and the girls sitting beside her draped in Mardi Gras beads. When Maurie left the girls had cried for days, even Melanie.

A burst of flat, canned laughter came from the television. Justine pictured her daughters, bundled in their coats on Lucy's worn sofa, watching it with deadened eyes.

Maurie said, "You know, I'd kind of like to see the old place one more time." She spoke as if it were a silly notion, but something wistful colored her voice, and her breezy tone didn't quite mask it.

Justine picked up the saltshaker. Her finger traced its empty smile. "What about Phil?"

"Oh, Phil. He was the worst of the lot, honey, the absolute worst. I'll tell you all about it when I get there. Tell my girls that Grandma's bringing kisses for Christmas."

Lucy

Independence Day was the one day the lake families returned to town, to watch the parade down Main Street and listen to the bands play in the square. So by nine that morning, I was dressed in a blue-and-red-striped skirt and a white blouse, my hair pulled into a tail that exploded in frizzy curls behind a red ribbon. Lilith and Emily wore their patriotic best, too, and Mother warned Lilith and me not to get dirty as she packed our picnic basket and aired our blankets. Emily, of course, was at no such risk; Mother took her everywhere with her as though they were joined by an invisible apron string.

Father sat on the front porch, reading as he waited to drive us into town. His straw hat with the red band sat on his lap. At one point, Mother sent me to him with a glass of iced tea. As I set it beside him, he raised his eyes from his book. "You look a picture, Lucy."

Until that moment I'd felt starched and ridiculous, but now I was glad of the pull of hair at my temples and the fussy skirt whose petticoats scratched my thighs. On impulse I gave a little curtsey, and he chuckled. I blushed and, unable to think of a way to prolong the encounter further, sidled away.

In our room, Lilith was in a wretched mood. Mother had bought her an outfit almost as childish as mine, a dress with a big navy skirt beneath a white bow and the same black patent leather Mary Janes Emily and I wore. She stood at our window watching Jeannette and Betty walk past in their narrow, bias-cut dresses and low-heeled shoes, envy and frustration written on her face.

"You look pretty," I said, to console her, because of course she did. She told me to leave her alone and went downstairs. From our window I watched her walk down our front steps and up the path after the older girls, her skirt swinging like a bell below the bow.

Without her, our room felt small and hot, so before long I went out, too. By the time I got to the lane Lilith had reached the lodge, and I watched as she disappeared inside.

Next door, Mr. Williams was loading a picnic basket into his car. His face shone with sweat above the white collar of his shirt, but he smiled in his good-natured way and wished me a happy Fourth of July. I said the same, but I didn't want to talk to him, so I went down to the lake.

The water was morning-still, and the sky was mounded with white clouds that were reflected on its surface as on a mirror. I wished I could take off my shoes and socks and feel the sand on my feet. It would still be cool from the night, and its coarse grains would be pleasantly sharp between my toes. But that would spoil my socks, so I skipped stones instead. I was good at skipping stones, and I was secretly proud of this. As I counted each stone's footsteps across the unruffled surface I began to feel better.

I'd just bounced a stone seven times when I heard a low whistle, and turned to see Matthew Miller standing at the edge of the grass. He wore a faded blue shirt with the sleeves rolled up and brown pants that were too loose: hand-me-downs from his brother, no doubt, and handmade, like most of the things they wore. He was carrying a metal toolbox. He wasn't going to the parade, I realized. Now that I thought about it, I supposed the Millers never went.

"You're good at that," he said, "for a girl." He smiled as he said it, though, so I didn't know if I was allowed to take offense. "What's your record?"

"Twelve."

"Mine's fourteen." He dropped the toolbox and walked onto the sand, scanning for a likely stone. I was skeptical, but he launched the stone he found in a looping, sidearm motion that surprised me with its grace. It flew low over the water like a bird scanning for fish, then dipped to the surface. We watched and counted. Ten. Matthew looked at me from under his bangs, a satisfied smile on his lips. I hated to admit it, but I was impressed, and he could tell. His smile became a crooked-toothed grin that made me laugh despite myself. I told him I could do better. He said, let's see.

As I looked for a stone, a voice called his name. Mrs. Miller was standing at the door of the lodge with a dish towel in her hand. "Get over here," she said sharply, her deep voice carrying easily across the hundred yards between us. "Bring that toolbox with you."

"Looks like you're off the hook," Matthew said, and ran off with the toolbox banging against his leg. I watched him go. When the lodge door closed behind him, I thought of

Lilith, Jeannette, and Betty sipping Cokes at one of the wooden tables, Lilith's dark head glossy in the light from the overhead lamps. I didn't feel like skipping stones anymore. I gave the sand a shove with my toe and headed back to our house.

Mr. Williams was gone, but Mother was in our side yard talking with Mrs. Williams, who had walked over for a chat. Emily, in a white eyelet dress, sat on a tree stump nearby. As I crossed the yard, she stood up, cast a sly eye at Mother, who was deep in conversation, and sidled off behind the Williamses' house.

Well, that was interesting. I hadn't thought of Emily as devious; in fact, she seemed to have no guile at all. But she was definitely up to something now. I cut across the Williamses' front yard in time to see her slip behind the Joneses' and head for the lodge. On that side, the lodge rose above the sandy ground on thick posts about three feet high, and Emily, with a quick look over her shoulder, disappeared beneath it.

I was delighted. I'd been so careful not to get my feet dirty, and here was Emily messing about under the lodge in her best white dress, something that surely would earn her an all-too-rare reprimand. I went up to the lodge and peered into the den underneath.

Emily squatted ten feet away with her skirt hitched up so her panties were showing. She clutched something to her chest, something small and squirmy, and in the frozen moment after she saw me I realized something was rustling on the ground before her.

"Don't hurt them," she whispered.

I walked toward her on my haunches, holding up my own skirt. "Don't hurt them," she said again, and now I felt a little bit angry: who did she think I was that I would hurt them, whatever they were? Then I saw what she'd found. A mother cat lay curled in a hollow in the sand, and writhing on her belly were kittens, each no bigger than the palm of my hand. They were so new that their eyes were still sealed shut. In the quiet I could hear the smacking sounds they made as they suckled.

I sank to my knees, my skirt forgotten. The mother looked at me with her eyes glinting and her ears bent back, but she didn't hiss or growl, which told me Emily had been there often enough to earn her wary trust. One kitten, yellow with a white spot on its forehead, slipped from the pile and burrowed frantically into the backs of its brothers and sisters. I scooped it into my hand. Its claws were tiny needles as it stretched out its paws, searching for the teat. Its pink mouth nuzzled the tip of my finger, the tongue barely a touch on my skin, and its head shook with the effort it took to hold it upright. I could feel its heart, a helpless patter in my palm.

"How did you find them?" I asked.

"Abe showed me."

"Abe Miller?"

"He's my friend." She was proud, even a little defiant. I remembered how Abe had walked over to her the day Lilith and I swam to the pontoon. I hadn't thought anything of it then, but now the notion of Emily and Abe being friends struck me as strange. Not on Abe's part: he was childlike, as I've said, and he liked to play with the littlest children among the lake families. I'd often seen him holding their hands, or carrying them on his shoulders. But never Emily, because Emily wasn't allowed to leave our yard without permission, and I was certain Mother would never have permitted her to play with Abe in any event. Her only playmate, infrequent at that, was Amanda Davies, a vivacious girl whose mother sometimes brought her when she visited but who found Emily too dull to seek out otherwise.

Mother's shrill voice calling Emily's name interrupted my thoughts. Emily took off running. I returned my kitten to the nest, where it latched hungrily onto a teat, and walked after her, looking back over my shoulder at the dark space beneath the lodge.

Mother was behind the Joneses', her hands twisted together. Mrs. Williams stood twenty paces off, watching her. When Mother saw Emily she said, "Oh, there you are," as if it was nothing, but it hadn't been nothing, and I felt a surge of angry hurt. Lilith and I could spend hours in the distant corners of the forest and Mother wouldn't care, but Emily couldn't leave her side for ten minutes without her panicking. I couldn't imagine how Emily had managed to spend enough time with Abe to become friends. Then I thought: maybe today wasn't the first time she'd been devious. I looked at her. She stood before Mother in her white dress with her round dark eyes, the picture of contrite innocence. Grudgingly, I was impressed.

Then Mother noticed me, and our disarray — not only was my skirt smudged, but cobwebs littered my hair, and the hem of Emily's dress, despite her efforts, was brown with dirt. "What have you two been up to?" she asked, her anger at our filth limned with astonishment that we'd been up to anything, together, at all. Emily looked at me, pleading.

I almost told. If Lilith had been there, she would have, and she would have enjoyed watching Mother forbid Emily to go under the lodge ever again. But Lilith wasn't there, and I remembered the warmth of the kitten in my hand, the furtive way Emily had sneaked away from Mother, and the timbre of her voice when she said Abe was her friend. I said, "We were just playing." The gratitude that flooded Emily's face was so naked I had to look away, but it made me glad I hadn't said anything.

I haven't been to the Independence Day parade since the late 1960s, when it turned into an unpleasant annual clash over the Vietnam War and we stopped going. When I think of the parades of my youth I hear the brass band playing on hay bales in a horse-pulled wagon, and I see the bunting around the square, the flags on the lampposts, the farmers in clean overalls and the girls with ribbons in their hair. It was just a small town parade, typical for its time, but to me it was no less memorable for being commonplace. Every year Lilith, Mother, Emily, and I stood with the Williamses on the sidewalk outside our pharmacy, waving little

179

flags as Father rode by in Mr. Williams's Ford with the WILLIAMS & WILLIAMS law firm banner on the grille and the EVANS PHARMACY banner on the back. Father looked so handsome, with his black hair slicked back, his seersucker suit neat on his slender frame, and his straw hat.

At night there would be fireworks over at the baseball field, but the lake families never stayed for them. We went back to the lake, where the Millers would serve us supper as they had on the first night of summer, and then we had our own fireworks show, put on by the oldest Jones brothers, Eddie and Brian. They were in their early twenties then, riotous men-children, survivors of countless scrapes — many involving fire — and they relished the opportunity to blow things up in a community-sanctioned cause. I'm sure the town's fireworks couldn't compare to the show they put on for our eyes only, the blossoms of color falling topsy-turvy in the sky, mirrored in the still night water.

When the fireworks were done, we lit a bonfire on the beach and gathered around it in chairs, on the picnic tables, or on the cool sand. The roar of the fire and the swirling ascension of sparks held us quiet for a time, the firelight throwing strange shadows on the faces of mothers and fathers, grand-parents and infants. I sat on the sand beside Lilith, and Mother and Father sat in chairs behind us. Mother's face was rosy and young-looking in the firelight. Her hair was like mine, frazzled and untamable, but that night it looked like a halo around her pale oval face. Father had his arm around her, his fingers playing with a thread on her shawl. Emily drowsed on his lap, her legs draped over his thighs. My face roasted in the heat of the fire, while my back felt the chill rising off the lake. But I was warm inside, and calm. In the lodge the lights were on; the Millers were cleaning up after our feast. I thought about Matthew scrub-bing dishes while the fireworks burst. I hoped he'd been allowed to watch them.

At some point I turned to Lilith, but she was gone. I looked around and saw her on the other side of the bonfire with Jeannette and Betty, the full skirt of her dress tucked close around her legs. They were giggling, their eyes sliding to Charlie and his friends, who sat nearby. The boys were shoving and showing off, as boys do. Then Charlie, urged on by his friends, came to stand behind Lilith. She smiled up at him, and her hand moved to rest on his forearm.

I looked at Father. He was watching them.

Even in the dim light I could see the rigid set of his face. Mother saw it, too, and our eyes met. I slipped back from the fire and walked around the group until I was behind Lilith. I leaned close and, masking my words with a smile as though I was sharing a joke, I told her that Father was watching.

For a moment she froze. Then she looked at Father across the fire and laughed, an openmouthed, flirtatious laugh, her teeth shining white. Father's face remained still, his eyes bent upon her, but his hand jumped where it sat on Mother's shoulder. Then Lilith turned to Charlie, slid her hand down his forearm, and took his hand in hers.

I stopped breathing. I couldn't bring myself to look across the fire to where Father surely was watching still. When Jeannette leaned across me to say something to Lilith I slid away, outside the circle, down the dark beach, past our row of houses. I walked to the end of the dock and sat on the cool metal. The moon was half full, and its light spilled on the water. The Milky Way was a gossamer veil across the sky. My thoughts were incoherent and filled with dread.

The night wore on. One by one and two by two people stood, stretched, and left the bonfire. I saw Mother and Father rise,

Mother carrying Emily. They didn't tell Lilith to come, as I thought they might, though Father paused and looked back at the fire before going inside. Only a dozen people were left now, mostly teenagers and younger boys allowed to stay up late on the holiday. I heard Lilith's clear laughter ring out, and once or twice Charlie's deepening voice. The littler boys hunted crawdads at the water's edge and then threw them into the fire to sizzle and explode. Up and down the row the other houses went dark. But in our house the parlor light remained lit.

At last, when the fire huddled down to embers, the last of the revelers stood to leave. I stood, too, my body tight from sitting so long on the dock and my neck sore from turning to watch them. Lilith and her friends said their good nights, and I caught up to her as she reached our steps. She took my hand, and in that gesture I knew she was afraid, and that she was glad to have me there. We walked up the steps together.

Father was sitting in the parlor alone. His legs were crossed and his fingers were templed under his chin. I thought about how long he must have sat there, in the wingback chair, waiting. I wanted to go straight upstairs, but Lilith stopped in the entryway and turned to him. Her face was composed, but her skin was waxen under the ceiling lamp and her hand clutched mine so tightly it seemed she would break its bones.

"Come here." Father's eyes were bottomless and without light, his slender fingers a cage beneath his jaw. Lilith let go of my hand and walked into the parlor. She sat on the davenport with her knees pressed together, folded her hands in her lap, and straightened her back.

"Go to bed, Lucy," Father said. But I didn't. I went halfway up the stairs and sat where he couldn't see me but I could see Lilith. She didn't look at me, but I knew she knew I was there.

"Daughter," Father said. "You must be careful. There can be sin in the smallest touch."

Lilith raised her chin almost imperceptibly. "I just held his hand."

"He is a boy becoming a man. His thoughts are not pure."

"It's Charlie. We've known him since he was little."

"Even so. Make no mistake. He wants to corrupt you."

I could see her neck tighten as she swallowed. Then she said, "What if he does?"

My heart slammed so hard against my ribs

I was sure they both could hear it. Lilith's face was impossibly still, as though she'd turned to marble. Father's chair creaked as he got up. When he appeared in front of her I tensed, ready to flee, but he didn't look my way. He knelt down and took her hands in his. I felt a small shock, and my own hands tingled. I couldn't remember him ever touching either of us with such deliberation. I couldn't see his face, but I could see hers, and as if it were my own I felt the power of his gaze press upon her brow.

When he spoke, his voice was barely above a whisper. "Perhaps I should bring you back to town with me."

A small muscle jumped below Lilith's eye. She went even paler. "You don't have to do that." When he didn't answer she said, "You can trust me, Father. I won't let him."

My hands were shaking. I wound them together and tucked them under my chin. Father considered Lilith for a long moment more. As the silence expanded, my stomach roiled to the point of nausea. He couldn't take her. I didn't know what I would do without her.

"Lilith," he said at last, "you need to understand that there is temptation everywhere. The sins of the flesh will call even in the voices of those you have known all your life. You alone have the power to keep your intentions pure. To remain clean, as a true child of God."

"I will. I promise." She lowered her eyelashes. Then, in the quiet church of our parlor, she underwent a strange and arresting alchemy. Without saying another word or moving a single muscle, she grew younger before my eyes, the restless longing of the teenaged girl melting into the unquestioning innocence of the child she had been. I pressed my fingers to my mouth. She was my sister again, the Lilith I'd thought I'd lost.

Father saw it, too. He took a breath that spread his shoulder blades. Then he bowed his head. "Have mercy on me, O God, according to your lovingkindness," he began. Lilith's lips moved with his through the rest of the psalm. But her eyes found mine, and in them I saw such a raw mixture of defiance and misery that I felt faint.

"Go to bed now," Father said, when the psalm was done. I ran up the stairs as quietly as I could. When I reached the landing I saw Emily's door close, the doorknob releasing its catch with a listening, cowardly stealth: Mother.

Then Lilith was there, and she pushed me into our room. She closed our door and leaned against it. I went to her, and she embraced me, and I cried, and felt awful, because she was the one whom Father had chastised and threatened to take back to Williamsburg; she was the one who should be crying, and I should be consoling her. But when we went to bed, she came and lay beside me beneath my covers. As we listened to Father's footsteps crunch on the path to the bridge, she wrapped me in her arms again, and this time I knew it was she who was the comforted, and I the comforter.

JUSTINE

In the diner on Monday, everyone was talking about a big storm coming. They sounded excited, like a crowd at a bullfight, anticipating the promise of disaster at a safe remove. Maisy, the shoe store owner, said she'd sold three pairs of boots just that week. Mike the barber sighed; he'd lose money with his shop closed, but even he had a thrill in his voice when he talked about the weather forecast. They reminisced about epic blizzards in the past — the 1995 storm that cut them off from the highway for a week, and the one in 1987 that caved in the roof of the Methodist Church. No, that was 1986, said Roberta Jones, a substitute teacher who had strong opinions about everything. A vigorous debate ensued, with arguments pegged to graduation dates, wedding dates, and birth dates.

It was the sort of conversation, rich with shared history, that Justine most enjoyed eavesdropping on. But this one worried her. If these people, who seemed to be inured to blizzards, were impressed by this upcoming storm, it was cause for serious concern. She remembered midwestern blizzards from her childhood. They always caught Maurie by surprise — they didn't say anything about snow! she'd say. Then they'd be stuck in the apartment for days eating peanut butter and saltines. Maurie thought it was fun, like camping. Justine thought about Lucy's isolated house and decided she'd better stop by the Safeway on the way back. She also worried about how the old house would weather the storm. A voice in her head whispered that if Patrick were here, he'd be able to check the roof, fix what needed fixing, keep them safe. She tried to muffle it.

The doorbell jangled. Quentin, one of the two brothers who had breakfast at the counter every morning, came in. His appearance shocked Justine — he'd aged a decade since she'd last seen him, the day before Thanksgiving. Everyone else stopped talking, their faces falling into expressions of sympathy. Without realizing it, they moved closer to one another. Something terrible had happened to Quentin, and it was clear that everyone but Justine knew what it was.

Quentin walked to the counter and sat on his usual stool. Ray put a hand on his arm, and Justine could see the fifty years they'd known each other in her touch. "I'm so sorry, hon."

He rubbed his face. He didn't seem to see the others standing in an awkward half circle with their coffee cups. He said to Ray, "You remember how I worried about my boy in Iraq? I always told Nate he was lucky to have Jake close. Even with all the trouble that boy got into, I never thought he'd get himself killed not five miles from home." He closed his eyes, gave a shaky sigh. "Nate hasn't even answered my calls."

Quentin's son was a captain in the marines who'd been decorated for valor during Desert Storm. He had a pretty southern wife and two little boys. The oldest was the pride of the Little League. The younger loved peewee football. Justine had heard Quentin tell Nate these things in the voice of a man who knew that, in the ledger of sons that all men keep, he was the richer. His face was gray with grief over his nephew's death, but Justine understood why his brother didn't want to talk to him right now.

The morning crowd broke their silence. They lowed a murmuring chorus of regret, and one by one they approached Quentin.

The men put their hands on his shoulders. The women embraced him. And as she watched him lean into the arms and hands of his neighbors, Justine felt an envy almost indistinguishable from sorrow. No one in the world — not one person — would touch her the way these people were touching Quentin, no matter the tragedy she suffered.

Arthur Williams slid into her booth, surprising her. "I hope you don't mind. I see you here every morning on my way to the office."

"Not at all," Justine said. She was glad for a reason to look away from Quentin.

Arthur glanced at the grieving man and shook his head. "A shame," he said. "Though not entirely a surprise." With that oblique comment he returned his attention to Justine. "I didn't just stop in to say hello. I had a phone call yesterday from someone looking for you. A Patrick Gallagher."

Justine put her hands in her lap. She tried to keep her face from betraying the flood of emotions that swamped her — shock, fear, anger, and, though she despised herself for it, a small ripple of pleasure.

"He said he was your boyfriend, and you'd disappeared without telling anyone you were leaving or where you were going. He saw my number on your phone bill and wanted to know if I knew where you were."

He paused. The air in the diner felt thick with foreboding. Justine licked her lips. "What did you tell him?"

"I told him I couldn't discuss our conversation."

Justine exhaled. Arthur regarded her keenly. He said, "My client is Lucy Evans's estate, not you. Our conversations aren't privileged. But I didn't feel comfortable answering his questions without checking with you first."

"Thank you." Outside, a pickup drove by, a huge brown mastiff pacing restlessly in the back. It was a Chevy, the same model as Patrick's, but it was black and filthy, where Patrick's was white and clean. Though if he drove it two thousand miles to Williamsburg, it wouldn't be clean, would it? Justine wrenched her gaze away. She needed to get out of the diner. She needed to get someplace quiet, where she could think.

"Well," Arthur said. "If he calls again, I'll answer him in the same way."

"Yes, thank you." Justine slid out of the booth, ignoring the startled look on his face. "I'm sorry, I have to go."

She went to the library, to her favorite chair, which overlooked the small back garden. A brown bird landed on the empty stone birdbath, then flew away, disappointed. Justine remembered how, the week Patrick moved in, he'd taken down the bird feeder Francis and Melanie had built from a kit and hung on the balcony. It hadn't come together right; the walls were askew and the floor slanted, but Melanie had loved watching the birds fly in and out. Patrick took it apart on the kitchen table and reassembled it so it was square, then held it up for them to admire how good he was at fixing things. Melanie never looked at it again.

She'd been so careful not to leave a trace. No credit cards, no checks. But he had looked at the phone bill. It hadn't occurred to her that Arthur Williams's number would show up there, but she also hadn't expected Patrick to try that hard to find her. Not that he wouldn't try at all. He'd ask Mrs. Mendenhall, he'd ask the girls' teachers, he'd call Dr. Fishbaum and Phoebe. But she'd assumed he'd give up after that. Because in her experience, when you left people, they disappeared in the rearview mirror along with the towns they lived in. You didn't leave an address, you didn't write or call or send Christmas cards, and you never heard from them again.

She knew other people weren't like her

and her mother, of course. Other people kept address books with the names of high school classmates and sent cards on their birthdays. They called when they came to town and got together for drinks. They sent graduation announcements, and holiday cards with pictures of the kids, and — she thought of Quentin — condolences when someone died. Still, they were easy to leave behind, if you really wanted to.

Here was the problem, and she should have seen it from the start: Patrick wasn't like other people either. Even the ordinary leaving that other people did was too much for him. That was why he needed to know where she was all the time. Why he touched her so often and wanted to be with her every possible moment. So she shouldn't be surprised he'd checked the phone records. He'd probably already figured out where the Williams law firm was. The phone was in Lucy's name, but her name was Evans, too; how long before he called to see if she was a relative? Thank God she hadn't changed the recording on the answering machine.

She should call him.

The thought echoed inside her brain. It was absolutely the right thing to do. She needed to do what other people did when they ended a relationship. She should have done it that way in the first place, if not to his face, then at least over the phone from Salt Lake City or Vegas or any of the other towns they'd stayed in on the way here. If she had, he wouldn't be looking for her now.

But what would she say? What were you supposed to say? I'm sorry? We're not right for each other? It didn't work out but I'll always love you? All Maurie had ever taught her was how to sneak out when your lover's back was turned. Plus she wasn't sure she could actually do it. If she opened the door wide enough to talk to him, he might push it open the rest of the way. Already that timid voice in her head was saying he could fix the oven and figure out the propane, and she couldn't let that voice win. She thought about this for the next four hours, in the library. She thought about it as she picked up her daughters. She thought about it so much she forgot to stop at the Safeway. She was still thinking about it when she walked into the kitchen and saw the light flashing on the answering machine.

Shit. It was Patrick; she knew it was. She sent the girls into the living room to the television. "It's freezing in there," Melanie complained. Justine snapped, "Turn up the radiator!" Melanie jerked her head in sur-

195

prise, then left the kitchen without another word.

Justine leaned over the machine, gripping the edge of the counter. She forced herself to calm down. It was too soon for him to have found this number. Wasn't it? It was probably just her mother, calling with an update on her drive. Or it was for Lucy, and she'd have to call the person back and tell them she was dead.

She pressed the button. It was a woman's voice she'd never heard before, businesslike, the vowels broad and unpleasant. "This is Elizabeth Sorensen, the assistant principal at Williamsburg Elementary," it said. "We've been having some trouble involving your daughter Melanie. I'd like to meet with you at your earliest convenience so we can discuss it." She left a number and hung up.

The answering machine beeped once, then sat, silent and impassive, on the white tiles. Justine stared at it without seeing it. Her face was numb. A low buzzing began in her temples.

I had a phone call yesterday from someone looking for you.

We've been having some trouble involving your daughter.

It didn't matter how far away you went. How far away you ran. Or how hard you shook the dust from your feet.

She walked into the living room. The girls were on the sofa fighting over which program to watch. Neither of them looked at her until she hit the power button on the television and the picture snapped into a white line and then a dot. Melanie opened her mouth to protest but stopped when she saw her face.

"You're doing it again," Justine said. Her voice sounded far away, blurred by the buzzing in her head.

Melanie crossed her arms. "Doing what?"

"The school called. They're having trouble with you. You know what that means."

"No I don't."

Justine smashed her hand on the top of the television. Both girls jumped. "Damn it, Melanie! I've seen how you do your homework, how you walk in and out of that school! You're getting a bad reputation already, you're ruining that school for yourself just like you ruined the school back home, and I won't let you! Not after we've come all this way!"

Angela gaped at her in shock. Melanie's back went rigid, and she clenched her fists. "No. I'm not doing any of that stuff."

"Why am I getting this phone call, then? If you're not doing anything why is the assistant principal calling me?"

"I don't know!"

"I don't believe you!"

Melanie jumped up. Her mouth was twisted, her face red. "I don't care what you think! I hate that school! I hate everyone in it! I hate the way they look at me! I hate the way they talk about me! I hate this house, this lake, and this whole stupid town! I wish we'd never come here!"

"You can't even give it a chance, can you?" Justine was shaking now. "You're the one who wanted to come! Angie didn't, but at least she's trying! But you've already made up your mind, and now you've got to ruin everything for your sister and me with your sulking and your pouting and your determination to be miserable! Because that's what you always do!"

Melanie stood straight and slender as a blade, her eyes bright with angry tears. "I didn't want to come! I didn't even want to leave San Diego! I just wanted to leave Patrick! You're the one who ruined everything, because we never would've had to go if you hadn't let Patrick live with us in the first place. If you hadn't made Daddy leave!"

This hit Justine like a cup of oil on a fire. She flew across the room and grabbed

Melanie by the shoulders, her fingers digging into the flesh beneath her daughter's coat. "I didn't make your daddy leave! I kept him there! I kept him there for years! I never said a word to him about the drinking or the drugs or the nights he never came home! No one could've kept him longer than I kept him!" She threw Melanie backward onto the sofa. The buzzing in her head became a roar, a howl, a wail of fury at Francis, at Patrick, at her mother, at Melanie, at a hundred other nameless things, and it filled up the room and drummed in her blood, the rush of it blocking out all other sound, even the sound of her own voice gouging her throat like nails.

Then, small and far away, she saw Melanie's spidery hands on the sofa cushion, her body cringing in the too-big coat, and in the corner Angela, cowering on the floor with her head buried in her arms. Justine's anger dissolved into horror. She brought her hands to her face. In the long, fractured silence that followed, Melanie looked at her mother, the fear in her eyes giving way to disgust, and Justine looked back, through the prism of her fingers, until Melanie leaped to her feet.

"Shut up! Shut up shut up shut up! I hate you! I wish you had left! Everything is your fault! Everything!" She pushed past Justine and ran up the stairs. The slam of the bedroom door echoed through the house.

Justine collapsed on the sofa as if someone had cut a string. Angela whimpered in the corner and Justine bent over, hugging her legs. Oh, God, it had all been a mistake. A terrible mistake. This house wasn't a starting-over place. It was cold and isolated and wrapped in a half-sentient pall of tragedy, and she hadn't escaped anything, she'd only made everything worse. They should go home. Patrick wanted her back, he would take her back, and maybe Dr. Fishbaum hadn't replaced her yet. They could leave today and they could walk right back into their apartment, to the worn brown carpet and the humming hallway clock, and it would all be familiar and theirs and exactly the same.

But at the thought she recoiled so viscerally she nearly retched. If she went back she'd never leave again. She'd live in that apartment with Patrick for the rest of her life, making his meals, managing his moods, massaging his fragile ego, snatching precious moments of silence at the kitchen table before his alarm went off, and every day in a thousand tiny ways he would remind her that she'd left; that she'd broken his heart;

that she could never love him enough, no matter how hard she tried to make amends. Angela would try to make everything all right, as she'd always done, and Melanie would watch it all, as she always had, the festering welt of her resentment growing more rancid every year.

No. They couldn't go back. So they would have to go somewhere else. Somewhere Patrick could never find them. It didn't matter where. They would just pile their things in the Tercel and drive to another town. To another apartment, another school, another job. She knew exactly how it was done.

"Angie, sweetie, come here," Justine said, and Angela crawled to the couch. Justine gathered her close, and into the silken froth of her hair she sobbed like a little girl.

LUCY

The morning after Independence Day, I lay in my bed and watched the sun creep from one floorboard to the next. Lilith was awake, too; I could feel it in her arm that lay around my waist. From the kitchen we heard the clink of forks on plates, but neither of us moved until Mother came upstairs and opened our door. Her hair was in its snood and her dress was pressed in crisp pleats beneath her apron. Time to get up, she said.

She'd made an elaborate breakfast: hotcakes, sausages, eggs, potatoes, and even corn muffins, Lilith's favorite. Father ate in his deliberate way while Mother scrubbed the pans, the sawing of the wire-bristle brush loud in the little room. I rearranged my food with my fork and stared at the butter dish in the middle of the table. The butter was soft, and brown crumbs crusted it where Father's knife had cut. No one spoke.

Lilith's feet didn't touch mine under the table. Emily's eyes worried between Lilith and me, sensing trouble she didn't understand.

Even though I wasn't hungry, I picked up my corn muffin and reached for the butter. Before I could pick it up, Father lifted the dish and set it by my plate. I looked up at him. He seemed his normal self, not the agitated man who'd waited for Lilith in the parlor the night before. He smiled at me, and I gave a small, tentative smile in return. Lilith's fork stopped for a moment on its way to her mouth, and suddenly I felt disloyal and guilty, as though with that one smile I'd taken Father's side against her. After that I didn't look at anyone.

When Father was done, he kissed Mother and Emily before he picked up his bag. We listened to his car drive away, the engine fading into the woods.

Then Lilith announced, "I'm going to Betty's." I stared at her, startled and hurt. She'd never done that; even after she began going to the lodge at night, she still spent her days with me. But I knew she was angry at me for smiling at Father, and this was her way of punishing me. I watched with misery as she washed her plate, put it on the drying rack, and walked out the front door without meeting my eyes. Mother twisted her hands together, pitying me, but I didn't want her pity, so I ignored her, and after I cleared my plate I walked out myself, letting the door slam.

Once I was outside, though, I couldn't think where to go, so I sat on the steps. The lake was listless in the sun. A loon swooped lazily, its wing tips pricking the water. Some of the littler boys fished off the end of the dock. Mrs. Lewis and Mrs. Pugh strolled by on their way to the lodge, fanning themselves. I picked at a scab on my knee until blood seeped through the crust.

The porch door opened, and Emily came to sit beside me. She turned her face to mine, hopeful and nervous. Her eyes were wide and black, like Father's. "Do you want to come play with the kittens?" she asked. I didn't answer her. I just stood up and left her there alone, as Lilith had done to me not ten minutes before, and it gave me a shabby sort of satisfaction.

I went into the woods, and without planning to, I followed Lilith's and my secret path to the Hundred Tree. We still hadn't gone there that summer, and I'd never gone without her, but my feet knew the way through the leafy light. I felt brave to be out in the forest alone. I also felt a smarting pride. I wasn't sitting around waiting for Lilith to come back; I was going on an adventure by myself. I imagined her asking me that night what I'd done without her. Oh, I went off to the Hundred Tree, I'd say. By yourself? she'd ask, and I'd shrug, as if it were no big thing.

But when I got to the clearing, everything looked different. The hole in the base of the tree didn't look like the door to our secret cave; it gaped like the entrance to a tomb. The great tree's branches that had always seemed so sheltering reached for me like the talons of an enormous bird. I thought about how far I was from the lake, and the forest through which I'd just come seemed to whisper with menace. Every nerve urged me to run back to the boys fishing on the dock, to Emily and her kittens.

The undergrowth behind me erupted. I screamed and spun around. Matthew Miller stood there, his hands raised in apology. I glared at him in shock and fury — just like that, his invasion made the clearing mine again. "You followed me," I accused. The thought of him creeping behind me through the woods was both frightening and a little bit thrilling.

"It wasn't hard. You're really loud."

"This is our place. It's private."

"I know all about this place. I found it years ago. I wondered who was using it." He gestured to the tree, filled with last summer's treasures, sodden and abandoned.

I opened my mouth to repeat my outraged defense of our property rights, but I remembered thinking, that first day, that the Millers might own much of this forest. If that were true, the Hundred Tree might not be Lilith's and mine at all, but Matthew's. I couldn't let him tell me that, so I changed my strategy. "Won't your mother be looking for you?" The terse way she'd called him when she saw us skipping rocks had made it clear she didn't want him playing with me.

Matthew laughed an odd laugh. "She's not my mother."

Despite myself I was intrigued. I'd never heard that Mr. Miller married a second Indian woman after the first; in fact, I didn't think anyone else at the lake knew this. I imagined telling Lilith later, with just a hint of the smugness that comes from having superior knowledge. If she'd come with me, she could have heard it for herself.

"Who is she, then?"

"My grandmother."

I scoffed to cover my disappointment. Then I wondered, where was his mother? I'd only seen his grandmother working in the lodge, and like all the lake children, I'd always called her Mrs. Miller. No one ever corrected us.

Matthew saw my curiosity. He debated with himself for a moment, then gave me a sideways glance. "I'll tell you the story," he said, "if you let me in your hideout."

No way was I letting him in the Hundred Tree. But I've never been able to resist a good story, so after some internal debate of my own I offered a compromise: we could sit on the ground beside the tree. He nodded, and we sat on the dry, brown leaves.

It was a terrible story, and therefore quite good indeed. Matthew's father had been the son of the Lutheran minister in Williamsburg, a good, God-fearing boy. Then he met a girl who lived among the impoverished remnants of the Chippewa who hadn't moved to the White Earth reservation south of here. Her father was a tribal leader who'd resisted the relocation, and he didn't want his daughter marrying a white man any more than Mr. Miller's parents wanted him marrying an Indian. They got married anyway, and both were disowned, moving in exile to our lake.

I'd known all this, more or less, but when I started to tell him so, he cut me off. "Something went wrong when I was born," he said, and I leaned forward — I could guess what was coming. He drew back, and I thought he might stop, but he dropped his eyes and continued. His mother was as proud as her father, so when Abe was born she hadn't called the white doctor or the Indian midwife. She'd done it alone, with only her husband to help her. She would do the same with Matthew, even though she had a fever when her pains came. At first Mr. Miller gave in, but after hours of fruitless labor his wife was so weak he became afraid, and he went down the lane, pounding on the door of Dr. Pugh's lake house in the middle of the night, for it was summer and the doctor was there. But Dr. Pugh didn't answer the door.

When Matthew's father got back to the lodge, his wife no longer knew him. The nearest hospital was in Bemidji, over poor roads in the dark, so he put her and Abe in his wagon and went to her family in Olema, the Indian town on the far side of the lake. But his father-in-law blocked the door. His daughter had forsaken her people, he said, and she couldn't come crying for help when that choice brought hardship. Go to the white man's doctor. It's too far, Mr. Miller said. He begged his father-in-law to come see his daughter where she lay delirious in the wagon. He wouldn't come; he was too hard a man; but there were tears on his wife's face, so to her Mr. Miller said, please, tell me where to find the midwife. She won't help you, said her husband, but under his words she whispered an address.

The midwife was a fat woman with long gray hair who smelled like gin even at four in the morning. She did her best, but Matthew's mother died on a bloody blanket on the linoleum floor just before dawn, her new baby screaming in her husband's arms and her firstborn crouched by her head, his hands twined in her hair, as though he could keep her in the world just by holding on.

Matthew's father buried his wife and returned to the lake with his sons. In his grief and ignorance, he struggled to care for them until one day, not long after, he opened his door to find his wife's mother. She walked to where Matthew lay wailing on a cot, picked him up, and never left. She'd raised and schooled him and Abe, and worked by their father's side ever since. She'd saved them, Matthew said. She never told them what her husband said when she left, but by coming she joined them in their exile: she hadn't seen her husband or any of her people since.

During this story Matthew's eyes never

left the leafy ground. I could see that once he started, he regretted bartering this miserable tale for a few minutes of my attention beside the Hundred Tree. In those days I was a stranger to empathy for anyone but Lilith, but I felt it for him as he sat under the great oak with his stained clothes, thin face, and lank hair. He must have been very lonely, to follow a girl he barely knew into the forest and pander his family's tragic and private history in exchange for her company. So I gave his tale the weight it deserved: I listened with grave attention and, when it was done, I let it have the forest to itself for a while.

During that silence I thought about Dr. Pugh, who did tricks with his stethoscope and always had a candy to ease the pain of a shot. I imagined him listening to Mr. Miller pounding on his door, begging for his wife and child. I knew my neighbors thought little of the Indians who lived in our county, but surely he wouldn't refuse to treat one, in an emergency? I thought, too, of taciturn Mr. Miller, who spoke to the fishermen who stayed at his lodge with quiet formality but never had much to say to us, even though he made the meals we ordered and served the ice creams we ate all summer long.

Matthew was watching me, trying to

gauge my reaction. "I'm sorry your mom died," I told him.

He shrugged, and I could see his armor slip back into place. "It's not like I knew her. It was worse for Abe. He's never been right, and sometimes I wonder if that's why."

I asked him when his birthday was, to change the subject just a little. August 30, he said, which was right before we would go back to Williamsburg. He would be thirteen, a man according to the Chippewa. I told him mine was September 23, and I would be twelve. We smiled, pleased to confirm we were, indeed, almost the same age. Then we eased out of the sticky place his story had led us into a discussion of the rite-of-passage ritual he would have undergone were he with his mother's people.

We talked for a long time, about this and other things, first sitting and then lying on the carpet of leaves. I learned most of the books I'd read were his. His favorites were Ellery Queen mysteries, which his father gave him every birthday and Christmas, and he kept them in the room he shared with Abe, never abandoning them to the lending library. He asked me what it was like to go to a regular school, and I said I thought he had it better, doing his lessons at home, even though I could tell from his wistful tone he thought differently. As we talked I forgot, for a while, the night before and that Lilith had left me this morning. Above us the old tree spread its branches protectively once more.

When at last we stood to go, reluctant but hungry, Matthew said if I liked, some other day he could show me more secret places in the forest. He looked down as he said it, almost as if he were shy. Sure, I said, and we walked back together through the trees.

Back at the house, Mother was in the kitchen, making our lunch. Emily sat at the table, and in the glow of the pleasant morning I'd spent with Matthew I found the decency to feel bad about the way I'd treated her before. I wondered if she'd gone to see the kittens without me.

I leaned on the counter, watching Mother spread butter on the thick white bread. She gave me a smile and asked where I'd been, by which I knew she meant, what had I done without Lilith all morning? Instead of telling her, I asked whether she'd known Mrs. Miller was Matthew and Abe's grandmother. She went back to buttering the bread. Yes, she said; the mother died when the youngest boy was born, and the grandmother showed up after.

"Why do we call her Mrs. Miller?"

"We don't. We've never known her name, so we don't call her anything."

"All the kids call her Mrs. Miller."

"Well, she must not mind it, then."

"Why wouldn't she mind it? It's not her name."

She frowned. "Who told you all this?"

I opened my mouth to tell her Matthew had, but at the last moment I changed my mind. "Some of the other kids."

"You shouldn't gossip. It's none of our business."

I crossed my arms. "It's awful what happened to them."

She turned to face me, something she so rarely did that I had to stop myself from taking a step back. "Awful things happen all the time. Even to good people who don't deserve them."

That silenced me. I'd never heard her offer an opinion on fate or, even indirectly, on God, and at first I was outraged that it was the opposite of Father's lessons about how our free choices and intentions dictated God's rewards and punishments — a lesson he had, just last night, reiterated to Lilith while Mother listened behind Emily's door. Then I thought about Matthew and his family, and for the first time I tried to apply

Father's teachings to someone other than myself or Lilith. What might they have done to bring down such tragedy? It would have to be Mr. or Mrs. Miller who was the sinner, and the sin must have been huge, to demand a life in payment. Would God really punish someone in a way that took away an innocent child's mother? It seemed so cruel. Yet it had to be so, because if Mother was right, it would be fate that had done it, unconcerned with deserts or consequences, and that would be worse. I shook my head, trying to find the words to ask Mother how she could believe such a thing. But she turned back to the plates, and in that motion became again the cloudy-eyed woman I'd always known, so much so that I wondered if I'd imagined her vehemence of the moment before. "Call your sister for lunch," she said.

To my surprise, Lilith was in our room, and she looked perturbed when I came in. "Where were you? I looked everywhere for you." She had makeup on. Pink lipstick and pale blush, colors suited to Betty's fair coloring.

I was pleased that she'd come looking for me, and I started to tell her where I'd gone. Then I thought about Matthew, stretched out in the leaves beneath the Hundred Tree, talking about Ellery Queen and Chippewa vision quests. I shrugged. "Just around."

JUSTINE

That night the snow began. It began gently, and Justine didn't notice it as she climbed the stairs with Angela for bed, but when she woke she could tell by the pale light that snow had fallen and was falling still. Through the window the flakes were so dense they hid the lake behind a curtain of white. She remembered the talk in Ray's and how she'd planned to stop at the Safeway. She leaned her head against the cool windowpane.

Angela was still asleep in Lucy's double bed, wearing one of Justine's sweatshirts. The night before, when Justine and Angela had come upstairs, Justine had eased open the girls' door to give Melanie a grilled cheese sandwich, since she'd missed supper. Melanie was in her bed, reading one of the Emily books. The books had sat on the floor of Lucy's bedroom since Justine had read them, but before she could wonder when or why Melanie had gotten one, Melanie shoved the book under her covers and froze her with a look as cold and black as the winter night outside. Angela pressed close to Justine, not wanting to sleep in this room with this sister, so Justine put the plate on the dresser, closed the door, and took Angela to bed with her. She was glad to do it. In the weeks between Francis and Patrick, Angela's small, warm body in her bed had been one of her few comforts. But this time, even with Angela beside her, she didn't sleep until nearly morning.

All night the image of Melanie huddled on the sofa haunted her. She had never struck her children. After enduring Maurie's volatile moods she'd wanted to be a different kind of mother: calm, predictable, knowable. So all through Francis's slow disappearing, the heady early days with Patrick, and the tension that seeped into the apartment after he moved in, she made sure to show her daughters the same face, unruffled and constant as the Pole Star. It was one of the few things she thought she'd done right. That, and keeping Francis with them as long as she had.

Though if she were honest, it hadn't just been she who'd done that. Francis had loved Melanie best; in fact, she might have been the only one of them he loved at all. He used to play his guitar after dinner while she stood on the coffee table and sang her little-girl songs, and sometimes he'd let her play, moving her fingers to shape the chords. He said she had music in her, and Justine could believe it, watching them there in the living room. For a while, she thought Francis would stay for Melanie, but in the end even she hadn't been enough to hold him. Now they were adrift in a cold country, while the man who'd replaced him scoured phone bills to track them down. By morning, the only comfort Justine had found was in her resolution to leave this place, start over somewhere else, and do it right this time.

She put her ear to the door of the girls' room. It was quiet.

In the pantry she took stock. Cereal and half a loaf of bread; they would have breakfast. Two cans of SpaghettiOs: lunch. She counted six of Lucy's frozen dinners, a box of spaghetti, and a jar of marinara. The milk was getting low, but they could make it last a couple of days if they used it just for cereal. They also had a few packets of microwave popcorn, a package of Fig Newtons, a half-empty box of saltines, a tin of tea bags, and peanut butter. Outside the snow fell fast and hard, and the wind had picked up, a breathy moan that echoed from the rafters to the basement. Justine wondered again who would plow the road.

Back in the kitchen, she unplugged the phone. She wasn't going to call Patrick. They were leaving; there was no point. And now, if he called Lucy's number, he'd get no answer.

When she heard Melanie on the stairs her stomach tensed. She'd already laid out bowls, spoons, and the cereal, so she turned to get the milk as her daughter came in, saying, "I let you sleep. There won't be any school."

Melanie didn't answer. Justine put the milk down and sat in her chair. For a long time the wind and the clink of Melanie's spoon were the only sounds. Then Justine ran one hand across the old table, a gathering gesture. "Melanie, listen. I know you're not happy here. None of us are. So we're going to leave. We'll find a new place, where we can start over." The air inside the kitchen shifted. It was just the wind, Justine told herself, but she had that odd feeling again, that the house was paying attention. "Grandma's coming for Christmas, but right after that, we'll go. We'll find the right place for all of us. I promise."

There were dark smudges beneath Melanie's eyes. The corner of her mouth twitched as she gave a small nod, and for a moment it was as though a veil parted and in the harsh lines of her daughter's face Justine saw not truculence but misery. She wanted to kneel beside her and gather her into her arms, but the fierce angles of Melanie's shoulders, of her elbows and wrists, kept her in her seat. She realized she couldn't remember the last time she'd put her arms around her. She looked away, out the window, where the air was as white as bone.

Angela came in. Her legs were thin beneath Justine's sweatshirt. She crawled into Justine's lap and settled her head into its accustomed place on Justine's shoulder. Justine pulled her close and kissed her forehead. Across from them Melanie returned to her cereal.

The worst thing about the storm, worse even than the drafts and the nearly bare pantry, was the fact they couldn't leave the house. Justine thought longingly of the Paul Bunyan Mall, its warmth and bustle. She'd have to turn on all the radiators on the first floor. At least if it were warmer they wouldn't have to stay in the kitchen; they could watch television. Television would fill the silences. "Do you want to turn on the TV?" she asked.

The girls looked up from their cereal, and Justine saw they, too, were dreading the long hours with only their mother and one another for company. She felt a familiar sadness as they took their places on opposite ends of the sofa, wearing their coats as they waited for the radiator to kick in. Other snowbound families, she was sure, were sitting around fireplaces playing cards or board games, making memories they'd share later, around other fireplaces. In the flickering light of the television her daughters' faces were gray.

After she got dressed she sat on her bed. Outside, the wind had a whine to it now, as if a pack of wolves was baying in the distance. Were there wolves in these woods? Probably; the woods seemed endless, primeval. Her latest mystery lay on the table, the plastic library cover shining dully in the filtered light, but the storm's energy enervated her; she couldn't read.

She looked at the box of Emily books, on the floor by her feet. Easy enough for Melanie to pick one out, really, though she couldn't imagine what had motivated her. She wondered which one she'd read. One of the earlier ones, with the young girl's unadorned sentences? Or a later collection, still simple, but ornamented with images from an older woman's memory? *The lake curved to the horizon like the back of a spoon. Fireflies swirled like golden smoke in the trees.* Images she herself remembered, from the summer she'd spent here.

She picked up the photograph of Lucy and Lilith from the bedside table. She studied their faces, Lucy's tilted up to Lilith's and Lilith's turned to the camera. It was the only photograph of any of the Evans sisters in the house, and she wondered why that was. Lilith's jewelry box was on the table, too — the box that didn't hold the engagement ring from the soldier who died before he could marry her. What had their lives been like, those two surviving sisters, growing from youth to old age in this house and raising a child in the shadow of tragedy? Why had they stayed? This had been their summer home; what happened to the house they must have had in town?

She wondered if Maurie would have been different if she'd been raised somewhere else. Or if she'd had a father. Would she have spent her life running from place to place, from one man to the next, if the soldier had returned to help raise her? She thought of her own father, whose name she wasn't sure Maurie knew. And of Francis, who walked away from his children without a backward glance. Of all the Evans girls' fathers, who hadn't left even their names behind for their daughters.

She knew, then, how she would spend these snowbound hours. She would go through the house. She'd sort out what to sell, what to throw away, and what to keep. Hopefully she'd find Lilith's ring, but she was more interested in what else she might find in the piles in the basement and the crowded closets. Maurie never kept scrapbooks or photo albums, so Justine had no record of her childhood. Maybe she'd find pictures of Maurie as a girl. Or of Lucy, Lilith, and the rest of the family she knew so little about. Maybe there would be things she could give Melanie and Angela, saying this was your grandmother's, your great-grandmother's. Things they could take with them when they left.

The girls were watching SpongeBob. She made them peanut butter and jelly sandwiches and told them they could eat in front of the TV. Then she went to the basement.

The basement was a low, dark room with a concrete floor and brick walls, and it stank of mildew and damp. The washer and dryer stood against the near wall, beside shelves filled with tools, canning jars, and other junk. Justine saw a snow shovel, too; a new one, with the label still attached. She didn't remember seeing it before, but she was going to have to shovel the walk, so she was glad it was there. Magazines were stacked as high as her waist along the far wall, and in the back, beside an old water heater, stood mountains of cardboard boxes. The rest of the space was crammed topsy-turvy with chairs, tables, lamps, and other furnishings. Dust and cobwebs covered everything, and it was even colder down here than in the rest of the house.

Justine shivered, momentarily daunted. But as her eyes adjusted to the dim fluorescent light, shapes began to emerge from the wreckage. In an armchair lay a wooden mantel clock, its brass face glimmering. A lamp shade with amber beading decorated an iron floor lamp. On a table was a stack of books. And the boxes in the back: she could make out the word EVANS on one, and on another, PHOTOGRAPHS. She felt a little thrill, suddenly, and started to pick through the pile.

Much of the furniture, she was pleased to find, looked to be good quality. The tables were made of dark wood with pretty brass handles, the arms of the chairs were elaborately carved, and the lamps were brass or painted porcelain. She knew nothing about antiques, but they had to be worth something. Anything intact she put next to the staircase. Things she wanted to keep — the mantel clock, a pair of bookends, an ivory box with *ELEANOR* filigreed on the lid — she put on the bottom step. She opened every drawer, finding pencils and screws but no diamond ring.

By midafternoon dust choked the room and caked her clothes, and she was sweating even in the chilly air. She'd sorted all the furnishings except the table of books, which she'd saved for last. She pulled over a chair, picked up the top one, and wiped the dust off with her sleeve: Kant's *A Critique of Pure Reason.* Underneath it was *Critique of the Power of Judgment,* and below that a number of other philosophical and religious texts, including Nietzsche's *Thus Spake Zarathustra,* books by Hume and Hegel, and thick, ponderous tomes with titles like *The Five Tenets of Calvinism; Grace, Free Will, and Perdition;* and *Predeterminism and the Rights of Man.*

Justine was disappointed. She'd hoped for fiction, even classics. She flipped through *A*

Critique of Pure Reason, feeling the old paper stiff beneath her fingers. It was filled with underlinings and notes in the same small, neat script as in the Bible upstairs. "Yes! Damnation is not predetermined" read one. "We make our own choices!" read another. She turned to the inside front cover, on which was written, "Thomas Evans, 1918." She picked up another book and another, finding the same name and approximate date in each one, and marginalia in the same hand.

Thomas Evans. Her great-grandfather. Despite the neat handwriting his words were passionate — he'd clearly been a man of ideas, maybe a minister or a teacher. These books weren't worthless; they were a treasure. They were a window into the mind of a man whose blood ran in her own veins.

As Justine moved them to her pile of things to keep, she saw a yellowed envelope wedged between the pages of one of the Kant books. She pulled it from its place and opened it to find a series of newspaper clippings from the *Williamsburg Gazette.*

The first was dated September 3, 1935, its headline large and urgent:

WILLIAMSBURG GIRL DISAPPEARS

Emily Evans, 6, daughter of Thomas and Eleanor Evans of Williamsburg, was reported missing from her family's summer home at Stillwater Lake this past Sunday.

The Evanses were set to return to Williamsburg that morning, but the child wasn't in her bed when they woke up. Search parties have found no trace of her in the nearby woods.

Williamsburg sheriff Merlyn Llewellyn believes the child ran away from home. Some of her clothes are missing, as well as other personal belongings, he said. According to Agnes Lloyd, wife of Mayor Robert Lloyd, whose family was vacationing with the Evanses, the child has tried to run away before.

Anyone who can help with the search should contact the Williamsburg sheriff's office.

The other articles described beneath progressively smaller headlines how searchers dragged the lake and combed the woods with search dogs until mid-October. Finally in early November a short article declared SEARCH FOR MISSING GIRL SUSPENDED DUE TO SNOW. The last clipping was dated

December 30, 1935:

LOCAL MAN FOUND DEAD

Thomas Evans of Williamsburg was found hanged from the chandelier in his living room on Christmas morning by his neighbor, Theodore Williams.

Mr. Evans's evident suicide is the last in a series of tragedies to strike the Evans family. Mr. Evans' six-year-old daughter, Emily, disappeared from the family's summer house on September 1, and no trace of her has been found. Mr. Evans had also recently suffered financial difficulties. His home is in foreclosure, and this fall he was forced to sell his family's business, Evans Pharmacy, now Lloyd's Pharmacy, in Williamsburg.

Mr. Evans was the grandson of Dafydd Evans, one of Williamsburg's founding fathers. He was also a member of the Elks Club and the Williamsburg Chamber of Commerce. He is survived by his wife, Eleanor, and his daughters, Lilith, 13, and Lucy, 12. No plans for a funeral service have been announced.

There was one final paper, a piece of thick cream stationery with a single sentence written in the now-familiar hand:

Let the wicked be ashamed,
and let them be silent in the grave.

Justine held the papers as though they might disintegrate. The books at her feet spoke differently now. They were no longer the living record of a curious mind; they were the hollow echoes of a man doomed to the worst of tragedies: his child, his home, his livelihood, all lost. And his life, taken by his own hand. "We make our own choices." His words, so exuberant in the pages of Kant, seemed like an epitaph now.

The day Lucy told her about the girl in the painting, that summer Justine and Maurie had lived here, Justine had asked what she thought happened to her. Lucy smiled, but it was a sad smile. "I used to pretend she was living somewhere safe," she said. "That she was happy." Then she shrugged her shoulders in her thin blouse. "But she's dead, of course." Her voice casual, certain.

Justine put the papers back in the envelope and set the envelope on top of the stack of books. She pulled the box marked PHOTO-GRAPHS from the pile in the back and hauled it up the stairs to the kitchen. Then she went to the living room. The girls' eyes

229

were dull from the television. "I have something to show you."

They shuffled in, Angela obedient, Melanie reluctant, already prepared to be bored. Justine waited until they sat at the table, then opened the box. Dust puffed into the air, making her sneeze. It was filled with leather photo albums.

"These are pictures of our ancestors," she said. "I've never known what they looked like, or even what their names were. I think we should find out." She opened the top album and turned it so Melanie and Angela could see.

Its pages were thick vellum with oval cutouts. Below each black-and-white portrait was the subject's name in Victorian script: "Sarah Pugh Evans, 1881," "William Evans, 1883," "Dafydd Evans, 1890." Justine scanned the unsmiling faces. Although most had dark hair like Melanie and a few had fair curls like Angela and herself, she saw no obvious likenesses. Yet something snatched at her eye, and as she reached the end of the book she realized what it was. They were all fragile of frame, like her and her daughters. Their collarbones were fine beneath high-necked blouses, and their hands were dainty in their laps. In the dark rooms where they posed in formal black, their skin as white as chalk, they looked like china dolls, easily shattered. It was a legacy of frailty.

"Who are they?" Melanie asked.

"I don't know. Great-great-grandparents, maybe?" Justine closed the book. The next one was newer and filled with snapshots held in place by yellowing tape. Now Justine smiled. "These are pictures of Aunt Lucy and Grandma Lilith." She pointed to a photo of two girls sitting on a set of porch steps, a baby on the older girl's lap. *Lilith, Lucy, and Emily, 1931* said the caption. The girls wore dresses and white socks above black Mary Janes and the baby was swaddled in white from her lace hat to the hem of her crinolined dress. The smaller girl's hair was a tuffet of curls as in the photograph upstairs, but her face was younger, about the same age Angela was now.

"She looks like you, doesn't she?" Justine said to Angela. As her daughter frowned she added, "Of course, you're much prettier."

Melanie tilted her head. "I don't think she looks like her."

Just then the doorbell rang. Justine thought about ignoring it, but it was obvious they were home. She wiped the dust from her hands. "Wait here."

Matthew Miller stood on the porch. His

boots were clumped with snow and his coat was covered in it. Behind him, through the screened porch windows, the storm was a wall of white. Justine couldn't tell how much snow had already fallen, but the wind raged and it was clearly going to snow for the rest of the day and all through the night. She really should have stopped at the Safeway.

"I wanted to make sure you were all right. In the storm." Deep lines ran from the old man's hawkish nose to the sides of his mouth. His cheeks sagged into jowls, and his eyebrows bristled almost comically, snowflakes clinging to them.

"We're okay." Justine tightened her hand on the doorknob, planning to thank him and close the door. Then she thought of him walking back to the lodge, a stooped black figure leaning into the wind and whirling snow, and she found herself saying, "We have tea. Would you like some?" She regretted it immediately, and willed him to decline. But he stomped the snow off his boots and stepped inside, hanging his coat in the closet as though he'd done it many times. Which he probably had. How many years had he, his brother, Lucy, and Lilith lived out here, just the four of them?

He took up a lot of room in the small

kitchen. Without his coat, his shoulders were broad and his arms were wiry and strong. Angela and Melanie looked at him and he stared back in the intense way he'd stared at them in the car, and at the top of the stairs, the day they'd arrived. Justine hadn't liked it then, and she didn't like it now. The noise of the television drifted in from the living room. "Angie, go turn off the TV," she said, and as Angela scurried away she fought the urge to send Melanie after her. He was just an old man, and he'd walked through a blizzard to check on them.

She put the water on and brought two of Lucy's delicate cups and saucers to the table along with the tin of tea bags. She went to move the photo album, but he had his hand on the picture of Lilith, Lucy, and Emily on the porch. Gently, he traced their faces with one square-tipped finger. In the softening of his craggy features Justine thought she saw something of the young man he'd once been.

"You knew them then," she observed.

"You look like her," he said to Melanie.

Melanie leaned closer. Lilith's image was blurred, by the lens or by time. "She does have the same color hair," Justine said.

"Not her." Matthew touched the face beneath the fair curls. "Different hair. But

233

she has her face."

Lucy was smiling a wide smile, and for this alone Justine thought she bore no resemblance to Melanie. Beside her the baby sat like a doll on Lilith's lap, her features indecipherable between the lace of her bonnet and the froth of her collar, as though she'd been erased. "Were you here the summer Emily disappeared?" Justine asked.

"Who's Emily?" Angela had come back into the room. Now she leaned against Justine, looking at the picture.

"The baby. She disappeared one summer when they were here at the lake."

"She ran away in the night," Matthew said. "She got lost in the woods."

Angela's mouth dropped open. "In the woods?"

Justine smoothed her hair. "It was a long time ago."

"What was she like?" Melanie asked.

Matthew met her level gaze with one of his own. "She was the favorite."

Justine thought that was strange — both that he would know it, and that it would be the first thing he would say to describe the missing girl. Melanie shook her head. "Not Emily. Lucy."

Matthew paused again. Justine wondered

if all of his conversations were this deliberate. At last he said, "She was loyal."

"Loyal?"

The longest pause yet. "Lilith had a baby,
and the father died in the war. She couldn't
go anywhere after that. A single mother,
unmarried. In those days, that's how it was.
So Lucy stayed here with her."

Melanie considered him. Then she nodded. "That was cool of her."

"Yes." Matthew smiled. "She was cool."

Melanie's interest in Lucy pleased Justine.
The sense of belonging to a family, even
one with a tragic history, was the one good
thing she'd found here. The kettle whistled,
and Justine filled their cups. "How long do
you think the storm is going to last?"

"All night. Tomorrow, too. Do you have
what you need?"

She glanced at the pantry door. "We can
get by if it's just for a couple of days."

"When it stops I'll plow a path across the
lake."

"When will they plow the road? I don't
think our car can drive on the ice."

"Lucy's can."

Justine didn't know where the keys to the
Subaru were, or whether it would even start
after all this time. She chewed her lip. Matthew said, "I can plow the road for you."

235

"Thank you." She'd misjudged him, she decided. He was odd, with his quiet manner and his silences. But Lucy had lived here for years with no other company — no doubt she'd depended on him through the long winters. Surely Justine and her daughters could do the same. Until they left, she reminded herself.

They finished their tea, talking more about the weather, which Justine had learned long ago was something you could talk about with anyone, anywhere. What she learned from Matthew about northern Minnesota winters made her feel even better about her decision to leave. When they were done, Justine walked him to the door. He told her to let him know if they needed anything. "You'll find a shovel in the basement," he said, and as he opened the porch door Justine remembered the shovel she'd seen by the washer. He had put it there, probably sometime in the past two days, while they'd been in town. Which meant he'd kept a copy of the house key he'd given her, and he'd used it to let himself into the house. Perhaps more than once. She rubbed her arms as she watched him walk down the steps and disappear into the storm.

"Can I turn the television back on?" Angela asked.

Justine closed the door. "Go ahead." So much for interesting her children in their ancestors. But when she went back to the kitchen Melanie was turning the pages of the photo album. Her face was open with interest — and the rarest of invitations.

"There's more pictures of them."

Justine kept her face composed, as if Melanie were a horse that might startle. She sat down, careful not to touch her arm, and together they looked through black-and-white windows at two little girls who lived in a Victorian house and celebrated Christmases and birthdays and first-days-of-school with the pale woman and the philosopher who were their parents, and the baby sister who would turn into a sober-eyed child and disappear.

That night Justine brought the box of Emily stories into her daughters' bedroom. "These are stories Aunt Lucy wrote. I thought it might be nice to read one. As a bedtime story." She wasn't going to say anything about Melanie reading one of the books last night. Melanie didn't say anything either, but she turned onto her side and rested her head on her hand in a listening posture, so Justine began to read.

She picked the story in the oldest book

and the youngest hand, because it was a sort of origin story for all the others. In it Emily was a princess who lived in a castle with her parents, and she was happy. As she grew, word of her beauty spread far and wide, and the queen feared the kings of the neighboring lands would steal her away for their sons to marry. So on Emily's sixth birthday the queen sent her to live in a cottage deep in the royal forest, where she would be safe. But although the cottage was cozy and the queen visited often, the little princess was very lonely.

Then one day, a prince stumbled upon her secret home. Taken by her beauty, he chased her so far into the forest that she became lost. As darkness fell, she sank onto a bed of moss and began to cry. The forest creatures gathered around: deer and chipmunk, fragile sparrows and shy foxes. The bravest of them, the mouse Mimsy, stepped forward and, to Emily's astonishment, began to speak. She said Emily had entered an enchanted forest, where fairies lived and all the animals could talk. Emily asked if Mimsy could help her find the way back to her cottage, but Mimsy shook her head sadly. No one who entered the enchanted forest could ever leave. *This is your home now,* she said, *but don't be afraid, for we will keep you company.* And Emily dried her tears, for she knew she wouldn't be lonely anymore.

Justine's voice started thin, but it gathered strength as she read. Angela and Melanie listened without moving. Even the air in the house was still. It caught her words and held them as if they were tufts of milkweed.

"I liked it," Angela said when she was done. She looked so small beneath the quilt. Before she could stop herself Justine pictured her lost and alone in the forest — the real forest, not the fantasy of Lucy's story — and saw again the ragged pile of bones and cloth she'd imagined when she first read the books.

"I did, too," she made herself say. She brushed a curl from Angela's forehead.

"Is it about her sister?" Melanie asked. "The one who disappeared?"

Justine looked at her in surprise. "Yes."

"Are all of them about her?"

"I think so."

"That painting in the living room. Is that her, too?"

"Yes." Melanie looked thoughtful, and Justine felt again the tenuous connection they'd shared when they looked through the photo albums. Though they'd declined Lucy's invitation to live here, she thought

Lucy would be pleased to know they were reading the stories she'd written about the little sister she'd loved.

"Can we read another?" Angela said.

"Tomorrow night." Justine slid the book in among its companions and put the box beside the girls' dresser. She would read a story to them every night, she resolved, and they'd take the notebooks with them when they left. This had been the best half hour she'd spent with her daughters in years.

When she closed their door she stood for a moment on the landing. The overhead light flickered; there must be a short in the wiring, or maybe it was the storm. A web of fine cracks lined the plaster around it like the glazing on a ceramic plate. She went to the door opposite and opened it. The little room smelled old and shut in, but when she turned on the light the lavender walls bloomed. The twin bed had the same white quilt she remembered. Above it hung a print of a young woman in a long white dress walking across a golden field, a straw hat in her hand. Justine remembered that, too, just as she remembered the crocheted curtains on the window, the plain dresser, and the rag rug on the floor. She remembered this room better than any other room she'd slept in as a girl.

She looked for a long minute. Then she turned off the light and closed the door.

LUCY

In the heat of the afternoon, when the fishermen dozed in their rooms, the Miller boys had a break from their chores. So every day after lunch, I waited at the edge of the forest beside the Millers' wooden toolshed until Matthew wandered down, his hands in his pockets.

We always played in the woods — never by the water, up at the creek, or past the Davies house where the rope swing hung. We knew there was something illicit about our friendship, so we were secretive. Anyone who saw Matthew serve my ice cream would think we were just Thomas Evans's daughter and the Indian boy whose family ran the lodge, but as soon as we vanished beneath the leafy canopy, we crossed the boundaries between us and became fellow explorers in a land that was ours alone. We went places Lilith and I never had gone, places so deep the rest of the world fell away. We built forts, set traps, and caught bugs. We stomped through the undergrowth, climbed trees, and listened to our voices reverberate in the green air. Matthew was always one for collecting things, like shells and rocks, so we looked for small treasures, and every afternoon when we left the woods his pockets would be crammed full.

We stayed away from the Hundred Tree. Even though Lilith never wanted to go there with me anymore, that place was still hers and mine. Instead, Matthew and I spent much of our time at a place Matthew called "the berms": six mounds of earth that rose as high as our shoulders in a clearing a quarter mile to the west of the Tree. We didn't know what, or who, had made them, but we decided they were Indian graves, because that made the way we played on them delightfully forbidden. Matthew brought cardboard boxes from the lodge that we flattened to make sleds to ride down their sloping sides, and we jumped from their tops into the deep, mulchy beds of leaves between. It was a more boisterous sort of play than I was used to. Lilith and I had played games of the imagination, pretending to be fairies or princesses in an enchanted forest. With Matthew, everything was physical. Running, climbing, jumping, hunting, building, destroying.

We had quiet times, too, when we sat, temporarily exhausted, on the soft tops of the berms and talked. I'd never talked with anyone but Lilith, not in that intimate way of shared confidences. But Matthew was easy to talk with. His words were few and careful compared to Lilith's lively and abundant chatter, but he thought about things in an interesting way, and I found the slow rhythms of his conversation comfortable. I especially liked hearing him talk about the other people at the lake. Mother would call it gossip, but it wasn't that, not really. He had a different perspective on us, that was all, and through his eyes I saw the people I'd known all my life in a new way. For example, he told me Jeannette's father, Dr. Lewis, brought him the sports pages each weekend so he could follow the baseball season. I told him Dr. Lewis had a son who'd died when he was three or four, and we calculated he would have been about Matthew's age now, had he lived. From then on, whenever Dr. Lewis barked at the boys who played loudly in the lane while he read his newspaper on his porch, I thought about him bringing Matthew the sports pages. I'd never pitied an adult before.

As Lilith and I had, Matthew and I also

talked about what we wanted to be when we grew up, but with him I found myself spinning different dreams than I had with her. What if I went to college? Some Williamsburg girls had done that, although not many, and most of those had gone to the teachers college in Duluth. But I thought I would like being a teacher, especially if there were children like me in class, quiet ones who liked learning about history and the natural world but who never raised their hands. I imagined living in a small town — not our town, but another place that could be known and managed — and teaching in the school. My husband would be the mild sort, like Mr. Jones; perhaps he'd have a general store, too. They were such little dreams, so plain and ordinary compared to the grand ones Lilith made for me, but they felt more real, as if they might come true.

Matthew's dreams were big, like Lilith's, but they were boy-flavored. He was sure people would go to the stars someday, and he wanted to be on the first ship. He had his brother to look after, but he could bring Abe along when he went to whatever big cities star-travelers lived in when they weren't on their rocket ships. Abe would like that. Their father would be sorry to see them go, but he couldn't expect them to live in this lodge forever, could he?

After that summer we never played together again. I suppose it was to be expected. We'd become friends at one of life's sweetest but most fleeting times — the last days before childhood gives way to adulthood and all its complications. Soon, like Lilith, we would be too old to play in the woods, and as teenagers we would grow shy and awkward around one another. This would make me sad, but I would tell myself it was the normal growing apart that happens to children as they get older, and nothing to be regretted.

But here, where I've sworn to tell the truth, I must confess I knew that wasn't it, not entirely. There was that last terrible day, of course, which also happened to be his birthday. And Emily. After Emily, he looked at me differently, as everyone did. Our family was a tragedy, and no one knew how to talk to us. Lilith, Mother, and I didn't help; we kept to ourselves, with all our hopes and secrets. It wasn't until Mother died and Matthew took over the lodge from his father that we saw each other as neighbors, and not until Lilith died that we became friends once more. Though our friendship remains seeded with a certain distance even now. I wonder if he ever thinks about that summer. He probably doesn't. It was so long ago, and it was just a summer.

But one of our playdates in particular I must recall here, because it changed things in a way I only appreciated after everything was done. It was late July, a close, cloudy afternoon that threatened rain. Matthew and I were walking home through the woods, filthy and sweaty, when we heard a sound not far off. It wasn't a forest sound; we knew all those. It was a low, whimpering cry that made the hairs at my nape rise straight up. We'd become so comfortable playing among the imagined dead that we no longer felt that wonderful tickle of fear in the berms, but this cry sounded exactly like the keening inhabitant of a desecrated grave.

I tensed to run. Matthew put his hand on my arm. He pointed to our right, where the sound came from, and stepped into the undergrowth. Being alone seemed even scarier than advancing toward the sound, so I followed him. We tried to walk quietly, but the untrodden brambles cracked with our every step. The whimpering stopped, but whatever had made it breathed in choked little gurgles, and I knew it wasn't a ghost, and that it was afraid.

It was Emily. She was sitting under a tree,

her arms around her knees. Her white socks were stained and her arms and face were scratched from the brambles she'd pushed her way through. I couldn't have been more astonished if we'd found a gorilla sitting there. She'd never gone into the woods, much less ventured way out here. When she saw us she gave a bleat of relief.

Matthew knelt in front of her. "Hey, it's okay. Are you lost?"

Of course she was lost. At first I was irritated. Then I saw something else. She was wearing the dress she'd had on at breakfast, but now she had several blouses over it and three or four skirts underneath. Beside her was the pink purse she'd gotten for Christmas. Something wiggled inside it. I squatted beside Matthew, picked it up, and opened it to find a kitten, a little calico. It blinked up at me with its round blue eyes and opened its mouth in a tiny, insulted mew.

I turned to Emily in stunned comprehension. "Were you running away?"

She gave a hiccupping sob. I could not believe it. Why would this girl — this pampered, favored sister — run away from home? My hand tightened on the purse, and the kitten squalled in protest. I took it out. It was bigger than it had been on Independence Day, but it was still too small to leave its mother. Emily took it from me and tucked it under her chin.

"Does it have a name?" Matthew asked.

"Mimsy."

He touched its head. His two fingers filled the space between its tiny, triangular ears. "Emily, listen. You can't run away. It's too dangerous."

"I'm not scared," she told him, though she was clearly terrified.

"What about your mother? She would be so sad if you left."

Two fat tears slid down Emily's cheeks. The kitten licked at them, its pink tongue dabbing in and out. "She wouldn't miss me."

"Don't be stupid," I said. "Of course she would."

"No." Her eyes were pools of ink above the kitten's tiny face. "She would just love you instead."

I sank to my knees on the rough, leafy ground. As if Emily had conjured them, I felt Mother's arms around me, in my bed in the brown house in Williamsburg.

"That's not how mothers are," said Matthew, the boy with no mother. Neither Emily nor I answered him. After a moment he reached out his hand. "Come on, we'll take you home."

Emily stifled a small sob, but she took his hand. Matthew walked her back through the forest while I followed behind. When we got close to the houses, he ducked his head once and turned toward the lodge. Emily stood looking after him, her purse with Mimsy back inside dangling from one hand, until I came and touched her shoulder. I left my hand there as we walked the rest of the way to our backyard.

Mrs. Jones and Mrs. Pugh were standing by our clothesline. Mrs. Jones had her hands on her hips. "Well, I don't know," she was saying. "I don't see mine between dinner and supper and you don't see me going to pieces."

Mrs. Pugh saw us and gave an exasperated sigh. "Emily, your mother's been looking everywhere for you." She took us around front, where mothers and children were calling for Emily along the beach, up the road, and in the marshy grasses past the Davieses'. They sounded unconcerned, even annoyed. I wondered how long she'd been missing.

A clot of women stood near one of the picnic benches. Mrs. Williams was there, and Mrs. Lloyd, and Mother, who made squeaking gasps, as though she were having an asthmatic attack. Mrs. Lloyd said, "Eleanor, get hold of yourself. She's not an infant. She's just off playing somewhere." Mother shook her head. Behind them Lilith leaned against the big elm, watching Mother with naked contempt.

When Mother saw us, she gave a cry, ran across the road, pushed me aside, and grabbed Emily's shoulders. She screamed something I couldn't understand and started shaking Emily so that Emily's head looked as though it might snap off her neck. Emily dropped her purse, and it lay wiggling on the ground until I picked it up.

Mrs. Pugh shouted in alarm, and she and Mrs. Jones grabbed Mother's arms. "For God's sake, Eleanor!" Mrs. Jones said.

Mother broke free, clutched Emily, and buried her face in her hair. The women stood around in an uncomfortable circle. Mrs. Williams patted Mother's back. "See, she was just off playing with Lucy, like Agnes said." Over Mother's shoulder Emily looked straight ahead, at no one.

Finally Mother got herself under control. She released Emily and gave a shaky smile. "You know I don't like you to go off by yourself without telling me." She stroked Emily's arm and noticed all the blouses she was wearing. She lifted her bulging dress to see the skirts she wore underneath. She looked at her youngest daughter with a stunned expression. Emily looked back, unflinching, just as Lilith had regarded Father in our parlor that first night, after she'd asked him when he stopped being a child. Mrs. Pugh and Mrs. Jones exchanged a look.

Mother tucked a stray lock of hair behind her ear, a furtive, embarrassed gesture. She picked Emily up and balanced her on her hip. Emily's legs hung past Mother's knees. She was way too big to be carried like a toddler, I realized, though Mother carried her like that all the time. Mother nodded at the women and said, "Thank you." As she carried Emily to our house Emily watched me over her shoulder. She was worried about the kitten, I knew. I nodded at her. I would return it to its mother, just as I'd returned Emily to hers.

Once they'd gone, Mrs. Pugh gave Mrs. Jones another look, and Mrs. Jones glanced at me. The two of them, joined by Mrs. Lloyd, walked off, whispering as they turned up the road. Only Mrs. Williams remained. "Lucy, where did you find Emily?" she asked me.

I liked Mrs. Williams. She was a short, round hen of a woman with friendly brown eyes in a plain face and a warm, sparkly manner. The whole Williams family had that aura of contentment some families have that makes you wish you'd been born in them instead of your own. But right then I couldn't look at her, because I knew she would see evasion in my eyes. "Just in the woods," I said. "Not too far off."

She was quiet for a moment, and at last she said, "Lucy, you know you can talk to me anytime you want." I studied the ground. I couldn't imagine what I would talk about with Mrs. Williams. "Remember that," she said, and headed down the lane.

As soon as she was gone Lilith came over to me. "What happened?"

I held Emily's purse behind my back so Lilith wouldn't see it. "I think she was running away from home."

Lilith squinted at the house, where Mother was undoubtedly stripping Emily of the shirts and skirts she'd thought she'd need in whatever life she'd been running to. Her face curdled, making her strong features ugly. "What's she got to run away from?"

I thought of Emily's legs hanging down as Mother carried her. I thought about the empty look on her face as Mother hugged her. I thought about never being able to play in the forest alone, or make a friend, or spend more than a few minutes by myself. I thought about not having even the privacy of my own bed at night. I thought, for the first time in a long time, about how those things had made me feel, when Mother slept with me.

But to Lilith I said, "She doesn't know how good she's got it," and for a moment she and I were united once more in our disdain for our little sister, our parents' favorite, who couldn't understand how lucky she was.

JUSTINE

The storm dumped three feet of snow in two days. After it passed, Matthew got up before dawn and cleared the road and Justine's driveway with a plow he attached to the front of his truck. Justine lay listening to the rumble of the big engine shuddering through the heavy air, and when he was done she got up and used his shovel to carve a path to the carport, then drove the girls to school. In the diner the crowd buzzed with stories — about the tree that fell on Mike Potter's truck and how Maisy was still stuck out at her mother's. When Justine ordered her coffee, Ray asked how she'd weathered the storm in a way that sounded as though she'd been concerned about her. Justine said they'd done fine, thank you.

A green station wagon with New Mexico plates was parked in the driveway when they got home.

"Who's that?" Melanie asked.

Justine ran her gloved hands around the steering wheel. "It's Grandma."

Angela shrieked, and Melanie gasped in delight. Both girls unbuckled their seat belts and clambered over their backpacks to get out of the car. Justine exhaled, then followed them.

Footprints led to Lucy's house and then away, toward the lodge. Neither the walkway to the lodge nor its front steps were shoveled — Matthew used the back door — so Justine and the girls were breathless from staggering through the snow by the time they reached the big porch. The door was unlocked, so they went in.

The lodge's main room was chilly and shut up for winter, but Justine remembered the red-painted log walls, the wooden dining tables, and the pool table. Maurie and Matthew stood by the bar. Maurie still had her coat on, and the snow hadn't yet melted from her boots. Melanie and Angela, who'd rushed here so quickly, stopped short behind Justine, the three years since they'd seen their grandmother making them suddenly awkward.

At first Justine thought her mother hadn't changed. Maurie was tan from the southwestern sun and her body was trim in tight black jeans. Her teeth were white, her lips

256

red, and her lashes thick with mascara beneath overplucked brows. But as she drew nearer, Justine saw the skin of Maurie's face was looser, and new lines traced the corners of her mouth and eyes. She was thinner, too, in a way that made her look haggard, even a little hunted.

Maurie conducted her own inspection, cataloging her daughter's worn jeans and unadorned face. Justine braced for the usual criticism: sweetie, why don't you ever make the slightest effort? Maurie said nothing, just drew her into a hug. Her perfume smelled like gardenias.

When she released Justine, she turned to the girls. "Look at these beauties! Do you remember your grandma?"

Angela smiled shyly. "You used to do our fingernails."

"That's right! And I brought all sorts of things for us to play with. Nail polish, hair things, even some very special makeup just for little girls." She pushed Melanie's lank hair away from her face with a well-manicured finger, and Melanie gave a lopsided smile that was a faint but recognizable echo of Maurie's own.

Maurie waved her hand, a gesture that took in the covered pool table, the bar, and the small square tables with their chairs, and said to Justine, "Not much has changed around here, has it?"

"It never does," Matthew said. The look he gave Maurie was heavy with history, and Justine realized this man who'd known Lucy and Lilith in their childhoods had also known Maurie in hers.

"I thought you'd have gone somewhere warm by now," Maurie said.

"I like it here well enough."

"And Abe? How's he?"

"He's the same, too."

"Where is he? I'm sure he'll want to see me." Maurie smiled. For a moment Justine sensed a silent crossing of swords between them. Then Matthew gave the smallest of shrugs and opened the door to the right of the bar. Behind it was a small alcove with a restaurant kitchen to the left, a set of stairs on the right, and another door at the back.

Justine hesitated. She still hadn't seen this Abe person, and she didn't know why that was. Was he crazy? Bedridden? Over the last few weeks she'd gotten used to thinking she and Matthew were alone here, even though she'd known about Abe. Now she wasn't sure she wanted to meet him. Curiosity won out, though, so she followed Matthew and Maurie, and Melanie and Angela came too — the three of them brushing the last of the snow from their jeans and crowding into a dim room heated to a near-sauna temperature by an iron stove. With its pine walls and low ceiling it felt like a burrow after the spacious main room, and it stank of cigarettes and the medicinal reek of the aged.

In one corner a man sat in a stuffed chair pulled close to an old television. He looked up, startled, as Matthew turned it off. "We've got company." Though his words were short, his voice was gentle.

Justine knew right away why she hadn't seen this man before. He was old, older than Matthew, and he hadn't aged as well. He'd been big once — it was there in the breadth of his shoulders — but now his limbs were thin beneath his plaid shirt and the blanket on his lap. Almost no hair remained on his purple-mottled head, and his thick, knobby fingers shook with tremor. His face was broad, with prominent cheekbones and a bony nose, and though his eyes lacked the keenness of Matthew's, the resemblance was there.

When Maurie saw him, the tendons in her neck strained, and one hand went to her chest. Justine thought she saw a ghost of satisfaction in Matthew's expressionless eyes as he watched her absorb what the years had done. Then Maurie bent down and took the old man's hand. "It's me, Abe. It's your Maurie."

His face lit with recognition. He touched her hair, and Maurie let his fingers twine through it. Her demeanor with him was tender, even protective — not an aspect of her mother with which Justine was terribly familiar.

Matthew said, "This is Justine. Maurie's daughter. These are her children. They're the ones living in Lucy's house." To Justine he said, "This is my brother, Abe."

"You mean they haven't met?" Maurie's eyes glinted a reproach at Matthew that he accepted impassively. But as Justine looked from one brother to the other, a dim memory crystallized. She was sitting at one of the tables in the lodge's main room with Maurie, Lucy, Lilith, and two dark-haired men. She'd finished her hamburger, and now she was eating the French fries that came with it. Maurie was telling stories and the others were laughing. At some point the grown-ups ordered drinks, so Justine went to the porch to read. Later she heard a crashing clatter of violence and ran to the doorway to see one of the men cradling the other's face in his hands. Maurie shouted something, and the next day — wasn't it? — the next day she and Maurie had gone.

That time Maurie hadn't said not to look back, so Justine looked through the rear window until the trees blocked the lake from her sight.

Maurie waved the girls over. "Aren't my granddaughters gorgeous?"

Angela looked at the floor, but Melanie studied the old man frankly. Abe leaned forward in his chair. His finger traced trembly circles in the air in front of their faces. "A little of Lucy here, a little of Emily there," he said in a thick voice clotted with consonants. "Nothing of Lilith, though, no sir. Nothing of that one." He patted Angela's arm. "Although you're even prettier than she was." He smiled up at her with wet lips opening on a nearly toothless mouth. Angela stood frozen as his touch became a caress, like one would use to pet a kitten. Justine resisted an urge to yank her away.

To her relief, Matthew said, "It's time to go. He gets tired." His voice permitted no argument, not even from Maurie, so the four of them left through the back door, Maurie promising Abe she'd come back soon and Justine resolving never to set foot in that room again.

On the way to Lucy's house, Maurie stopped at her car, which was crammed with boxes, a couple of prints in cheap frames, a lamp, and a laundry basket stuffed with shoes. Two enormous suitcases filled the backseat. Justine sighed. Sixty years old, and everything her mother owned still fit in a hatchback.

"Let's just grab the suitcases," Maurie said. "And the shoes."

In the lavender bedroom, they put the suitcases in a corner and Maurie sank onto the bed. As her mother looked around at the plain furnishings Justine saw remembrance settle into her bones, bringing with it a rare moment of stillness. Then Maurie summoned a smile and turned to Melanie and Angela, who stood in the doorway. "This room didn't look like this when I lived in it. I had this fabulous Indian blanket, and posters everywhere. Buddy Holly, Elvis Presley, Little Richard. Bill Haley. Marlon Brando." Her hand swept the air, indicating a place for every name. "This was my room for seventeen years. But as soon as I left they changed it back. Turns out I was just borrowing it." Her tone was wry, but shadows darkened the fine-boned hollows of her eyes. Justine wondered how many hours she'd driven that day, and the day before that.

"I'm making grilled cheese for dinner. Did you eat?"

"God, no. I haven't eaten since Montana."

On their way out Justine turned up the radiator.

At dinner they heard all about Phil-the-boyfriend, cheating bastard and scam artist, who'd told Maurie of a sure thing in the form of a friend's tax-free offshore business, then dumped her for the hostess at the golf club and denied taking any of her money. Maurie, of course, hadn't gotten anything in writing.

"He took everything. All that money I'd been saving for my old age. Almost five thousand dollars." She said this with equal parts pride and shame. Justine felt a stab of pity, even though she'd seen her mother run this game on dozens of men: the hard-luck girl who needed a knight in shining armor. She'd even run it on her, three years and twelve hundred dollars ago.

She changed the subject. "How long have you known those men in the lodge?"

"They've been here since before I was born. Their father built that place."

"Are they —" Justine glanced meaningfully at Angela. "Are they okay?"

Maurie snorted. "Do they look dangerous? No, they're just two old bachelors. Harmless."

Justine nodded, though she wasn't re-assured. Maurie's judgment when it came to men was notoriously unreliable. She got up to clean the dishes.

Maurie twirled her glass of the rosé she'd brought with her, watching the pink liquid rise and fall. It was her third. "I'd forgotten how cold this house gets."

"I imagine it wasn't built for winter," Justine said.

"No, but Matthew always said they could put a wood-burning stove in the living room, and the downstairs, at least, would actually be habitable. He said he'd put it in himself. I bet he still would, if you asked him."

It was the opening Justine needed. "We're not staying. We're leaving right after Christmas."

Maurie took this in, her fingernail tapping the table. "You're going back to Peter?"

"Patrick. And no."

"Where, then?"

"I don't know yet."

Maurie laughed. "Shake the dust off, right, sweetie?"

Justine kept the dishrag moving without comment. Maurie reached into her purse and pulled out a half-empty pack of Vantage cigarettes and a lighter. She lit up and took a deep drag. "Of course you're leaving." She smiled at Angela. "This is no place for pretty girls."

"What was it like to grow up here?" Melanie asked. She'd said nothing during the meal, but now she watched her grandmother with feline intensity. Justine put the last plate in the drying rack and sat down. She was curious, too. She'd never dared ask that of Maurie.

Maurie draped one arm over the back of her chair. She seemed relaxed, her pupils dilated from the wine. "Oh, you know how small towns are. People have nothing better to do than talk about your business. And there's no town smaller than the town you grow up in. Everybody thinks they know you, just based on who your parents are. Or who they think your parents are."

"Who did they think your parents were?" Melanie asked.

Maurie's eyes narrowed, and Justine thought she wouldn't answer, but Melanie kept her pinned with her gaze until Maurie shrugged. "My father died in the war, before he and Mother could get married. That was enough of a scandal right there. And Mother was apparently a bit of a tramp in her younger days. The most popular theory was she messed around with Abe Miller while

Daddy was off fighting Hitler." She gave a bitter laugh. "Which made me part Indian, part slut, and one hundred percent bastard."

Justine glanced at Angela, but she was drawing aimless circles on the table with her finger and hadn't heard. She thought about the creepy old man at the lodge, shriveled beneath his blanket, and how his hands had caressed Maurie's hair and Angela's arm. Could he actually be Maurie's father? Her own grandfather? The thought appalled her.

Maurie rolled her eyes. "Honey, please. Abe Miller is not your grandfather."

Justine flushed. "I know. It's just that he was so happy to see you."

"He always liked me. He's a little slow, but he's sweet. Matthew keeps him locked in the back like he's some sort of crazy uncle, but I used to sneak in to see him." She shook her head. "God, Matthew was pissed when he found that out. I thought he'd kill us both." Then she leaned forward and pointed her finger at Justine. "Here's the truth. My father was Charlie Lloyd, the son of the family that owns this town. But Mother wasn't good enough for them, so Agnes Lloyd told everyone she'd been running around behind his back. If she'd done the honorable thing, I'd be rich now. Charlie's sister got herself killed in a car crash before she had any kids, so it all would have come to me. Instead she gave it to the damned library."

Maurie's face was drawn with bitterness and hurt. Justine's hands tightened in her lap. The library had a mahogany checkout counter, picture windows, and raised brass letters above the door: AGNES M. LLOYD LIBRARY. Maurie had waited tables for forty years to save her five thousand dollars, only to have it stolen by a middle-aged hustler in a trailer park. Was it really so simple? Had her mother's miserable fate been decided before her birth by the prejudices of a small town and the malice of a reluctant mother-in-law? After all, her own fate had been decided by a great-aunt she'd barely known — another woman who'd decided to ignore her relationship to Maurie.

Maurie picked up her wineglass. The rim was crusted with feathered red stains from her lipstick. "It doesn't matter. We Evans girls make our own luck, that's what I always say." She waved her glass at Melanie and drank.

Justine looked at the clock on the micro-wave. It was ten. "It's past bedtime," she said to the girls. Reluctantly, they allowed her to shepherd them up the stairs.

Maurie put out her cigarette and followed, as Justine knew she would. She watched as they brushed their teeth and Justine helped Angela pull on her nightgown, but she didn't say anything until Justine told Angela it was too late for their story. Then she pushed her way into the room, swaying a little from the wine. "How about Grandma reads you your story, since Mommy's too tired?"

Justine tugged at the sleeves of her sweatshirt, smarting from the implied criticism, even though she'd been expecting it ever since they'd climbed the stairs. Maurie took a dim view of Justine's parenting. Justine was never any fun, she said. She never — in one memorable phrase from years ago — made magic for her children. It was ten fifteen, and the girls had school tomorrow, but Justine got out of her mother's way. It wasn't a battle she could win.

Angela pointed to the box of Emily books. "They're over there."

Maurie picked up a notebook. "Oh my God. Where did you find these?" When Justine told her she said, "Lucy used to read these at the library. She let me turn the pages." She turned one now. She wore a wistful expression that made her look younger, or at least less tired. "I always

268

wondered what happened to them."

When Justine was little, on the rare nights Maurie stayed in, she would sometimes read Justine a bedtime story. Justine had loved the weight of her mother on her bed in her chiffon bathrobe, the scent of her night cream, fresh and sweet. Maurie read as well now as she had then: slowly and with great expression. Both girls were mesmerized, and Justine, too, found herself drawn in by Maurie's voice, mellow and tinged with a lyricism that transported them all to the magical summer forest of Lucy's imaginings.

The story was called "Emily and the Indian Princess." In it Emily found a series of earthen mounds in the woods. She didn't know what they were and they scared her. Then, on the night of the midsummer full moon, the ghost of an Indian princess appeared and told her the mounds were where the Indians had buried their treasures. If Emily were to dig in the mound she indicated, she would find the princess's own riches. So, with the help of Mimsy the mouse and her cousins the moles, Emily dug until she found a golden crown and scepter, and necklaces and bracelets of gold and silver and gems. She put them on, and all the creatures of the forest called her Princess Emily. The ghost of the princess smiled and said Emily was the true heir to her forest kingdom.

Maurie closed the book. In the silence they could hear the house breathing, soft and slow. Then she laughed, breaking the spell. "Well, damn. I sure could use an Indian princess right about now."

"Couldn't we all," Justine said neutrally.

Maurie gave her an irritated look. She pushed Angela's curls aside and kissed her forehead. "I'll tell you what, baby. While I'm here, I'll read you your stories every night. How's that sound?"

Angela nodded as she slid down her pillow. Melanie's eyes met Justine's, but Justine looked away. It was okay if her mother read the Emily stories to the girls for a while. She was their grandmother, after all. And they would be leaving soon.

LUCY

Father wasn't Mother's first love. I didn't know this until she was dying. She died slowly, so she had lots of time for deathbed reminiscences. Most were about her childhood on her family's farm, and how desperately she'd wanted to escape her father, our tiny, hunchbacked Grandfather Roberts, whom I barely remembered, so long had he been dead. Lilith and I ignored those stories; they didn't interest us. But this one did interest me, so I listened.

His name was Samuel. I never heard the family name, but he was a Williamsburg boy. They were the star pupils of the one-room schoolhouse that used to sit on First Street, and when they were in the upper grades the teacher often asked them to stay after school to help her. He lived in town, but every day he walked her home to her family's farm — three miles there and back. By the time they graduated, they were promised to one another. He was going to take over his father's cabinetry shop and build her a house. It would have been yellow, she said.

Then came the Great War. Williamsburg's young men shipped out in the fall of 1917 in a frenzy of flag-waving and band-playing, and Samuel the cabinetmaker's son never came back. Mother wasn't the only war widow, or almost-widow, in the county by any means, but she was a shy, plain girl who'd just held one boy's hand. She thought Samuel was her only chance, she told me through milky tears, and I did feel a little sympathy for the girl she must have been.

Father was six years older than she, so although she knew of him and his prominent family, they'd never had much to do with each other. While she and Samuel were courting, Father was away at the Methodist seminary. After he broke with the seminarians, he came back to Williamsburg, and when his brother was killed in France and his father died of the influenza, he took over the pharmacy that was supposed to have been his brother's inheritance. So he was there when the shy, plain girl came to pick up the sleeping powder her mother was stockpiling against the day, not much later, when she would make her own escape from the hunchbacked farmer.

He was so charming, Mother said, her eyes swimming with an apology she didn't know she was making. Of course he was. He was educated and intellectual, and to a smart girl who never got to go to college, listening to him talk about Kant and Hegel and the power of free will had to have been thrilling. He was older, too, and had the aristocratic superiority of his well-to-do family. I can see it. I did see it, every day of my life until the summer of 1935.

A picture of them on their wedding day sat on the fireplace mantel at our house in town. I don't know where it is now; probably in the basement, where many of the things from that house went once the bank claimed it. In it they're standing side by side, their faces unsmiling in the manner of the time. He is as compelling in the photo as he was in life, his eyes mesmerizing, his cheekbones sharp and argumentative. She is small, her head just reaching his shoulder. Her arms are thin beneath the silk of her gown, and she clutches her bouquet so tightly that the tendons are visible on the back of her hand. Her eyes are full of surprise and gratitude. She thought, then, that she had been saved.

Saved. What a word that is! So full of power, yet so passive. It speaks of a force greater than we, of an agency that is strong enough to redirect the flow of our lives when we cannot. God, the love of a man or a woman, the birth of a child, the simple act of growing up — these are all things we think can save us. Father, Mother, Lilith, and even Maurie believed they could be saved by these things, at one time or another. I had no such delusions, but it didn't matter; in the end I'm no more saved than they. As I sit in this dark house, listening to its exhalations that have worn the walls as smooth as vellum, it occurs to me that the whole tragic history of our family comes down to this: none of us knew how to save ourselves.

I've often wondered what Lilith thought of Mother's story. Because she, too, lost a sweetheart to war. Charlie proposed in early 1942, during a weekend leave between training and deployment, with that enormous diamond ring that had been his grandmother's. He was a serious young man then, and he'd become handsome in that big-featured Lloyd way. It wasn't the life Lilith had dreamed of on those summer nights at the bridge, but it would have been a good life all the same. He'd been accepted to the state medical college once his service was done, and someday they'd live in the Lloyds' fine house and she would be the doctor's wife instead of the pharmacist's daughter. And, of course, he'd loved her since they were children. Even through her wild days, when everyone tutted and said she wouldn't have become so wayward if her father had lived. That was worth something, right there.

The telegram came just six weeks after he'd gone. Lilith sat with it on the porch for hours while Mother and I pretended to go about our business so she wouldn't see us watching. Then, when I was preparing our supper, she came and set it on the table. She looked at me with that level gaze of hers, and her eyes were dry. I stood with my hands covered in flour, my faded plaid apron hanging from my shoulders. I couldn't think of anything to say. I suppose, by then, nothing I could have said would have made any difference.

A month later she told us she was pregnant with his child, conceived during that one, brief visit.

The Lloyds were awful about it, of course. Agnes had been against the marriage from the start; she had higher hopes for her son than a small town beauty with a sullied reputation. She even demanded the ring back, saying she never gave Charlie permission to take it. Lilith said no. Then, after Agnes stood on the sidewalk outside Lloyds' Pharmacy and told her Maurie wasn't Charlie's child — no Lloyd was ever so dark, she claimed, and we knew what she meant — Lilith never spoke to anyone in that family again.

Years later, when Maurie learned her father was the son of the richest family in town, she was furious at Lilith. If only Lilith had given the ring back, she said, Agnes would have acknowledged her grandchild and Maurie wouldn't have been stuck out here living on my library wages and Lilith's hostessing paycheck. I knew Agnes would never have acknowledged Maurie under any circumstances, but Maurie didn't see it that way. To her, Lilith had thrown away her birthright out of selfish pride. But Lilith was right to keep that ring. While she didn't love Charlie, she appreciated his devotion, and, as I said, they would have had a fine life. I don't blame her for holding on to the one talisman she had of the one dream she dreamed that could have come true.

Besides, Maurie wouldn't have been happy even if she'd gotten the Lloyd name and money. She craved change too much, and the thrill of choosing. As soon as she could walk, she'd disappear the instant we looked away, into the woods or around the shore, reappearing covered in dirt like a wild creature. Lilith named her for Maureen O'Hara, the young ingenue — just two years older than she — who'd starred in the film *How Green Was My Valley* the year before, and the name was apt, for Maurie loved drama. She reinvented herself constantly, changing her hair, her clothes, and her way of talking. She was incapable of conforming. Or belonging.

Still, she brought such life to this place while she was here. I used to take her with me to the library, and at my lunch break we'd go for fountain sodas at Father's old pharmacy. I knew what people thought of us by then, three women living in the woods with an unsolved mystery and a bastard child, but Maurie was irresistible. Iain Mc-Neil at the counter gave her extra syrup. At the library, Jeannette Lewis let her stamp the return dates on the checkout cards. When I read my stories in the children's circle, she sat on my lap like a queen, turning the pages while her schoolmates watched.

We were happy, I think now. It's a thought that surprises me. But when Maurie was young, we thought less about what we'd lost, and more about what we had in front of us. Less about the things we'd done, and more about what amends could be made. Lilith and I even began to look at Mother differently, as a grandmother instead of a mother, and there seemed the possibility of forgiveness.

But as soon as Maurie stormed out of here, her sails filled with rebellion and pride, we became mother and daughters once more. Into the space Maurie left crept memories of that other child, memories that had lurked patiently in the corners, waiting for an absence large enough to fill. Mother sat in her chair while the television muttered. Lilith's travel and celebrity magazines piled up on the coffee table. I lay awake as I hadn't in years, thinking of things long past. We became again what we'd been at the start: three women living with their sins and their ghosts, keeping an unspoken vigil, growing old.

One day I looked at Mother and knew she was dying. It was autumn, an ordinary day, and she was stringing beans into a bowl, and in the stuttering movement of her hands I knew it. For a time she spent her days in the parlor watching television as usual, the only evidence of her decline the afternoon naps that became longer and longer. Then came the morning she couldn't get out of bed, so we moved the television to her room, and propped her on pillows. When she could no longer feed herself, we held the spoon to her mouth. We carried her to the tub and washed her papery skin while she crossed her arms over her chest as though keeping a secret. Once a week we set her hair, a limp memory of the curls she'd wrested into a snood for all those years. Toward the end we diapered her, changing her often so she wouldn't get sores. We sat by her bed with our books and magazines, letting the endless tremor of her voice wash over us.

We were good daughters. We were dutiful.

At the very end she talked only of Emily. It was all I could do to sit out my assigned hours by her bedside, listening to her voice tremble on about how she'd loved her. I was going to keep her safe, she told me, her eyes imploring my understanding, my forgiveness. She was going to be the one I saved. I wouldn't look at her in those moments. I looked at my book, the words a blur, and tried to keep my hands from shaking.

She died at night. Lilith was keeping watch, and she came to wake me when she heard Mother's breathing change. I sat on one side of the bed and she the other. We didn't turn on the light, but the moon was bright; we could see her and we could see each other. We didn't speak. We watched her, and we waited. Mother's mouth was open and her lips were cracked from the air that seeped in and out. Her hands twitched on the sheet, unable even at the end to be still. At last the sky to the east began to grow pink and the stars to fade, and it was time.

I expected her to back out of her life without waking, just as she'd lived it. I thought this would be fine with me. But she opened her eyes, and I was overcome by a sudden, wretched need for her to see me. For mine to be the last face she saw on this earth. I leaned over her, looking into her eyes that were as pale as smoke and as dry as ash, but she didn't see me. She looked beyond me, over my shoulder. She raised her arms. They shook with the effort it took to hold them up, but I could see them curving, the palms softening, as though cupping a face. I felt the air change, as if a veil had shifted just beyond my sight, parted by those seeking hands. Emily's name was a whisper on her breath.

I sat back. My chest was tight, and I swallowed hard to loosen it. Lilith watched me. Her cheeks were wet with tears she had shed without a sound. Then she seized Mother's

280

hands and pulled them down to the bed. She held them there as they fluttered like moths, trying to break free. She held them as the lake took on the color and sheen of mercury in the gathering light. She held them as Mother's eyes pleaded and then were still. She held them until Mother was dead.

JUSTINE

The next morning Maurie came with Justine to drive the girls to school, saying she wanted to see what the town looked like these days, so after they dropped the girls off, Justine drove around the square. It was overcast, and in the milky light the buildings looked even more timeworn than usual. The few passersby walked with their shoulders hunched into the wind, past mounds of graying snow that clogged the street corners. Maurie looked out the window through huge black sunglasses, her face expressionless.

Justine pulled the Tercel into a spot in front of Ray's. She felt an oddly proprietary desire to show her mother the diner and its inhabitants. She'd felt the same way about Dr. Fishbaum's office when Maurie visited her in San Diego. She'd invited her mother to come with her to work one day, and Maurie spent the morning chatting with the

282

old and befuddled patients in the waiting room. They seemed younger with her there. Dr. Fishbaum and Phoebe liked her, too. Justine had been proud of her, and proud of the office — it was her office, her job, her coworkers. Her place.

Now, though, Maurie kept her sunglasses on as they slid into Justine's usual booth. Not until she'd established that she didn't know anyone did she take them off. Justine cataloged the now-familiar faces — Maisy and Mike and Roberta, Lorna and Steve from the general store — and felt a rush of affection for them even though she'd never exchanged a word with any of them. She was about to tell her mother how she came here every morning and how great the coffee was when Ray came out of the kitchen.

"Maurie. What a surprise."

Maurie gave Ray her most brilliant smile. "Ray Spiver. I thought you got out of this place years ago."

Justine looked from Ray to her mother. It had never occurred to her that they were the same age. Maurie seemed so much younger.

Ray shrugged. "I came back."

"And whatever happened to — what was his name? Jimmy?"

"Vietnam."

"Oh, what a shame," Maurie said, with what seemed like sincere sympathy.

"What can I get for you?" Ray's manner was friendly, but Justine knew her well enough by now to sense the distance. It made her think about what her mother had said the night before, about this town and her reputation in it.

"Just coffee," Maurie said, again with that wide smile. As soon as Ray left she leaned across the table and hissed to Justine, "God, I hated that bitch."

"What?" Justine shot a glance at Ray, who thankfully had her back to them. "Why?"

"She always looked down that fat nose of hers at me, even though she was nothing but trailer trash from Mahnomet. When she got that scholarship, you'd have thought she'd been crowned queen of England. Now look at her. Right back where she started." Maurie's face contorted with malicious satisfaction, but when Ray brought her coffee she smiled at her as if she hadn't just called her an ugly bitch, and asked after a few old classmates. Ray, unsurprisingly, knew the latest on all of them. When Ray asked what she'd been up to all these years, Maurie waved a hand. "Seeing the world," she said, and Ray nodded, as though she knew exactly what that meant.

Justine drank her coffee quickly, anxious to get out of the diner. She'd brought Maurie here to show her a place she considered hers, but as soon as Ray recognized her it had become Maurie's instead. This whole town, Justine reminded herself, belonged to Maurie far more than it would ever belong to her. So did Lucy's house, no matter what Lucy's will said. That was yet another reason to leave.

When they got back to the lake, Maurie launched into the living room with a fury, and it was soon apparent her mission was broader than just a missing ring. By the time Justine cleaned the breakfast dishes, the Hummel figurines from the curio cabinet lay stacked in one paper bag, and the knick-knacks that had littered the living room tables were piled in another. A third bag was crammed with papers from the rolltop desk. This was fine, Justine told herself. She needed to sort through the house anyway, and she could use the help. Still, watching Maurie cram unused stationery and broken reading glasses into the trash bag made her queasy. It was a little like watching a grave robber.

So she went upstairs. She started in Lucy's room, where she spent the morning packing her great-aunt's clothes for donation. Lucy seemed never to have gotten rid of anything, including her own mother's prim dresses, which still smelled of flowery perfume. Justine assumed there'd be nothing here worth keeping, but way in the back of the bedside table drawer, behind a Kleenex box and two bottles of Sominex, she found something odd. Carefully wrapped in a small silk handkerchief was a crude wooden pendant the size of a quail egg on a leather string. In its heart was carved the letter *L.* The wood was stained and worn smooth, as though it had been held often in someone's hand. A dear possession, obviously. Was it Lucy's? Or Lilith's? Maybe Maurie would know, though Justine doubted it. She set the pendant on the bedside table beside the photos of herself and her mother and of Lucy and Lilith.

Downstairs she heard metal hangers being tossed in a pile — Maurie must be plowing through the hall closet — so she went to the lavender bedroom. A quick survey of the dresser confirmed that Maurie, the consummate vagabond, had already moved in. The rest of the room was empty, except for a large, dust-covered trunk in the closet. Justine pushed open the heavy lid. The acrid smell of mothballs made her eyes water.

The trunk was filled with a child's clothing: dresses and skirts and blouses with round collars and pearl buttons, all in soft pastels; a little girl's underwear and socks, a pair of white sandals, and black patent leather party shoes. Everything but the shoes was neatly folded in white paper.

They must be Emily's. All the things her mother had brought to the lake for her daughter that last summer, she had kept. Of course she had. She'd hoped Emily would come back and wear them again, and as the years passed she hadn't been able to give them away. So she'd kept them here, in the room Maurie had borrowed. Justine remembered how the old woman had tottered to the chair when her surviving daughters lit the candles beneath the painting. At nine, Justine had been too frightened of her to pity her. Now the thought of her folding these clothes with such care brought an ache to her throat.

Gently she placed the clothes in paper bags. They were too small for her daughters, but she couldn't leave them for the house's next owner to throw away or give to Goodwill, to be sold for fifty cents or a dollar. There must be a vintage clothing shop in Bemidji that would take them and sell them to someone who would value them.

At the bottom of the trunk, she found a Buster Brown shoe box. Inside was a child's blue slipper, trimmed in satin. Its sole was caked with long-dried dirt. Justine picked it up with her thumb and index finger. That Emily's mother had kept even this solitary, dirty slipper was somehow more heartbreaking than everything else put together.

"I see you found the Emily shrine."

Maurie stood in the doorway. Startled, Justine nearly dropped the slipper. "It's awful, what happened to them."

"I know. That damned Emily messed everything up for everybody. Though you'd never know it to listen to them. Growing up, it was like having a sister that everybody loves better than you, except she's dead, so you can't say anything bad about her and she'll never grow up and crash the car." Maurie laughed. "You're lucky you're an only child. You didn't have to share me with anyone." Before Justine could think how to respond to this, Maurie held up a pair of ancient white ice skates. "Look what I found!"

They were hers, she said, a present from Abe Miller. He'd seen how bored she was during the long winters, so he used his plow to clear a patch of ice on the lake. She skated there every fair day, and every time it snowed he plowed the lake again. She got pretty good; she could skate backward and do spins on one foot, even. Abe watched from his upstairs window while she did shows for him like in the Ice Capades. As she talked Maurie held the skates to her chest, and Justine could picture her as a young girl skating in circles, her arms out for balance and her breath in white clouds.

When Justine brought Angela and Melanie home from school, Maurie presented them with the skates as though they were Hans Christian Andersen's silver prize. "Who wants to learn to skate?"

Angela threw off her boots, but Melanie looked around with horror at the brown paper bags that were everywhere now, filled with Art Deco letter openers, midcentury ashtrays, and Victorian vases.

"We're going through Lucy's stuff," Justine said. "We have to do it before we leave."

Melanie walked to the closest brown bag. She picked up a candlestick, one of the two that had sat on the table beneath the portrait of Emily. She looked at Justine and tightened her lips. For once Justine knew what her daughter was thinking. "Before we go we'll see if there's anything we want to keep," she told her.

The skates were way too big for Angela,

and her face fell as Maurie yanked them
off. "Let's try you," she said to Melanie.
Melanie eyed them dubiously, but after a
bit of coaxing she eased one foot into the
old leather. They were too big for her, too,
but Maurie tore up a page from one of
Lucy's old tax returns and wadded it into
the toes. Then she wedged Melanie's feet
into the skates and drew up the laces. "Let's
try them out!" She grabbed Melanie's hand,
her smile splitting her face into a quarry of
lines and fissures.

"But I can't skate," Melanie protested.

"Of course you can't! I'm going to teach
you!" Maurie pulled Melanie by the arms
until she staggered to her feet, her ankles
wobbling. "Justine, go get the shovel."

It was three thirty, and the sun had already
sunk behind the trees, but the sky was still
bright as they headed down to the lake.
They made an odd procession, Maurie
holding Melanie's arm as she limped
through snow that reached her knees, Justine carrying the shovel, and Angela huffing
along beside her. When they got to the lake
Maurie took the shovel and attacked the
snow. It was heavy and deep, and after ten
minutes she had cleared only a few square
feet.

"There's too much," Justine said. She

wanted to go back inside. This was the longest she'd spent outdoors since they'd gotten here, and already her fingers were numb inside her gloves. The temperature must be close to zero.

"Oh, no. We're not giving up. Wait here." Maurie clambered back to the road and half-ran to the lodge, where she clomped up the snow-covered steps and banged on the door.

"What's she doing?" Angela asked, her teeth chattering.

"I don't know," Justine said, although she was pretty sure she did. She watched as Matthew opened the door to the lodge and let Maurie in.

"I don't want to skate," Melanie said, looking at the lake and its blanket of snow broken only by the tire tracks of Matthew's truck. Justine couldn't blame her. But she knew they were powerless against Maurie when she was like this. Some of her worst childhood memories were of those times when Maurie, caught up in a dervish-like frenzy, led her on some bizarre adventure from which she could not escape. Though, to be fair, they were just as often her best memories. When she was fifteen, she'd met Carole King at a party her mother made them crash, and Justine still remembered how beautiful the singer was, with her blond curls in a headband, a cigarette in one hand and a drink in the other.

"Just try it," she said. "Your grandmother wants to teach you."

Angela looked at the skates. "I wish they fit me." Melanie glared at her, but didn't say anything more.

An engine started up, and Matthew's truck, plow attached, lumbered across the road and onto the ice. Maurie waved from the passenger window as the truck cleared a space the size of a basketball half-court. When it returned to shore she climbed out and skidded over to them. Matthew got out, too, and walked more slowly to stand behind Angela and Justine.

"Okay, Melanie, come with me." Maurie took Melanie's hands and began to walk backward through the snow, Melanie staggering in her wake. When they reached the ice Maurie stepped onto it and pulled Melanie after her. The heavy steel blades scratched as they grabbed at the ice and held. Justine took Angela's hand. In San Diego, Melanie hadn't wanted to join the rec soccer team or the local Girl Scouts, nor had she played softball or basketball, taken ballet classes, or sung in the after-school choir. She'd rejected all these things without even trying them. Maybe, Justine thought, Maurie could get her to skate, and she'd like it. Even warm places had ice rinks.

"When I move my right foot back, you move your left foot forward," Maurie instructed. Melanie shook with the effort it took to balance. Her ankles turned in and her hands clutched Maurie's, but when Maurie moved her right foot backward Melanie inched her left skate forward. They took several steps like that in a frozen parody of a waltz, and Justine felt a singing flood of relief and pride. Then one skate slipped and Melanie fell, taking Maurie with her, both of them hitting the ice hard.

"Shit!" Maurie pushed herself to her feet, creaky but resolute. She wrapped her arms around Melanie and pulled her up. Come on, Melanie, Justine thought. She willed Melanie to pull the skates under her, and after scouring at the ice for several desperate seconds, Melanie did. She teetered on the blades, her mittens digging into Maurie's forearms.

"I don't want to," she said.

"The trick is not to be afraid." Maurie shook off Melanie's hands and Melanie's feet wobbled for a second before she fell again, landing on her knees. She cried out, her face contorting as she bent forward. Justine cried out, too, her own knees faltering in sympathy. Then Melanie looked up at Maurie, and Justine could see from the set of her daughter's face that it was over; her mind was made up; she was never going to skate. Justine felt a tremor in her chest, and she gripped Angela's hand tighter.

"It won't hurt if you don't fall," Maurie said in a jaunty voice. Again she pulled Melanie to her feet. This time Melanie grabbed her around the ribs. They were both gasping in the frigid air. Maurie managed to push Melanie away, and Melanie fell again, the skates shooting forward so she landed flat on her back.

"Melanie!" Justine cried. Her mother needed to stop, but she knew she wouldn't. Because it wasn't about the skating anymore. When Justine was nine, Maurie had taken her on a roller coaster at the Six Flags outside St. Louis, and Justine had been so terrified she'd thrown up. Maurie made her ride it again and again until she'd convinced her mother she loved it; loved the upside-down part; loved the speed. *That's my brave girl,* Maurie had said. Now Justine couldn't move. Her feet were immobile in their boots, as though they'd become part of the snow. On the ice, her daughter struggled to sit up.

Maurie flapped her arms in exasperation. "For God's sake! You're not even trying!"

"Stop it!" Melanie shrieked. "Stop it!" She lifted one foot and pounded the back of the skate blade into the ice. Maurie started toward her again, but Melanie backed away, skittering like a crab. Her mouth was a gaping red hole in her face.

"Get up!" Maurie told her. "Evans girls never quit!"

Justine let go of Angela's hand. Melanie wasn't going to get up. She wasn't like Justine. In Colorado Springs, when Justine was twelve, Maurie's boyfriend had a small ranch and a big bay horse. The horse's back had spread Justine's legs wide, and the world spun upside down, and the dirt tasted like horse shit, again and again and again. *Get up, Justine. Evans girls never quit.* She wrenched one foot forward. "Mom, leave her alone! She doesn't want to do it."

The sky had faded to pearl, edged with rose along the tops of the western trees. Maurie's face was in shadow as she turned to Justine. "I'm not going to let her be a quitter!"

Matthew walked onto the frozen lake. Justine jumped as he passed her; she'd forgotten he was there. His boots with their deep treads navigated the ice as though it were gravel. Melanie scooted away from him, but she was no match for his long strides. When he got to her he squatted. Justine couldn't hear what he said, but she could see her daughter's face crumple, and she put her arms around his neck. Then Matthew carried her back to shore and toward the road.

Maurie rushed after them. "Matthew, no! She has to learn —"

Matthew turned to her. His face was so black with warning that Maurie actually stepped back. He scowled at her for a moment more, then walked away, carrying Melanie through the snow to the front porch of Lucy's house while Maurie watched with the outrage of a child whose favorite toy has been stolen.

Justine pushed past her. When she reached the porch steps Matthew came down them. He neither spoke to her nor slowed down. She opened the screen door to find Melanie on a porch chair unlacing one of the skates. Melanie shook her head without looking up. "Go away."

Justine stopped, fidgeting with the zipper on her coat. I'm sorry, she wanted to say. I couldn't stop her. I've never been able to stop her. Then the door opened again and Maurie and Angela came in. Melanie kicked off the skate, sending it clattering to the floor at Maurie's feet. Her face as she looked at her grandmother was chiseled and forbidding. Maurie just smiled. "Angie, what do you say we get you some skates and you can give it a whirl?"

Melanie looked away, working on the laces of the second skate. Angela watched her for a moment. Then she nodded.

"That's my brave girl," Maurie said, and Justine flinched. Melanie kept her eyes on the laces.

LUCY

After Independence Day, Lilith behaved with impeccable modesty when Father was at the lake. During the week, she still went to the lodge in borrowed clothes and makeup, but on the weekends she wore her own, demure dresses and kept her face clean. Father scrutinized her as though looking for Charlie's fingerprints, but he found nothing that made him take her back to Williamsburg, and I was glad, for her sake and mine. Though we spent our days and evenings apart, I still loved having her with me at night.

During this time, though, I began to notice a change in Father. I'd always known, from the way he breathed here, that he loved the lake the way I loved it, as a balm for the spirit. He came directly from the pharmacy on Fridays, still in his white coat, and within hours the stress of the week melted from his shoulders, so by family time he was relaxed, ready to consider and impart the tenets of his faith and philosophy. Lately, though, the tension that followed him from town never left him. He was snappish with Mother, terse even with Emily. His sermons were less about family, personal responsibility, or the need for us children to remain innocent, and more about charity, the forgiveness of debts, and the terrible wages of usury — lessons I could not understand. He grew thinner, too, which deepened the hollows of his cheeks. I worried about him. I began to spend more time at the house when he was there, so I could watch him.

"You should go play outside," Mother told me one such afternoon. I was on the porch swing, reading. Father was on the far side of the porch, reading also. Emily was playing a game of jacks on the floor by my feet. She'd taken to following me around when I was in the house, but I'd decided I didn't mind. Now she looked up, waiting to see what I would do. For the first time, I thought about taking her to the woods to play. It was a sunny day, not too hot, and the woods would smell of peat and clover.

Father looked over, distracted by our conversation. "What are you reading, Lucy?"

Mother retreated to the kitchen. I held

the book so Father could see. *"Huckleberry Finn."* I was reading it for the second time; it was one of my favorites from Matthew's collection.

He closed his book and set it on his lap. "And what do you think of young Mr. Finn?"

I tried desperately to gauge him. What did he think of Huck? Huck was a disobedient rascal, uninterested in the book-learning Father so prized, and he was a petty thief to boot. But he had strong morals for all that, and he was appalled by the self-interested manipulations of Tom Sawyer, as was I. Then there was the matter of Jim. Jim was actually my favorite character, because of the unfailing loyalty he showed to his new friend. It was a quality I thought I had, too, and one that, like Jim's, I felt wasn't sufficiently appreciated.

Father rattled the ice in his glass, waiting.

"I like him." When Father raised one eyebrow, I added, "He's good to Jim."

He smiled, which made him look more like his pre-Independence Day self. "Yes, he is. He's one of my favorite characters in all of literature. He does what he knows is right, despite what the so-called Christians tell him." He gave me an appraising look while I tried to project my Huck-like moral center through every pore of my skin. When he turned back to his book, I felt light-headed. Emily, who'd been watching us intently, resumed her game. The whump-swish of the ball and her hand sweeping up the jacks echoed the blood pounding in my ears.

Later that afternoon, as he sometimes did, Father went to the lodge to play pool with Mr. Williams, Dr. Pugh, and Mayor Lloyd. I followed him. I was consumed by a new notion, ignited when he questioned me about Huck Finn but still inchoate, and I couldn't let him leave my sight while I turned it around in my head. So I ordered a pop and sat at a table on the other side of the room while they played.

As usual, they talked about politics and business, and the others called Father Tommy, his schoolboy name. I loved to watch him with the other men, because I could tell they respected him. They admired him as a man who'd taken over his father's shop and kept it running even in hard times, which counted for a lot in those days, but it wasn't just that. They were churchgoers, and you might think they would look askance at a man who stayed home on Sunday mornings, but at Father's memorial service, Mayor Lloyd would say the most prominent men in town often came to him for moral guidance. He'd say this was because of Father's character, but I suspect it was also because, except for Mr. Williams, his childhood friend, he had no favorites among them, and was beholden to none of them. He was the closest to an impartial arbiter they had, like a priest in a confessional.

They were beginning their second game when Lilith came in with Jeannette and Betty. Lilith wore a modest smock dress and no makeup, which made her look much younger than the other two, but they didn't treat her any differently for it. They sat at a table with their pops, giggling and talking. She didn't even glance at me. Father looked her up and down, but when he found nothing troubling in her demeanor he turned back to his game. He hadn't noticed me at all. The small notion that had taken root in my mind shriveled, and I decided to go.

As I stood up, a panicked wail came from the kitchen, and Abe carried little Amanda Davies through the back door. Amanda was about Emily's age, a pert, towheaded tomboy with a sassy mouth — she would be the first woman to sit on Williamsburg's town council — but now she was in hysterics, with a bloody gash across her forearm. The men exclaimed in alarm, and Dr. Pugh rushed forward. He took Amanda from Abe, set her on a chair, and began to examine her wound.

Matthew had followed Abe and Amanda into the room, and Dr. Pugh said to him, "You, boy. Bring some towels." When Matthew obeyed, Dr. Pugh folded a towel and laid it on the cut, applying pressure. Amanda's crying subsided, and once she was calmer Dr. Pugh looked at Abe. "What happened?"

"It was a hacksaw, sir." Abe shuffled his feet and looked at the floor. "She fell and cut herself on it."

"Where the devil did she find a hacksaw?"

"In the shed."

"Is that what happened, Amanda?" Dr. Pugh asked.

Amanda's voice shook. "We were playing."

"You and Abe? In the shed?"

Amanda nodded. Dr. Pugh and Mayor Lloyd shared a look. Even from fifteen feet away I could feel Matthew tense.

Dr. Pugh ran the hand that wasn't applying pressure to Amanda's wound down each of her legs to her ankles. "Are you hurt anywhere else?"

Amanda looked at Abe. She pulled her lower lip with her teeth.

Abe said in his thick voice, "She's not hurt anywhere else."

Mayor Lloyd set down his pool cue and took a step toward Abe. Abe's face darkened, and to my surprise, his hands curled into fists. I'd never seen him angry. He was so gentle most of the time that, even after that summer, his anger would always take me unawares.

Matthew put a hand on Abe's arm. Mr. Miller moved from behind the bar and stood in front of his sons. Mayor Lloyd put his thumbs in his belt. He'd been an amateur boxer, and though he'd gone to fat he looked like he hadn't forgotten how to knock people down.

"I'm going to need to talk to your boy," he said.

Mr. Miller crossed his arms. "You can talk to me." He was a big-shouldered man and his arms were muscular from the labor it took to run his business. Matthew's thin arm slid across his brother's chest. He looked young and afraid, and I was afraid, too. Lilith, Betty, and Jeannette watched from their table, all of us braced for violence.

Then Father said, in a mild voice, "Let's hear what the girl has to say." Everyone turned to him, standing at ease by the pool table. When he had everyone's attention he knelt by Amanda. "Amanda, tell me what you and Abe were doing." Every eye was on Amanda now, and she, who always did like it when people's eyes were on her, sat up despite her pain and trepidation.

"We were playing king and queen."

"What sort of game is that?" Father asked.

"It's where I get to be the queen," she said, as though that should be obvious.

"And how did you cut your arm?"

Again Amanda looked at Abe. Abe's face was still flushed, and I could tell from the rapid movements of his eyes that he was afraid of what she might say next. Amanda said, "I fell. There was a sharp thing on the wall, and it cut me."

I looked at the men, expecting to see them relax, but they remained tense. "Did Abe do anything to hurt you when you were playing?" Father asked.

"No." Her voice was suddenly so quiet I could hardly hear her.

"Anything at all?"

Her eyes flicked again to Abe. The room was quiet except for the faint buzz of the ceiling fan high in the rafters. A small movement caught my eye, and I saw Lilith had leaned forward in her chair.

Amanda shook her head.

Father patted her knee. "Good girl." He walked to Mayor Lloyd and led him away from Mr. Miller and Abe. Mr. Williams came, too. Father was slight and a little stooped; to anyone else he would have been an insignificant figure beside these larger men, but to me there seemed to be a light that fell only on him from the ceiling lamps. I edged closer so I could hear them.

"I don't like it, Tom," Mayor Lloyd said. "The two of them, alone in that shed."

"Playing," Father said.

"But he always plays with the girls. Never the boys. I saw him come out from under the lodge with your youngest not two weeks ago. What do you think they were up to under there?"

Playing with the kittens, I wanted to say, but I didn't have the nerve.

"You know what he's like," Father said. "He may be nearly grown, but he's still a child in his heart. He doesn't think like that. And God doesn't judge us on the things we do, but on the intentions of our hearts." As always when he invoked God, his voice rang with authority. He smiled at Mr. Williams and, by the faintest glance, at me, which sent a small delighted shock tingling through my fingertips. "Mens rea, isn't that the term you shysters use?"

306

Mr. Williams smiled, too, and shook his head. "You should have studied law, not religion."

Mayor Lloyd ran one hand over the top of his balding head. His hand trembled a little, with relief, I thought. "Maybe so. But it's not right." He turned to Mr. Miller, who still stood with his sons by the bar. He pointed a finger at him, belligerent again. "You tell him. We can't have it. Not anymore."

Mr. Miller's eyes wavered for the smallest instant, and he gave a curt nod. He said to Abe, "Get back to the kitchen," and Abe disappeared through the door. Matthew followed. Mr. Miller returned to the bar, turned his back to us, and began wiping the glasses in the drying rack. Soon Dr. Pugh and Mr. Davies took Amanda to town to stitch up her arm, Lilith and her friends left, and everyone else carried on as though nothing had happened.

But later, as I was looking through the books on the lending shelf, I heard Mr. Miller's voice, raised in anger, through the back door. The lodge was empty save for me; it was that dead time between the afternoon and the early supper crowd. I went to the door and stood with my ear close to it.

"It's got to stop," I heard him say. "You

can't play with them anymore. Not with the girls."

"I didn't mean to hurt her."

"That's not what I mean. You're grown now. It doesn't look right, you playing with the girls. It's going to bring trouble on us. Play with the boys all you want, but if I catch you with one of the girls again, I'll strap you, so help me God."

That was all he said on the matter, at least within my hearing. But for the rest of that summer, and for all the summers after, Abe stayed away from the lake children, girls and boys alike. Even when the town folk stopped coming and the summer people became vacationers from distant cities, Abe worked in the back of the lodge, out of sight. None of the mothers had minded Abe's attentions to their daughters; in fact, Abe with his gentle ways was the only Miller they liked. The fathers, though; that was something else. The fathers didn't like their little girls playing with older boys. Especially older half-breed boys.

Which is why it was interesting that, of all the men in the lodge that day, it was Father who wasn't bothered by what happened. Father, who couldn't abide Lilith sitting next to Charlie Lloyd at a bonfire, had no trouble with Abe and Amanda playing in the Millers' shed, or with Abe and Emily playing under the lodge. The difference, I decided after giving it much thought, must lie in that thing he'd said to Mr. Williams. *Mens rea.* It wasn't until years later I learned what that was: a legal term meaning "guilty mind." Some acts, no matter how dire the results, aren't considered crimes without proof of an intent to do harm. To Father, Charlie Lloyd had mens rea; Abe did not; and that was all that mattered.

He was right, of course. About Charlie, about Abe, and even, to some extent, about himself. Charlie had had lustful thoughts about Lilith for years, and would until the day he died. Abe was not incorruptible, as I later learned, but I'm certain he never meant to hurt anyone. As for Father, no matter what you think of him when my story is done — and I expect you will judge him harshly indeed — I will say only this. I believe he tried, as best he could, to keep his intentions pure in the eyes of his God. And when he saw that he had failed, he imposed upon himself without complaint the harsh punishment his God demanded.

JUSTINE

Justine only checked Lucy's post office box every few days, so she wasn't sure how long the letter from the assistant principal had been there. "I would like to schedule a meeting with you about your daughter Melanie," it said. Justine was alone in the kitchen when she read it, and she thought about throwing it in the trash. It had been three weeks since the assistant principal called, but Justine hadn't done anything about it. She'd decided to ignore the whole thing. They were leaving anyway, so what was the point?

But the tone of the letter was stern. It used the words *consequences* and *unacceptable,* and Justine worried about what the woman might do to punish Melanie without consulting her. Better to meet with her and apologize for whatever Melanie had done. So, on the Monday before the winter break, she told her mother she had some errands to run and went to the school an hour before the final bell.

She pictured Elizabeth Sorensen as a gray-haired woman with reading glasses and a buttoned-up mouth. That was how the assistant principal in San Diego looked, and that was how she remembered all the assistant principals she'd met as a child. She'd spent a lot of time in assistant principals' offices. Sometimes her mother was there, too, and when she was, the assistant principal would talk about the importance of a stable home in a voice that sounded just like Mrs. Sorensen's had on the phone.

Instead, Mrs. Sorensen turned out to be a tall, attractive woman about Justine's age with straight, straw-colored hair in a blunt cut. She wore brown tweed pants, a soft brown sweater, and a cream scarf, all with a casual elegance that made Justine feel short and frumpy in her T.J.Maxx jeans and pullover. Her office was small and outfitted with cheap public school furniture, but framed Audubon prints hung on the wall, and a kilim rug lay on the industrial carpet. The effect was cozy, which Justine also found discomfiting.

She sat with her purse on her lap while Mrs. Sorensen opened a manila folder. "I've read Melanie's records from her school in

San Diego." She looked down at the file. "The counselor there said she had become resistive. Refusing to follow instructions and do classwork. Over the past few months she had several physical altercations with her peers."

Justine hadn't known Melanie's disciplinary record would follow her here. So much for a clean slate. The mother of the girl whose backpack Melanie threw in the mud had snatched the new backpack and shut her front door before Melanie could finish her apology. Justine felt again the helpless anger she'd felt that day, both at the woman and at Melanie. She gripped the vinyl handles of her purse. "Just tell me what she's done so we can make it up."

Mrs. Sorensen's blue eyes were cool and intelligent, like a scientist's. "She hasn't done anything. I was surprised to read all this in her file."

Justine was confused. "Then what — ?"

Mrs. Sorensen softened almost imperceptibly. "Look, it's a small town. We don't get new kids often. I keep an eye on them, because I moved here in fourth grade myself, so I know how hard it can be." She paused, inviting Justine to appreciate her solicitude. Justine doubted whether pretty, blond Elizabeth Sorensen had any idea how hard it could be, so she said nothing. The assistant principal continued, "Angela's doing fine, all things considered. She's a sweet girl and she's working hard. Melanie's situation is different."

So that was what this was about: Melanie hadn't made a friend yet. Justine was relieved it wasn't a disciplinary issue, but Melanie's lack of social skills wasn't a new problem, either. Melanie hadn't had a friend since the third grade. Alicia Clark had been the last, a cute, red-haired girl who came over on Saturday afternoons until her mother stopped calling without explanation.

Then Mrs. Sorensen said, "Unfortunately, she's being targeted by some of the other girls."

Justine wasn't sure she'd heard her correctly. "Did you say targeted?"

"Bullied, I should say."

"*Melanie*'s being bullied?"

Mrs. Sorensen picked up a pen and turned it over in her fingers. Then, her expression as bland as though she were describing the weather, she told Justine how a group of girls — the "queen bees" she called them, daughters of the town's oldest, most prominent families — had organized a campaign against Melanie almost from the day she'd arrived. They called her Smelly Melly and made up cruel rhymes about her. They said she was dirty and anyone who touched her had to wash their hands. Even things she touched, like pencils, books, or her desk, had to be wiped before anyone else used them. It was a small school, Mrs. Sorensen explained, and all the students in the fifth grade, even the boys, were under the social control of these four ringleaders.

Stunned, Justine waited to hear how Melanie had struck back. Hit someone, wrecked someone's backpack. But Mrs. Sorensen said nothing about that. Instead she said, "Melanie was so distant when she arrived. She acted like she didn't care about these girls, or their power. They saw it as a challenge."

The assistant principal regarded her with studied, bureaucratic sympathy. Justine looked away, over Mrs. Sorensen's shoulder at a print of a red bird with an orange crest. She'd grown accustomed to Melanie spurning other children, but for her to be the object of these attacks, so similar to the social torments Justine herself had experienced as a child? And she'd had no idea. She remembered how Melanie had walked up the school steps just that morning, her feet heavy, her head bowed. Still, she'd trudged into the San Diego school, too, hadn't she? How was Justine supposed to have known the difference? The red bird stared back with one bright, black, accusatory eye.

Mrs. Sorensen was waiting for her to say something. Justine thought for a minute, then said, "What are you going to do about it?"

This was the right question; the one the assistant principal expected. Her tone became, if possible, more officious. "Well, in addition to serving as the assistant principal, I'm the school counselor. What I'd like to do is use this situation to start a school-wide discussion about bullying that, frankly, is long overdue. Melanie's difficulties will be a learning opportunity for everyone at Williamsburg Elementary. It's a teachable moment, as they say."

Justine's mouth opened in disbelief. She couldn't imagine anything Melanie would like less than to serve as the poster child for an antibullying campaign. But what would other mothers say about this? Would they give permission? They probably would. It was the expected thing, to want to help your children. And of course she did want to help Melanie. She also didn't want to make trouble for her, because trouble apparently

315

followed you, in your records, from town to town.

Then she remembered the winter break was four days away. "Can it wait until after the break?" she asked.

Mrs. Sorensen nodded. "That would be best."

Justine relaxed — they would be long gone before Mrs. Sorensen could seize her teachable moment. She picked up her purse, preparing to leave. The assistant principal cleared her throat. For the first time she looked a little uncomfortable.

"There's one more thing. I'm worried Melanie may have deeper problems that need to be addressed. With your permission, of course." She took another folder from beneath the first and slid it toward Justine. This, Justine figured with a sinking dread, was going to be the same thing the San Diego school always wanted to talk about. Melanie was unhappy. Melanie was angry. Melanie missed her father. All of it true, all of it immutable. In San Diego she'd assured them Melanie lived in a stable home with a good man who wouldn't leave, and that had mollified them somewhat. She wouldn't be able to say that here.

But the folder didn't hold the counselor's report she'd expected. It held a stack of drawings on lined papers torn from a spiral notebook. They were clearly done by Melanie, but unlike Melanie's usual delicate sketches the lines of these drawings were heavy, as though she'd driven the pencil hard into the paper.

The first was of a girl crouching in a forest. She wore a white dress and had black hair that covered her face except for her eyes, which were wide with fear. The forest was a tangle of scribbled trees that pressed down upon her from all sides. In the branches loomed a man's face, his hair a dark mass, his eyes black holes. The drawing was crude, but the menace in the woods was visceral, like something done from a nightmare. Justine's pulse quickened as she turned the page over. The next drawing was of the same girl, her arms reaching as she fell into a circling black vortex. Her mouth was open in a scream.

There were a dozen more, each of a terrified dark-haired girl, usually in a tangled forest, sometimes in a swirl of black circles, many with that same face watching from someplace close and dark. In each, the pencil had scored with a passion that made Justine's fingers shrink away as though the paper were hot. As she turned the pages the air in the assistant principal's office became heavy, smothering.

"She was drawing in class, and her teacher took away the notebook," Mrs. Sorensen said.

Justine licked her lips. "She likes to draw."

Mrs. Sorensen turned the pen in her fingers. "The registration papers you filled out don't list a father's name."

Oh, God, here it was. "Their father left. Over a year ago. I don't know where he is."

"I see." The pen turned and turned. "Is there another man now?"

"No. We left him in San Diego."

"Why?"

"Does it matter?"

"Was there violence?"

"Of course not."

"Did he touch the children in ways they weren't comfortable with?" The assistant principal's face was mild, as if she were asking the girls' shoe size, but a faint pink tinged her cheeks.

"No! Patrick would never do that!" Justine snapped the folder shut. He wouldn't. She knew it with absolute certainty. Whatever his faults, he wasn't a child molester, and he loved Melanie. Melanie hadn't loved him back, but that wasn't because he'd done anything terrible. He just wasn't Francis, that was all.

Elizabeth Sorensen's face was quite pink now. "Surely you can see how these drawings might arouse suspicion."

"No, I can't. They're just drawings! How do they mean Patrick hurt her?"

"I'm troubled by how distressed the girl is in these pictures. And by how much she looks like Melanie. And there's a man in several of them."

"That man looks nothing like Patrick." Justine felt a hot rage. This woman! So perfect, so smug, so certain she knew everything about the single mother and her children who'd showed up in her insular little town dressed in cheap, ill-fitting clothes. So troubled, by the dismal life of abuse and neglect they must lead!

"Even so, may I have your permission to talk with her about them?" Mrs. Sorensen prompted.

"No." Justine snatched the folder and walked out, leaving Elizabeth Sorensen sputtering about not removing documents from a student's file. She walked past the secretary, out of the school, and got in her car. It took every one of the ten minutes remaining before her daughters came out for her hands to stop shaking.

LUCY

August came. August in Minnesota is a miserable month, thick with heat and the buzzing of horseflies as big as grapes. In the towns it's something to suffer through, especially in those days before air conditioners, when people sat inside with the windows shut and the drapes drawn and children spent hard-won nickels on fountain sodas that cooled them only for a moment. But our lake was so deep it never fully gave up the cold of winter, and the shock of it against our hot skin made even the worst days bearable. At night we slept with our windows open, listening to the crickets and the frogs, in sleeveless nightgowns under white sheets, as water-fed breezes cooled our faces.

One morning, not long after the scene in the lodge with Abe and Mayor Lloyd, I woke to find Father sitting on my bed in his fishing clothes. It wasn't quite dawn, and everything floated in shades of gray, so at first I thought he was the afterimage of a dream. I managed to keep my breathing even so he wouldn't know I'd woken. I couldn't imagine why he was there. He just sat, with his elbows resting on his thighs and his hands clasped between them, his head bowed, as if he were praying. The lines of his shoulders, the curve of his back, the clenched muscle in his cheek, all betrayed the weariness and tension that had haunted him the past few weeks. After a minute or two I couldn't help myself; my breathing hitched, and he looked at me. He relaxed a little when he saw I was awake, and smiled. "Lucy. Do you want to come fishing?"

Fishing! I had to fight to keep the joy and, yes, triumph, from my face. He'd never taken any of us fishing. None of the men took their daughters; fishing was only for the sons. Lilith used to say we were lucky to be girls, because no one pulled us out of bed before dawn on Saturday mornings, but now that Father had asked me, I wanted nothing more than to get up and go fishing with him.

He waited on the landing while I dressed. Like Lilith before her evenings at the lodge, I dithered over what to wear, then chose my simplest skirt and plainest shoes. When I came out, Father smiled again. "It's not the usual fishing attire," he said, "but it will do."

All but two of the boats were already gone. Mr. Jones stood in one of them, stowing tackle boxes and rods while two of his sons waited on the dock. Bobby and Davy were younger than I, and they looked at me with open surprise. Mr. Jones said, "Going to try a little fishing, Lucy?" He had a gentle way about him, and was the unlikely father of six wilding boys who were in and out of trouble their whole lives. At his funeral those boys, grown men then, would sob like children as they carried his casket from the church.

Father said, "I decided I shouldn't have to fish alone just because God gave me daughters."

"Your girls are so pretty, they'll be doing fishing of a different sort soon," Mr. Jones said, winking at me. Father didn't say anything to that; he just went to the shed, where he got two fishing poles. While he was gone the Joneses' boat pulled away. Mr. Jones waved, and I waved back. I was pleased he'd said I was pretty.

Father loaded the boat with his tackle box, a bucket, a thermos, and the poles. Then he helped me in and started the motor, heading the boat out into the lake. We didn't go very fast, but the air teased my hair and face. It smelled wet and musky with leftover night. Since Lilith and I had swum to the pontoon, I hadn't ventured into the lake beyond where my feet could touch the bottom. Now, as we forded the dark water, I thought about how it had lured me down, and for a moment I imagined myself jumping in, clothes and all. I tightened my hands on the metal side of the boat.

Just inside the eastern point, where the land curved to form our bay, was a marshy area thick with grasses and lily pads. Here Father cut the motor. It was as if I'd gone deaf, so sudden and absolute was the quiet. Then, as my ears adjusted, I caught the small sounds of morning: a whippoorwill call, the peeps of frogs in the grass, the first buzz of insects. The mouth of the creek was nearby, and its water trilled over rocks to meet the lake.

Father patted the metal bench beside him. Wary of the pitching boat, I climbed over and sat. He was patient as he explained how it was done. He showed me how to put the worm on the hook, winding its body three times through the barbed tip, leaving enough at each end to wriggle in the water. I stifled my revulsion as I picked up a worm and fed it to the hook, clumsy, Father's hand guiding me. He turned me sideways so I straddled the bench, and he sat behind me the same way, his chin brushing my hair as he reached his arm around me to drop the line in the water. The red and white bobbin slapped the surface, then floated.

"Now we have to be quiet," he said, "and wait for the fish to come." I nodded, relieved. Whenever I'd dreamed about being alone with Father I'd been unable to imagine what we might talk about. But being quiet — that was something I was very good at.

The fishing line lay as light as a spider's thread on the perfect stillness of the water. Far away I heard a motor start; one of the other fishermen was moving to a new spot. The other boats were past the points, in the deeper water beyond our sight. I was glad we were inside the bay, here by the reeds, where the lake's surface lay like a glossy membrane over the silty, caramel-colored bottom a mere dozen feet below.

After a while my eyes grew heavy. Father was warm and close, sheltering me from the cool air. We breathed together, in and out, and he stroked my arm, his fingers lightly tracing my skin, as they often traced Emily's when she sat on his lap. Love was in his touch, but reverence, too, a worshipfulness that felt as though he were drawing a great calmness from my body. Happiness, thick and liquid, flooded even my smallest veins and settled below my stomach. The newly risen sun was warm on my head.

"You're not one to be noticed, are you, Lucy?" Father said quietly. "You're like the church mouse that no one sees but who hears the entire liturgy."

His words shivered in my spine. I didn't know what to say, or if I should speak at all. Should the church mouse speak when it was noticed? Thankfully the fishing pole bowed in my hands.

"You have a fish," Father said. He put his hands behind mine on the pole, his arms on either side of me. The bobbin was nowhere to be seen; the tip of the pole was bent almost to the water. With his right hand Father worked the reel, winding it up then spinning it out. "We're letting the fish get tired," he said, "so it won't fight so much when we pull it in." The reel whizzed and clacked, the line whipping up and bowing again. I held on to the rod, though Father's were the hands working it, his long, thin fingers nimble and strong. "Good job, Lucy," he said, "you're doing great. Now we'll bring it in."

He began to wind and wind the reel, stopping when the rod bowed too much, then starting again. I looked over the side, eager to see the fish. When it rose through the water, glimmering and struggling, I gasped, and Father laughed. "It's a big one," he said. "A fine, big fish for your first catch." He stood as he wound in the last of the line, rocking the boat, hauling the brown-speckled fish from the lake. It was as long as my arm, a walleye, and it twisted in the sun, its mouth gaping for air and its scales glinting with gold.

Father took the line just above the fish's mouth and pulled it into the boat. It flopped on the bottom, its thrashing tail loud against the metal. I lifted my feet, startled. Its eye was as big as a dime, dumb with mindless terror, looking up at the sky, which must have seemed a new and terrible thing. Its mouth opened wide then closed again, and again, and again, and the hook through its jaw and gill dripped bright red blood. Father watched it, his head tilted. Its spasms slowed, then renewed with an even greater frenzy. I covered my face with my hands. "How long until it dies?"

I heard Father pick it up and strike it against something. "It's dead now."

And it was. Its jaws were still and its eye was blank. Father yanked the hook out and threw the fish in the bucket, which was filled halfway with water, and it floated there with its white belly up. The water in the bucket turned pink. I felt dizzy. I held on to the side of the still-rocking boat, hoping Father wouldn't see.

"This is a good spot," he said. "Let's cast the line again."

Over the next half hour we caught three more walleyes, all smaller than the first, all dying for too long on the bottom of the boat until Father picked them up and crushed their heads against the metal bench and threw them in the bucket. I didn't doze anymore. I watched the bobbin with dread, hoping it would stay on the surface, my heart lurching each time it twitched and sank. When at last we turned for home I sat in the bow, facing away from the pale bodies that swayed in the bucket. I leaned into the wind, feeling the air cool my face as it blew my hair back.

In the kitchen Mother was making breakfast. When she saw me with Father she stopped mixing the pancake batter. "You took her fishing?"

"She caught four fish." He laid them on the counter.

Mother wrapped them in paper and put them in the refrigerator. "We'll fry them for supper," she said, smiling a tight smile at me.

At the table I surprised myself by how hungry I was, reaching for more than my usual share of pancakes, eggs, and biscuits. Father laughed, saying I was a fisherman and deserved a fisherman's breakfast, and when he smiled at me I felt something shimmer between us like a ribbon. But I also remembered the fish flailing on the bottom of the boat and the pink water in the bucket, and the eggs tasted like dough in my mouth and I had to turn away.

Lilith hadn't asked where I'd been, and she'd hardly looked at me since I'd returned. She was awake, I think, when I got dressed, and as I pictured her watching through the window at our boat trailing black chevrons across the water I felt a wretched mixture of spite and regret. I hoped she was envious that Father had chosen me, the quiet church mouse, to take fishing. I hoped she'd felt left out, the way I did when she was with Jeannette and Betty. I also wished she'd been in the boat with me, because she would have understood about the fish, and about Father's hand on my arm, and I didn't know how to explain any of it to her.

Now she set down her fork with an air of

announcement. "Guess what? We're going to put on a cabaret."

"A what?" Father said.

"It's like a talent show," she explained. "With singing and dancing and magic tricks. We're going to do it on the last night of summer, for all the families. We've been practicing."

She hadn't told me about this. Not once, in all the nights I'd stayed up until she got home just so I could listen to her gossip, had she said anything about putting on a show. I'd been keeping my own secret, of course — she didn't know about my friendship with Matthew. I was afraid she would ruin it; that she'd make fun of how we still played like children or tell me what a little boy Matthew was compared to Charlie and the others. I could think of no reason for her not to tell me about the cabaret other than that she simply hadn't cared to tell me or, worse, hadn't even thought about it.

"Who's we?" Father asked. I could sense Mother stiffen, and I realized Father might not approve of this at all, and might forbid it. I wasn't sure what I wanted him to do. Lilith, though, seemed unconcerned as she began ticking off her fingers. Jeannette and Betty. Ben. Harry and Mickey Jones. Felicity and Sincerity. Opal would play the piano.

329

Opal was the Williamses' daughter, shy and immature at seventeen, and Father had been fond of her since she was a little girl. Everyone else Lilith named was the teenaged son or daughter of a lake family, and she hadn't mentioned Charlie.

"What kind of music?" Father said.

"Songs from the movies, and from musicals. Like 'Lullaby of Broadway' and 'Blue Moon.' I'm going to sing 'On the Good Ship Lollipop.' "

Shirley Temple's films were the only live-action movies we were allowed to see when they came to the Williamsburg theater. I hadn't heard of any of the other songs. Father nodded. "When I was a boy, we put on a puppet show one summer," he said, his face soft with nostalgia. Mother turned back to the dishes.

After breakfast I didn't linger at the house. I wanted, more than anything, to be in the deep forest with Matthew, even though it was Saturday and we didn't play together on the weekends. So I sat on the fallen log by the shed where we always met. I hoped he'd see me and come down. If he didn't, I told myself, I'd go to the Hundred Tree alone.

Abe was behind the lodge, tinkering with his motorcycle, a black, catlike machine he kept in fine condition and that, when he rode it up the lane, never failed to bring the younger boys running. My log was thirty feet from him, but he had his back turned, so he didn't see me. The grass was high here, and tickled my knees. A cloud of gnats swam around my head, and I swatted them away. I wouldn't wait long.

I heard the familiar squeak of the hinges on our back door and, to my surprise, Lilith came out. I'd assumed she'd gone to join her friends for what I now knew was cabaret practice. She looked around and called my name. I didn't want to talk to her; my thoughts were too muddled with the fishing and the cabaret she hadn't invited me to join, so I didn't answer, and she didn't see me sitting low on the log. But she did see Abe. She walked toward him through the Williamses' and the Joneses' backyards. When she got about ten feet away, she stopped. She put her hands on her hips. "I like your motorcycle."

Abe looked at her, then lowered his eyes. "Thanks."

"Would you take me for a ride on it sometime?" Lilith's mouth curled up on one side in that way I'd come to recognize. She arched her back slightly, pressing the cones of her breasts against her yellow blouse. Abe stared at them. He wiped his greasy hands on his pants. My heart beat an alarm inside my ribs: what was this?

"I can take you now, if you want," he said.

Without thinking, I stood up. At the same moment Matthew came around the side of the lodge. He stopped when he saw Lilith and Abe, and he frowned. I remembered how he'd fumbled with the change that first day at the lodge, and I felt a stab of jealousy. "Abe, you're wanted inside," Matthew said.

Abe jammed his hands in his pockets and walked toward him. As Matthew turned to go, he saw me. He looked at Abe, then at me again, and shook his head. He couldn't come with me, but he wanted to, and that was enough.

Lilith had seen me, too, and once the brothers were gone she came over. She smoothed her skirt under her and sat on the log. I sat beside her, and we were silent for a while. It was not a comfortable silence. Before this summer, our silences had been of the best sort, thoughtful and communicative. I'd often thought, during them, that we were thinking the same things. I didn't think that now. Her body hummed with a tension I couldn't translate.

I said, "Why didn't you tell me about the show?"

She relaxed. I thought I'd guessed right, and she was relieved I'd brought it up. "I didn't want you to feel left out."

I turned this over for a bit. "Why would I feel left out?"

She sighed. "Oh, Lucy, you would never want to be in a cabaret. You could never be on a stage, having people look at you."

The sun was hot on my knees. I pulled my skirt down to cover them. She was right, of course. I'd never have the nerve to be in a cabaret. That was for her, whom no one could fail to notice, even if she were sitting quietly in a corner. Still, she'd always made me feel that with her by my side I could be more than what my nature would have me be; do more than I would have dared on my own. I would have expected her to encourage me to be in it — just a small part, off to the side, singing in the backup chorus. I know, now, that she had her reasons for excluding me. But at the time I thought it was because she'd never really believed I could leave anything but the faintest of footprints, no matter how much she tried to help me. I wanted Matthew to come back.

"I'm sorry I didn't tell you," she said. She put one arm around me and rested her head against mine. I sat, feeling the weight of her, until she got up to go. This time, she did head for the Lloyds'.

I sat there for a while longer, despite the droning insects. Then I went to the house. Emily and Mother were in the kitchen. "Emily, do you want to come and play?" I said. Emily gave a small clap, and a quick look at Mother. Mother didn't want to give her up; I could see it. "Just for a little while," I added, and she relented, though I could feel her watching us as we walked out. Emily skipped with delight.

"Let's play in the woods," I said, because I was the big sister, and I decided the game.

JUSTINE

Justine sat on Melanie's bed, watching her sleep. Melanie lay on her side with her knees pulled up to her stomach, her eyelashes dark, perfect crescents. She looked achingly young. Justine hadn't said anything to her about the meeting with Mrs. Sorensen the day before — about the bullying or the drawings. Especially not the drawings. Although she was still confident they weren't of Patrick, their urgent lines pulsed with an anguish that worried and confused her. She didn't know what to say to Melanie about them. But she did think she knew what to do.

She put her hand on Melanie's leg. Melanie opened her eyes and her face fell into its familiar dour lines. She looked exhausted despite the night's rest.

"It's time for school," Justine said, "but you don't have to go."

Melanie studied her suspiciously. "Why?"

"There's only four days until the break, and we'll be gone before school starts up again. So you might as well stay home. If you want."

Melanie continued to frown. Angela raised herself on one elbow, the quilt falling around her pink nightgown. With her mussed curls she looked like a child in an old-fashioned calendar. "I don't want to stay home," she said.

"I thought you didn't like that school, either."

Angela glanced at Melanie. "I don't. But we're having a Christmas party today."

"We'll have just as much fun here, I promise. We'll go to the mall. Hang out with Grandma." Bake Christmas cookies, she almost added, then remembered the broken oven.

"But I want to go to the party. And I want to sing in the chorus concert. It's tomorrow night."

"I didn't know you were in the chorus."

"Everybody's in the chorus," Melanie said. "They make you."

Justine had seen the sign outside the school advertising the concert but hadn't thought anything about it. If Angela hadn't brought it up, they would have missed it. Which wouldn't have been such a bad thing.

She'd never driven the forest road at night. "Do you really want to sing in it?" she asked. Angela nodded. Justine turned to Melanie. "But you don't, do you?"

Melanie's eyebrows drew down in a vee. Justine felt a wave of gobsmacked delight: Melanie liked the chorus! Melanie scowled in confusion at her mother's grin, which made Justine laugh. It couldn't be that hard to drive the road in the dark.

"Fine. I'll take you to school, Angela. Melanie can stay home. And we'll all go to the concert tomorrow. After that, we'll all stay home. Sound good?" Both girls nodded, and Justine smiled again. It wasn't often she got things right with her daughters.

When she returned from driving Angela, Melanie was helping Matthew shovel the walk to the lodge's front porch. Justine slowed as she drove by them. She couldn't imagine what had prompted Melanie to do that, and she debated telling her to come inside. They hadn't had much to do with the Millers since the ice skating incident, which was fine with her. She still found them both unsettling.

Then she told herself: stop it. He plows that road for you even though he drives his truck across the lake. Helping him with his walk was the least they could do. Like when Mrs. Mendenhall went to see her daughter and they'd gotten her mail and watered her plants. That was how it worked, being someone's neighbor. And he was their neighbor, even if only for a little while longer.

In the kitchen Maurie was going over her lists of things to keep and things to sell. Her papers were all over the table and her breakfast dishes sat unwashed on the counter. It had been like this since she'd arrived, and would be like this as long as she stayed. The only housecleaning done in any of their apartments had been done by Justine.

"How long has Melanie been outside?" Justine asked her.

Maurie peered over the top of her red cheaters. "I didn't know she was."

Justine sighed and turned to the dishes in the sink. After she'd washed them she poured herself a cup of coffee and went to the living room, where she could keep an eye on the shovelers through the window. Matthew worked with efficient deliberation, heaving great mountains with each slow stroke. Melanie moved more quickly but managed only a snowball's worth at a time, her shovel hitting the mound askance or slamming into the ice beneath.

It was warm in the living room. Cozy, even. In fact, it was cozy in the entire house, now that Justine had decided she didn't need to ration the propane anymore. Maurie's brown bags were still scattered about, and she reminded herself to go through them, to see if she wanted anything. She noticed the candlesticks were back on the table beneath the portrait of Emily. The original candles were gone — Maurie must have thrown them away — and in their place were the candle stubs Justine had pulled from the drawer for Thanksgiving. She glanced toward the kitchen. She hadn't thought Maurie cared about Emily, but apparently she'd held a little ceremony of her own. That was interesting. She looked at the portrait again. The little girl stared back at her with those inhabited eyes, and Justine turned back to the shovelers.

They were almost done, though it was a mystery why they were doing it at all. Surely no one used the front door in the winter. Then it hit her: they had. They had used it the night Maurie arrived, and again when Maurie needed Matthew to clear the ice. The shoveled walkway was a courtesy for them. A courtesy, and an invitation. Justine's hand tightened on her coffee cup. She didn't like visiting people. She certainly didn't want to visit the Millers — didn't want to sit in that cramped, smelly room, "visiting."

Still, she had to admit she was touched by the gesture. Maurie had said Matthew Miller had lived here since before she was born, and that he'd never married. He'd probably spent decades in that lodge with no one for company but his brother and the guests who passed through in the short summer season then returned to their cities and forgot him. And Lucy, of course, and Lilith and their mother. It must have been a lonely life, made even lonelier now that Lucy was gone. Of course he would want them to visit.

She herself wasn't lonely, though. The thought surprised her. She'd been lonely for so long and so thoroughly that she never thought about it anymore. But here in Lucy's house, where she was more alone than she'd ever been, she wasn't. The snow-covered lake lay like milk between the charcoal of the points and the gray of the far shore. Its empty quiet, so unnerving when she'd first arrived, was soothing now, a balm upon her nerves. It was the sort of quiet she'd listened for each morning in her San Diego kitchen, that no matter how still she sat she'd never quite heard beneath the weight of Patrick sleeping down the hall and the humming of the hallway clock moving relentlessly toward seven fifteen. Here, even with Maurie making her mess, she could hear it: deep, mournful, and embracing.

She'd barely thought of Patrick since Maurie had arrived, she realized with surprise. That was one thing, at least, she could thank her mother for.

The walkway was done. Matthew reached out a hand and Melanie shook it. He patted her shoulder, nudging her up the steps to the lodge. Justine didn't want Melanie going in there alone with him, so she went for her coat and boots, cutting off her mother's question with the closing of the door.

She found Melanie and Matthew at a table in the main room, drinking cups of cocoa. They looked up at her and she stopped, feeling foolish.

"Would you like some cocoa?" Matthew asked. He knew why she was there; it was in his face.

"No, thank you." She stood there awkwardly in her half-zipped coat as they continued to look at her. "Well, if it's not too much trouble."

"It's a mix," he said. "So it's no trouble."

She went to the table, feeling like an intruder. When Matthew brought her cocoa he set it in front of her with his callused

hand and said, "She worked hard. I appreciate it."

Justine put her hands around the mug.
The cocoa was very hot; she wouldn't be
able to drink it for several minutes. She
didn't know what to talk about to fill that
time. Finally she said, "We're grateful to
you for plowing the road."

"That's no trouble, either." He gave a hint
of a smile.

"Well, you won't have to do it much
longer," she said. "We're moving away after
Christmas."

His smile faded. He turned to Melanie.
She bit her lower lip, the muscles in her
neck working. The lines of his face seemed
to deepen. He nodded, as though agreeing
with something only he heard. "It is a hard
place to live."

Justine wished she hadn't said anything.
After all, he'd shoveled his walk in hopes
they'd come visit; that they'd drink his
cocoa and sit at his table. And she'd just
told him they would never do that, or
wouldn't for long. It would have been better to leave without saying anything.
Wouldn't it?

"It's not so bad," she assured him. "It's
quiet. I like that." He didn't respond, so she
rushed on, "It's just so cold. For us, I mean.

We're from a warm place. And the school is so far away."

"I wouldn't know about that." He shrugged his shoulders in the dirty brown coat. "I didn't go to the school."

Melanie watched him, her fingers picking at one another behind her cup. "Why not?"

"My grandmother taught us here." He saw her envious look and gave a gravelly laugh. "I would rather have gone to the school."

"Why?"

"I wanted to learn things my grandmother couldn't teach me. And I wanted to be with the other children. Play on a baseball team. Go to birthday parties." He spoke as though none of this mattered anymore, and looking at his ancient, weary face, Justine couldn't imagine him as a boy who wanted to play center field and wear party hats.

"I've never wanted to do any of those things," Melanie said.

"Why not?"

"Because they're stupid."

That small smile again. "Maybe they seem less stupid when you can't do them."

Melanie blinked. Justine had never seen her at a loss for an argument, but she was now. Matthew took a long, calm drink from his cocoa, watching her from beneath his bushy gray brows.

"Do you like it here?" Melanie asked. For once her voice held no challenge, only an honest curiosity. Justine turned to Matthew, surprised by how eager she was to hear his answer.

Matthew paused for so long that she thought he wouldn't respond. He looked at the door that led to his small living quarters. His fingers considered the ceramic mug. "It's been a good place for us," he said at last.

As if he had been waiting for a cue, Abe opened the door. Justine was surprised to see him standing; he'd seemed too weak to walk. He held on to the jamb, his head shaking with his palsy.

Matthew turned to him. "I thought you were sleeping."

Abe shuffled over. He wore sagging pants, a plaid shirt, brown woolen socks worn through at the big toes, and no shoes. He sat beside Justine, and she slid her chair back a little, away from him. He smelled like nicotine and menthol. He folded one purpled hand over the other and smiled at Melanie, who sat across from him. "Go back inside," Matthew said. The sharpness of his tone startled Justine. "Company makes you tired."

"This is different company. Not cabin

people." Abe sounded petulant, like a boy arguing with a parent. Justine had noticed his childishness the night she'd met him, but now it seemed like more than senility. He was probably mildly retarded. That would explain the odd way he'd touched Angela that night, she thought.

"That doesn't matter," Matthew said.

Melanie said, "Can't he have some cocoa?"

Matthew ran one square hand across his face. His eyes were the same near-black as Melanie's and Maurie's, Justine saw. His hair had once been as dark as theirs, too, as had Abe's. It was no wonder there had been talk about Maurie's parentage. She studied Abe, hoping she wouldn't find other traces of her mother, though surely Maurie was right; this simple man couldn't have been Lilith's lover. To her relief, other than the eyes and Maurie's dusky complexion — which was probably the result of years in the sun, not genetics — she didn't see any resemblance.

Matthew gave in, and went to the bar. Abe smiled at Melanie again. "What's your name?"

Melanie smiled back. "Melanie."

He tilted his head. "Emily?"

"No. Melanie." She pronounced it slowly,

345

but kindly. Justine couldn't remember the last time Melanie had spoken kindly to anyone.

"I knew an Emily once."

"That was my grandma's aunt."

Abe nodded. "I liked her."

"You did?"

"She played with me sometimes. I showed her the kittens." He pursed his lips. "Mimsy was her favorite."

Mimsy was the name of the mouse in the Emily books, Justine realized with a jolt. The cheerful friend to the lost girl. When Melanie heard that name, she leaned forward with an intensity that was strange even for her, and Justine remembered how she'd asked Matthew about the photograph of the Evans sisters; the stealthy way she'd slid the Emily book beneath her covers; how she'd asked if the painting in the living room was of Emily. Justine had assumed, like Mrs. Sorensen, that Melanie's drawings were self-portraits. Now she saw they weren't of Melanie at all. They were of the lost child. Not lost in the fantastical summer forest of Lucy's stories, but alone and frightened in the winter woods, pursued by a man with the savage face of a killer. Justine knew she should be glad the drawings had nothing to do with Melanie. Instead she licked her lips, which were suddenly dry.

"Do you know what happened to Mimsy?" Melanie asked Abe.

Abe drew his mouth down. "I don't like to think about that."

Matthew put one hand on Abe's shoulder as he set his cocoa on the table. "We don't talk about Emily. It upsets him." He said this to Melanie, and his voice held a warning.

"Of course," Justine said, gratefully.

Abe's eyes were cloudy again. "She was too small," he said, almost to himself. "Too small to be out at night."

"That's right," Matthew said to him, soothingly.

"What about Lucy?" Melanie asked. "Can we talk about her?"

Matthew frowned. "Why do you want to talk about her? She has nothing to do with you."

"You said I was like her."

"I said you looked like her. There's a difference."

Melanie looked so hurt that Justine felt bad for her, but she didn't say anything. Like Matthew, she wanted this conversation to be over.

Matthew drummed his fingers on the table. Then he reached for his brother's cocoa, even though Abe had barely touched it. "It's time for your rest." This time Abe didn't resist, and neither did Melanie.

When Abe and Matthew had gone, Melanie slouched in her chair, watching the door. On the wall behind her hung half a dozen faded photographs of men and boys holding large silver fish. None was more recent than the 1970s. The place really was a time capsule, Justine thought, its past separated from its present by the thinnest of veils. Maybe it wasn't so strange that Melanie would be fascinated by the old story. After all, Emily had disappeared from the house they were living in, which, like this lodge, seemed unchanged from the day it happened. She herself had been intrigued by it the summer she'd spent here. "You seem interested in Emily," she said.

Melanie's head snapped around. Justine saw a flash of anger, then her features shuttered. "It's okay," Justine said. "I think about her, too. It's hard not to." She raised her fingers and lowered them flat upon the table. "Does it scare you, what happened to her?"

"No." Melanie's voice was flat.

"Well, it scares me. If you disappeared like that, I don't know what I'd do."

As the dim light cast shadows beneath

Melanie's cheekbones, Justine glimpsed again the adult face that waited beneath the girl's, all hard edges and smooth, icy planes. "Would you stay here for the rest of your life?" Melanie asked. "Like Emily's mother?"

Justine knew the answer: of course she would. She would stay here, waiting, just as Emily's mother had. She would die without knowing, just as she had. And the not knowing would be almost worse than the loss itself. She looked down, gathering herself. Before she could speak, Matthew came back. He collected their empty mugs and began washing them in the small sink behind the bar.

The message was clear. Justine stood and zipped her coat. Melanie rose too, reluctantly. As they turned to leave, the back door opened and Abe was there again, holding a small wooden box. Matthew looked up in frustration, a mug in his hand, but Abe spoke to Melanie. "I have a present for you." His manner was shy, like a boy giving a flower to a crush. Justine took the box before Melanie could reach it, then felt ridiculous. What did she think it was going to be? All that talk about missing daughters had rattled her.

When she opened it she found a little girl's

blue slipper. It was stained with dirt, and it was the match to the one she'd found in the trunk in Emily's room.

Justine heard the crash of ceramic in the sink and turned to see Matthew picking up the pieces of the mug. She could sense his heart pounding and felt a corresponding surge in her own blood. What was this? Why did this old man have a missing girl's dirty bedroom slipper hidden in a box?

Abe gestured at Melanie. "I want her to have it."

"Where did you get it?" Justine asked.

"I found it by the creek. The night she left."

"I thought they found no trace of her." She was sure that's what Dinah the librarian had said, and the newspaper clippings in the basement, too.

Abe stammered under the pressure of everyone's attention. "I — I wanted to keep it. To remember her. She was my friend."

Matthew put his hand on his brother's arm. His manner was calm, but Justine could still sense the rapid pace of his heart. "You found that the next day, when we were looking for her, right?"

Abe's fingers worked at his pant leg.

"It's okay. You didn't know they would want it, did you?"

"They were looking for her. Not her slipper."

"That's right. We were looking for her."

Melanie's eyes were wide as she watched them. Justine felt a tickle along the back of her neck. Abe had said he'd found the slipper the night Emily disappeared, not the next day, when the searchers had gone looking. Had he meant to say that? Or was it just the lapse of an old, simple man — a fumbling of time, or of words? For a moment she pictured the dark-haired figure who'd stalked Emily in Melanie's drawings, but of course that didn't mean anything. Melanie had no idea what had happened to the little girl, and it was in her grim nature to imagine the worst fate possible.

Justine put the slipper back in the box. "You should keep this," she said to Abe as she placed it on the table. "Thank you anyway."

She left then, nudging Melanie before her. As she shut the door she saw the brothers standing in the light from the back room. Matthew placed his hand on Abe's shoulder and turned him toward the back door. He picked up the box as he followed.

LUCY

Matthew was here this evening. We had tea on the porch and watched the lake settle into darkness. Since Lilith's passing, he comes by once or twice a week. We don't talk much, but our silences are comfortable, and I'm always happy to see him walk up the road.

Tonight, as he sat in Lilith's chair and I in mine, I found myself wanting to ask him if he remembered our time together as children. It was a difficult question, because we never talk about the past. Our conversations are always in the present or the immediate future: how are his guests, how is the library, what will the weather bring. I've always thought it a generosity on his part, to avoid raising memories of the worst time of my life. I still think that. But now that I'm writing this and remembering so many things I thought I'd forgotten, something else occurs to me. He and Abe are the only other people still living who were there, and they were witnesses to much of it. I wonder how much he remembers.

So I said it, straight out, the way Lilith would have: "Do you remember how we used to play in the forest?"

The question surprised him, as I knew it would. He looked at me, and then away, and in the quick turn of his head I saw the boy he'd been, smooth skinned and black haired and clear-eyed. "I do," he said. His voice was melancholy, but there was happiness in it, too, as if this memory, at least, was a treasured one. Then my mind leaped ahead to the end of that summer, to our last day together, and the old shame bore down on me. I couldn't speak anymore, and he, respectful as always, let it be.

When he left I watched him walk to the lodge. In the last, blue light his figure was straight and tall. He is nearly seventy-seven, but he could have been sixty, or forty. He will live a long time after I'm gone, and he'll outlive Abe as well. He'll be lonely here by himself, but I don't think he'll leave.

If you read this, I imagine you'll think it strange that so many of us stayed. Strange that Maurie was the only one to go. Of course, we always knew she would. As a girl she found her adventures in the forest, but

353

as she grew she wanted adventures of a different sort. She hung around the lodge, teasing and flirting and God knows what else with the summer boys. Every year she had a new one on a string; some lawyer's son or prep school baseball star who was "going places." They played along, because she was alluring in a wild sort of way, but in the end they drove away with their parents, casting her off like an outgrown pair of shoes, and she cried behind her bedroom door. She had her pick of the local boys, too, but she treated them the way the summer boys treated her: as nothing but easy fun. Like Lilith, she got a reputation, but she didn't care. Neither did Lilith, though it drove me to exasperation. She's ruining herself, I told Lilith, but Lilith wouldn't hear it. Let her play, she said. She's not long for this place anyway.

Still, we weren't prepared for the suddenness of her departure. That was my fault. I shouldn't have kept those letters, the ones that boy Justin sent. They spanned about six months before he gave up and, I suppose, began to forget her, but I couldn't bring myself to throw them away. Maybe it was because I remembered the way they played in the early days, off in the woods, as Matthew and I had. I used to imagine them finding the Hundred Tree, with the cushions rotting where we left them. As if those things were still there, after all these years. Whatever the reason, I kept his letters in a shoe box in the back of our closet. And one night Maurie found them.

We were in the parlor. Mother and Lilith were watching the television, and I was reading. Maurie had been upstairs for some time. She'd taken to wearing some of Mother's and Lilith's old things — brooches, scarves, and wraps that she made lively in that way she had — so I suppose that's what she was looking for. She came running down the stairs in her jeans and those cowboy boots she wore everywhere then. The tears on her face ran black with the mascara she slathered on. She went to Lilith, opened the shoe box, and threw the letters in her lap. Her fury had that elemental quality Lilith's used to have, a crackling, combustive charge that lit her up from the inside. I was glad of the enormous wings of my chair, like a protective shell.

"He wrote me! And I never knew! I thought he didn't care. But you took them! You opened them, and you read them, and you never gave them to me!"

Lilith picked up an envelope and read Maurie's name in that boyish hand. "I've never seen these."

I crossed my legs beneath my skirt. My panty hose scraped together. It was a hot night, and they were wet behind my knees. I said, "She didn't take them. I did."

Maurie whirled on me. "Liar. You don't do anything she doesn't tell you to do."

Well, that hurt me. I wanted her to know she was wrong. I wanted it very badly. So I gripped the arms of the chair and said, "His mother asked me to do it. She didn't want him with you. They were a nice family."

I shouldn't have said that, I know, even though it was true. Maurie's face wrenched. I'd never thought she looked like Father, except for the coloring, but her anger did something to her eyes, giving them that intense, deep-seeing quality his had. "You bitch," she said.

Lilith stood up. The letters fell to the floor. "Don't talk to Lucy like that."

"It was better this way," I said, and my voice shook only a little. "Those things never last." She was right; I'd read the letters. I'd read them many times. I knew how much he loved her. But they were only fifteen.

"How would you know?" Maurie's voice was acid. "Nobody's ever loved you."

"I said leave her alone," Lilith snapped.

Maurie spun back to her mother. "Do you understand what she did to me? Do you? Do you? All I've ever wanted is to get out of here! He was the only one who ever loved me, who ever wanted me. And she wrecked it!"

A quivering silence followed. I was terrified Lilith would look at me, and of what I might see in her eyes if she did, but she didn't. With a forced calm, she said, "Stop it. He was just some boy you played with for a month every summer. He wasn't some knight in shining armor."

Maurie jabbed a finger at her. "You don't know what it's like for me, stuck out here with my mother, a dried-up virgin, and an old woman who can't stop talking about a girl who died twenty-five years ago." She waved her arm at Mother, who shrank as though from a blow. "Do you even know what people say about you? About me?"

"I don't care what they say. And if you don't like it here you can leave. You don't need some boy to take you."

"Really, Mother?" Maurie's voice raged with bitter contempt. "Like you did? After my daddy died you just sat here on your ass, and you're going to keep sitting here until you die. So will Lucy, because she doesn't have the guts to leave. I know what this is about. You both lost your chance. So you had to ruin mine."

It took everything I had not to move. Lilith stepped close to Maurie until her face was inches from her daughter's. They were the same height, with the same dark hair, the same strong bones from which Lilith's skin had begun to slip. When Lilith spoke, her voice was quiet and hard. "I didn't lose my chance when your father died. I lost it when you were born."

Maurie went white. In her chair by the television Mother gave a low sob. I closed my eyes. To this day, I don't know why Lilith said such a cruel thing. Maybe it was to give Maurie the shove she needed to get out. Maybe she even believed it. If that were true, it would be a great relief to me. But in all the years that followed, I never found the courage to ask.

"Fuck you," Maurie said. Her voice was quiet now. "Fuck all of you. You're going to die in this dump. But I'm getting out."

And she did. The next morning, before we woke, she drove the car to town and took the first bus that pulled into the station. We got the postcard two months later, from Minneapolis. She'd gone looking for him. She must not have found him, or it hadn't turned out well, but she would never let us know that. Instead she wrote about her sophisticated life, sharing an apartment with two other girls, working in a restaurant, going out at night. Honestly, it all sounded pretty low to me, but she had a job and a place to live, and that gave me great comfort. Lilith hadn't seemed worried that her daughter was a runaway at seventeen, but the thought had made me sick with fear.

Six months later she was in Chicago, and it was the same story, but this time there was a boyfriend she was sure she'd marry. A year after that she turned up in Detroit with no mention of the boyfriend. On it went: Kansas City, Cleveland, and Pittsburgh, and then towns so small we'd never heard of them. Sometimes there were boyfriends, sometimes not, but it never stopped, even after you were born. The way she dragged you back and forth across the country, it was clear she never caught up to whatever she was chasing.

When she came back that summer, though, something was different. On the surface she seemed relaxed, glad to be home, but she jumped when the phone rang, and I knew she wasn't chasing anymore. She was running. That was what made me think she might be back for good. Because there's no better hiding place than here. And, I told myself, she had you to think about. She'd rarely mentioned you in her postcards, and apparently she never told you about us, but you were old enough to want to belong somewhere, and where else could you have that? We were your only family, even though we were strangers. I watched you read in the hammock and walk barefoot down the lane to the lodge, and I could feel you unwind as the summer went on. Surely, I thought, Maurie would see that staying here was the best thing for you.

I will admit, too, that I wanted her to stay. Despite all the trouble she'd been, despite all the worry she caused me and the things she said the night before she left, I loved having her home. She acted like nothing had ever gone wrong between the three of us, and I believe she was glad to see us. She lay on the beach in her bikini, her body too thin but her skin rosy in the sun, or sat with her legs over the arm of the porch swing, dangling her sandals from her toes, and laughed with her mouth wide open. Best of all, she did something to Lilith, something that made Lilith's eyes glow as they used to do, before Emily and Father and the rest. I would have done almost anything to keep them that way.

Then one night in late August, the four of us went to dinner at the lodge. We didn't often eat there, especially after Matthew added those cabins, but most of his guests were gone now, so when Maurie suggested it we agreed. It was as empty as we'd hoped, with just two other families who were well along in their meals and three Indian men at the bar. After Matthew's summer girl took our order, he brought the food himself. By then the other diners had left, so he pulled up a chair and we had a nice, easy time for a while, listening to Maurie's stories about the places she'd been. She could tell a story, even when she was the butt of the joke, so she made her life sound like a wild, funny ride instead of the miserable, vagabond existence it was. "Remember, Jus?" she'd say. "Remember when we went to Six Flags, and rode the roller coaster?" You were so proud of her, your beautiful mother, reshaping your life into a grand adventure there at the table.

After a while, Maurie asked why Abe didn't join us. Matthew told her he was closing down the kitchen, but she shook her head. "Why don't you ever let him out of there?"

"He works in the back," Matthew said, in a tone that told me he didn't want to discuss it. Maurie said that was just an excuse.

"Do you think he's some sort of pervert?"

She was smiling, but Matthew's arm tensed next to mine. I didn't like this conversation either. Matthew's father had kept Abe in the back for one reason, but I knew Matthew did it for another.

"I'm going to get him," Maurie announced, and walked to the back door.

Matthew looked at you, where you sat fiddling with the last of your French fries. "You don't have to sit here with us old folks. Why don't you get a book from over there and go read on the porch?"

It was clear you wanted to stay, but it hadn't been a question, so off you went.

A minute later Maurie came out with Abe. He was still a handsome man then. His shoulders were broad and he hadn't gotten fat the way some big men do. His hair had almost no gray in it, and his face was as unlined as a man twenty years younger.

Maurie went to the bar, where she ordered beers from the girl. The three Indians watched her while she waited and she smiled at them. When she brought the mugs, two in one hand and three in the other like the practiced waitress she was, she set them on the table. "Now that it's just us grown-ups, we can have a party." She didn't ask where you'd gone.

I've never been much for beer, so I sipped

mine. Abe drank his as if it were a Coke, and Maurie wasn't far behind. The conversation wasn't as much fun as it had been. Matthew stopped talking altogether, and Lilith sat stiffly, watching Maurie as she draped herself over Abe's arm and talked about some man she'd known in Abilene who ran a dog racing park. Abe blinked his slow eyes, always at Lilith. I was glad Matthew had sent you to the porch.

When Maurie finished her beer, she picked up her glass and Abe's and went to the bar for a refill. This time she stood a little closer to the Indians and said something to them with a toss of her head. They were rough-looking, with long hair past their collars and pants dirty from outside work. They'd come over from Olema, just for the beer; they weren't overnight guests. I'd noticed more Indians hanging around the lodge since Matthew's father retired. I didn't know why — Lord knows they had plenty of bars in Olema — but I knew Matthew had longed to be part of his mother's tribe as a boy, so I'd been happy for him.

Now one of them put his hand on Maurie's hip below the belt loops of her tight jeans. She shook it off playfully, then took the beers and came back to us. The Indian said something to his friend, and they looked over their shoulders at her. When she sat she wound her arm through Abe's and ignored them in a way that wasn't ignoring, if you know what I mean.

I said it was getting late. Lilith agreed, and Matthew told Abe he should finish with the kitchen.

"Let him finish his beer," Maurie said. "You never let him have any fun." She patted Abe's hand. "Come on, let's toast to old times."

In Lilith's eyes I read an agreement: we'd stay long enough for Abe to finish his beer, then we'd leave.

"Speaking of old times, how come you never left this place?" Maurie asked Matthew. "Didn't you want to be an astronaut or something?"

I didn't remember telling her that. Matthew didn't look bothered, though. In fact, he smiled at me. "Life has a way of turning out differently. I'm happy enough."

I believed him. I still do. After all, he could have left. When his father retired, he told him he could sell the place if he wanted, but Matthew expanded it, taking out a loan to build those cabins. Now he has a nice business going, with many of the same families coming up year after year. I know he stayed because of Abe. But I do think he likes it here. Sometimes the dreams of children are just that.

Maurie shook her head. "I don't know how any of you stand it." I looked toward the porch, where you were reading. She caught my glance. "She only likes it because she's a kid."

"Did you like it when you were a kid?" I asked.

That stopped her. She turned her glass around on the table. "I did," she said. "For a while."

Then she said she was visiting the restroom. On the way she passed the Indians, and when the one who'd touched her winked at her, she poked him with a finger, laughing. He grabbed her around the waist. "Come on, stay here," I heard him say. She looked at us, then shook her head. She leaned in and said something with a smile as her hand tried to dislodge his arm. He pulled her tighter against his leg.

Abe stood up. His chair crashed to the floor behind him. Matthew told him to sit down, but Abe walked to the group at the bar. His shoulders were massive in his white tee shirt and cook's apron, and he outweighed the man who was holding Maurie by thirty pounds. He lifted him off the stool by his upper arms and set him on the floor.

"It's time to go."

The Indian was drunk enough to be stupid. "Why don't you let the lady pick her own man? It's obvious she don't want no retard."

Abe shoved him so hard he staggered into the closest table, tipping it over in a violence of wood and cutlery, and everyone was on their feet. The Indian's friends pulled him toward the door. Abe followed, his large hands in fists, but Matthew blocked his way. In the commotion Maurie scurried to the center of the room. I checked the door to the porch and saw you standing there, the book forgotten in your hand.

"Get him out of here," Matthew said to the men, and they hustled their friend out while Matthew talked to Abe, his voice low and soothing. "It's okay. The guy was drunk. You're good. You're a good man. You're a good man, Abe." His hands were on Abe's upper arms, rubbing up and down. Abe's shoulders slumped. Matthew took his face between his hands. "There you are."

"What the hell was that?" Maurie's hands were on her hips and her eyes were fierce. "Jesus Christ, Abe. I'm thirty-eight years old and you still won't let me talk to a guy? Get over yourself. You're not my god-damned father."

Abe swung his head to her. His mouth opened. Slowly, his eyes slid to Lilith. Her face was as blank as a doll's. For a long moment nobody moved. Then Maurie snapped her chin up, grabbed her purse from the table, and walked out.

The next day she left. She'd been here too long, she said. She needed to get back to her life. We asked her to leave you with us; we tried to persuade her it would be best for you to have a stable home, but she said you were better off with your mother. And so you went. We heard nothing for almost two years, and then the postcards started again just as before. She never came back. Not when I wrote her that Mother had died, or that Lilith was sick. Not even when Lilith was buried next to Mother and Father, the small circle of mourners drawn tight around her grave.

JUSTINE

That afternoon Maurie volunteered to pick Angela up from school, and when they came back they had a bunch of Lloyd's Pharmacy bags filled with Christmas decorations. The girls unpacked plastic Santa Clauses, tinsel, ribbons, candles, and lights while Maurie fished out a bottle of Jack Daniel's and a carton of eggnog and made herself a drink. Then she handed Justine an invitation. "This was in the P.O. box."

Justine wondered why Maurie had checked Lucy's mail, then decided it was exactly the sort of thing Maurie would do. The invitation was to a holiday party at Arthur Williams's house on Christmas Eve. "We don't have to go," she said.

"Sure we do. This is their big annual thing."

Justine glanced at her mother. There would probably be a lot of people there she knew. People who'd known her when she was a girl. "Are you sure you want to?"

"Why not," Maurie said, as if it were a perfectly normal thing to want to do. Which it was, unless you were Maurie. Although Maurie did love a party.

Maurie pulled a receipt from one of the bags. "Here you are, Mrs. Vanderbilt."

Justine had to look at the total twice to make sure she read it right: $121.86. That was two weeks' worth of groceries. She'd been planning to get decorations — she just hadn't gotten around to it yet — but she'd have gotten them at the Walmart for less than half what these cost. "Mom, this is too much."

Maurie raised an eyebrow. "I wouldn't have done it if I'd thought you were going to."

Melanie and Angela stopped unloading the decorations. They looked from their mother to their grandmother. Justine said, "Never mind," and put the receipt in Lucy's junk drawer next to her list of things to do.

Maurie went to the living room with Angela, their arms full of baubles. After a moment Melanie followed. She hadn't spoken much to Maurie since the ice skating incident, in that way she had of never letting a good grudge go. Maurie had pretended not to notice, in that way she had of never admitting she'd done anything wrong. Justine poured herself a glass of eggnog and, after a moment's deliberation, added a splash of Jack Daniel's.

When she was a girl, they didn't have Christmas ornaments because everything they owned needed to fit in the back of their car. But every year, sometimes before Thanksgiving and sometimes as late as Christmas Eve, Maurie would have a fit of seasonal enthusiasm and buy light strings and holiday candles. Then she'd play Christmas music and drink eggnog with Jack Daniel's while she and Justine strung the lights along the walls. Justine had loved how the lights' determined, colorful cheer transformed whatever drab apartment they were staying in. It was the only time she wished the girls at school could see where she lived.

Now her mother turned on the old radio in the living room. Eartha Kitt was singing "Santa Baby." Melanie and Angela debated where to put the nativity scene while Maurie ripped open packages of lights. Justine watched from the doorway.

"Don't just stand there," Maurie said. "Go get the hammer and some nails from the basement."

When Justine got back, Maurie was standing on a chair in the corner, a string of lights over one shoulder. She pounded the nail to the beat of the music, then turned around on the seat, swaying her hips and snapping her fingers. Angela laughed and Melanie smiled, her head nodding in time. Justine picked up a piece of tinsel from the pile on the floor and, using the other chair, hung it over the door to the entryway.

When it was done, they stood in the middle of the room and looked around at the tinsel glinting in the lights and the Santa Clauses smiling their elfin smiles from every surface. They'd moved Maurie's paper bags to the dining room, so the room didn't look like a recycling project anymore. "It looks pretty good, doesn't it?" Maurie said. And it did. The house, with its heavy, well-crafted furniture and high ceilings, wore the gaudy trappings with a dignity none of Justine's childhood apartments could have hoped for.

Maurie brought cups of unspiked eggnog for the girls and a plate of Keebler Christmas cookies that she put on the coffee table next to the manger scene. Then they all sat and listened to the pings and coughs from the radiator and the music from the radio. The girls looked happy, and proud of what they'd done. Maurie sat cross-legged in her chair, beaming with childlike delight, but in her papery skin and the shadows around her eyes Justine saw the old woman she soon would be, and she felt a rush of tenderness for her. She was glad she hadn't made more of a scene about the money.

"My mother was the queen of Christmas," Maurie said. "Decorations, cookies, tree, the whole shebang. She'd hang lights all over the porch. Even though nobody could see them but us and the Millers. Not everything needs an audience, she'd say. Then after Christmas dinner we'd invite the Millers over. Although Matthew was the only one who ever came."

"Why didn't Abe?" Melanie asked.

"Oh, Matthew always had an excuse for him. He wasn't feeling well. He needed to clean the kitchen. It was ridiculous. After living out here with us all those years, you'd think —" She paused, looking past Justine at the window. Then she smiled, shaking it off. "Anyway, Matthew would come over after dinner and I'd get to stay up late. It was fun."

Justine tried to picture it: Lucy, Lilith, their sad mother, a young Maurie, and the taciturn Matthew Miller. Having fun.

"We should invite them over," Melanie said. "On Christmas."

"Of course we will," Maurie said.

"What?" Justine said.

"Why not? We'll have a party. It'll be like old times."

Melanie turned a hopeful face to Justine. Justine thought of Matthew mixing powdered cocoa in his chilly, half-lit lodge. Had he spent his Christmas evenings here even after Maurie left? He probably had. He'd probably spent fifty Christmases in this room, including Lucy's last Christmas a year ago. She turned her glass in her hand. What would it be like, to have a friend for half a century?

Melanie's skin glowed in the Christmas lights. Soon they would leave the Millers and the ghosts of the Evans girls behind for a sunny apartment in a warm town, and the Millers would be here alone. "You're right," Justine said. "We should invite them."

LUCY

Matthew's thirteenth birthday was the Friday before Labor Day. It was the last real day of summer. On Saturday, the lake families would pack their summer clothes and prepare their houses for winter. The end-of-summer party, with Lilith's cabaret, would be that night, and on Sunday we would drive back to the sturdy houses that waited for us on Williamsburg's orderly streets. But on Friday we were still summer's children, and the day was open wide.

I'd asked Matthew if his family would have a birthday celebration for him. He said they would, but not until after we'd gone. They had too much to do before we left, what with cooking and serving the food for the party. I thought it was a shame that he'd have to wait to celebrate such an important birthday, but he said it would be better to do it when his family had the lake to themselves again. That stung me a little, but I tried not to let on.

Besides, I'd made my own plans for his birthday. I'd been thinking about it for a while, and when the day came, I was ready. After lunch, I waited until Lilith left and Mother took Emily to the beach, and then I changed out of my playsuit and into my best summer dress. I took off my worn brown Mary Janes and put on the new white sandals that had sat in the closet since we'd unpacked back in June. I usually wore my long hair in a braid, to keep it out of the way, but today I left it down. I wasn't one for looking in the mirror, but I did glance once, before I left our bedroom. With my curls falling about my face I looked different. Younger and older at the same time. I looked away, and felt like myself again.

When I was ready, I went down to the fallen log. I'd taken longer than usual, so Matthew was shuffling his feet in the grass, waiting. When he saw me, his eyes widened. "What's with the fancy duds?"

"I'm going to a birthday party," I said. He blushed, then laughed and looked at the ground. I felt my face reddening, too, and in our sudden awkwardness I felt a small, strange unease. I shook my head, my loose hair brushing against my arms. Don't be silly, I told myself. "Follow me," I said, turning into the woods, making sure to walk the same way in my sandals as I always had in my Mary Janes.

It was one of those hot, buzzy, late-summer days, and as I walked a light sweat broke out on my face and arms. Matthew followed close, nearly stepping on my feet, asking every ten paces where we were going. You'll see, I told him, enjoying his curiosity and good-natured pique. The odd moment at the fallen log was forgotten now that we were walking the paths we'd walked all summer, among trees we knew as well as we knew our own hands. It wasn't until the end that we walked on a trail we'd traveled only once before.

When we got to the clearing, I stopped, struck as always by the cathedral the Hundred Tree made, its branches like flying buttresses and the ground beneath it stippled with light that looked as though it had filtered through stained glass. A chorus of cicadas dipped and swelled, registering our presence, then forgiving it. I crossed my arms, waiting for him to see what I'd done. When he did, he brushed his hair out of his eyes and smiled his crooked-toothed smile. "You're letting me in the tree?"

I shrugged, like it was no big deal. "Lilith doesn't want to come here anymore." That morning, I'd taken all of Lilith's and my things out of the hollowed tree except the pillows and the flat log we'd used as a table. Then I'd hung a dozen sheets of Emily's colored art paper, with stenciled holes cut in them like Chinese lanterns, from the inside of the trunk. On the log I'd put a white pillowcase, two of Mother's flowered tea plates, and a bowl that I'd filled with the best skipping rocks I could find. I'd brought two bottles of root beer, and in a small bag were some of the homemade cookies Matthew's grandmother sold at the lodge. It looked neat, organized, ready. My fingers picked at the dry patches on my elbows as I watched him.

"Wow," he said. He'd picked up a stick along the way, and he fidgeted with it, passing it from one hand to the other. He looked caught off balance, as though the ground under his feet had tilted unexpectedly, and I felt sick. I'd made a horrible mistake. The dressing up, the decorating, the root beers, the cookies — it was all wrong. I'd wanted to give him a birthday party. I'd wanted to show him I was his friend. But now I saw it through his eyes, and I saw that it was something a girl would do, when I was sure the thing he liked best about me was that I wasn't like a girl. I should have just tossed him his present during a break in our games, saying, oh, by the way, happy birthday. Like a boy would. I looked at my feet, knobby with calluses in their pretty shoes ordered from Sears at the first hint of spring, and wished I could run away.

He walked into the tree and looked up at the colored papers. "This is neat," he said. He set down the stick. "Aren't you coming in?" He sat down beside the table, so I did, too, fixing my skirt so it covered my legs, longing for the easy modesty of my playsuit. I hoped he couldn't see how red my face was, but when I looked at him, he was looking at the plates and the root beers. "I've never had a real birthday party before," he said. "You know, with friends and everything." His expression was wistful.

I stopped fiddling with my skirt. I realized that despite what he'd said before about how his birthday would be better once we'd gone, he envied us town children, blowing out candles with our friends, while he marked his birthdays with his broken family, alone at their empty resort. I thought of my own birthday parties, with three or four girls from my class sitting at our dining room table in our best dresses while Mother, in her starched apron, served cake and lemonade. I thought about how lonely I'd felt at every one of them.

I opened the root beers and filled our glasses with a small flourish, like a waiter. Then I pulled the cookies from the back. "They're your grandmother's," I said.

He smiled that lopsided smile. "You know, her cookies aren't very good. I don't think Chippewa do much baking." I told him they were better than any I could bake, so we'd have to make do. I took a big, decisive bite to show him I meant business, and that made him laugh, and take a bite for himself.

After that, I felt better. It was strange being inside the Tree with someone other than Lilith, but the air was the same sheltering cool it had always been, and Matthew and I talked in the easy way we had all summer long, our backs against the pillows, drinking our warm root beers, my dress and sandals forgotten in the dim light. After a while I pulled his present out of the bag I'd put the cookies in. "It's not much," I said, and it wasn't. After buying the cookies and root beers, I hadn't had any money left, but it wouldn't have mattered. The lodge was the only place to shop, and the only gifts for sale were the dusty souvenirs on the shelf behind the pool table — the dream catchers and birch-bark baskets that his grandmother made.

He unwrapped the wax paper bundle. Inside was a small cloth bag with a drawstring. I'd made it using pieces I'd cut from my denim skirt, and although I wasn't much of a seamstress, it hadn't turned out too badly. As he held it in his hands, I rushed to explain: you tie it to your belt, and when you find something you want to keep, you put it inside. It was the only thing I could think of that he needed.

He fingered the drawstring. The Chippewa carried pouches like this, he told me, when they hunted. They made them from buffalo hide, and they kept knives in them, and arrowheads and fishing hooks. He'd seen pictures. I hadn't known that, but it made me glad. He tied the bag to his belt and smiled at me. For a moment something passed between us that made us both look away, but then he said, "Let's go see what we can find to put in it," and we walked out of the Tree and into the forest.

Because we'd avoided the Hundred Tree, we'd never explored the area around it. But even Lilith and I hadn't gone where Matthew and I went that day, far to the north and west, farther from the lake than I'd ever been. There were no paths here, just small tracks made by deer and raccoons. The air seemed hushed and alight with discovery, and I found myself walking with stealth, my nerves awake to the small sounds in the brush and the flashing of birds in the leaves. Sticks poked my feet between the straps of my sandals, and my dress and hair snagged on branches, but I didn't think about that, or about what I'd say to Mother when she saw I'd ruined my best summer outfit. I was an ancient explorer, alone in the wilderness with my comrade, breaking humanity's first trail through a brand-new land. I could tell by the lithe, alert way he moved that Matthew felt these things, too.

Soon, just as those ancient explorers had, we began to talk about staking our claim to the territory we traveled. We would build a tree house out here, using salvage from Matthew's family's backyard. We'd fortify it with fences we'd build from fallen branches, so they'd seem like part of the forest. We wondered if we could live in it year-round, and decided that of course we could. We talked about the equipment we'd need: bows and arrows, knives, rope for snares, and hollowed-out rocks for catching rainwater. We'd skin the bears we'd hunt, and use the pelts to keep us warm. If the Chippewa could do it for the thousands of years they'd roamed this country, so could we. We kept our voices low, in deference to the new terrain we traveled. Once in a while Matthew bent to pick up a rock or leaf, showing it to me before sticking it in the pouch, and whenever he did, I felt the small, private happiness that comes from giving just the right gift.

After we had walked long enough to imagine we had crossed into Canada, we emerged from a thicket to find ourselves on the edge of a road. It was just a narrow, empty strip of blacktop, and the forest continued beyond, but I recognized it: it was the road to Williamsburg. On Sunday I would travel it in the backseat of Father's Plymouth, between Lilith and Emily, my sunburned legs sticking to the vinyl as we covered in minutes what Matthew and I had believed to be almost a nation.

Heat waves slithered in the air where the road crested a small hill to the west. Almost below the range of sound, I could hear a pulsing hum that might be faraway cars, or electricity coursing along the wires that ran on posts beside it. As Matthew and I stood there, our faces scratched by branches and our clothes pricked with thistles, I felt what the Indians must have felt when they first stumbled upon a railroad laid across the wild prairie.

Matthew whacked the scrabbly roadside

grass with his stick once, hard. Then he threw the stick across the road, where it vanished in the wall of green leaves on the other side. A flurry of gnats spun angrily in the air where it passed. "Let's go," he said.

We turned back, and in a few steps the road was hidden. But the forest was different now. The mystery that had shrouded it all summer had dissolved like fog in the sun. The trees were just trees; the underbrush just a clutter of leaves and sticks; the only animals the squirrels and chipmunks we'd always known. We didn't talk as we walked back to the Hundred Tree, and then on toward the lake. Though I couldn't hear the hum of the world anymore, I knew it was there, waiting.

At last we reached the paths the other children had worn as wide and bare as sidewalks, and we walked side by side. I saw that Matthew had grown that summer; my chin barely reached his shoulder now. For some reason this made me even sadder.

"It was a great birthday," he said. "Thanks."

"You're welcome," I said, my voice woolen.

Gently, as if by accident, his fingers brushed against mine. Then he took my hand and held it. His hand was heavy and warm, and rough from the dishes he washed, the fish he cleaned, the trees he climbed. Above my dirt-streaked calves my ruined skirt swung against my knees, and I could feel every part of my body at once. Matthew didn't look at me, nor I at him, but he didn't let go of my hand and I didn't pull it away.

We were still holding hands when we came upon Lilith and Abe. They were in a small clearing, a chapel of green and golden light about two hundred yards from the houses. We didn't hear them before we saw them, and when we saw them we stopped walking.

Lilith lay on her back in the dead brown leaves, her legs bent at the knees, her skirt crumpled at her hips. Abe was on top of her. His pants were around his ankles and his naked buttocks rocked in and out between her legs. Her white fingers clutched at his shirt, pulling him closer, and her head was back, her neck arched, her teeth bared, her eyes staring sightlessly up at the trees. The sounds they made — fleshy and wet, sucking and rutting and moaning and gasping — drowned out even the blood pounding in my ears.

I don't know how long we stood there, watching, our hands tight together, listening, as the whole forest, known and unknown, telescoped upon that one glade, until Abe gave a long, shuddering thrust and Lilith cried out, and when that happened I screamed loud and high, and Lilith heard me and shoved Abe off of her. Her dress was unbuttoned and her bra had slipped down, and I saw her pale new breasts, the pink nipples small and hard, and it made my head swim to see them naked like that, those tender things I'd helped her hide away behind white cotton cups with delicate metal hooks only a few months before, in her bedroom.

She began buttoning her dress. Abe scrambled to his feet, his hands covering the dark and swollen thing that hung between his legs. Then he pulled up his trousers and stood with his shoulders hunched. Matthew let go of my hand, which felt suddenly light, the air cool on my empty palm. He called his brother in a voice I didn't recognize. Then he walked away, and Abe followed. I don't know if Matthew looked at me, or what might have been in his face if he did, because I didn't look at him. I looked at Lilith.

She got to her feet more slowly. She was wearing her white dress with the blue sash, and it clung to her sweaty skin from her collarbones to her calves. Her long black hair was tangled and littered with leaves. Her lips were red and wet and her cheeks were flushed. She stood before me, one hand at her throat, in a shaft of light that filtered through the leaves, and for a moment she looked like a wild nymph, exposed to the world, beautiful and damaged. Then I saw her white panties, crumpled in the leaves at her feet.

I turned and ran, pushing at branches and tripping on roots, crashing through the forest that slammed shut behind me with savage green teeth, not stopping until I burst onto the grassy verge where our clothesline stood and our dresses, their bows limp and wet, hung motionless in the hot, still air.

JUSTINE

The school gym was too small. It was filled with metal chairs, but still people stood in the back and along the sides, clustering around a holiday bake sale by the door. Justine and Maurie found a place to stand along the left side of the chairs. Maurie looked stiff, the skin around her mouth tense. The gym was an annex to the main school building, and the dedication above the door said it was built in 1945. Justine tried to imagine her mother as a girl here, in gym class or maybe a school play, but she couldn't.

A woman Maurie's age was staring at them from her seat three rows away. She said something to the man next to her, and he turned, too.

"Do you know them?" Justine asked.

"No." Maurie looked the woman square in the eye until she turned back around.

Justine didn't know anyone, of course, but

she recognized some of the mothers who waited for their children on the sidewalk after school. She also saw Elizabeth Sorensen in the front row with a Nordic-looking man and an older blond couple. Her profile was elegant beneath a sleek French twist. Justine scanned the program and saw Claire and Maxwell Sorensen. She wondered what grade Claire was in.

The chorus, which had been running through warm-ups despite the din, stopped singing. The chorus teacher moved the children closer together and relocated a boy from one row to another. She directed the older children to sit, then waited with the stiff back of a circus ringmaster for the audience to stop talking and the herd of squatting fathers with video cameras to settle into their places in the center aisle. When it was quiet, she raised her baton and launched the younger singers into an energetic rendition of "Jingle Bells."

Justine focused her instant camera on Angela in the second row. Angela's ash-blond curls floated around her perfect, china-doll face as she sang. The girl beside her, also adorable, with a pixie haircut and a red dress, smiled at her and bumped her arm between the first and second verse. Delighted, Justine snapped a picture, including the pixie girl. Someday, she knew, Angela would look at it and try very hard to remember that girl's name. She tried not to think about that.

When the littler kids were done the chorus teacher waved the older children to their feet. Justine studied the girls. Four, standing together, reeked of status in satin headbands and pressed collars. Even their hair looked like it had been done in a salon. Justine, who remembered fifth grade very well, didn't like them.

Melanie stood at the end of the top row. She'd placed herself there on purpose, Justine knew, because then she'd have only one person beside her. Only one person who would avoid touching her for fear of contamination. That person was a chubby girl with glasses who kept a careful six inches between them. Melanie pushed her hair behind her ear, and when it immediately fell forward, did it again. In that gesture Justine saw Francis, sweeping his hair out of his face as he played his guitar. The image pricked her heart with a quick stealth before she could defend it. Francis would have loved that Melanie was in the chorus, she thought, then corrected herself: obviously Francis hadn't given a damn what Melanie did.

The chorus wasn't very good, of course, but they sang "In the Bleak Midwinter" with simple, quiet piety, and "Deck the Halls" with a verve that more than compensated for the painful intonation. And the chorus teacher was oddly compelling. When she raised her baton to begin a song, Justine could feel the children's hearts pause, like sledders at the top of a hill. They watched her with rapture, this plain woman with her brown hair falling out of its bun and her wide bottom straining at her black skirt. Even the queen bees forgot themselves, their mouths chewing the music like cows working a cud.

But it was Melanie whom Justine watched. Melanie, who sang with something shining in her eyes and something aching in the line of her throat, something rich and unaware that made Justine remember the Melanie who'd sung on the coffee table in her nightgown, long ago. Then, when the last notes of "Silent Night" washed over the crowd, and the teacher, having frozen with her hands raised and her body alive to the fading echoes in the air, dropped her baton at last, a remarkable thing happened. She looked at Melanie — only Melanie — and nodded at her. Melanie's mouth stretched into a wide, delighted grin that lasted through the applause, which lasted a long time. Justine willed Melanie to see her; to smile that smile at her; but she didn't. Later she would realize she hadn't taken her picture.

The concert was over. The audience rose in a crashing of metal chairs, collecting coats and toddlers, but Justine stood still. In the next town there would be a chorus, and Melanie would join it. Justine would see to it. She imagined a sun-drenched, white stucco apartment building with patios and bougainvillea and a swimming pool. She imagined her daughters walking through warm air to the nearby school, where Melanie sang in the chorus and no one washed their hands after they touched her. She wished they were there already.

"Let's get out of here so I can have a cigarette," Maurie said.

It took them a while to find the girls in the swarm of people, but then Angela, bouncing with excitement, wriggled between a pair of elderly aunts. "You were fantastic, sweetie," Justine said, running her fingers through her hair.

"What did you think, Grandma?" Angela asked, her face shining.

"I thought you were the prettiest girl on the stage," Maurie said, which was such the perfect thing to say that Justine smiled at her in gratitude.

They found Melanie beside the risers. Her face had settled back into its usual sour expression, but her hands betrayed her, the fingers thin and needy as they worked at one another. Justine touched her shoulder. It was the first time she had touched her with intention since she'd flung her onto the sofa. Through a sparkle of tears she saw that Melanie's head now came up to her chin. "That was beautiful," she said. Melanie shrugged and looked down.

The chorus teacher was talking to another family nearby, but when she saw Melanie and Justine she excused herself and came over. Up close, she was far from plain. Her face was strong, with full lips and small, bright eyes, and the bones of her hips and shoulders were flung out with an exuberance her sober pencil skirt and high-buttoned blouse couldn't quite contain. "I'm Rose Scozzafava." Her voice had a faint accent. "You have a very talented daughter."

"Thank you," Justine said. She wasn't sure this was the right thing to say. Mrs. Scozzafava leaned close.

"I have a chorus for high school students. Not a school program, a private one. Even though she's in fifth grade, I would take her." Her voice was clipped, almost military with its foreign consonants. Justine wondered how she'd wound up in Williamsburg.

"We'll think about it." She wasn't going to tell the chorus teacher they were leaving, but even if she'd considered it, the look on Melanie's face would have stopped her. Then a blond woman pushed forward to press Mrs. Scozzafava's hand, and Justine and her family slipped away through the emptying room.

In front of the door Patrick was waiting for them.

Justine stopped. The world funneled in, then spun out again. A mother in a tan parka walked past, towing a girl in pigtails. An elderly man and woman shuffled after them. Patrick came closer. He was wearing a faded blue jacket Justine didn't recognize and a baseball cap over his ginger hair. He looked thinner. Justine put her hand over her mouth. She wasn't sure what it was doing.

Maurie said, sharply, "Who's this?"

Justine couldn't answer. When she was sure her face was under control she turned to her daughters. Their faces were shocked. Then Angela's dissolved into confusion and Melanie's hardened into fury and revulsion.

"I didn't know he was coming," Justine said to her.

When she turned around again Patrick was right in front of her, and she took a stutter-step backward. His eyes looked fragile. He said, "Can I walk you to your car?"

She didn't know how to say no. So they walked, she and Patrick several steps behind Maurie and the girls. Maurie canted her head, clearly trying to overhear anything they might say. Melanie's back was straight, and she'd taken Angela's hand. Justine wrapped her arms around her chest, not from the cold. The school had no parking lot, so they had parked two blocks away, on the street. It seemed like two miles now.

"I hope you don't mind that I came," Patrick said after they'd walked the first block in silence.

"How did you find us?" Justine's lips were stiff.

"It's the only school in town. I saw the sign for the concert and thought it was worth a shot." He jammed his hands in his pockets. "You called a lawyer out this way. I got laid off, so I decided I'd come see if you were here."

She stopped walking. "You lost your job?"

He stopped, too. His shoulders slumped

and his hands burrowed deeper into his cheap coat. "I couldn't do it, Jus. After you left I didn't care about those copiers and faxes. None of that mattered. All I've been thinking about is you. I need to talk to you. Please."

The sidewalk was nearly empty. The last of the concertgoers hurried to the warmth of their cars. Justine clutched her purse as though Patrick were a mugger. He'd driven two thousand miles because of a number on a phone bill. It was insane. It was also exactly what he would do. God, she'd messed everything up so badly. She should have called him. If she had, he wouldn't have left San Diego. He might not even have lost his job. She'd been an idiot. A coward. Shaking the dust off her feet. Goddamn it. She looked at his hands, deep in his pockets. He didn't even have any gloves.

She steadied herself, lowered her purse to her side. He was here, and it was her fault. She needed to fix it. She owed him that much. "Where are you staying?"

"The Motel 6."

"I'll call you there tomorrow. We can meet somewhere, and we'll talk."

He blew out a huge breath, as though he'd been holding it this entire time. "Thank you, Jus." They walked on again in a silence broken only by the crunch of their feet on the snow. Tomorrow, Justine thought. Tomorrow she would tell him the things she should have told him before. Tonight she would rehearse them, alone in her room, so she'd get them exactly right. She would end it properly, he would go home, they would leave, and everything would be okay.

They got to her car, where Maurie and the girls waited, shivering. Patrick said, "Hey, Angie. Mellie." Angela pressed closer to her sister. Melanie was still holding her hand.

Justine unlocked the doors and Patrick opened hers for her. Then he stepped back and began to walk away. She saw, at the far end of the street, his white Chevy truck. She hadn't seen it before; he must have come after the concert began. As he walked up the sidewalk she took a moment to regain her equilibrium, then turned the key in the ignition.

Nothing happened. She turned it again. Click-click-click. "Mommy?" Angela said from the backseat.

Patrick, halfway to his truck, looked over his shoulder. When he saw they hadn't left, he turned back. "Oh, no," Justine said. She turned the key again, and again. Nothing. When he got to her window she rolled it down. "It's just cold, it'll start in a minute."

"Let me hear it," he said. He leaned in. He listened to the click-click-click and shook his head. "I hate to tell you, but your starter's out. You'll have to call a garage tomorrow and have them tow it."

Justine's fingers were numb in her gloves. She had $983 left in Lucy's checking account. How much would it cost to fix the starter? Pay the tow truck? She owed her mother $121.68. She hadn't bought any Christmas presents yet. A rime of ice coated the bottom of the windshield. Maurie sat beside her, watching but offering no assistance.

"It's okay, I can drive you home," Patrick said.

No. She didn't want him to take her to Lucy's; didn't want him to know where she lived. She looked up and down the street. It was empty beneath the lights. Maybe he could take them to a hotel. But not the Motel 6. Then where? What other hotels were there? One night at a hotel: $19.99. They needed money for the next town. Gas and hotels on the way. First month's rent, security deposit, money to last until she got her first paycheck from the job she hadn't gotten yet.

"Come on, it's not like I had plans for

tonight. Let me drive you home."

Shit. It was five below zero. They needed to go somewhere. And even if they did go to a hotel, they'd need to get out to the house tomorrow, because how long would the car be in the shop? More than a day, surely.

Justine tightened her hands on the steering wheel. He was going to find out where they lived anyway. It was a small town. All he had to do was ask around and somebody would tell him Lucy Evans's great-niece was living in the lake house.

In his truck, she sat in the front seat and tried not to think about all the times she'd been in it before. The times she and Patrick had eaten their doughnuts, drunk their beers, and made love on the back bench seat where her daughters and her mother now crowded together.

The reflectors lining the county road flared to life, one by one, then faded, like small flames. No one spoke. At the turnoff to the lake, the truck rose and fell, its suspension swinging through the ruts of the dirt road. "Damn," Patrick muttered once, as branches laden with snow scraped the top of the cab.

When they reached the clearing he pulled to a stop in front of Lucy's house. In the dark it looked even more slump-shouldered than usual. "This is where you're living?" he said, disbelief coloring his voice.

Melanie opened the door and climbed out; Maurie and Angela followed. Justine reached for her door, but Patrick put his hand on her arm. "Please. Stay a minute."

Maurie stopped at the bottom of the porch steps and looked back. Justine nodded at her, and she and the girls went up, Melanie last, glancing over her shoulder before she went inside. Justine kept her hand on the door handle.

"You'll need a ride back to town tomorrow," he said. "I should stay."

She'd known he would say this, and she had her answer ready. "My mom has her car."

He didn't press. But then, he didn't have to. He knew where she was. He could come back any time. "Why are you living way out here anyway?"

"My great-aunt left me the house."

"But it's in the middle of nowhere. And it's a wreck. Even in the dark I can see that."

Justine couldn't help bristling a little. "It's not as bad as it looks. I came here once when I was a kid, and it was beautiful then. It could be nice if someone fixed it up."

"And that's going to be you?"

"Why not? It's a house. I never thought I'd have a house of my own."

Patrick shifted in his seat. Something small skittered across the beams of the headlights and was gone. "We could have a house, you know. I've been thinking about selling cars. There's good money in that."

She hadn't meant to criticize him, but it was plain he'd taken it that way. She felt terrible all over again. He'd worked so hard at the Office Pro, trying to get his boss to let him sell the copiers, and it had all been for nothing. Because of her. The truck smelled like road food and the mothbally odor of his coat, probably bought at a secondhand store along the way, as hers had been. She thought of him driving across the high desert, alone in his truck, to a place he'd never been and where he had no real assurance she would be, and guilt overcame her. "Patrick, I'm sorry for the way I left."

In the dim light from the dashboard she could see the muscles of his face tighten. "It was the worst day of my life. I came home, and you weren't there, and then I found that note, and it didn't even say good-bye."

"I know. It was the worst thing I've ever done to anyone."

"But why did you go? That's what I don't

get. We've got such a great thing. I saved your life, then you saved mine, that's what I always said."

This was it: the conversation. It wouldn't be tomorrow, it would be now. We aren't right for each other. It's better this way. I'll always remember you. Good luck with your life. But when Justine tried to say the words, nothing came.

He leaned closer and took one of her hands. "Jus, I need you. I came all this way because I want to make you see that."

Her breath snagged in her chest. Because she did see it. It was the one thing she knew for certain. She looked at their hands, linked on the vinyl seat. Beneath the smell of McDonald's burgers and mothballs she could smell his fresh-bitter scent. She remembered what it felt like to sit beside him on the sofa, their hands clasped just like this, and to wake up next to him, his arm across her stomach, his nose against her neck. What it felt like to be so loved, so needed. For just a moment, she let him in again. What if he stayed? What if they all stayed? He could fix up the house. He could paint it the sunny yellow it used to be; he could fix the plumbing and the drafts and the oven and put in that wood-burning stove. Maybe this could be a starting-over place for all of them.

Maybe he would be less anxious, less controlling, if they lived here, where he'd have her all to himself. Maybe — just maybe — they could be like other families. Happy.

She looked up at the house. The girls' bedroom light was on, and through the tall window Melanie watched them with her arms hugging her ribs. In silhouette she looked fragile, and very alone. The house watched, too, bowed beneath its nameless, solitary burden.

"I'm not very good at being alone," Justine said. She hadn't considered this before, but it was true. She'd always been lonely, but there had also always been that one companion, that one pillar around whom her life had been centered for better or for worse. First it was her mother, then Francis, then Patrick. Those weeks between Francis and Patrick, she'd failed at being by herself. She was failing at being by herself now, too, and that was why she was thinking about letting Patrick stay. It was also why she'd needed to leave him the way she had, she realized. Not because she'd been worried about what he'd do — though she had been — but because if she hadn't run somewhere far away, without telling him good-bye, she'd never have had the strength to leave him at all.

"You don't have to be by yourself," he said. "That's what I'm trying to tell you."

Justine turned back to him. Her chest loosened, and her words came more easily. "But I think I need to be. I'm sorry I couldn't tell you that before."

He shook his head, getting agitated. "Why would you want that? Why would you want to live here, in this shitty house? When you could have our life together, back home?" His face was turning the blotchy red it got when he was very upset. Justine wanted to take her hand back, but she didn't want to upset him more, so she didn't, even though he was holding it very tightly, and as his face reddened he squeezed harder. "Look, Jus, I'm not giving up. I saw your face back at the gym. You were glad to see me, you can't deny it. I don't get why you left, but I'm going to make it right. I'm going to show you that you need me as much as I need you." He gestured to the truck and the house. "See? You've needed me already."

That was when she knew he'd messed with the starter. Somehow, in the frigid Minnesota night, while she'd been in the gym taking pictures of Angela, he'd slipped his gloveless fingers under the hood and broken it. Not to find out where she was staying, but to be her savior again, as he

had with the bus. She felt instantly claustrophobic, as if the truck's cab had shrunk
around her in the space of a second. She
yanked the door open. "I have to go."

He didn't try to stop her. "I'll see you
soon," he said, from the shadows that filled
the cab.

As he drove away Justine's claustrophobia
melted into the wide, empty night, and she
berated herself. She hadn't ended it; he still
thought he had a chance. Now she'd have
to see him again to do it right. She walked
to the house, trying to calm down. It was
okay. Christmas was still four days away;
she had plenty of time. And if she couldn't
do it, or if he wouldn't take no for an
answer, they were leaving anyway, and she
wouldn't let herself feel guilty about disappearing on him again. Leaving no trace this
time.

Maurie was waiting in the entryway, and
Justine braced for her inquisition about
what had happened in the truck. But Maurie didn't ask. Instead she crossed her arms
and said, "That man came out here to find
you."

"Yes."

"How did he know you were here? Did
you call him?"

"No. He came looking for us."

Maurie digested this. "Why did you leave him?"

Justine took off her coat. "It's hard to explain."

"Oh, honey, I'm sure you had your reasons. I'm just wondering, what special brand of crazy is he?"

Justine thought about the men who'd sat at the breakfast table in apartment after apartment when she was young. They'd been nothing but man-shaped cutouts to her smaller self, changing from short to tall, loud to quiet, Firefighter Paul to Songwriter Steven to Crazy Jerry. "Have you ever had someone who loved you too much?"

Maurie gave a bitter laugh. "No one I've left has ever come looking for me, if that's what you mean."

"That is what I mean. At least I think so."

"You think if someone cares enough about you to check your phone records, figure out where you are, and drive halfway across the country to get you back, then he loves you too much?"

"I don't know. Maybe."

"Let me tell you something. If even one of my men had done that for me, I'd still be with him."

Justine stared at her. All her talk about shaking the dust off her feet, and now this?

Maurie's index finger tapped a rapid staccato on her arm. She needed a cigarette, or a drink. Probably both. Justine made herself smile. "Even Crazy Jerry?"

"Okay, not Crazy Jerry." Maurie's own smile faded, leaving her looking tired. "But just about anybody else."

LUCY

I sat in the dark under the lodge with my arms wrapped around my knees. Despite the afternoon heat, I was shivering. Lilith's face as Abe hunched over her hung before my eyes. The cry she'd made echoed in my ears.

Father would be here by suppertime. Would he know, from looking at her? Was it written on her skin somehow? I didn't know how I could look at her again, or talk to her, or share a bedroom with her. Everything was different now. I rested my face on my knees and sobbed into the filthy dress I'd worn for Matthew's birthday party, which seemed so long ago it felt as if it had happened to someone else.

I cried for a long time, and when I stopped I was tired straight down through my bones. The sweat on my arms had dried to a fine salt. My eyelashes felt cool and wet. To my left, the kittens rustled, undisturbed by my blundering entrance or my tears. In their nest were bits of cloth, some yarn, and a dish that had held milk. Beyond them I could see the lakeshore. It was crowded; everyone was getting the most out of summer's last day. Mother was playing cards with Mrs. Williams and Mrs. Jones at a picnic table. Emily, in a blue swimming suit, sat on the beach alone. From my cave the scene was flat and bright, as though I were watching a movie in a dark theater.

After a few minutes Emily stood, went to Mother, and asked a question. Mother nodded, and Emily walked toward the lodge. She could have been coming to get a pop or an ice cream, but I knew she was coming to play with the kittens. She'd told Mother about them, giving up the one secret she had in exchange for a bit of freedom. I thought about leaving before she got there, but I couldn't face the sunshine, so I sat with my chin on my arms and waited.

When she crawled under the lodge, she checked each of the kittens, stroking their heads, then picked up the sleeping Mimsy and sat cross-legged in the dust-covered sand beside me. In the slight bouncing of her knees I could tell she was glad I was there, and I was glad she was there, too. Her innocence soothed me.

I wiped my tear-streaked face with my hands. "Has the mother gone for good?"

Emily looked around, but the mother cat was nowhere to be seen. "She still brings them things to eat sometimes." She gave a worried sigh. "But I found Mimsy outside yesterday, almost in the forest."

I didn't tell her that soon all the kittens would be prowling the forest, where they would be both predators and prey. She must have heard something in my silence, though, because she said, "Who will protect them when we go back home?"

I looked out at the beach, where Mother played cards with the other women, glancing frequently over at the space beneath the lodge. "Their mother will teach them what they need to know," I told her. "And the rest will be instincts they were born with. It'll be enough."

Emily touched the calico's paw, feeling the tiny claws. "Do you think Mother would let me keep one?"

Mimsy lay on her back. Still asleep, she stretched her paw toward Emily's chin. Suddenly I wanted her to have that kitten so badly that my throat ached. "I bet she would."

We sat for a while. Emily talked to the kittens, calling them by name, scolding the one who would never share, praising the clever one. Her voice was high and young and pure, and as I listened my mind pushed the thing I'd seen in the woods into a corner where it paced but did not approach until Father's car drove up the road and Mother called for Emily. Then, as we walked to the house, it came slithering back — Lilith in the leaves, Abe on top of her — and my skin felt hot again.

Emily put her hand in mine. It was cool, and much smaller and softer than Matthew's. She smiled at me. She was a serious child, but she had dimples when she smiled, and perfect baby teeth.

Lilith was on the porch reading a magazine. She'd changed into a flowered dress, and her hair was smoothed back in a pink headband. My stomach felt shaky when I saw her. She looked at Emily's and my hands, joined as hers and mine had been for so long, and though she tried to hide her surprise, I knew her too well. I felt her watching me as I went upstairs with Emily to change for supper. She was wondering if I would tell Father what I had seen. She should have known I would not, no matter whose hand I held.

Mother had made a pot roast, which was the best thing she cooked. It was tender and full of flavor, the potatoes and carrots dissolving in your mouth. The smell filled the house, and it made me hungry even though I hadn't thought I could eat. After Emily and I changed we went to the kitchen and sat at the table as Mother pulled the roast from the oven. Her cheeks were rosy from the sun, and she smiled at us. I felt a rare flash of pity for her. In Williamsburg she'd serve supper to three silent children and a husband who never told her how good the pot roast was. In the dark house that her husband's grandfather had built, behind curtains her mother-in-law had hung forty years before, the sun-glow would fade from her skin in less than a month.

Supper was quiet even for us. Father ate in his slow way and didn't give any sign that he saw the stain Lilith bore. Though he must, I thought. Those eyes that saw everything, they had to see it.

After supper, we gathered in the parlor and waited for Father to read. I hadn't looked directly at Lilith since I'd come inside the house, and I couldn't look at her now, knowing that Father's voice would soon shake the air, lacerating her with righteousness. She sat with her ankles crossed and her hands folded, and I could feel the tension in her. Surely Father could

411

sense it, too.

But for the first time in my memory, he did not read. He pulled Emily onto his lap as usual, but his eyes were unfocused, rimmed with red, and his face was drawn, with lines at the corner of his mouth I'd never seen before. Mother watched him with worry that she tried to hide. My heart beat faster. Lilith didn't move, and I followed her lead, though my hands and feet ached to fidget.

Father wrapped his arms around Emily's waist, drawing her closer. He bent his face to her neck and pressed his lips to her skin beneath her hair, his eyes closed. Emily, startled, squirmed away, and Mother reached for her. But Emily slid from Father's lap and sat beside me on the davenport. Mother's lips parted, then closed again. Father just sat, his brilliant eyes dull. Emily shifted closer to me, her arm almost touching mine. I could feel the slight tremble in it.

Father sighed. He said, "I'm glad you're all coming home soon."

I felt as though I'd swallowed a stone. I hadn't known until that moment how much hope I'd placed in him. He was the only one who could bring Lilith back, the only one she might listen to, but he wasn't even going to try. After another minute, Lilith dared to pull a magazine from the rack. She opened it and began to turn the pages. Mother picked up her needle and sampler. I, like Father and Emily, sat unmoving in the deepening light that seeped through the curtains. I listened to the laughter of the children outside, and I found myself wondering what the other families were doing. They were probably on their porches, watching their children run about. They weren't sitting silently behind curtains that shut out the sun. For the first time I wanted to be out in the warm evening eating a chocolate ice cream from the lodge, like all the other children.

When Mother and Emily went upstairs, Lilith rose to go to bed, and I followed. I dreaded being alone with her, but I wanted even more to get out of the parlor where this strange version of my father sat without reading or speaking. In our room I changed with my back to her. I climbed into bed, turned my face away, and closed my ears against the familiar sounds of her undressing. When she turned out the light I forced myself to lie still, as though I were already asleep.

Then she got into my bed. My skin erupted in gooseflesh. She put her arm around my waist and pulled me close, my back against her stomach, as she'd done on Independence Day, but this time her embrace held no comfort. "What were you doing in the woods with Matthew?" she whispered in my ear.

I screwed my eyes shut, still feigning sleep even though my entire body was rigid. She pressed her knee against the back of my leg. "Did you kiss him?"

My jaw was stiff. "No."

"You should kiss him." Her breath was warm on my neck, and I could feel her breasts against my back. "I bet he tastes good. His brother does."

I thrashed against her, kicking her legs. "Stop it!"

She let me go. I pushed myself against the iron poles of the headboard. My voice echoed in the room, and for a wild moment I worried that Mother — or Father! — might come to see why I had shouted. But they didn't.

Lilith was on her knees in front of me. She looked at my face, at my nightgown hitched up around my thighs, at my shaking body. Then she brought her hand to her mouth and made a harsh sound, as though she were retching. "Oh, God, Lucy. I'm sorry. I'm sorry." She rocked back and forth, cupping her face in her hands. It took me a moment to realize that she was sobbing, soundlessly, as though her throat was squeezed shut. I touched her arm, light and tentative, and then flinched as she grabbed my hand and held it as fiercely as she had when she pulled me from the lake. Lucy, she was saying, over and over, I'm sorry, and I was crying, too, and I didn't know when I'd started.

At last she fell silent, and her grip on my hand eased, though she didn't let go. "It's all going to be different now," she said. Her voice was so bleak it chilled the air.

I nodded. I knew she was right. We knelt there like that, facing one another and holding hands, for a long time. Finally we lay on our backs, side by side in my small bed. I kept my eyes open on the ceiling. I rubbed my thumb along her fingers, back and forth, feeling her breathing ease until her hand lay limp in mine. Only then did I sleep.

When I woke the next morning, I was alone. I heard birds, and the faint slap of water against the sand. Far away, the motor of a fishing boat — it was very early. I got dressed and went downstairs. Lilith was not in the house. I went out to the porch and looked up and down the road. I didn't see her.

I ate a bowl of cereal. I'd never eaten a meal alone before, and it was a surprisingly powerful thing to do, as if the kitchen were a foreign territory I'd conquered. I saw things I'd never noticed, like the way Mother stacked the graying dishcloths in careful squares on the counter and the way the floor was worn between the sink and the oven by my mother's feet and my grand-mother's.

As I finished, Lilith crept in the back door, careful not to let the hinges squeak. When she saw me, she smoothed her hair behind her ears. I asked where she'd been, and she said she'd woken when Father left to go fishing and gone for a walk. She sat at the table. She gave me a small smile that held the ghost of her hand in mine the night before, but an odd charge crackled about her. Our silence was edgy with it.

Soon Mother came downstairs with Emily. When she saw my empty bowl she pressed her lips together. I'd known she would make a big breakfast for our last day, but I hadn't cared. Now, looking at her narrow back as she made coffee, I felt guilty, and angry with her for making me feel that way. Emily tried to catch my eye, but I didn't look at her. I just wanted this day to be over. For us to be on the road to Williamsburg.

"As long as you're up, you may as well start packing," Mother said without turning around.

The next hour passed in a somber mirror of our first day, as Lilith and I laid our clothes and shoes in our shared trunk. I watched Lilith from the side of my eye. The way she folded her things, with a care unusual for her, made me uneasy, though I couldn't have said why. Then Father came back with two small walleyes, and Mother called us to the table, where I ate her eggs, bacon, and toast as though I hadn't already eaten a bowl of cereal.

It was a cloudy day, with rain certain, but it held off until Lilith and I were washing the lunch dishes. Then, as the first fat drops began to splat against the windows, Mother told me to get the towels that were hanging on the clothesline. I stepped outside with the wicker basket, glad for the excuse to leave the house. The air was thick and warm, tangy, not yet rain-cooled. I closed my eyes and drew it deep into my lungs. When I was younger, I was terrified of thunderstorms. Lilith tried everything — songs, games, stories about dogs rolling around in the sky — but nothing helped. Then one day she brought me into this very backyard as a storm was coming. Wait, she said as I trembled beside her, and we waited in the heavy stillness. Slowly, the top branches of the trees began to shift and shudder like a great beast shaking its harness. Wait, she said again, as the electricity in the air raised the hairs on our arms and the wind turned the leaves upside down. Then, in a crash of thunder, the rain poured down. I screamed, but Lilith laughed, flung her head back, opened her mouth wide to the rain, and shouted, *See? See?*

I didn't see, not the way she saw. But I was no longer afraid, and I'd even learned to enjoy the slow, pent-up gathering of the world before a summer storm. So I took my time taking the towels off the line as great, gloppy raindrops fell slow and rare, not yet enough to make me wet.

When I put the last towel in the basket, the wind had begun to toss the high branches. I saw Matthew walking across the Williamses' backyard. His white shirt was blotted with gray where raindrops had fallen on it. I wanted to go inside, but he was looking at me, so I shifted the basket from one hip to the other and waited.

When he reached me we stood uncertainly. The memory of the day before lay like a stain on the ground between us. Then he said, "I wanted to give you something before you go. For your birthday." He pulled from his pocket a piece of wood the size of a small plum, carved into a teardrop shape. In the center was an *L,* and in the top was a small hole through which he'd threaded a leather string. It was as smooth as a skipping stone, and it fit my palm exactly.

"The wood's from the Hundred Tree." He smiled in that shy way he had, and suddenly I wanted to throw the pendant as far as I could. Because I couldn't look at it, this gift from my only friend, without seeing Lilith and Abe grinding their bodies together. I couldn't even look at Matthew without seeing them. Around us the wind gathered force. I shoved the pendant in my pocket and ran inside, the basket bouncing on my hip. I could feel his eyes on my back, hurt and confused, and all I could think was that tomorrow morning we would go, and this would all be over. All of it.

When I got in the house, Lilith was drying the last of the dishes, and from the knowing look she gave me I knew she'd seen Matthew and me through the window over the sink. She wasn't the only one.

"What were you doing with that boy?"

Mother said.

I put the basket on the table. "Nothing."

"What did he give you?"

"Nothing."

"I saw him give you something."

"He gave her a present," Lilith said. "So what?"

Mother ignored her. "You stay away from him."

I opened my mouth to say I would, but Lilith spoke first. "Why does she have to stay away from him?"

Mother's eyes flicked to the hallway. "Keep your voice down."

Lilith spoke louder. "Why? Don't you want Father to know Lucy has a boyfriend?"

"Shut your mouth," Mother hissed.

"There's nothing wrong with having a boyfriend. Didn't you ever have a boyfriend, Mother?"

"He's not my boyfriend," I said, but neither of them heard me.

Mother grabbed Lilith's arm. She was taller, but she seemed smaller, and although she was gripping Lilith tightly, Lilith didn't seem to feel it. "Stop it," Mother said. "We're going home tomorrow. Everything will be all right then." It was so close an echo of my own thoughts that I had to look away for a moment. Mother was not my ally.

Even though we both wanted the same thing.

Lilith smiled without a hint of sympathy. "Do you promise?" The energy that had hummed around her all day sizzled and cracked. Outside, the skies opened and the rain roared down.

Mother's mouth quivered. I felt a sudden, seething contempt for her, hunched between us like a cornered animal. Of course she couldn't promise. She couldn't promise us anything.

Then the screen door opened, and Emily came in. She was dripping rain from her dress onto the floor. In her arms she held a blanket. The little calico raised her head from its folds and looked at us with her round eyes. Mother's hand went to her throat.

"This is Mimsy," Emily said. "She's the one I told you about."

Mother tried to smile, but she looked dizzy. She reached behind her for the counter, and I knew right then how it was going to go.

"Can I keep her?" Emily said. "Please? I'll take care of her. I won't let her make a mess."

Mother started shaking her head before Emily finished speaking. "No. No. I can't have a pet in the house. It's too much." She pressed back, against the counter. "And it's wild, sweetie. A wild animal. It belongs here, in the forest." She tried to make her voice reasonable, placating, but I saw the way her neck constricted, the tendons straining, the way her hands gripped the counter. I saw the way she looked at that kitten and at the way Emily held her close, and I knew. I knew Emily wasn't allowed to have anything but her. My face grew hot.

"Why can't you let her have it? Why can't she have this one thing?"

Lilith looked at me, perplexed. She had no idea what I meant. But Mother did. The shame of it was there in her face, but she shook her head again. "Your father would never allow it."

"Father wouldn't care if she had a kitten. He's not the one who sleeps in her bed every night." That was a mistake. I knew it as soon as the words left my mouth, and I could tell from Emily's flinch that she knew it, too.

Mother drew herself up. "She can't have it. And that is final."

Emily cried then, as only a six-year-old can cry, her face crumpling and tears mixing with the rain on her cheeks. She said please, Mother, please, but Mother was unmoved. "Take it away, right now," she said, and sent her favorite child back into the rain.

When the door had shut behind her, I stared at Mother with eyes that felt like coals in my head. She couldn't promise anything, but she could take things away. It was her only power. I could feel Lilith looking at me, but I saw only Mother. Mother, who wouldn't meet my eyes, because she was a coward. Neither of them said a word as I followed Emily out the door.

It was raining so hard I could barely see her, a dark shape crossing the Williamses' yard. She ran with her head down in a vain attempt to keep Mimsy dry. I ran after her, my feet splashing in the puddles. But when she disappeared under the lodge I stopped. I didn't follow her into the crawl space. I didn't sit beside her and put my arms around her while she cried. I didn't help her smooth the kitten's ruffled fur as it settled into sleep. I didn't tell her Mother might change her mind if she asked again tomorrow, or that the kitten would still be here next summer, or that it didn't matter because I would be the sister she'd always wanted. I just stood in the rain between the Joneses' and the Williamses', feeling the water soak through my clothes until even my underwear was wet. Then I walked around to the front door of our house and went up to my room to change.

JUSTINE

Justine didn't call Patrick at the Motel 6 the next day, or the day after that. She hadn't figured out what to say to him, and when he didn't come to the house she convinced herself she was right to wait; he wasn't ready to talk to her, either. Maybe, she hoped, she could avoid the whole thing until the day after Christmas, when they'd leave — though the greater part of her knew that was unlikely. This was Patrick, after all.

Maurie, Angela, and Melanie acted as though Patrick hadn't shown up at all, though a couple of times Justine caught Melanie looking at her. When she did she looked away. She left the lake only once, to pick up her car from the repair shop, and she watched for Patrick's truck all the way there and back. She didn't see it. Yet his presence, seeming to lurk just beyond her vision, kept her on edge. So when Maurie insisted they go to Arthur Williams's Christmas Eve party, Justine welcomed the distraction.

She put on the only dress she'd brought, a beige pleated silk with white buttons and a peter pan collar that she'd planned to wear for job interviews. It was not a festive look: in the mirror above Lucy's dresser she was drab and sexless. Even the freckles the San Diego sun had dusted across her cheekbones had faded, leaving her skin the same washed-out color as the dress. On impulse she dug out the mascara she'd bought from the makeup counter girl and brushed it on. It made a small but gratifying difference.

Maurie, of course, looked fabulous. When she came out of her room in a black suede circle skirt, black leather boots, and a red scoop-necked sweater cinched around her waist with a gold belt, Angela applauded. Maurie shook her head so her gold double-hoop earrings chimed against her cheek and curtseyed, spreading her skirt like an ink stain on the floor.

Melanie and Angela were wearing jeans because Justine hadn't brought any of their dresses; they weren't suitable for winter. Maurie told them not to worry — jeans could be dressed up, if you knew how. She took them to her room and laid out scarves, ribbons, necklaces, makeup, and nail polish.

"Accessories are how you give your outfit a sense of occasion," she said as she opened a jar of bobby pins. Justine watched Angela finger a light blue scarf and smiled. In this grandchild, Maurie finally had a girl who wanted to play dress-up.

Maurie turned first to Melanie. "You have a strong face. For you we need rich colors, the colors of royalty." Melanie's eyes widened at this flattering reinterpretation of her stern, haughty features. Maurie wrapped a ruby pashmina around her shoulders and turned her to the small makeup mirror she'd put on the dresser. She was right: the red scarf made Melanie look exotic, like an aristocratic gypsy. Melanie lifted her chin, studying her reflection. Maurie groped through her jewelry case, pulled out a gold necklace studded with red glass, and clasped it around Melanie's neck. "You'll wear red lipstick, of course."

"Mom," Justine said. "She's eleven."

"Oh, please. It may suit you to look like that" — Maurie waved at her — "but this one's got fire. You've got to let her express herself."

Stung, Justine wrapped her arms around her waist. When she blinked, her eyelashes felt heavy beneath the mascara.

Maurie rearranged the necklace so the

427

heavy pendant in its center lay in the hollow of Melanie's throat. "Let's think about your hair, shall we?"

An hour later, standing beneath the streetlight outside Arthur Williams's house, Melanie looked years older than she was. Her hair was pulled tight in a French braid, her eyebrows were tweezed into Audrey Hepburn arches, her lips were bright red, and she touched her necklace with red-painted nails. She reminded Justine of that infamous shot of a ten-year-old Brooke Shields with her oddly adult, made-up face above her naked little-girl chest. Justine's stomach tightened, even though she knew that there'd been no stopping Maurie once she got started.

Arthur Williams lived in a big Victorian on a tree-lined Williamsburg street. Tasteful white lights sparkled along the wrought iron fence and in the bushes. It was five o'clock; the party had started an hour earlier, and through the windows the front rooms were crowded with people.

"That's the one that used to be ours." Maurie pointed to the brown house next door. It was smaller, with simpler gables and a more modest porch, but genteel nonetheless. It was neatly maintained, with plastic candy canes lining its front walk. Justine recognized the front steps from the picture of Lilith, Lucy, and Emily in the photo book.

"It's pretty," Angela said. The blue scarf was around her neck, and Maurie had tied blue ribbons in her hair. With her curls teased she looked like Shirley Temple.

Maurie sighed. "It's all right. Nothing like the Lloyds', though." She pointed to a brick monstrosity on the corner that was twice the size of the brown house. Its flat, small-windowed facade gave it a sinister presence, like an abandoned asylum, and the paint on the front porch was peeling. Justine would pick the brown house if she had the choice, but Maurie said, "That's the one that should have been ours," and her mouth was bitter.

They opened Arthur's door to an assault of color and sound. The entryway was full of people with drinks in their hands. A twelve-foot Christmas tree twinkled in one corner and a staircase trimmed in red ribbon curved up in the other. Through wide doorways on either side more people filled a living room and a dining room. A few turned to look at them, and Justine felt conspicuous, even though it was Maurie they were looking at. She caught a few quick exchanges, just audible in the hubbub: Is that Maurie Evans? Her aunt passed, you know. Left everything to the granddaughter, I heard.

A server walked by with champagne flutes on a tray, and Maurie grabbed one. A moment later another server appeared and collected their coats. The Williamses had spared no expense, it seemed, which surprised Justine. Arthur didn't seem the ostentatious type.

Maurie led them to the living room, where twenty or so people stood in groups, chatting. Justine did a quick, nervous survey for Patrick — his appearance at the chorus concert made her think anything was possible — but he wasn't there. Most of the guests were about the same age as Arthur and Maurie, and the party had the relaxed feel of a gathering at which everyone had known everyone else for a long time. Justine recognized Dinah the librarian by the window wearing Christmas tree earrings with blinking red lights, and in the far corner she saw Quentin from the diner, talking to a man who was not his brother. Nearby, Maisy the shoe store owner gabbled to a woman who looked covertly for an escape. Several other faces looked familiar, too, although she couldn't place them. Maybe she'd seen them at the Safeway, or the library. She felt a rush of pleasure, then discarded it. What did it matter that she knew people at this party?

Maurie grabbed her arm. "I can't believe it," she hissed. "The bitch is still alive."

Justine followed her gaze to a love seat and a group of chairs around the fireplace. They were empty except for two of the chairs, where an old woman and a doughy blonde in blue scrubs sat. The old woman's skin was as wrinkled as a dried fruit, and her sparse white hair lay in a thin, careful net over her scalp. She was dressed in a black pantsuit and a blue blouse. On her lapel was a green and red pin the size of a silver dollar. She sat very erect, balancing a plate of sausage rolls on her lap with a gnarled but well-manicured hand. "Who is it?" Justine asked.

"Agnes Lloyd."

Justine felt Melanie press closer for a look as she did some quick math. If Charlie was Maurie's father, then this woman — his mother — would have to be close to one hundred years old, maybe more. Then again, she was the oldest person Justine had ever seen. She glanced at Maurie. Her mother was pale, her mouth a grim line. Before Justine could say anything to her, Maurie broke to the left and grabbed the arm of a portly man in a green sweater. "Johnny Swensen!"

Johnny looked taken aback, but said, "Hey, Maurie." Maurie kissed his cheek and wedged herself into his group, which included two other men and a woman who, judging from the disapproving look she gave Maurie, was Johnny's wife. Maurie kept her back to the old woman by the fire as she launched into an energetic patter about how Johnny hadn't changed a bit. Johnny's face reddened as Maurie kept hold of his arm. She made no move to introduce Justine.

Justine, uncomfortable standing there with no one to talk to, eyed the empty love seat by the fire. Feeling quietly daring, she led the girls over to it. She was careful not to look at the old woman; instead she watched Maurie with Johnny Swensen. Usually her mother was fearless in a crowd, and Justine had always envied her that. Now, though, her expansive gestures seemed brittle rather than brave.

"We haven't met. Are you new in town?" The question came from Agnes Lloyd. Justine turned with what she hoped was a friendly smile. The old woman's voice was thready, but her eyes were sharp.

"Yes. We've just arrived."

"Agnes Lloyd. Pleased to meet you."

Instead of introducing herself, Justine said, "Agnes Lloyd? Are you the person the library is named for?"

Agnes gave a small, gratified nod. "I am."

"It's a beautiful library," Justine stammered, while she tried to find something of Maurie — or herself — in Agnes's face. Age had sunk the old woman's cheeks, scored deep lines around her mouth, and faded her eyes to the color of weak tea. But they once had been dark brown, Justine decided. Almost black.

"They were going to tear it down," Agnes said. "They couldn't afford the repairs. I told them there'd been a library in this town as long as I'd been alive, and would be long after I was dead if I had anything to say about it." She smoothed an invisible crumb from her lap, a proud little gesture. Her suit was cheap, like something Justine might buy at Ross, and her purse, a black clutch that sat by her feet, had a broken clasp. Her brooch, though, looked to be studded with real emeralds and rubies. Inherited, probably. Like the diamond ring Charlie had given Lilith. And her house, which was sliding into ruin. How much of her money had she given to the library? According to Maurie, Agnes's children — Charlie and the unnamed sister — had died long ago. Her husband was dead, too, no doubt. The attendant, whom Agnes hadn't bothered to introduce, stared into the middle distance. Justine thought she knew what books had come to mean to Agnes Lloyd.

Ray, her thick legs in panty hose, her large bust swaddled in a cardigan embroidered with brightly colored and inappropriately placed Christmas balls, strode over to them. Her dyed black hair rose in an even more exaggerated bouffant than usual. She held two cocktail glasses. "God knows what Suzanna puts in this nog," she said in her deep rasp, "but it's fantastic." She sat in one of the chairs and gave Justine a glass. "I didn't bring you one, Agnes. Did you want one?"

Agnes's lips pursed. "No, thank you."

"I didn't think so." Ray nodded at Melanie and Angela. "Are these yours?"

"Yes," Justine said. The eggnog smelled of nutmeg and burned her throat.

"It's good to see children at this party. It used to be filled with them. Now it's like happy hour at the nursing home. No offense, Agnes."

Agnes narrowed her eyes. With her thumb and forefinger she inserted a sausage roll into her mouth like a token into a slot machine. It was odd seeing someone so old eat, as if, at Agnes's age, the body should have outlasted the need for sustenance.

"Who are you?" Melanie asked Ray.

Justine frowned at her; her tone was blunt, even rude. Ray extended her hand with exaggerated propriety. "My name is Rachel Susan Spiver, and you may call me Ray."

Melanie took her hand with equal gravity. "My name is Melanie Annabel Evans," she said, "and you may call me Mel."

Ray threw back her head and laughed. Justine stared at Melanie, then started to laugh, too. Melanie smiled her crooked smile. Justine could sense Agnes watching them. Melanie's last name hadn't escaped her notice.

Arthur Williams appeared then and took the seat next to Ray. "Justine, I'm so glad you came."

"Well, my mother wanted to," Justine said. "I did, too," she hastened to add.

"This party is a family tradition. My grandparents had it every year, and so did my parents. Maurie used to come when she was young, with Lucy and Lilith. So did her grandparents, I imagine. Didn't they, Agnes?"

"I'm not as old as you think I am, Arthur." Agnes gave a cagey laugh that did little to ease the lines around her lips and didn't reach her eyes at all. Her gaze darted from Melanie to Angela to Justine. Was she, too, looking for resemblances?

"It's strange to meet people who knew my family," Justine ventured. "I never knew them."

"There have been Evanses here as long as there have been Williamses," Arthur said. "Dafydd Evans and Rhys Williams founded the town. Along with Merlyn Lloyd, of course. Although Rhys got the naming rights."

"Because Lloydburg would have sounded silly," Ray said. Justine covered a laugh with a cough. She rather liked this tipsy version of the diner owner.

"I'll settle for the library," Agnes said. "It's legacy enough." The attendant, to whom no one was paying any attention, rolled her eyes. Arthur looked down and smiled despite himself. Then he turned to Angela and Melanie.

"You must be excited to see all this snow."

Angela said, "I like the ice. I want to learn to skate."

"Skating is very popular here," Arthur told her. "There are hockey leagues even for little girls." Angela nodded, even though her aspirations ran more to Michelle Kwan than Wayne Gretzky, and Melanie refrained from saying anything negative about ice skating in general. Justine relaxed, feeling the eggnog warm her muscles and dull her worries about Patrick. Even with Agnes's disconcerting presence, it felt good to be sitting here, in front of the cheerful fire.

A flash of red caught her eye. Her mother was standing just inside the door, talking to Quentin from the diner. Justine recognized the invitation in the cant of her body, one shoulder higher than the other, and heard the laugh she used on men as she drained her glass. She waved it at Quentin, then tugged him by the hand and disappeared into the entryway. Justine glanced at Agnes, who appeared not to have seen her. She told herself it was fine. They wouldn't be here long enough for her mother to get into any real trouble.

Ray said something that made Arthur laugh, and Justine turned back to them. Soon others joined their group, pulling up more chairs and sighing as they released stomachs held in too long above belts cinched too tight. Servers brought drinks and platters of cheese blintzes. Stories were told, news traded, and laughter rolled and broke in warm waves. Melanie followed the conversation with alert interest, and Justine's attention flickered between her and Agnes, who said little but seemed to draw energy from the small crowd, her cheeks growing pink as she listened. The attendant picked at her chipped fingernail polish, ignoring everyone.

Then, without warning, Maurie was there. She'd refilled her champagne glass, Justine saw. She put one hand on the fireplace mantel above Ray and said, "Hello, Agnes."

Agnes pressed her lips into a thin line. "Maurie, it's lovely to see you."

"It's lovely to see you, too." Maurie's tone was breezy, as though she'd run into an acquaintance at the supermarket, but her consonants were clipped the way they got when she was trying very hard not to slur them. Everyone in the group stopped talking. The attendant stopped picking her nails. Justine's nerves flickered with foreboding.

Arthur said, "We're glad you could come, Maurie."

"Glad to be here. Actually, I've been meaning to ask you something, Artie. Do you know where Mother's engagement ring is? We can't seem to find it." Maurie's voice was still light, but she glanced at Agnes for the barest instant. "As you can imagine, it's of great sentimental value."

"Yes, I imagine it would be." Arthur's voice was neutral. "I told Lucy so. But Lilith wanted it buried with her, and Lucy honored that wish."

Maurie could not hide her shock. For three seconds, she didn't move. Then, in the same easy tone as before, she said, "Really. Does Agnes know that?" She turned to the old woman. "Agnes, did you know my mother is wearing your ring in the Methodist Church cemetery?"

Her voice wasn't loud, but the room quieted as people, feeling the prickle of malice as only people in a small town can, turned to watch. Justine said, "Mom, don't."

"Don't what?" Maurie said. "I just came over to ask Agnes if she's enjoying my granddaughters' company. They're beautiful, aren't they?"

Angela looked worried. Melanie watched Maurie with a stony glare that made her look even older.

"Of course they are," Agnes said acerbically.

"I think they look a little bit like Charlie, don't you?"

Justine heard several gasps. Agnes said nothing but drew her lips into a sphincter.

"Maurie, that's enough," Arthur said.

Maurie's voice was still measured, but now rage quivered beneath it. "Enough? It may be enough for you, Artie. After all, your daddy sent you to law school and gave you

439

this fancy house. Nobody ever called you a half-breed, or your mother a whore."

More gasps. Agnes's thin voice cut through them. "How dare you talk to Arthur like that in his own home?"

"Oh, I don't know, Agnes. Maybe it's because I've known this guy since we were five, and in all that time he's never said one word to defend me to all the people in this town who treated me like shit. Maybe because I'm looking at the woman who turned her back on my mother because she didn't think she was good enough for her perfect, dead son." Maurie pointed at Agnes. "Let me tell you something. When your precious boy got himself blown up, my mother could have had any man in this town, but she didn't want them. And when she died, she wanted Charlie's ring on her finger forever. Does that sound like a whore to you?"

Justine said, "Mom, stop. Please. It's all over and done with."

Maurie's eyes snapped to her. Then she looked around the room. Every last person in it was watching her. She forced a smile. "Right. We're here to celebrate Christmas. Love thine enemies and all that." She raised her glass in a toast, drained it, and walked out, careful not to wobble in her high-

440

heeled boots.

In her wake the room filled with shocked conversation. Justine turned to Arthur. "I'm so sorry. I'll take her home."

"It's not your fault." He looked shaken.

Agnes was white beneath her face powder, with two spots of high color on her cheeks. Justine felt sorry for her; no one deserved to be spoken to like that, least of all a frail old woman. Then again, according to Maurie, Agnes had been very cruel to Lilith, and even though it was long ago, her cruelty had inadvertently led to the wandering, dissatisfied misery of Maurie's life. That Maurie had gotten to tell her off pleased Justine in a way she didn't feel all that bad about. "I'm sorry about what my mother said," she told Agnes, as diplomatically as she could manage.

Agnes raised her napkin to her lips. "I don't hold you to account for your mother's behavior." This statement was so steeped in unintentional irony that Justine stood up without answering. She could feel everyone's eyes on her as she thanked Arthur, told Ray good-bye, and led her daughters from the room.

She found Maurie in the entryway, talking with Quentin and two other men. "Mom, we need to leave."

Maurie linked her arm through Quentin's. Her eyes glittered. "No. I'm having a good time with my friends. Why don't you go eat some more Christmas cookies with Agnes? Maybe she'll give you some of her money. That's what you're after, isn't it, other people's inheritances?"

Justine stepped back as though Maurie had pushed her. Don't cry; she told herself. Don't let her make you cry in front of all these people. She felt a hand take hers, and looked down: Angela's. Melanie pulled her pashmina higher on her shoulders and looked at the men, her face a mask of distaste.

Then, thankfully, Arthur appeared with their coats. Once he was there Maurie co-operated, pressing against Quentin as he helped her into hers. She made a bit of a show of walking to the door, her head held high, but she stumbled on the steps, and by the time they got to the car she was leaning on Justine. On the way home she rested her head against the window, her eyes closed. Justine drove slowly. It was almost utterly black on the county road, and she saw just one other car, a pair of headlights that held steady a half mile behind them. When she turned into the forest the headlights drove past, into the night. They belonged to a pickup truck, color indeterminate.

At the house, Justine helped her mother up the steps as Melanie and Angela followed in shocked silence: how had the vivacious grandmother who had draped them in jewelry and shawls two hours before become this woman who leaned on their mother and swore every time her foot missed a step? Francis had come home drunk often, but not until three or four in the morning, and even Maurie, though she'd been tipsy plenty during her last visit, hadn't gotten staggering drunk. Justine's anger made her pull her mother along more roughly than necessary. "Wait down here," she said to the girls. Then she half dragged Maurie up to the lavender bedroom and let her fall onto the bed.

Maurie smiled a wobbly smile up at her. Her lipstick was smudged, which made her mouth look bruised. "I think Quentin liked me. Don't you think so, sweetie?"

Justine didn't answer, and within seconds Maurie was out. Justine stood for a minute longer, catching her breath. In the corner she saw a shopping bag with a vase sticking out of it: Maurie's loot from the house, no doubt. She peeked inside. Besides the vase the bag held one of the flowered plates from the kitchen, a stained plaid apron, and one of the Hummel figurines — a little girl with a puppy tugging at her underwear. That was all.

Justine ran her hands through her hair. The apron and the plate. Maurie hadn't given Justine the nurturing stability they represented, but apparently in some neglected corner of her heart she cherished it from her own childhood. Now that was irony, Justine thought bitterly. Maurie snored gently through her open mouth. Justine took off her mother's boots. She'd leave her clothes on; it was easier. She removed the gold earrings, then turned off the light and closed the door behind her.

Melanie and Angela were sitting close together on the living room sofa. The Christmas lights were still on, glowing like the lights of a distant emergency. Angela's cheeks were wet. Melanie had wiped off her makeup, leaving dark blotches beneath her eyes.

"What's wrong with Grandma?" Angela asked in a tiny voice.

Justine sat in one of the armchairs. The house creaked, high in its rafters, like an old woman shifting in her rocker. "Grandma had too much champagne. It makes you very sleepy."

"Why was she so mean to you?"

Without warning Justine's eyes filled with tears. Her breath wheezed in her chest, and for a precarious moment she thought she might lose it completely. She closed her eyes for a moment, and that steadied her a little. "She gets that way sometimes. It doesn't mean she doesn't love you."

Angela climbed onto her lap. Justine slipped her arms around her. Angela was too big to sit on her lap, she realized; her feet reached the floor, and Justine wasn't sure when that had happened. Meanwhile Melanie sat on the sofa, alone, picking at her fingers as she watched them.

Justine eased Angela away, keeping hold of her hand. She reached her other hand to Melanie, who, after a moment's surprised hesitation, took it. "Let's go upstairs. I'll read to you."

So they got in their pajamas, and when Justine said she was too cold to sit on Angela's bed they all got into Lucy's. Justine lay with the Emily books at her feet, Angela's head on her shoulder, and Melanie loose limbed on her other side. She read until her voice faded, and her daughters drifted to sleep, and the snow began to fall in the small, still hours of Christmas morning.

LUCY

That evening, when it was time for the end-of-summer party, we wrapped ourselves in our raincoats and hurried through the drenching downpour to the lodge. Lilith had gone early to get ready for the cabaret, so it was just the four of us. Father and Mother walked together, Father carrying Emily, and I walked behind. We could see our neighbors coming as well, hooded like pilgrims in the miserable light.

The lodge was crowded and warm from the press of bodies. The Millers had arranged a buffet on the bar with fried chicken, bean salad, corn bread, and Matthew's grandmother's cookies for dessert. Matthew and Abe stood behind the bar, serving. I looked for Lilith. Several of the other teenagers were there, but Lilith, Jeannette, and Betty were not. At a corner table, four weekend lodgers ate their meals, no doubt wondering what had happened to their quiet fishing retreat. They were whiskered and unwashed, a sharp contrast to the scrubbed and polished small-town gentry that filled the room.

Mother, Father, Emily, and I were an island of silence among the chatter of our neighbors, who seemed energized by the closeness of the too-small space. Now that we were around other, happier, people, Father's face looked even more haggard. Mother looked tired, too, and rested her hands on Emily's shoulders, as though for support.

When I got to the buffet, Matthew gave me the same smile he'd given everyone else, but he picked me a nice, fat chicken breast, and placed it on my plate with the smallest flourish of the tongs. I kept my head down. Abe, ladling the bean salad, looked away from me. I felt queasy as I passed him.

The Williamses had saved two seats at one of the tables. Mother told me to take Emily and sit with the other children, so I found a spot on one of the couches where we ate with the two youngest Jones brothers and the younger Pughs and Davieses. We didn't talk, to them or to each other. I looked around again for Lilith, but I still didn't see her.

As dinner wound down, the teenagers

moved us off the couches and carried them from the porch into the main room, where they set them to face the front wall, leaving an area about fifteen feet across. Then they moved the tables and arranged the chairs in rows behind the sofas. There weren't enough seats for everyone, so people stood along the bar and the back wall, and the littlest children sat on the floor at the front. Mother and Father sat with the Williamses in the first row of chairs, while Emily and I sat on a couch with Josie Pugh and Melody Lewis. Mr. Miller and Matthew's grandmother came from the kitchen to stand with Abe and Matthew behind the bar. The four weekend fishermen stood near the back door, unsure of their welcome but curious about what was afoot. Lilith still was not there.

The teenagers went back to the porch, where they conducted further boisterous preparations for several minutes. Finally, after the backstage noises crescendoed and then quieted, Ben Davies came out wearing his father's coat, tie, and fedora. Above his lip he'd drawn a Clark Gable mustache. The adults gave an appreciative round of applause until Ben raised his hands for quiet. "Welcome to the first annual Miller Lodge Cabaret!" he said in a circus-huckster drawl.

"Prepare to be dazzled, amused, amazed, and entertained! I, Ben Gable, will be your master of ceremonies, and your guide through an evening you won't soon forget!"

Delighted laughter rippled through the room: Ben was a bit of a show-off, and he was in his element. With a grand wave he introduced the musical accompanist, Opal Williams. She was small and plump like her mother, and she walked to the piano with a pile of sheet music. I had to admit I was impressed. Lilith's and her friends' managing to get their hands on all that music reflected a level of planning I hadn't expected.

Once Opal was settled, Ben introduced the first act: The Great Magician "Evan Roberto," who wore a mail-order black cape and top hat. He had a trick wand that sprouted flowers, and he did card tricks and pulled quarters from the ears of the children on the floor while Opal played a jaunty ragtime tune. He was pretty good; despite my black mood, I found myself smiling with everyone else at his exaggerated movements. Then Felicity and Sincerity Pugh sang a sweet duet of "Red River Valley," their blond heads nodding in time, followed by Charlie Lloyd, who juggled Coke bottles — three, then four, then five — sweating with concen-

449

tration and cutting his eyes to his father, whose florid face betrayed such relief that his son wasn't making a fool of himself that it was an embarrassment in itself.

In between the acts Ben kept up a funny patter that distracted the audience from the hisses and shuffles of the performers backstage. In every crisp entrance and neat bow I detected Lilith's hand, bossy and sure, directing these older children just as she'd always directed me in every game we'd ever played. The crowd applauded enthusiastically. The four lodgers had stayed, I saw, and applauded along with everyone else. Even the drum of rain on the roof sounded like applause.

With every act I looked for Lilith, but it wasn't until midway through the show that Ben introduced "The Boswell Sisters." I'd never heard of this jazz trio, but it was clear from the anticipatory murmurs that most people in the room had. Lilith, Jeannette, and Betty walked out and stood in a row, Lilith in the center, and I saw why she hadn't shown her face during dinner: she had cut her hair. The long, sinuous black curls were gone, leaving a shiny bob shellacked in waves that curved around her ears. Her face was made up with powder, rouge, and red lipstick, highlighting its dramatic

450

angles and planes. She wore a fashionable, waist-hugging dress, and she posed with her chin high, looking regal and much older than thirteen.

Beside me Emily said "oh!" and I heard coos of approval from several of the women. I stole a glance at Father. His face was expressionless, save for two grim lines bracketing his mouth. Mother touched her snood with nervous fingers as Mrs. Williams whispered a smiling comment in her ear. I felt a restless fear stir to life behind my ribs.

Opal began the music, a slow, jazzy intro that her fingers fumbled only slightly. Lilith, Jeannette, and Betty rotated their shoulders from side to side with the beat. When the music accelerated, they began to sing:

If you want your soul set free,
lift your voice and sing with me!
If the Devil grabs your hand,
Here's one thing that he can't stand!

The tune was joyful, their harmonies decent, and they had choreographed simple moves that they performed in unison, stepping from side to side, flipping their hands back and forth. The crowd, caught up in the rollicking, syncopated beat, tapped its feet and clapped. I didn't move. I couldn't

451

take my eyes off my sister.

Something had happened to Lilith when she took the stage, and it was more than just the hair and makeup. She was luminous, as though something beneath her skin had ignited. The odd, gypsy bones of her face seemed unified at last, and she was beautiful in a way that was no longer perplexing. Jeannette and Betty, with their pert noses and thin-lipped smiles, looked like ordinary girls in a makeshift teenaged cabaret. But Lilith was something else. Greta Garbo must have looked like this at thirteen, I thought dizzily, and Bette Davis, in whatever unremarkable towns they'd grown up in. All those years that Lilith had talked about becoming a movie star, I'd believed her because I adored her. That night it seemed possible to me, even by the harsh standards by which such dreams must live or die.

The accompaniment slowed again. It switched keys, becoming mournful. Jeannette and Betty stopped swaying and began to hum in a low drone that rose and fell. Lilith stepped forward. The crowd quieted, uncertain. Then, in a husky alto, Lilith sang:

If that old Devil should grab your hand,
Here's one thing that he can't stand:
Shout sister, shout sister, shout!
Oh Lord! Shout! Oh Lord!

She sang the rousing words as if they were a dirge, every note dripping with warning, and she sang them directly to me. My mouth was dry. The fear in my chest stretched out its clawed feet. I could sense the audience's collective intake of breath. Behind Lilith, Jeannette and Betty looked at one another.

Then the song recovered its joyous major key. Lilith stepped back, and the three girls finished together in hip-swinging, finger-snapping rhythm,

Just tell old Satan how you feel,
Get that old Devil right off your heel!
Shout sister, shout sister, shout!

By the time they finished the tenth repetition of *shout sister,* the crowd was on its feet. When the girls curtsied, everyone roared their approval: it was, by far, the best act of the night. Opal curtsied, too, and deservedly so; playing that song must have taxed her skills to the utmost. Jeannette and Betty squealed and hugged Lilith between them as they ran backstage. I looked at Father and Mother. Although neither joined in the standing ovation, they were clapping. Maybe it would be all right. Maybe Father wouldn't mind the makeup and the dress, since it was for a show. Maybe he wouldn't even mind the haircut. Although it was modern, it was the same style that every woman we knew wore, even proper matrons like Mrs. Lloyd and Mrs. Pugh. But my fear receded only a little.

After the Boswell sisters came Richard Pugh, who made a just passable Charlie Chaplin. Then we had another magic act, by Eddie Jones, that wasn't as good as Evan's, and as the quality of the acts declined I could sense the audience growing restless. The show had gone on for over an hour, and the adults wanted to send their children to bed and move on to their last cocktail party of the summer. Two of the lodgers had gone upstairs, and the other two leaned against the back wall, drinking whiskey. The room was quite hot now, and the windows were coated in steam. Outside, the rain poured on.

At last Ben Davies took the stage with an air of finality. The last act of the night, he promised, would bring us all to our feet. "Will you please welcome," he intoned, "America's sweetheart, Shirley Temple!"

The audience gave a tired round of applause. Then Opal started playing "The Good Ship Lollipop," and Lilith skipped out. She was wearing the blue dress with the white bow that she'd worn on Independence Day, but she'd shortened it to the top of her thighs like a little girl's play dress. She'd traded the red lipstick for pink, and her newly shorn hair fell about her head in loose black ringlets, far curlier than it had been when it was long. She wore her hated black Mary Janes and white ankle socks, and she held a lollipop. When she got to the center of the stage she stood with her legs akimbo, pouted her lips, opened her blue eyes wide, and blinked twice.

The crowd laughed, its enthusiasm reignited. My insides turned to concrete.

"On the good ship Lollipop," Lilith sang in a high lilt, *"it's a sweet trip to a candy shop."* She marched across the stage, copying the twee gestures of Shirley Temple: the exaggerated swing of the arms, the straight-legged, little-girl strut. But her mouth tilted in that off-kilter smile she'd used on Charlie, on Matthew, and on Abe. *"Where bonbons play, on the sunny beach of Peppermint Bay,"* she sang as she sashayed from side to side, her dress flouncing up to show the white bloomers she wore underneath. Through it all she kept her eyes wide open, as innocent as a doll's.

The audience didn't know how to respond. A few, like Mayor Lloyd and Dr.

Pugh, laughed appreciatively, but many, especially the women, looked uncomfortable. *"Happy landings on a chocolate bar,"* Lilith sang to Mayor Lloyd, and Mrs. Pugh and Mrs. Jones raised their eyebrows at each other.

I willed Lilith to look at me, but she wouldn't. She stood in the center of the stage again, her hands on her waist. *"See the sugar bowl do the tootsie roll,"* she sang, swaying her hips, *"with the big bad devil's food cake."* From the back of the room one of the lodgers let loose a catcall. The crowd muttered, and several turned to glare. Lilith gave no sign that she'd heard, but her eyes held a manic glint that made me wrap my arms around my chest, where tiny claws scrabbled like rats. She skipped to where Father sat white-faced and stiff. *"If you eat too much, uh, oh, you'll awake with a tummy ache,"* she sang to him. She waved the lollipop in front of his face. *"On the good ship Lollipop, it's a nice trip, into bed you hop —"*

Father stood up. He grabbed Lilith's arm, and she shrieked in pain. I screamed, too, my hands flying to my mouth. Opal stopped playing. There was a shocked silence.

Lilith blanched at the look on Father's face, and her courage failed her at the moment she most needed it. Standing there in the dead-quiet room with her lollipop and her childish dress, she looked as young as the little girl she'd been mocking. Father threw his coat over her shoulders and marched her out the door with Mother trailing behind. Emily and I followed, washed out on the wave of shocked and excited chatter rising behind us. The rain had stopped at last, but a thick mist lay upon the ground and on the lake.

As soon as he got in the house, Father threw Lilith away from him. She stumbled into the newel post of the staircase, and his coat fell from her shoulders, revealing her little girl outfit. Father took a step toward her. He was beneath the foyer light, and it spilled around him as though he were an actor in a play, unreal and real at the same time. Lilith held on to the newel post with one hand. The eerie beauty she'd had on the stage still clung to her, and I could feel her gathering it closer about her. She did not drop her eyes from his now.

Father said, "You have shamed me. You have made a mockery of everything I have ever taught you."

I shrank against the wall beside the pictures of Grandmother and Grandfather Evans. Mother backed up to the front door, clutching Emily. "Thomas, please," she said.

Lilith gave a laugh that sent invisible fingers along my scalp. She tilted her head and sang, lightly, *If that old Devil takes your hand, There's one thing that he can't stand —"*

Father slapped her. Emily screamed, and I jerked backward. Lilith sang again, louder: *"Shout sister, shout sister, shout!"*

He slapped her again, so hard she had to sit on the stairs. Emily started to cry. I pressed against the wall, where the photographs of my grandparents watched their son with dead eyes.

"You were clean," Father said, and his voice broke.

Lilith's smile was gone, and her lips were swollen from his blows. The light that had shone in her guttered out, leaving a slight girl with oddly harsh features in a ridiculous dress. In her face was fear, and maybe sorrow, but also triumph, crouching there small and fierce, and it pulled all the air from inside me. "Not anymore," she whispered.

In the silence that followed none of us moved. Then Lilith stood unsteadily, her dress hitching up so the bloomers underneath blazed white. She turned and walked up the stairs with her back straight. Father watched her go. His hands were shaking.

The sound of our bedroom door closing echoed throughout the house.

Mother sidled up to Father. "Thomas," she said, her fingers picking at his sleeve.

"Take Emily to bed," he said without looking at her. And she did. She took Emily by the hand, and pulled her up the stairs. She didn't look at me. But Emily did. Her eyes were hollow with fear. Fear for me, left alone in the foyer with Father.

He was between me and the stairs. I edged forward, thinking to slip past him, but he turned to me. His face was so wracked with pain that I felt faint. "Lucy," he whispered. "Help me." He fell to his knees before me and pulled me into his arms. When he pressed his face into my neck I felt the buttons of his shirt like pebbles against my chest. His wiry hair scratched my face, and his arms were so tight around me I could hardly breathe. He dug his fingers into my back, kneading between my ribs, as if digging for my heart, and he muttered words, fast and slurring, into my ear: *Have mercy upon me, O God, according to thy lovingkindness,* he said, as his hands ran up and down my back, clawing for purchase. *Wash me thoroughly from mine iniquity, and cleanse me from my sin, for I acknowledge my transgressions, and my sin is ever before me.*

The hallway light fell in its circle around us. Beyond it the entire house was dark. *Against thee, thee only, have I sinned, and done this evil in thy sight,* he said, and his voice shook with a violent emotion I didn't understand, and I wanted to cry in terror and incomprehension — how was I supposed to help him? I stood with my eyes closed as he buried his face deeper in my neck, murmuring, *Behold, I was shapen in iniquity; and in sin did my mother conceive me,* and pulled me tighter against the whole of his body from his thighs to his shoulders, saying, *Behold, thou desirest truth in the inward parts: and in the hidden part thou shalt make me to know wisdom.*

"Oh, Lucy," he moaned. "Help me." Now his hands lay upon my buttocks, cupping them through my dress and my underwear, and he said, *I will wash my hands in innocency; so will I compass thine altar, O Lord.* And he took my hand in his, and drew it to that place between his legs, and held it there. He whispered into my ear, *Purge me with hyssop, and I shall be clean: wash me, and I shall be whiter than snow.* I did cry then; I did; with fear and a dark shame. With his other hand Father smoothed my hair. "Don't cry. Don't cry. *Make me to hear*

460

joy and gladness; that the bones which thou hast broken may rejoice. Hide thy face from my sins, and blot out all mine iniquities." His hand on mine in that place between his legs tightened, as did the hand that held my hair, and his voice strangled, Create in me a clean heart, O God; and renew a right spirit within me.

"Lucy," he said again, into the joining of my neck and my shoulder, and create in me a clean heart, again and again, rocking me back and forth, as though I were a babe and he were comforting me, but I couldn't help the tears that flowed down my face and into his hair. Was I helping him? Or was I the iniquity? A madness was on him, and I didn't know if I was its cause or its cure, and I was so afraid, and he held me so tightly that sparks danced before my eyes.

At last he shuddered, and my hand felt him shudder, and then he gave a deep sigh, the breath of it entering into my pores. He let go of my hand and my hair and wrapped both his arms around me again, tenderly now, his body heavy against me. My skin crept across my shoulders and down my back. "Daughter," he said. "My innocent. You have saved me from sin. I am clean without transgression, I am innocent; neither is there iniquity in me." Without lifting his face from my neck he rested his hand upon my forehead. *"Cast me not away from thy presence; and take not thy holy spirit from me. Restore unto me the joy of thy salvation, and uphold me with thy free spirit. Amen."*

He released me, and my head spun with the rush of blood that returned to it. "Go, now, my daughter and my salvation," he whispered, but in the shadows in his eyes I saw no one who had been saved, and no one I could recognize. I stepped around him, my limbs stiff, my jaw clenched, and walked up the stairs in the dark, leaving him kneeling there on the floor.

Emily's door was shut tight. I heard no sound from Mother or Emily behind it. In our room Lilith was lying fully clothed on her bed, her eyes open, looking at the ceiling.

"Lilith," I whispered.

She didn't answer.

"Lilith," I said again, and my voice shook. But she turned her face to the wall.

"I'm sorry, Lucy," she said. "I can't help you anymore."

JUSTINE

It was barely light when Justine left her daughters sleeping in Lucy's bed. From the basement she got the presents that Santa Claus would leave on the living room floor: hair ribbons, socks, a diary for Melanie, a doll with golden hair for Angela. A couple of cheap cotton sweaters. The usual pathetic haul. But she'd also bought a pair of imitation suede boots like the ones Angela coveted, and for Melanie she'd bought a secondhand guitar. It cost $40 at the pawnshop, almost more than everything else combined, and way too much, given Lucy's dwindling account balance, but when she saw it she thought about Melanie singing in the chorus and Francis moving her fingers across the frets and she wanted, immediately and powerfully, for Melanie to have it.

When she'd laid out the gifts, she sat with her coffee on the sofa, waiting for the girls to wake up. It hadn't snowed as much as she'd thought it would, and the flakes that fell now were sparse and small. This worried her. She'd awoken with the certainty that Patrick would come today — he wouldn't be able to resist seeing her on Christmas, surely — so she'd hoped it would snow enough to keep even his sturdy truck from reaching them. Now she hoped he'd come later in the day, for Christmas dinner. She thought she could manage that. It would only be for a couple of hours.

As she finished her coffee she heard Angela's feet scuff across the landing. A moment later her youngest daughter appeared in her pink nightgown. She stopped halfway down the stairs, a question in her face. Justine smiled at her. "Santa came. Go get your sister."

Angela said, with an anxious look, "Should we wake up Grandma?"

Justine had been thinking about this. Maurie had driven here, she claimed, to spend Christmas with them. But she'd gotten plastered on Christmas Eve and lacerated Justine with the bitter meanness that always lurked below the campy veneer she wore to disguise it. She could be just as cruel hungover as she could be drunk. And Justine could still feel her daughters' sleeping bodies, warm and trusting beside her, in her bones. So she told Angela to let her be.

For a little while, despite her mother sleeping off her hangover and Patrick lurking at the Motel 6, it was the best Christmas she could remember since the early days with Francis. She had bought cinnamon rolls, and she put them on a plate on the coffee table. Melanie and Angela unwrapped their Santa presents with no more enthusiasm than they warranted, but Melanie seemed to like the diary, and Angela petted the little golden-haired doll even though, as Justine watched her with it, she realized she'd gotten too old for dolls. Outside the window the lake was gray and quiet, and for now at least, Patrick seemed very far away.

When the Santa presents were done, Justine told them she had her own presents for them. This wasn't the usual thing; Santa had always been their only Christmas benefactor. Even though Melanie had outgrown the Santa myth and Angela soon would, Justine felt better pretending it was Santa, not she, who brought the annual gifts from Walmart. But these gifts, she wanted credit for. So she told the girls to close their eyes, and pulled the guitar and boots from their dining room hiding places.

Their reactions were everything she'd

hoped for. Angela squealed as she reached for the boots and didn't seem to care that they weren't the brand the other girls wore. Melanie was struck still when she saw the old guitar, scratched and dinged but strung with new strings by the woman at the pawnshop, who played herself. "Later we can find someone to give you lessons," Justine said.

Melanie put three fingers on the frets, and a C chord sang in the room. Angela looked up from her feet, which were already in the boots. "Hey, that's good!"

Melanie raised one eyebrow at her, played the chord again, and the three of them laughed together for the first time in what felt like forever.

Then, above them, the floorboards creaked. Both girls turned to Justine. "I'm sure she's feeling better," Justine said. They heard water running in the bathroom sink. Scrambled eggs, toast, and coffee; that was what Maurie would need. As Justine stood up, Melanie set the guitar aside, carefully.

Justine was scooping the eggs into a bowl when Maurie appeared at the kitchen door, still in her blue robe. Her skin was sallow beneath her makeup. "You had Christmas without me."

"We thought you'd want to sleep."

"You thought I'd want to sleep through Christmas with my granddaughters? The last Christmas I'm ever going to have in this goddamned house?"

Justine felt the listening silence from the living room. She held the bowl in front of her stomach. "I'm sorry. The girls got up early. And they haven't opened your presents yet."

Maurie's mouth twisted. She turned her back on the eggs and toast. In the living room she clapped her hands. "Are you girls ready for your presents from Grandma?" Melanie and Angela watched with palpable misgiving as Maurie got her packages from the corner, but, though she looked like hell and her hands shook, her familiar, make-the-best-of-things energy soon enlivened the room, and Justine felt her daughters relax as they saw the grandmother they recognized.

Angela gasped in delight as she unwrapped a pair of ice skates, clean and white and new, the silver blades shining. "I got the right size from your shoes," Maurie beamed at her.

"Mom, those are great," Justine said. She wondered how much they cost, and where her supposedly broke mother had gotten the money. She was glad she'd given Angela the boots.

Melanie's gift was a plastic purple case with a pair of eyes painted on it. Inside was an array of eye shadows, lip glosses, and blushes. Maurie pushed the guitar aside and sat beside Melanie. "These are jewel tones, and they are the perfect colors for your hair and skin. Remember how gorgeous you looked last night?" She drew Melanie into a hug. "You and I, we're the dark beauties in this family," she said in her ear, and beneath the forced brightness in her voice Justine heard such a yearning ache, such a weary homelessness, that her throat tightened. But while Melanie didn't resist the hug, she didn't surrender to it either, and when Maurie felt that, she let her go.

The afternoon eased by. Patrick didn't come. Justine cleaned the wrapping paper from the living room floor; then, while Maurie napped, Melanie strummed her guitar, and Angela played with Melanie's makeup, she slipped upstairs and packed her clothes. She'd never fully unpacked, so it didn't take long. Tomorrow morning she'd put the girls' things back in their pillowcases; that wouldn't take long, either. She put her bag in Lucy's closet beside the Emily books, two boxes of family photos, a box of her great-grandfather's books, the old leather Bible, and the few other heirlooms she'd stashed there the day before.

She had it all figured out. Tomorrow she would tell Maurie they were leaving. She'd ask her to finish going through the house, and tell her she could keep whatever money Lucy's belongings would fetch. Maurie would be sorry to see them go, but she'd known they'd planned to, and the money would please her. Once Justine and the girls were settled in their new apartment, Justine would contact Arthur and ask him to wire her Lucy's money and the house sale proceeds when the probate was done. They were going to Atlanta. She'd never been there, and it was warm.

They'd invited the Millers at seven, so at six they ate their precooked turkey, microwaved mashed potatoes and sautéed beans. Patrick still didn't come, and Justine began to nurse a tiny, flowering hope that he wouldn't. They sat in the dining room, and Maurie opened a bottle of wine, and it was all rather nice. It wasn't until they finished that they heard the truck drive out of the woods, and Justine's frail hope died. At least, coming this late, he wouldn't be able to stay very long. She stood up without looking at anyone, and carried her plate to

469

the kitchen. When the doorbell rang, she went to answer it, feeling her daughters' eyes hot on her shoulder blades.

Patrick stood at the door with a shopping bag full of presents. His pickup was parked in the driveway, and Justine was surprised to see that the snow came halfway up the tires. It couldn't have been an easy drive. "Merry Christmas," he said. His voice was too loud. He strode past Justine into the living room, put the bag on the coffee table, and took off his coat to reveal a blue shirt and a red tie. He grinned, his shoulders thrown back, and he vibrated with nervous energy — he was in his salesman mode. Justine took a moment to collect herself as she hung up his coat. He had something planned, something more than just the visit and the presents, and he was excited about it. She needed to marshal her strength.

"You're just in time for our party," Maurie said, and Justine knew her mother was not her ally. She'd decided she liked Patrick.

Patrick's grin faltered, then recovered. "Party?"

Justine shut the closet door. "We're having the neighbors over."

"Don't tell me other people live out here." It was a joke, but it sounded forced. Justine watched him closely. He hadn't planned on other people being here, and it threw him. She wasn't sure if that worked to her advantage, or against it. It could go either way.

"Two old men live in the lodge." She went to the kitchen, avoiding Melanie and Angela, who still sat at the dining room table. Patrick followed, Maurie close behind, and as Justine washed the dishes they leaned against the counter and talked — about his drive, the weather, and the relative merits of Motel 6's and Travelodges — until the doorbell rang at seven.

Matthew stood there alone, with a loaf of pumpkin bread and a bottle of wine. "Abe isn't up to coming," he said, without looking at Maurie.

"This is Patrick," Justine told him. "He's a friend from San Diego."

Patrick gave Matthew his salesman's handshake, two quick pumps. Justine took the pumpkin bread and the wine to the kitchen. Patrick followed her. While she sliced the pumpkin bread, he opened the wine and started pouring drinks. Just like any other couple with people over, she thought. Except they'd never had people over. Unlike Francis, for whom mysterious men were always leaving cryptic messages, Patrick had slipped into her insular, friendless world as though it was exactly the sort of place he was used to.

"That guy's kind of creepy," he said. His tone was light, but it had an edge to it.

"He's okay. He's helped us a lot."

He set down the wine bottle. "Helped you how?"

That had been the wrong thing to say. Patrick hated it when anyone helped her but him. She shrugged, like it was no big deal. "Just little things. Like plowing the road so the girls can get to school."

He gave a short, hard laugh. "Jus, do you hear yourself? You're living so far in the middle of the backwoods, down a road that's not even a road, that you have to ask some geezer to plow just so you can get out." He pointed at the stain on the ceiling. "In a house that's falling apart around you."

"You're right. It's not what I expected," Justine temporized. That mollified him, and he went back to the drinks. She picked up the sliced pumpkin bread and returned to the living room, where everyone else was sitting. She pulled another chair from the dining room and turned on the radio. Now that it was Christmas Day the stations were all solemn orchestras and reverent choirs singing hallelujah. She missed Bing and Aretha.

Patrick came out with the drinks on a

serving platter he must have dug out from one of the cupboards. He passed them around and raised his glass in a Christmas toast. The testiness of the kitchen had vanished; now he was the picture of gracious bonhomie, and a part of Justine had to admire him. He hadn't planned on Matthew Miller being here, and he felt threatened by him, but somewhere between the kitchen and the living room he'd pivoted, neatly and quickly. That's what a good salesman did, he'd told her many times. He changed his script to meet the circumstances.

"I bet you're wondering how I know Justine," he said to Matthew.

"A friend from San Diego, she said." His deep-set eyes were noncommittal.

"I saved her life."

Justine's cheeks grew hot. Matthew's eyebrows lifted, but he didn't say anything. Maurie leaned forward, her breasts rounding over the neckline of her black wool dress, and gave Patrick what he needed. "Really? How?"

"Well, let me tell you. I was walking to work one day when I saw this little slip of a girl step off the curb right in front of a bus. It's a good thing I used to play football, because all those instincts came right back.

The bus missed her by this much." He grinned at Justine. "I saved her, and then she saved me, is what I always say."

Everyone looked at Justine. Patrick's grin was brittle; he was wound tighter than he wanted to be, and trying not to show it. Justine said, "It's true. That's how we met."

Patrick's grin widened. Maurie made the appropriate congratulatory exclamations. But Melanie's face pinched with a bitter contempt that made Justine look down. She picked up Angela's glass of apple juice, even though she'd barely touched it, and took it to the kitchen, where she leaned on the counter and forced herself to breathe slowly. Melanie was right. She was doing it again; that complicated waltz with Patrick's fragile ego and his moods that she'd done for almost a year. Still, she reminded herself, she only had to do it for a couple more hours.

She took her time topping off Angela's glass. When she came back, Patrick had moved on to other stories. The Indiana farm. The Mustang. The Office Pro. All the stories he'd told her at their first lunch date, all told with that same easy charm, but as she listened to him now she saw why, despite his gregariousness, he didn't have any friends. He talked only about himself, and he didn't let anyone else talk at all. He didn't notice that Melanie listened with open distaste and Matthew with weary politeness, or that no one but Maurie laughed at his punch lines. He just talked, on and on, for over an hour, until, during a small break in the monologue, Matthew said he had to go.

Patrick followed him with the tail end of one of his football stories while Justine got Matthew's coat. He looked exhausted as he put it on. After the effort it had taken to dress up and navigate the slippery road, the evening must have been a sad comedown from Christmases past. Impulsively Justine put her hand on his arm. "Thanks for coming," she said.

Matthew's face warmed with the hint of a smile. Out of nowhere Melanie had her arms around him and her face buried in his coat. He touched her head lightly before he walked out. The wind had picked up, tossing the snowflakes like confetti.

After she closed the door Justine stood for a moment with her hand on the doorknob. Then she turned around. "Patrick, you have to go, too. I need to get the girls to bed."

She expected him to plead and wangle, but he played his trump: "Can't I watch them open my presents first?" Justine rubbed her arms in the cold air that had come through the front door. She couldn't deny him that. But it wouldn't take long. Then, somehow, she'd make him leave.

They went back to the living room, where Patrick laid his presents on the coffee table. Melanie arched her nose in the air, as though he were laying dead fish in front of her.

"Go ahead, open them," Justine said.

Angela's gift was a pink Hello! Kitty tee shirt covered in spangles. She loved it, and the conflict that raged in her face was sad to see. Justine said, "You'll look pretty in that. You should thank Patrick."

Angela nodded, relieved. "Thank you, Patrick."

"Now you, Mellie," Patrick said. Melanie opened her package to reveal a San Diego Padres shirt. As it fell into her lap she drew her hands back as though it were electric.

"It's so you can remember that time I took you to the game," Patrick said, smiling.

Melanie raised her eyes to him. They were utterly opaque. Justine reached over and took the shirt. It was just an ordinary child-size Padres shirt. But Melanie's hands still hung motionless over her lap, and Patrick was still smiling at her. Justine felt a tremor of unease. The Padres game was one of the best memories she had of the four of them together. Patrick had bought the girls Red Vines and ball park dogs. The grass was greener than any grass she'd ever seen. Now Melanie stood up, and her face was pale. "I'm going to bed." She walked out of the room without looking back. The inside of Justine's mouth felt like paper as she watched her.

"Angie, go up with your sister." When both girls had gone she said to Patrick, in a voice she hoped struck the right notes of pleasant and firm, "You really should go now."

He got up and looked out the window, then shook his head. "I don't think I can drive back up that road."

She pushed back the curtain and saw that he was right. The snow was up to the fenders of his truck. This explained the nervous energy he'd hummed with all night, and why he'd waited until evening to come: he'd seen the snow and hoped for this. For a wild, desperate moment she thought about asking Matthew to plow the road, but it was so late. And he'd been so tired; he was probably already in bed. "You can sleep on the couch," she said, her jaw tight.

"Thanks." He smiled his wide smile. It made the house seem very small.

Maurie said, "Well, if you're staying, I'll get the bourbon." She went to the kitchen and reappeared with her Jack Daniel's. Patrick raised one hand.

"Maurie, do you think I could talk to Justine alone?"

Don't go, Justine pleaded silently. Maurie looked from Patrick to Justine and back again, and for a moment Justine thought her mother's reluctance to be left out of anything would make her stay. Then her hand tightened on the neck of the bottle. "Of course." She took the bottle upstairs with her.

A tenor crooned "O Little Town of Bethlehem" as Patrick sat on the sofa. Justine took a chair, keeping the coffee table between them. She was keenly aware of the snow all around, pressing on the roof, creeping up the walls.

"I have a present for you, too," he said. "I probably shouldn't give it to you. But I want you to know where I stand."

Justine had no doubt what it was. She took the small package with fingers that fumbled with the red wrapping paper and the black velvet box. The ring was gold and the diamond small and bright.

"It was my mom's. My dad said if it was for somebody Mom would have liked, I could have it. And Mom would have loved you."

This was what he'd been doing these past three days, she realized. He hadn't been in Williamsburg at all; he'd driven to his father in Indiana and gotten this, his dead mother's ring, to offer her. For a moment her trepidation gave way to a pity so profound that she almost wept. It was such a beautiful, sad, desperate gesture, and it held everything she loved about him, and everything she needed to escape.

The colored Christmas lights danced on the facets of the little stone. It was a simple thing, a farmer's ring for a farmer's wife. Justine touched it. Seven weeks ago, this would have been everything she wanted. Marriage. Security. A man who would never leave. She would have taken it without question, grateful for everything it promised.

He leaned forward. "Jus, come back with me. I'll get a job selling cars, and in no time we'll have enough for our own house. A new one, where we can make our own family."

She could see it, shimmering in the white-cold heart of the diamond. A small house, in one of the new subdivisions going up east of town. Mountains in the distance, a good school a few blocks away. A two-car garage with Patrick's latest restoration project inside. Neighbors, barbecues, kids playing kickball in the cul-de-sac. The four of them around the dinner table, and the baby in his high chair. All of it seeming, to someone looking in the window, exactly like the life she'd always hoped for.

When she had looked long enough, she closed the lid. She put the box on the table between them. "I'm sorry." She raised her eyes to meet his. "I'm really, really sorry."

He shrugged, a wounded jerk of his shoulder. "I guess I didn't expect you to take it." He glared around at the walls of the faded living room, as if it were the house's fault Justine had said no. Then he picked up the wrapping paper and crumpled it, the sound harsh in the quiet room. "But I'm not giving up. Because you do need me. And the next time I ask, you'll say yes." He had that hectic look he'd had in his truck the night of the concert, the night he'd messed with the starter. Justine felt again the wormy unease she'd felt then.

She stood up. "I'll get your things."

She brought two blankets from the linen press. While Patrick spread them on the sofa she turned off the radio and took the empty glasses to the kitchen. When she headed for the stairs he blocked her way, towering over her, his shoulders hunched.

"Can I have a kiss?"

For a long moment the only sounds in the room were the pings of the radiator and the faint hum of the Christmas lights. Then Justine lifted her face a little, and he kissed her, tenderly and lightly, on the lips. "Good night, Jus."

She went to the girls' room. They were awake under their covers.

"Is he gone?" Melanie asked.

"It's not safe for him to drive. He's sleeping on the couch."

"You said it was going to be just us."

"It is. He's leaving in the morning."

"Is he going back to San Diego?"

Justine was tempted to lie, but she couldn't. "I don't think so."

The house was quiet, but Patrick's presence filled every corner of it. "Come sleep with me," she said. The girls got out of their beds without a word. After they climbed into her bed she slipped the deadbolt into place and crawled between them. She didn't put on her pajamas, and she didn't turn off the light.

Patrick wasn't going to leave in the morning. He would find a reason to stay, then another, and another. But it didn't matter. They were going to go. In the morning Matthew would plow the road, and they'd wait for their chance. Maybe tomorrow night, when Patrick fell asleep. They would be very quiet as they put their things in the Tercel and drove away.

"We're going to leave tomorrow," she whispered to her daughters.

She lay awake for a long time, listening to the silence downstairs.

LUCY

I don't know what woke me in the quiet of that last night. Perhaps it was the front door closing as she left, or the sound of her feet on the path. My eyes opened, and her bed was empty. I went to our window. The clouds of yesterday's storm still cluttered the sky, but stars glinted, and the moon shone on her slender figure walking up the road. Though she carried nothing, I knew she was leaving.

I put on my shoes and forced myself to move quietly down the stairs, every slow step an agony. I opened the front door by excruciating inches, tiptoed across the front porch with its treacherous, creaking floorboards. When I reached the road I could no longer see her, but I knew where she'd gone. She was on the journey she'd begun on Independence Day, when she'd taken Charlie's hand: across the bridge, to the road, to California, without me.

I ran, no longer caring how much noise I made. I didn't know what time it was, but the lodge and all the houses were dark. The only sound beside my hurried footfalls was the soft drip of water from the leaves. The air smelled amphibian with leftover rain.

When I got to the top of the hill, I saw her standing by the bridge, a half-lit shape. She was wearing the dress she'd borrowed for her Boswell Sisters routine. A bag lay at her feet, a small satchel. It must have been soaking wet, for I knew she had hidden it by the bridge that morning, when she rose so early. She'd scripted her exit perfectly. But she hadn't planned on the rain, and she hadn't planned on me.

She saw me right away, because she was looking back for someone else. She reached out a hand, and I stopped. "I left you a note," she said. "You'll see it in the morning."

Below us the creek, swollen with rain, rumbled on its way to the lake. The roaring in my ears was louder still. All through this long summer, as I'd watched her move away from me, I'd never thought she'd truly leave me behind. Not this way, by taking the journey alone that we'd always planned to take together. And not now, after I'd finally become a citizen of that strange and terrible country she'd occupied alone for so long.

"You're supposed to take me with you. That's what we always said."

"Lucy." I heard sorrow in her voice. "You know you were never going to come with me."

"I will. I'll leave with you right now." But even as I said it tears filled my eyes, because I knew she was right. I wouldn't go. I was never going to go. Even after what Father had done, the thought of the world beyond the lake and Williamsburg filled me with fear. What would two girls alone, with no money and no one to protect them, do in such a world? I hated myself, hated my cowardice, but when she said, "No, you won't," all I said was, "Please. Don't leave me."

A breeze shifted the leaves above us. Water fell like rain, then stopped. I crossed the space between us and touched her arm. Every night we'd spent talking in our starry bedroom, every time I held her hand, every day we escaped to the Hundred Tree, and every game we'd ever played was in my touch, and she felt these things and pulled away. "Read my note. It will tell you what to do. You've started doing it already. And —" She paused, a careful weighing. "And there's Emily."

Something pressed against me. Something heavy. I said, "Emily?" Even though, in that moment, I knew.

She grabbed my arms. Her fingers dug into my skin. "Lucy, listen to me. It doesn't have to be you. It can be her. It's going to be her anyway, someday. Mother can't protect her forever. Even she knows it."

My ears filled with cotton. I saw Emily on Father's lap, his lips against her neck. Mother's hand, reaching. Emily beside me on the davenport. Her arm trembling. I saw Lilith's hand, slipping through the firelight to take Charlie's as Father watched. The thing that pushed at me pushed harder. Your turn, it said. Your choice. I shook my head. "No."

"Lucy, please," Lilith said. But she didn't say anything more, because behind us came footsteps on the path. She looked over my shoulder, and her face closed.

I turned. Emily was standing there. Like me, she was in her nightgown, but hers was smudged with dirt, and I knew where she'd been. She had slipped from Mother's smothering, saving embrace to spend one last night with her calico, not caring what the punishment might be. She'd seen us, one after the other, glide past under the moonlit sky, and she'd followed. Now she stood with her hands clasped, her nightgown paler than the moon, her hair blacker than the night. Unlike Lilith, who looked so grown-up, she looked younger than her years. She was such a small, fragile thing, then and always.

"Come here," Lilith said. Her voice was hard. Emily came, slowly, her blue slippers scuffing in the dirt. Lilith bent so her face was just inches from hers. "Here's what you're going to do. You're going to go back to bed right now, and you're not going to tell anyone you saw me."

Don't do it, I begged her in silent desperation. Go home. Tell Mother Lilith is leaving. We can stop all this. We can stop it right now. I caught her eye and shook my head. She shifted from one foot to the other. She didn't understand me.

Then she saw Lilith's bag. She looked up at Lilith, and her voice was small. "Are you running away?"

"Yes. Tomorrow, I don't care who knows. Tonight, you can't tell anyone."

Emily picked at her nightgown. "But I don't want you to go."

"Well, I am."

Emily cut her eyes to me, the barest glance, then back to Lilith. "What about Father? He'll be so sad."

487

The inside of my mouth went dry. She knew. She knew what I had never guessed. But she thought it was love. Lilith was right; she would go to him so willingly. As willingly as I had gone fishing with him. In the rush of water below I heard a voice whisper, *create in me a clean heart,* and he was beside me, talking about the unnoticed who hear the entire liturgy. He traced his fingers along my arm. The fish were dying in the bottom of the boat, terrified of the sky. His face was in my neck and the buttons of his shirt were sharp in the cold halo of light.

Lilith gave a bitter laugh. "No he won't. He has Lucy now."

Something inside me shattered. With a howl I ran at her, my hands clawing at her face, at her hair. I couldn't see her, a blackness hung before my eyes, but I felt her fall back and I felt her skin beneath my nails, her bones beneath my fingers, my beloved sister, my enemy, my protector, my betrayer — *you sent him to me!* — and then she was hitting me, shoving me to the ground, kicking my stomach, my side, my ribs, my head. She was screaming *I saved you, all those years it was me, I saved you, I was the only one who saved you, nobody but me* and above it Emily was wailing, stop it! stop it! you're hurting her! Then her small body was

488

between Lilith and me, pushing Lilith away, but Lilith's hands were on her throat, *not you, you got none of it, ever, you were safe, safe, safe, SAFE* and I couldn't get up, my ribs were in agony, the world was spinning, but I got to my knees and I shouted, "Let her go!" because Lilith was shaking Emily back and forth so that her hair whipped and flew — and she did stop, for just an instant, Emily's pale, fragile throat in her hands, and the whole dark earth held its breath. Then she shoved Emily backward, and Emily fell over the bridge.

We froze. Lilith with her arms outstretched, I on my knees. The only sound was water, crashing over rocks.

I pushed myself up and ran, stumbling, holding my side, past Lilith, who still stood unmoving, her face stunned, to the end of the bridge, where the bank was slick with mud and the creek was so high it ran fifteen feet across in a massive, swollen distortion of the timid brook it had been the day before. I didn't see Emily, in the water or out. I screamed her name again and again, scrambling along the bank, following the water, looking for a dark head, pulling my way with the roots of trees that stuck out into the creek bed, my ribs jagged, an eternity of falling, slipping, grabbing, and sliding, branches tearing at my nightgown and my hair. But the stream was loud, and my voice such a weak, high bleat that not even I could hear it.

Finally, two hundred yards below the bridge, in a last torrent, the water spilled over a fallen tree into the lily patch where Father and I had fished. It was there that I found her. She floated beyond the push of the creek water, facedown in a knot of sticks and grasses the creek had ripped up by the roots, a clutch of flotsam among the lilies.

I plunged in. The water came up to my chest. The muck on the bottom sucked at my shoes and slipped cold tongues between my toes. The waterfall thundered in my ears, and creek water grabbed me, trying to push me away. When I reached her, I turned her to the sky and pulled her on her back, as Lilith had pulled me to the pontoon that early summer day so long ago, to a spit of land on the far side of the creek. I dragged her until she was clear of the water. Then I fell to my knees beside her.

She lay still, with her arms flung wide. Her white nightgown clung to her like wet tissue paper. Her eyes were open and blank. I took her face in my hands and whispered her name. But those eyes that were so like Father's did not blink, and when I lay my hand on her chest it did not move.

All around us the night teemed with silent life. In the reeds and in the sand, frogs and crickets and crayfish. In the lake, fish. In the trees, birds. Hundreds of tiny hearts beat no farther from me than I could skip a stone, and I heard them all in the marrow of my bones. But in my sister's limbs was a terrible stillness, an incapacity of movement that was nothing like sleep. I had never seen death before. I had never seen the body cast aside, like flotsam from the creek. There was nothing of Emily in it. Nothing at all.

When I took her to the woods that day, just the week before, we went to a glade Lilith and I knew, and I tried to play with her as Lilith and I had played. Let's pretend we're princesses, I said. Let's pretend there are fairies here, and animals that can talk to us. But Emily didn't know how to play that way. She hadn't learned the essential childhood art of imagining a life better than your own and pretending to live it. So I took her to the berms, and we slid on the cardboard sleds, and she laughed, and I laughed, too. Now, as I knelt beside her on that ragged beach, I thought about how she'd never once played pretend, and I wept.

I don't know how long I knelt there before Lilith came. I didn't see her appear on the far side of the creek, or wade into the lake. I saw her only when she walked out of the water onto the little strand. I put my hands on my knees, and I did not wipe away my tears. Lilith stood still for a moment, water dripping heavily from the hem of her dress. Then she knelt on Emily's other side and touched her chest. When she felt the silence there, she squeezed her eyes shut. In the moonlight, her face was gray. "I just wanted her to go home," she whispered.

One of Emily's bare feet lay in the water. The lake licked at it in little rills. Her mouth was open, and between her lips I could see her small white baby teeth. She hadn't lost one yet.

"What do we do?" Lilith asked. She was trembling.

It took me two tries to say the words. "We have to tell Mother."

"We can't. They'll think I did it."

She had done it. She had pushed Emily over the bridge, and Emily had died. But I said, "We'll tell them she fell."

She shook her head. She pointed to Emily's throat. In the moonlight I saw the dark marks below the delicate jaw, the imprints of Lilith's hands, which would blaze red in the light of morning. On Lilith's face the scratches my fingers had made were darkening with blood. She was right. No one would believe Emily had fallen.

Lilith wound her fingers together under her chin. She was shaking now. "Lucy, please. Help me." Behind her the creek spilled into the lake. It was such a little thing. Three feet of silty froth sliding over a log into a lily patch. Just a summer creek, swollen with rain.

A breeze kicked up, chilling me in my wet cotton nightgown. A cloud slid across the moon, and our small beach fell into a darkness that hid Lilith's face from me, and mine from her. The blood in my veins slowed. She had thrown our sister into the creek, where her lungs filled, not with the silken lake water I once breathed, but violent, muddy water that forced its way in uninvited. Now she knelt before me in her cabaret dress, which was drenched and stained with dirt. The dress she'd planned to wear to California, without me. Leaving me with Father.

Then the cloud passed, and the moonlight fell again upon her angular, haunting features, and I knew that I would help her anyway. Just as I knew, with terrible clarity, what I would ask in return.

I said, "You have to stay."

She went absolutely still. I waited. I waited

for her to think it through. She couldn't leave that night. They would come for her with police and dogs, not with "lost" posters. She also couldn't leave later. That was my price. That was what she needed to understand. For the quiet space of a dozen heartbeats we knelt there, unmoving in the light of the stars, above the body of our sister, while I waited. Waited for her to believe that I would do it. All of it.

Then she closed her eyes, and I knew it was done. I touched my finger to my lips, then to my heart, and held up my hand. She did the same, and pressed her palm against mine. It was cold.

I told her to get a boat. She left me on the shore with Emily and walked back up the creek. It was only half a mile along the curving edge of the lake to the dock, but it was a long time before I saw her black silhouette walking along it. Someone was with her, and I knew it was Abe; that he had come to the bridge to meet her as they'd agreed, to ferry her to freedom on his motorcycle.

"I didn't tell him why we wanted it," she said when she'd rowed, alone, to our small strand. "And he won't tell." I knew he wouldn't. There was nothing he wouldn't do for her, then or later. I waded into the water and helped her beach the boat. I didn't ask what excuse she'd given Abe for why she looked such a mess, or why she wouldn't leave with him as they'd planned. I didn't care.

"I couldn't find her slippers," she said. "It was too dark."

"Maybe tomorrow," I said.

We laid Emily on the bottom of the boat, where the fish I caught with Father flopped and died. Her dark hair floated in three inches of rainwater like the shadow of an aura. The moon was out again, shining full on her face. I'd closed her eyes, and in her white nightgown she looked strange and beautiful, like a water sprite brought up in a fishing net.

I took one oar, and Lilith took the other. Slowly we made our way, pulling in time. My nightgown dried stiff against my skin, my ribs stabbed me with every stroke, and the water in the boat sloshed around my feet. There were still no lights on the shore. I wondered if Abe was still there. I found myself hoping that he was, another soul awake in the night.

When we were a hundred feet from the pontoon I stopped.

"Here?" Lilith said. "It's not too close?"

"It's very deep."

We pulled in the oars. The night waited, infinitely patient. The wind had died away, and the water glinted like obsidian between the dark shoulders of the forest. The sky was a cathedral of stars, their reflections glowing like candles in the depths, held aloft by a silent, watching congregation.

The anchor was behind me, tied by a rope to a ring on the side. I untied the rope from the boat and handed it to Lilith, and she passed it beneath Emily and tied it around her waist. When this was done she sat with her hands in her lap until the boat quieted. Then she drew a deep breath, and leaned down.

"Wait," I said. I closed my eyes and reached for the words. When I found them I kept my eyes closed and let them leave my lips and settle around us, both heavy and light, like birds.

Have mercy upon me, O God, according to thy lovingkindness; according unto the multitude of thy tender mercies blot out my transgressions.

Wash me thoroughly from mine iniquity, and cleanse me from my sin.

For I acknowledge my transgressions; and my sin is ever before me.

Behold, I was shapen in iniquity; and in sin

did my mother conceive me.

Behold, thou desirest truth in the inward
parts: and in the hidden part thou shalt
make me to know wisdom.

Purge me with hyssop, and I shall be clean:
wash me, and I shall be whiter than
snow.

Make me to hear joy and gladness; that the
bones which thou hast broken may
rejoice.

Hide thy face from my sins, and blot out all
mine iniquities.

Create in me a clean heart, O God; and
renew a right spirit within me.

When I opened my eyes, Lilith was weeping. With one hand I smoothed the wet hair from Emily's cheek. I alone knew where she was going. I alone knew the dark welcome, the eternal stillness, and the cold peace that awaited her. Silently, I promised her I would watch over her always. A poor promise, I know. But I have kept it.

Then Lilith and I lifted our sister, Emily Rose Evans, and laid her upon the water. She sank soundlessly, her nightgown opening like a flower. I took the anchor and lowered it by its rope beside her until my arm reached into the lake up to my elbow. She was already far away, a pale shimmer among the reflection of the stars. I released the anchor, and she was gone.

JUSTINE

It was the darkest part of the night when Justine woke. Although it was quiet, her head echoed with the sound that had woken her. Her children were asleep. She pulled the quilt closer around them. The air was still, and in the light from the lamp everything in the little room was in its place: the photographs on the table, the jar with Lucy's hairpins, the bags of Lucy's clothes in the corner. All of it, like Justine, alert. Waiting.

As Justine watched, the doorknob turned with slow stealth. The door pushed against the deadbolt, then fell back. Just as quietly, Justine climbed over Angela's sleeping form and got out of bed. She stood in the middle of the room, her body rigid, watching the doorknob. Her skin prickled with revulsion. She knew what he wanted. He wanted to slip into bed beside her. To wrap his arms around her, to seduce her. He didn't know her daughters were in here.

"Justine!" Patrick kicked the door violently. Justine's muscles leaped beneath her skin. The old wood splintered but held. Melanie and Angela sat up, groggy and frightened. He kicked it again. "Justine, wake up! There's a fire!"

All around Justine, Lucy's things gathered themselves with a silent drawing in of breath. This was what they had been waiting for. Justine inhaled, too. She could make out the faint smell of smoke, like the memory of a dream. He didn't want to get in her bed. *The house was on fire.* Her mind fluttered wildly, like a panicked bird. Then it snapped into a bright, singing lucidity.

"What's happening?" Melanie said.

"The house is on fire," Justine said. Her voice was calm. Angela covered her mouth with both hands, her eyes wide. Melanie's face drained of all color. Justine put on her shoes, tying the laces with slow thoroughness. Patrick kicked the door again, but she ignored him. She helped Melanie and Angela from the bed. She looked around, one last time, at all the helpless, waiting things. Then she scooped up the photographs, the jewelry box, and the *L* pendant from the bedside table. Everything else she left. She opened the bedroom door.

Patrick stood on the landing with the skin of his face tight against his bones. Smoke flowed up the stairs, tasted rather than seen, puddling just below the ceilings. "Get my mother," Justine said. Her voice sounded far away to her own ears.

"I have to get you —"

"We're fine. Get my mother."

His mouth opened and closed. Then he went to Maurie's door.

"Take your sister outside," Justine said to Melanie. Melanie took Angela's hand and they ran down the stairs into a darkness lit by a faint red glow. Justine waited until Patrick had disappeared into Maurie's room before walking after them. The foyer was blurry with smoke, dark ropes of it moving like snakes across the faces in the photographs. Down the hall, in the kitchen, flames swam around the cupboards. As Justine watched, the gingham curtains went up like twin torches. She thought: I liked those curtains.

She opened the closet and gathered their coats and snow boots. Then she walked out, closing the door behind her. On the porch she helped Melanie and Angela put on their coats and boots. She put on her own coat, too, tucking the things she'd taken in the pockets, and then she led her daughters out to the road. There, calf-deep in fresh snow, they turned to face the house.

From here they could see no sign of the fire. The house looked as it always had, heavy and regretful. Slow, fat snowflakes fell, the only things that moved in the whole world. Justine stood between her daughters, holding their hands. One minute went by. Two.

In a violent crashing of doors, Patrick and Maurie burst from the house. They stumbled down the porch steps, and Justine, still calm, met them at the bottom. Patrick was gasping. Maurie had the quilt from the lavender bedroom around her. Her hair was a black nest, and her eyes were blank and confused. She slipped to her knees, and Justine smelled the bourbon as Patrick lifted her in his arms and carried her toward the road. The quilt fell and Justine picked it up. She would wrap her daughters in it. They would go to the lodge and call the fire department. The firefighters would come and put out the fire. It was a small fire. It was just in the kitchen.

Then something passed her in a blur: Melanie. She ran up the steps, across the porch, and into the burning house. The door slammed behind her, and the glassine calm in Justine's mind shattered in to a million pieces.

"Melanie!" She lunged after her daughter but tripped on the quilt, fell, scrambled to her feet, then ran up the steps. As soon as she got in the house she knew it was doomed. The fire had already swallowed the kitchen. Now, tasting fresh oxygen from the door, it leaped into the hallway. The heat of it slammed her backward. Too fast, she thought wildly. It was burning too fast.

Melanie vanished into the smoke upstairs, and Justine stumbled after her, choking on the hot and swollen air. Flames from the kitchen below flickered outside Emily's window, and the little room glowed like the inside of an ember, waiting to burn. Justine ran into the green bedroom and closed the door behind her. It was dark, a thick dark suffocated with smoke, but there was Melanie, silhouetted against the lesser black of the window, scrabbling in the bedside table drawer.

"Melanie! Get out of there!" Justine shouted. Melanie's head jerked up, her hair flying over her shoulder. Justine coughed so hard she doubled over. The air was poisonous, it would kill them, they had to get out right now. She grabbed Melanie's arm and yanked her back to the door. But as she reached for the knob a roaring crash shuddered the walls, and the cracks around the doorjamb flared with angry red light. The whole back of the house had gone up — Emily's bedroom, the dining room, the kitchen, all of it. A high keening split the air as the house's dry wooden bones writhed and snapped. Above it Justine heard Melanie's thin scream, choked off by the smoke.

She shoved her back to the window. Melanie sank to the floor as Justine wrestled the sash through the warped frame. *Open!* Justine begged it, but after two inches the window wouldn't budge, so she picked up the bedside lamp and hit the glass. Not hard enough; again. Every breath was a knife in her lungs. Finally the window shattered, and cold air rushed in. Justine gave a sob, pulled Melanie up, helped her crawl through the jagged glass in the frame onto the porch roof, then followed. Her arms sank to the elbows in snow. Melanie's blood spotted the white. Above them, black smoke poured from the window in a thick column.

She dragged Melanie to the edge of the roof and they knelt there, Justine's arms clutching her, both of them sucking in lungfuls of icy, clear air. The snow in front of the house glowed a dull red, and Justine saw Angela in the road, her mouth open in a scream. Maurie crouched beside her, her

504

face a rictus of terror. Behind them, Patrick walked in a tight circle, his hands on his head. Matthew Miller was coming down the road in a stiff-legged run, his coat half-buttoned. Justine tried to call him, but her voice rasped uselessly. Then Angela saw them and her mouth moved — "Mommy!" — and Matthew saw them, too. He ran past Patrick and up the walkway.

Heat pressed against Justine's back. She looked over her shoulder — the fire was in the green bedroom now, devouring the twin beds and the thin lace curtains, which exploded into plumes of sparks. The snow on the porch roof began to soften and slide. Horrified, she looked down to where Matthew now stood in the snow that had drifted up against the house. The drop was twelve feet or more.

She took Melanie by the shoulders. "You have to jump."

Melanie's eyes were blank with fear. She had one of the Emily books clutched to her chest. "Give me that," Justine said. Melanie shook her head and held the book tighter. Justine ripped it from her grasp and threw it off the roof, pages flapping. "Get on your stomach." Melanie was quaking so hard she could barely move, but she managed to get onto her belly. Justine lay down, too, her legs stretched back toward the house, her hands rigid with panic, gripping Melanie's wrists as her daughter slid backward, her legs dangling over the snow.

"Grab the edge," Justine said, and one by one Melanie locked her shaking hands around the old metal gutter. "Now let go." Melanie clung to the gutter, half on and half off the roof, straining against gravity, her eyes pleading. Justine, her voice breaking, said, "Please. You can do it," and Melanie clenched her teeth, and then, with a strangled cry, she dropped. Her fingers strained on the gutter for a split second before they slipped away and she fell. Justine crawled to the edge, and when she saw her daughter safe, Matthew's arms around her, relief made her so dizzy it felt like the porch roof was spinning.

Then the window of the green bedroom exploded. Justine covered her head as flames belched through the window's jagged mouth. Matthew pushed Melanie back, horror in both their faces, and Justine knew Lucy's window was gone, too, and the living room; the house was going up like kindling now. Fire seared her back and the snow under her feet slid away. She stood up and launched herself off the roof, hurtling into the red-black night, her arms opening like wings, soaring on the hot breath of the fire. Down she fell, through the roaring air, until she hit the snow hard, sank up to her knees, and crashed face-first into the silent, blessed cold.

A moment later Melanie's and Matthew's hands were upon her, turning her to face the sky. She stared up at it, stunned. The fire blotted out the stars, yet it made no sound. Snowflakes, melted by the heat, fell on her face like rain, but she didn't feel them.

Melanie's face bent over hers. "Mom! Mom!" Justine coughed, blinking the snow from her lashes. Sound returned, and with it, sensation. Cold. Heat. She moved her arms, then her legs, feeling them move thickly in the snow. She was okay. Nothing was hurt. She laughed out loud at the miracle of it, and Melanie's face loosened with relief. Then Matthew took her arms, and he and Melanie pulled her away from the flames that sprang from the living room to the porch swing to the porch roof, pulled her to where Angela's and Maurie's hands, too, reached and clung.

They watched from the road as the house burned. It didn't take long. They wrapped themselves in the quilt from the lavender bedroom, their faces warmed by the fire and their backs chilled by the cold air pushing in from the lake. Just before the fire trucks came, the roof fell in and the green bedroom and the yellow bedroom and the lavender bedroom crashed into the kitchen and the elm table and the parlor with the Christmas lights and the guitar and the ice skates that fell in their turn upon the photo albums and the dust-covered furniture in the basement, all gone already, of course; just as the Emily books and the little girl's clothes and the picture of Melanie and Angela at the Padres game were also gone. When the house collapsed, it gave a long, rolling moan, and a thousand billion sparks swirled into the night like fireflies. Ash drifted down all around, mixing with the snow that also fell.

Justine laid a hand on Melanie's head where it rested under her chin. The edges of the Emily book she'd saved, locked once more in her arms, dug into Justine's ribs. Maurie buried her face in Matthew's coat and he put his arms around her while Patrick stood beside them and watched, without a word.

There was no fire hydrant, and the only water was frozen in the lake, so when the firefighters came they gave them oxygen to breathe and bandaged Melanie's arms where the broken window glass had torn them. Then they, too, stood and watched the burning, the lights of their trucks swirling and blending with the light from the fire until the whole world pulsed red.

LUCY

There were no fishermen at dawn. It was
the last morning, so it was for packing
trunks and loading cars. Lilith and I had
changed into dry nightgowns. We had covered the scratches on her face with makeup
as best we could. Now we lay together in
my bed, waiting. As the air warmed, we
heard the first risers open their doors and
greet one another. A wind rose, filling the
morning with whispers.

At last we heard Mother cry out: Emily?
Lilith's arms tightened around me as
Mother ran first to the room where Father
slept and then to ours. Mother's eyes were
dark, as though her pupils had eaten the
blue of her irises, and I could see the
knowledge there. She knew already that
Emily would not be found in the house, at
the beach, or under the lodge. She knew
already that she was lost.

All that morning we searched, fanning out

through the forest, our neighbors calling anxiously now, for this time was not like before. This time a child had disappeared in the night, every mother's greatest fear. Lilith and I stayed together as we walked the forest with our neighbors. I couldn't look at the wind-blown lake, the color of chipped sapphires in the sun, so I kept my eyes on the dead leaves on the forest floor. Wherever we went we heard Mother's voice above the others', a high, feral cry shaped into a human sound only by the syllables of Emily's name. I shook when I heard it, my body clenching until finally I vomited, crouching behind a tree. "Poor thing," Mr. Jones said when he found me covering my mess with leaves. "Don't worry. We'll find your sister."

It was midmorning when Dr. Pugh and Mayor Lloyd suggested that "the Miller boy" should be questioned. The police had been called, but they hadn't yet arrived, so this was the last opportunity for vigilantism. Lilith and I had just come from the woods. It had occurred to me that someone might notice one of the fishing boats was missing an anchor, and the thought had made me so ill I needed to go to the docks to make sure no one had. They hadn't, and they never would. I don't know what the Millers thought when they stowed the boats for the winter, but they never said a thing.

Abe wasn't hard to find. He and Matthew had been helping the searchers that morning, but as lunch drew near, Mrs. Lloyd had asked them to make sandwiches for us. Mayor Lloyd walked into the kitchen as though he had the right and brought Abe out to the main room where Dr. Pugh, Mr. Davies, and their wives waited. Matthew and his grandmother followed, and the men made a half circle around them. Mr. Miller wasn't there, and I wished he were. His wife's mother wasn't going to be able to protect her grandson; I could see that in her face, which was the color of mahogany, and in her thick fingers knotted in her apron.

Abe looked at the men in confusion. As he had that first summer day when Lilith and I came for groceries, Matthew moved to stand in front of his brother. His muscles were tense. He knew what Mayor Lloyd was after.

"Son, I'm going to ask you a question, and I'm going to want your honest answer," Mayor Lloyd said. I hated him, I realized. I hated his red, beefy features that might have been handsome on the young boxer but were swollen and pitted on the overfed politician. "Did you see Emily Evans last night or this morning?"

Matthew said, "He was in his bed all night. I can swear to it. We're in the same room, him and me."

"And were you awake all night?"

"No. But if he'd gone anywhere, I'd have woken up."

It was the only thing he could say, but of course it was a lie — Abe had left, and Matthew knew it. I could see it in his face. He had woken up, sometime during that quiet hour when Lilith and I rowed out to the pontoon, and Abe hadn't been there. When his brother came back, creeping through the damp dark, had Matthew asked him where he'd been? What had Abe told him? I was in plain view, but Matthew didn't look at me.

The men exchanged glances. Mayor Lloyd was puffing himself up. They were going to take Abe and hold him for the police, and my head felt light. It was never part of our plan to have blame fall on any innocent person. I looked at Lilith: now was the time to lead them to the conclusion we needed them to reach. She was watching the scene with a small frown, but she didn't say anything. So I did.

"Maybe she's just run away again." Every head in the room swiveled to me, even Matthew's. I swallowed, though my throat was dry. "She's done it before."

At this Mrs. Davies nodded her head. "About a month ago. We found her pretty quickly, but she was wearing a lot of dresses and skirts, and she had a little bag with her."

"Why would she run away?" Dr. Pugh asked, and I knew why they would doubt it, just as I had at first. Sweet, docile Emily, beloved daughter of a decent family — such girls did not run away. In our haste the night before, Lilith and I hadn't talked about the answer to this critical question.

Then Lilith said, "Mother told her she couldn't take this kitten she'd found back to Williamsburg. She was very upset about it." In a smooth voice she explained about the kittens and how Emily had a favorite she'd hoped to adopt as a pet. The ugly current that charged the air weakened as the grown-ups listened, and though I wouldn't look at him, I could feel Matthew's relief.

Mrs. Davies sent Ben to find Mother and asked her, in the gentlest way, to check Emily's things. Mother stiffened as she realized what Mrs. Davies meant, but she went to the lavender bedroom, where she found several dresses were missing along with Emily's saddle shoes and her Christmas purse. Then Lilith came and said Emily's kitten was gone from under the lodge. Mother put her hand to her mouth and moaned, a wrenching, shuddering sound that came from a territory beyond weeping. She would have fallen if Father hadn't caught her.

Later that afternoon, Lilith and I were in the woods beyond the Lloyds', where no one else was searching. We walked a little ways, then we stopped in a clearing. Lilith sat on a large rock, closing her eyes and letting her shoulders slump. I sat beside her. I closed my eyes, too, and the sun made the insides of my eyelids red. From this distance, the faraway calls of the searchers sounded almost like birds. Long minutes passed. I wished I could stay like that forever; I was so tired. Then I felt Lilith move beside me. I opened my eyes to see Abe standing there. In his hands he held one of Emily's blue slippers.

"Give that to me," Lilith said, and he did. The slipper was caked with dried mud on the bottom, but it was dry. It hadn't gone into the creek. I had a small bag with two of the sandwiches the Millers had made, so I took it and put it inside. Later I would hide it deep in our closet, and I would keep it even after Lilith and I burned Emily's clothes and purse in the clearing by the Hundred Tree. I have it still.

"Do you know where she is?" Abe asked Lilith.

"Why would you think that?"

"I found that on the bridge last night, while I was waiting for you." His cow eyes were gloomy and afraid. "And the boat. You wanted the boat."

"What are you saying? She's my sister." I was struck rigid by the utterly convincing indignation on Lilith's face. She put her hand on Abe's chest. "You're not to tell about the boat, remember? Other people might wonder the same thing if they knew."

I waited for him to ask the obvious questions: What had she wanted the boat for? Why had she been wet to the skin when she'd met him? I didn't know what she would say if he did. But he didn't ask. Maybe because he was so slow. Or maybe for the same reason I never asked what she did with the kitten: he didn't want to hear her answer. Instead he said, "Are we still going to California?"

Lilith shook her head. "I can't go until I know Emily is safe. I'm sorry."

Days passed. The sheriff came with his deputies, and they sent for volunteers from Williamsburg and Olema who walked for miles in every direction. More days passed as they searched through trees turning russet and gold, their hunting jackets red and their dogs bounding through the bracken. Much later, in the quiet of another autumn day, Mother would tell me she heard those dogs every year when the leaves turned. I never did, but I've not forgotten the sound they made, either. The excited yowls, like laughter. Then, at odd moments, a lonely, mournful cry, the sound of loss itself.

Near the end of September they dragged the lake, but only to a distance of a few hundred yards, because no one thought Emily could swim farther than that. And, of course, no one thought she'd gone swimming. Lilith and I watched from our bedroom window, our hands clasped together, until they stopped well short of the pontoon and brought the boats back in.

In early October, when the frost came, the search became a weekend enterprise and the searchers became fewer. They were no longer looking for a living child. Then, when late October brought the first snow, Sheriff Llewellyn came to Mother, hat in hand, and said with gentle gravity that they had done all they could. After he left, Mother sat in the parlor staring into the gray air, her face still but her hands kneading.

Through all of this, Father diminished. In

the beginning, he seemed to recover some of the strength he'd lost since Independence Day: he strode through the trees, his great baritone roaring out Emily's name. Each evening he gathered us in the parlor and led us in prayer: *Gracious Lord, Father of all children, shine a light in the darkness for Your lamb, that has wandered from Your fold.* But each day that brought no news of her made him smaller and quieter. He kept his distance from Lilith and me, and his nightly prayers became open pleas for absolution, for forgiveness for sins he could not name. I pitied him, for I loved him still. Lilith watched him with merciless eyes.

When the sheriff's car drove away, he stood in the doorway, watching it go. We were the only lake family still there. Many had stayed long past the end of summer to help us search, but one after another they returned to their jobs and homes in town. Just Mrs. Williams was left, bringing us food we barely ate and comfort we barely took. Now she sat beside Mother on the davenport. The little house was cold; it had no radiators yet. Outside, the trees were bare except for the new snow that dusted their branches.

"Eleanor," Father said, "we have to go."

Mother hadn't left the lake once since

Emily disappeared. Father had been to town many times, meeting with the bankers who held off on collection in deference to our loss. Two weeks later he would sell his grandfather's pharmacy to Mayor Lloyd for less than his debts. By January the lake house was all we had, and Father was in his grave.

Mother said, "I won't leave her here alone."

"The house isn't fit for winter," Mrs. Williams said.

"I'll manage." Mother was so thin. Insubstantial, like a ghost. But her voice was resolute. As long as I could remember, she had bent to Father's will. Now, when it didn't matter and she couldn't save anyone, she would not.

Before he left, Father came to Lilith and me in our room. "You'll come with me," he said from the doorway. He said it to both of us, but he was looking at me. I remembered the first day of summer, when he'd stood there, looking first at Lilith in her Cinderella headdress, then sliding his eyes to me. My legs went wobbly with fear.

Lilith said, "Mother needs us here."

"I need you, too."

I knew he did. I could see it in the way his hand shook on the doorjamb. And I am certain — I have no doubt at all — that I would have gone with him if Lilith hadn't said, as though stating an unarguable fact, like the month of the year or the color of the sky: "You can't have us."

He dropped his eyes, and for the first time in my life I beheld him without those dark, mesmerizing irises. I saw a tired man, bowed and old before his time. When he raised them again he raised them to Lilith, not to me, and unlike on that first summer day, she didn't look away. She stood between our beds, every muscle frozen save for her hands, which trembled a little. A filament of understanding crackled between them, like the one that had joined him to me for that brief moment at breakfast the morning we fished, then snapped with a sound that was almost audible. Lilith's hands stopped shaking. Father took a step back, as though he'd lost his balance. He went to Williamsburg later that afternoon, alone.

Mrs. Williams brought us our winter clothes and space heaters. When the snow came in earnest, Mr. Miller plowed the dirt track to the county road so Lilith and I could walk to where the school bus picked us up. The other children whispered about us, but we didn't care. Lilith's summer friends, Jeannette and Betty and the lot, were at the high school across town, and she never mentioned them again. At night, Mother made our supper and we did our homework in the kitchen, warmed by a little heater. Father, busy with the business of bankruptcy, came on the weekends, and after supper Lilith and I went upstairs while he and Mother sat in the parlor without speaking. On Christmas Day, when he didn't come, the three of us sat in the thin light filtering through the front window and waited for the phone to ring.

Every day of that first winter, Lilith and I returned from school to find Mother sitting in the kitchen with her eyes on the back door. She wasn't waiting for us. Long past the time anyone could think a six-year-old girl might survive in that wild country, Mother hoped Emily would walk out of the woods. She never stopped hoping it. As the years passed she stopped watching the door, and if anyone asked why she stayed at the lake she said it was where she felt closest to her lost child. But she left the back porch light on every night for the next forty-four years, until the day she couldn't get out of bed. And it is only now, as I look back upon that summer and find my bitterness toward her has mellowed enough to permit something almost like pity, that I understand what it was I did to her the night I gave my sister to the lake.

Lilith killed Emily. But I kept her alive.

JUSTINE

The morning after the fire was one of almost impossible beauty. The skies were a scrubbed and perfect blue, and the sun starred the new snow with millions of tiny lights, winking and sharp like diamonds. But the chaos of the night was written in the tire treads and footprints that dirtied the road and in the blackened husk of the old house. The smoke seeping from the ruins tainted the air even inside the lodge.

Matthew had made up three of his upstairs guest rooms. Melanie and Angela fell asleep in one of them around dawn, the thin summer blankets pulled up to their chins. Maurie and Patrick took the other two. Justine and Matthew were still awake when, at nine, the last of the fire trucks drove away, leaving the lake to its accustomed quiet once more.

Matthew went to the bar and started washing the mugs in which he'd served the firefighters coffee. Justine picked up a towel and dried them. Matthew's hands shook a little, and when Justine saw this she was overcome with gratitude and affection for him. All night long he'd been steadfast. Without being asked, he'd made up their beds. At five he'd made a breakfast none of them thought they could eat until he placed it before them. At seven he'd stood beside her as the fire chief told her what she already knew, that the fire started in the kitchen and they were lucky to have gotten out alive.

She said, "You should get some sleep."

He nodded, but when she went upstairs he was still there, behind his bar, wiping the counter that needed no wiping.

Her daughters lay in narrow twin beds in the first room at the top of the stairs. She went to their window to pull the shade so the light wouldn't wake them, and as she reached for the cord she saw the Emily book sticking out from under Melanie's pillow. Justine slipped it out and opened the cover. But it wasn't a book of Emily stories. On the first page, in an old woman's shaky hand, was written, "For Justine." On the second began what appeared to be a journal.

Justine took the book to the room she was sharing with Maurie. While Maurie slept she read it, turning the pages first with curiosity, then with dread, and finally with horror. When she was done it was late afternoon, and Maurie was still sleeping.

She went down to the main room, which was empty. Matthew had gone to bed at last. She sat at a table with the book in front of her and drew her knees up under her chin. The sun poured through the mullioned windows on the western wall in columns of gold, and dust motes hung motionless in the air. Justine closed her eyes. The insides of her eyelids were scratchy with soot. Against them a little girl in a white night-gown sank through dark water to the words of a prayer.

They were her family. The family she'd brushed against as a girl and forgotten, the family whose legacy she'd planned to take with her now, in photographs and books and brass-faced clocks. As if legacies lay in things that could be bought and sold. As if families could be left behind or taken with you as you chose.

She tightened her arms around her legs, feeling the weight and wonder of it. Their history, Lucy's story, had directed her life even though she'd known nothing about it. It was a legacy of loyalty and betrayal. Weakness and regret. Love, and tender, harrowing violence. Lucy and Lilith, Emily, Eleanor with her nervous, ineffectual hands: they'd followed her everywhere she'd ever been, no matter how many times she'd shaken the dust off her feet in Maurie's car and her own.

She felt someone watching her and opened her eyes to find Melanie standing in front of her, wearing the adult extra-large sweatshirt Matthew had given her to sleep in. It had a silk-screened orange sun and the name of the lodge in kitschy log letters, and it hung to Melanie's knees. Justine thought: she has no clothes. Everything is ashes.

Melanie sat in the chair opposite Justine's. The book lay between them. It looked like all the others, the same black-and-white marbled cover, just as old. But its binding wasn't creased with decades of openings and closings. It hadn't been in the box Justine had gotten from the librarian, she was certain. "Where did you find it?"

"In the table by my bed." In the faint challenge of Melanie's gaze Justine saw that it hadn't been an Emily book Melanie had hidden beneath her covers the night they fought. It had been this. She'd had it for weeks, reading it in secret and illustrating it in dark strokes in notebooks of her own. It was she, Justine realized, who'd lit the candles beneath Emily's portrait, creeping down the stairs in the night, striking the matches while Justine and Angela and Maurie slept.

She pulled her feet off the chair and rested her arms on the table. "Why didn't you give it to me?"

The last ray of sun burst through the window like a solar flare before guttering out. It took the colors of the day with it. Melanie said, "Because I can give her what she wants. Better than you."

"She wanted me to know what happened to Emily."

"That's not all she wants." One of Melanie's fingers touched the corner of the book, lingering on the binding in a small caress.

Justine slid the book away and folded her hands on top of it. Melanie's finger picked at a divot on the table instead. The white bandage was bulky on her thin wrist. When had she become so thin? She didn't even look like a child anymore. She looked like an old woman with the smooth skin of a girl. "You shouldn't have gone back for it," Justine said. "You could have been killed."

A small muscle in Melanie's cheek tightened. "I know," she said, and for a time they sat with the memory of the choking heat in the green bedroom and the wailing of the house as it died, the stain of Melanie's blood on the snow and the cold metal of the gutter in their hands.

Then Justine said, "What happened at the Padres game?"

Melanie blanched. She looked away and gave the smallest of shrugs. "Nothing. He just told me I should be nicer to him."

Part of Justine wanted to accept this half-truth as the whole. Even after reading Lucy's book, that part of her could still make its cowardly argument. But she could not let it win. Not now, when she had seen the terrible wages a mother's cowardice could reap — had already reaped. So she said, "What else?"

Melanie's fingers worked at one another. Justine gathered the courage to push harder, but before she had to, Melanie's fingers stopped. She raised her chin. "He said sometimes kids disappeared, and nobody ever found them. But if anything happened to me, I shouldn't worry. Because he'd take good care of you."

Justine kept her face still. At the Padres game she'd left Melanie with Patrick while she took Angela to the bathroom. She thought it would let Melanie get to know him, see what a nice guy he was. She'd told herself it had worked; that Melanie had decided to give him a chance. Because afterward Melanie accepted his place in their lives without complaint. Now she remembered it was Melanie who had convinced Angela to leave the San Diego school, and she felt faint.

He wouldn't have hurt her. He didn't have real violence in him, she was sure. He was a man of neatly overturned sofas, sly fingers under a car's hood. But. If Melanie had disappeared, he would have been Justine's rock. He would have talked to the police, coordinated the search parties, made the flyers. He would have bought groceries and made their meals, and driven Angela back and forth to school. He would have comforted Justine in her shattering terror and, ultimately, her grief, which she would pour into his arms as he held her in their bed each night. He would have saved her, to the extent she could have been saved.

"We're going to go somewhere he'll never find us," she said, thickly. "I promise."

Melanie folded her bandaged arms, their bones skeptical in the too-big sweatshirt. They were as thin as Eleanor's arms in her wedding dress, in the photograph in the foyer. Above them her eyes were as black as her great-great-grandfather's must have

been, as black as her great-grandfather's —
for so Abe was, Justine now believed — still
were. She said, "I don't want to go anywhere. I want to stay here."

Justine sat back in her chair. Her wool
sweater scratched against her shoulders.

Melanie's fingers picked at one another.
"Please, Mommy." She hadn't called Justine that in a long time. The two syllables
were as soft and round as a baby's cheek.

Before Justine could answer, before she
knew how she wanted to answer, she heard
footsteps on the stairs. Melanie sat up, every
muscle tense, as Patrick came into the main
room and slumped into the seat next to Justine. He looked exhausted, as though he
hadn't slept at all. "How you girls doing?"
he asked. "Okay?"

"We're fine," Justine made herself say. She
had gone as rigid as Melanie.

Patrick rested his hands on the table. He
smoothed the right with the left in a nervous
habit Justine knew well. He cut his eyes to
her, then back to his hands. She knew what
he was going to say. He kept his eyes on his
hands as he said it. "I guess you'll have to
come back to San Diego now."

She didn't answer. And as she studied
him, she realized something. His face was
clean. Unlike hers and Melanie's, which

were dusky with soot. He hadn't run into a burning house after a book. He hadn't run into it after a child. He hadn't even run into it after the child's mother. He'd paced in circles in the snow instead. And he was ashamed of this. Justine's pulse quickened. She leaned forward. "Patrick, you need to leave. We don't want you here."

Melanie's eyes flicked to her in surprise. Patrick looked as if she'd slapped him. "But — I saved you. I saved all of you." He saw her disbelief and rushed on. "The fire started in the oven. I smelled the smoke, and I went in there, but it was already too late. So I came to get you. If it weren't for me, you'd all be dead."

Justine felt a flapping in her chest. It was true he'd woken them up, and he'd helped Maurie out of the house. But he hadn't saved Melanie, and he hadn't saved Justine. In the end, Justine herself had done the saving he'd wanted so desperately to do. She'd changed his script. Now he was trying to pivot.

She still had her hand on Lucy's book. The edges of its pages were warped with damp from lying in the snow where she'd thrown it. Long ago, two girls knelt on a beach in the moonlight, pressing a secret between their palms. But not only a secret.

The promise the secret bought was pressed there, too.

The flurry of wings quieted. She felt again that surreal, distant calm she'd felt in Lucy's bedroom. She said, "The oven hasn't worked since we got here."

"What?"

She raised her head and looked him in the eyes. "I said the oven is broken. And if you don't leave, I'm going to tell the firefighters that."

Patrick's mouth fell open. He looked like one of the fish in the photographs on the wall, with their gaping jaws and stunned eyes. The rest of the room seemed to disappear, and Justine could see every small hair on his face, every blood vessel in the whites of his eyes. Seconds ticked by. She waited. She waited for him to think it through. To understand exactly what she meant, and to believe she would do it.

Finally he blinked several times, and she knew it was done. He looked away, at the window. Then he pressed his hands on the table and stood. Now his face was shadowed; she couldn't see his expression. His arms hung from his shoulders, and his body seemed heavier than when he'd walked in. He said, "You will never find anyone who loves you like I do," and she knew he was right. Then he walked out.

When the screen door slammed she dropped her head into her hands and felt the breath leave her body through every pore. Across from her, Melanie picked up Lucy's book and put it in her lap.

Justine didn't know how long Matthew would let them stay in the lodge, or where they'd live when summer came and he needed the rooms. How they'd deal with the girls at school, or the assistant principal and her antibullying campaign. How she'd find a job. She couldn't think about any of these things until she'd slept fourteen hours in one of Matthew's beds, with her daughters safe and whole down the hall. But when she woke up, she would come down to the kitchen and help Matthew make breakfast. Then, as she cracked eggs into a bowl, no longer trying to make them exactly right, she would ask him if they could stay for a little while.

In the silence they heard Patrick's engine start. Justine reached across the table and took Melanie's hand. Though it was smaller, their fingers were the same. Slender and strong.

LUCY

I'm in my old bed, in Lilith's and my old room. It seems the proper place to write the last lines of this, my last story. Tomorrow I will go to town to read to the children, and when I'm done I'll drop this journal by Arthur's house and tell him to give it to you if you come. He won't have to keep it long. There's a sickness in me; I've felt it growing for many months. Unlike Lilith, who was dragged into death one cell at a time, I have no stomach for hospitals and tubes and dying under fluorescent lights. So I will die here, in this place that is still my favorite place, despite everything.

Matthew came by this evening. He brought pumpkin bread, his grandmother's recipe, which I love. It's gotten too cold to be on the porch, so we sat in the parlor, drinking tea from flowered cups and eating bread from flowered plates, like the old people we have become. We talked about the first snow, which is coming next week, or so they say. Later this year than usual. It's been strange to see the lake frozen but the earth brown all around. It makes me uneasy, with the millennium turning just over two months from now.

We talked a bit about it — the end of the millennium. Matthew said that when he was a boy he thought by the year 2000 there would be space travel, time travel, and cures for all diseases. Instead, all we got were faster cars and flu shots. He laughed ruefully, a boy disappointed. I told him flu shots were no small thing. But I agreed with him. Not much has changed in all these years. More wars. New countries. All that technology neither of us has much use for. Still, it's much the same world as it was when we were young, in all its most important particulars.

I asked if he wished he'd done anything differently. It was an odd question, and I surprised both of us by asking it. As I said, we don't talk about the past, but I've spent so much time in my memories of late that I suppose it was on my mind. I could see I'd made him uncomfortable.

"I made a choice once," he said, "but I'm not going to regret it."

I smiled: it was the sort of thing I'd

expected him to say. And I did understand him. I knew he meant the choice he made to stay here with Abe, in the place for which Abe was best suited, rather than go be an astronaut or follow whatever dream might have supplanted that one. He'd made his peace with it, no doubt because he'd made it out of love. The things we do for love are the hardest things to regret.

"Do you?" he asked. He wasn't just being polite, asking me the question I'd asked him. He wanted to know. I could see it in the careful way he held his plate. Between us lay all the decades that connected the children we'd been with the old man and old woman we'd become. And something more: that listening thing that, from time to time, infuses the air of this house and brushes against my cheek. Emily, but not quite Emily. Or not just Emily.

I set my teacup on the table. For a long time I'd wanted someone to ask me that question. I'd wanted to tell someone that I regretted nothing. That I, too, had acted out of love, and could claim that absolution. That I kept Lilith's secret because I was a good sister, loyal to the end to the only person who ever truly cared about me, who ever needed me. And that anyone who was hurt by what I did deserved their suffering.

But I don't believe these things any more, if I ever truly believed them. I regret it all. I regret that I didn't leave Lilith and Emily on the shore that night, and go get help. I regret that I didn't tell everyone, when they came, that Emily's death was an accident. I wish I'd let Lilith go wherever her spirit led her. I wish I'd let Emily lie in the earth, with a stone to tell the world she'd been here for a little while. I wish I'd been a different person entirely. A person with courage. If I had been, many lives would have been different.

Matthew was watching me with that patience I've always loved in him. I wanted to reach across the space between us, across all the vanished moments, and take his hand. The hand of the boy who had been my friend. Who walked with me all those years ago, as the light shimmered through the trees and the hem of my dress brushed my calves.

But I couldn't answer him, so I didn't.

One afternoon that summer you came, you asked about the girl in the painting and I told you the lie I've always told. I was very practiced by then. But I couldn't look at you while I told it. You, with your wispy hair and fragile features and your eyes like water under a pale sky. A child delivered of the past, born of the choices I made, whose life would span two centuries, not just one. You are the only person at whom I could not look when I said my little sister had run away in the night and disappeared in the forest. Not Matthew, not Maurie, not even Mother. Only you.

Then, when you asked what I thought had become of Emily, I told you the truth. I said it out loud, there on the porch. It's the only time I've ever said the words. I bound my secret up in the trappings of speculation and cynicism so you wouldn't hear it as anything but the clear-eyed guess of a person who accepts a great likelihood as certain. But I told you the truth.

Lilith would say I owe her, still, the secrecy she gave so much to purchase, and she is right. But now that she's gone, and I soon will be, there is another, greater debt I must pay. Long ago, I cast my sister into a grave over which her mother would never weep, and over which no one but I would ever mourn. She would have grown up to be beautiful. She would have grown up safe. I would have grown to love her. I have kept the promise I made to watch over her all my life, but it is not enough. After I am gone, I want someone who cared about her, even for just an afternoon; and who loved this place, even for just a summer; to know where she is and what happened to her.

So I'm telling you. You, the nine-year-old girl who lives in my memory.

Please, remember her. Remember all of us. We are the ghosts of lives stolen, and lives never lived. Once we were heavy, but now we are light. I promise we will not burden you.

JUSTINE

The water was a perfect mirror for the sky. Matthew turned off the motor, and the metal boat coasted to a stop, suspended between two heavens. The air on that early spring day was warm and cool at the same time. The last of the ice had melted just the week before, but the brown grasses at the water's edge already were streaked with green.

Justine opened the cardboard box. She expected a fine dust, noncorporeal, that would blow away on the wind or float on the water, but it was heavy, like sand. It would sink quickly.

Melanie sat beside her, and Angela and Maurie faced them. Matthew and Abe sat in the stern. Everyone was watching her. She'd thought she would recite Psalm 51, so she had a Bible — the King James version, with its words like music. Now she decided not to. The lake, so bright in the sun, seemed unconcerned with sin, or for-giveness.

She caught Matthew's eye. He nodded. She tipped the box over the side so that some of the ashes slid into the water. They plumed into the clear green depths and dis-appeared. Then she passed the box to Mela-nie. Melanie pushed her hair behind her ear, and it fell forward again. She took the box and tipped it over the other side. The ashes entered the water with a *shhh.*

Maurie helped Angela send a few fine grains to join the others. Then she put the box on her own lap and straightened her back. For a moment Justine was afraid she was going to say something, some grand, hollow words about death and family. She thought, please don't. And Maurie did, indeed, seem to think better of it. She poured the ashes over the side with only a whispered, "Good-bye, Lucy."

She would leave the next day. The probate had come through two weeks earlier, and Justine had given her the five thousand dol-lars her boyfriend took from her and told her, gently, to go. Maurie's face had closed tight on her hurt, and Justine wavered. But she remembered Melanie's red, open mouth on the frozen lake and her daughters' faces after Arthur's party, and she said nothing when Maurie said she'd been planning to leave anyway. Now, looking at Maurie's upright posture, she realized she might never see her again. There would just be the postcards that would keep coming until the end, and a couple of phone calls a year.

As Maurie gave the box to Abe, she squeezed his hand. Matthew hadn't wanted him to come, but Justine insisted. He lifted out a handful of the ashes and let them filter through his fingers into the water. "She'll be glad of the company," he said, almost to himself. He didn't see the look on his brother's face, but Justine did. Later she would find Matthew in the kitchen of the lodge, make them both a cup of tea, tell him Lucy's secret, and give him the pendant he had made for her long ago. Grief and regret would settle into the lines of his face as he took it, and he would seem much older from that moment on. Justine would wonder if she had been right to tell him, but he would thank her.

A flock of geese flew overhead in a raucous chevron, heading home. Matthew waited until they passed. Over his shoulder Justine could see the gap in the row of houses, like a missing tooth. The builders would come once the ground thawed. There had been a small policy on the house, enough to build something simple. Two bedrooms, a kitchen, a living room, a front porch. She would paint it yellow.

The birds were gone. Silence returned. A light breeze lifted Justine's hair and fell away. Melanie leaned over the side of the boat and drew her fingers across the surface of the lake, breaking her reflection into ripples. Then Matthew, with the greatest of care, laid the last of Lucy's ashes upon the water, and the water took them down.

ACKNOWLEDGMENTS

First things first: I would never have written this book without the unfailing encouragement of my husband, Chris. His faith in me, even as years passed without a finished draft, gave me the strength I needed to get it done. Saying yes to him twenty-five years ago was the best move I've ever made.

I also want to thank my children, Kyle and Matthew, for their patience, their willingness to put up with their father's cooking while I was at workshops, and the pride and wonder in their eyes when I told them this book had sold. If I've taught them nothing else, I hope I've taught them that even the wildest dreams are possible.

Thanks to my parents, Don and Audrey, and my sister, Tracy, who are the opposites of the parents and sisters in this book, and make me feel almost like the smartypants they seem to think I am.

I owe an incalculable debt to the writers

who've helped me along the way, especially Elizabeth Clark, my muse and fellow dreamer, who made me do it and showed me how. Also Ellen Collett, Judith Edelman, Sharon Hazzard, Sharon Knapp, Jeanne Koskela, Deborah Michel, and Kathy Stevenson, the Bennington "Old Ladies" who make me grateful every day that I got on that plane to Vermont. Thank you to my teachers, Douglas Bauer, Lynne Sharon Schwartz, Martha Cooley, and especially Alice Mattison, who always took the time. To Melissa Cistaro, in whose footsteps I have tried to walk, and Carey Lifschultz, who went into the trenches with me. And to Jenny Brown, Aya de Leon, Abby Fabiaschi, and Louise Miller, my comrades in this crazy debut journey and whose friendship kept me sane.

Thank you, also, to the many friends who asked how it was going and listened to my tales of woe, especially Jocelyn Lamm, Karla Martin, and Rona Sandler, sharers of wine, wisdom, and twenty-five years of friendship; Jules Campfield, who knows how hard some hills are to climb; and the ladies of the Mill Valley Book Club: Lisa Carmel, Sara Fortine, Tammy Grant, Katy Kuhn, Annika Miller, and Dawn Smith-Holmes.

A *massive* thank you to Michelle Brower,

my agent, who picked my manuscript out of the slush pile one snowy February day and changed my life, and whose positive energy and stalwart support made it all so much fun. An equally enormous thank you to my editor, Kate Nintzel, whose guidance took this novel to places I didn't know it could go.

Last, but of course not least, I want to thank everyone in the publishing world who took my dog-eared manuscript, made it into a beautiful book, and sent it into the world, especially Lauren Truskowski, Molly Waxman, Shelby Meizlik, Jennifer Hart, Margaux Weisman, Annie Hwang, Ben Bruton, Joy Johannessen, and Sally Arteseros.

ABOUT THE AUTHOR

Heather Young earned her law degree from the University of Virginia and practiced law in San Francisco before beginning her writing career. She received an MFA from the Bennington College Writing Seminars, and has studied at the Tin House Writers' Workshop and the Squaw Valley Writers Workshop. She lives in Mill Valley, California, with her husband and two children. *The Lost Girls* is her first novel.

The employees of Thorndike Press hope you have enjoyed this Large Print book. All our Thorndike, Wheeler, and Kennebec Large Print titles are designed for easy reading, and all our books are made to last. Other Thorndike Press Large Print books are available at your library, through selected bookstores, or directly from us.

For information about titles, please call:
(800) 223-1244

or visit our website at:
gale.com/thorndike

To share your comments, please write:
Publisher
Thorndike Press
10 Water St., Suite 310
Waterville, ME 04901